Praise for th

Matters of the Heart

Matters of the Heart is a lesbian medical romance where a doctor and patient find love together. I don't know how Catherine Maiorisi did it....I recommend *Matters of the Heart* to anyone who's looking for a solid, traditional romance.

-*The Lesbian Review*

I'm a sucker for a slow-burning romance, and this one nicely hit that spot. As is made clear in the introduction, it's Maiorisi's first attempt at a full-length romance—previously she has been known for murder mysteries. If she wants to continue in this genre, she's off to a great start.

-*Rainbow Book Reviews*

A Matter of Blood

This is an excellent mystery and whodunit with well-developed characters, an interesting backstory and great potential. The action is fast-paced but nicely interspersed with moments of stillness and humanity....Well written, enjoyable reading. I literally can't wait for the next one to see where Ms. Maiorisi takes us with both the crime-fighting team and the prospective romance.

-*Lesbian Reading Room*

This book was a long time in the pipeline for Catherine Maiorisi, and it shows. The pacing is perfect, and there has clearly been a lot of work done over a long period on making sure that everything is just right. As a result, this is a really easy read that will hold your interest until the final page.

-*The Lesbian Review*

The Blood Runs Cold

While I did not read the first book in Catherine Maiorisi's Chiara Corelli series, this did not prevent me from thoroughly enjoying *The Blood Runs Cold*. Maiorisi populates her story with some much-needed diversity, but never strays into exhortative territory: these characters feel like individuals rather than stereotypes intended to fill a role (or purpose). The mystery is suitably complex, sure to keep readers guessing until late in the game.

-The Bolo Books Review

In most cases, I will say readers can start with the current book and not miss anything. With Chiara ostracized by other members of the department, readers should start with *A Matter of Blood* to get the full effect and the background of Chiara and PJ working together. Both books are fast-paced thrillers, where every minute could be their last, with no one to trust and nowhere to hide….Love page-turner thrillers? Pick these books up—then try to keep up with Chiara. It'll be a breathtaking ride.

-Kings River Life Magazine

An excellent police procedural with twists, turns and surprises. Looking forward to other mysteries featuring Chiara Corelli.

-Map Your Mystery

A MESSAGE IN BLOOD

About the Author

Catherine Maiorisi lives in New York City with her wife Sherry. She is a full-time writer. And writing is what she most loves to do. But she also reads voraciously, loves to cook, especially Italian, and enjoys spending time with her wife and Zooming with close friends.

A Matter of Blood, the first book in Catherine's NYPD Detective Chiara Corelli Mystery series, was a 2019 Lambda Literary Award Finalist. The second in the series, *The Blood Runs Cold,* was a 2020 Lambda Literary Award Finalist and a Golden Crown Literary Society Finalist. *A Message in Blood* is the third in the series.

While writing that first mystery, Catherine wrote a short story to develop the backstory for Brett Cummings, Corelli's love interest. To her surprise, the story turned out to be a romance, a genre she had never read and hadn't considered writing. "The Fan Club" was published in the *Best Lesbian Romance of 2014* edited by Radclyffe.

She has since published four romances: *Matters of the Heart, No One But You, Ready for Love* and *Taking a Chance on Love.*

Catherine has also published mystery and romance short stories. Go to www.catherinemaiorisi.com for a complete list and while you're there sign up for her mailing list.

Catherine is a member of The Golden Crown Literary Society, Sisters in Crime and Mystery Writers of America.

A MESSAGE
IN BLOOD

CATHERINE MAIORISI

BELLA
B O O K S
2021

Bella Books, Inc.
P.O. Box 10543
Tallahassee, FL 32302

Printed in the United States of America on acid-free paper.

First Bella Books Edition 2021

Editor: Ann Roberts
Cover Designer: Judith Fellows

ISBN: 978-1-64247-197-7

Acknowledgments

I wrote about a third of *A Message in Blood* in 2019 and picked it up again in March 2020, just as New York City went into Covid19 lockdown. Dear reader, I know I don't have to tell you about what that's been like. But I'm lucky. Though it isn't easy and everything takes longer than usual, I've been able to concentrate and write in the middle of the pandemic.

Child sex trafficking is a difficult subject. However, while I read a lot of upsetting information as background, Chiara and P.J. focus on punishing those who abuse children not on the actual abuse. And though several characters reveal they've been abused, the abuse is not described graphically. This is an important subject that needs more light shined on it.

As always, first thanks to my wife Sherry for her support and encouragement and her patience with my obsessive need to be writing and reading. I can't think of anyone I'd rather be locked down with.

Thank you to my editor Ann Roberts who managed to edit this long and complex manuscript in the middle of the pandemic with fires raging all around her. A brave woman on all fronts.

And thanks to my friend Judy Levitz for really helpful comments on the book.

No acknowledgement would be complete without a shout out to Jess and Linda and the other women of Bella Books for their support and encouragement. I appreciate all you do. Thanks.

And to my readers. I hope you enjoy *A Message in Blood*. Thank you, for buying my books, for reading them, and for letting me know how you feel about them. I love every email, every comment on Facebook and Twitter, and every review. Keep them coming.

Dedication

To all the first responders, to all the doctors, nurses, aides and hospital workers, to all the unheralded low-paid support workers staffing supermarkets and delivering food and medicine, and to all the behind the scene workers keeping the lights on, the gas flowing, and the world running in the time of the Covid19 pandemic.

CHAPTER ONE

Out on the tip of Pier 54, huddled in their coats against the battering wind, NYPD Detectives Chiara Corelli and P.J. Parker peered through the icy rain and the mist rising from the choppy water intent on keeping the floater in sight. But the pale face, streaming hair, and waving arm seemed like a trick of the eye, appearing, disappearing then appearing again.

Corelli clamped her jaw closed to keep her teeth from chattering. A floater in the Hudson River was better than being trapped behind a desk, even if it was a lot warmer behind that desk today. She was thrilled that a scheduling fluke put them on top of the catch list. But she hadn't planned to be in the middle of the Hudson River spotting a floater in a freaky November storm so she was underdressed in the leather coat and silk scarf she usually wore this time of year. She closed her eyes against the shifting wind and biting rain, stomped her feet, and wrapped her arms around herself. Nice irony. Survive the bullets, die from pneumonia.

Her surgeon would be pissed. She'd strongly advised Corelli to take another month to allow her body to fully recover. But the better she felt the harder it was for Corelli to stay home so she'd pushed and pushed until the surgeon reluctantly approved her for limited duty. To the doctor *limited* meant sitting behind a desk, to her it meant anything other than brawling with the bad guys.

Another blast of wind whipped her dripping hair in her face and pulled at her soaked leather coat. She shivered and hunched her shoulders trying to stay warm. "If the divers don't get here soon, they'll have one frozen body in the water and two on the pier."

"Over there." Parker pointed to a boat slowly making its way toward them.

The activity on the boat was a blur but if she squinted, she could make out four or five people milling around and two in wetsuits adjusting their air tanks for the dip into the freezing Hudson River. Though a recovery mission like this one didn't have the same imperative as a rescue operation, it seemed to her the crew was moving in slow motion while she and Parker were freezing their asses off. Of course, she had no one to blame except herself. She could have delegated this to one of the many police officers on the scene but she would never ask anyone to do something she wouldn't do herself. She pulled the collar of her coat tighter but it wasn't meant for this weather and didn't do much to stem the trickle of water running down her neck and back or to protect her from the wind and sleet. But at least she wasn't the one swimming in the Hudson River.

The divers slipped into the water and swam toward the pier in line with Corelli and Parker. They quickly located the woman, waved, and went under, taking her with them. A minute or two later one diver surfaced and towed the body toward shore.

"Let's go, Parker." With the gusting wind and sleet battering them, it was slow going on the icy boards and as they neared the end of the pier, Corelli stumbled.

Parker grabbed her and kept her on her feet. "Let me help you to the car. It's unlikely the medical examiner will find anything. I'll check and let you know."

Corelli pushed Parker's hands off her. "Damn it. Stop treating me like an invalid. And just because I've been away two months doesn't mean you're in charge. I decide who does what, when. Remember?"

"Limited duty doesn't include standing for hours in the middle of the Hudson River in a freaking ice storm. Damn, Corelli, not even two full days back and you're suicidal."

Parker veered in the direction of the tent set up so the Medical Examiner could do his job without his eyeballs freezing. Corelli followed. One of the diving team was leaving the tent and held out a hand to stop them. "There's another girl trapped deeper. Meg will bring her in once she frees her."

"Girl?"

"Yeah." He shook his head. "Kids."

"Shit." Be careful what you wish for. That warm desk was looking better and better.

They moved into the tent and stared down at the small body marbled blue and white from the icy water, long blond hair, unseeing blue eyes, tiny mouth hanging open, and small hands limp at her side. Every cop's nightmare. The guy standing over the girl looked up. "Hey, you can't come in here."

Parker flashed her badge. "Detectives Corelli and Parker."

"Oh, sorry, I'm Rob Willis, the new Medical Legal Investigator."

Corelli ignored the hand he extended and focused on the girl. She appeared to be about eight or nine years old, the age of her niece, Gabriella.

"Bastards," Parker said, as another body was gently placed next to the first.

The second girl was darker, long brown hair, brown eyes, olive skin and maybe a little older. Corelli studied the bodies.

"The kids are the hardest, aren't they?" Willis' question pulled her attention to him.

"Yeah, they are. I have a niece about the same age."

"And I, a daughter." Willis checked the girls for broken limbs and head wounds. He studied their necks, made some notes, then called for body bags to transport them to the morgue. "They haven't been in the water very long but as I'm sure you know, even a short time will eliminate any trace evidence. Right now my best guess is they were strangled."

"Thanks, Willis." Corelli and Parker moved aside to make room for the morgue technicians and left them to it.

Wondering whether she'd ever be warm again, Corelli headed for the two divers packing their gear. Seeing her approach, one of them muttered "traitor" and turned his back. The blood rushed to her face. Interesting, she was surprised her body was capable of flushing right now. Parker tensed. The ostracism hadn't been bad since she returned but it was still there. Though being shot while catching a murderer helped the men and women in blue remember they once respected her, some police would always see her as a traitor.

"Sorry, Corelli. You don't need that shit while you're dealing with two dead girls." Drumond, the supervisor of the diving team, saying her name brought her back to the freezing riverside.

"Not your fault he's an ass." Corelli pointed to the pier. "Bodies don't usually wash up down here. Why did these two end up out there?"

"Normally the tides and river flow would have dragged them downstream but all the recent storms have washed a lot of debris downriver and some of it accumulated around the piles under the pier. The girls got snagged on the debris. If one of them hadn't pulled loose enough to float to where she could be seen from the pier they might never have been found."

Corelli put her hand on the shoulder of the other diver who'd retrieved the girls, someone she'd known since the academy. "Meg, I have to ask, are you sure there were the only two?"

"It's pretty murky down there so no guarantees, but I poked around and I didn't find any others."

"Thanks. Good job, as always. Stay warm." Corelli fought the impulse to wrap her arms around herself but with each icy gust of wind she clenched her whole body. Damn. If she didn't get inside soon she would be shivering and her teeth would be chattering. Her gaze swept the clusters of police watching them. Determined not to show weakness, to project strength instead, she willed her shoulders to straighten and her voice to remain steady and greeted those who acknowledged her. As they approached their car she extended her hand. "Give me the keys to our car. It'll be more comfortable than the backseat of an unheated patrol car so meet me there with the witness."

Corelli started their unmarked vehicle, raised the heat to high, and moved to the backseat. She allowed herself to shiver and her teeth to chatter for a few seconds before rubbing her hands together to warm them and then drying her face with tissues they kept in the car. She was pretty sure she was soaked down to her underwear but she couldn't do anything about that or her ice-cold feet right now. She looked up when Parker opened the door.

"Ms. Connors, this is Detective Corelli," Parker said. She waved Jean Connors, the witness, into the car, closed the rear door and slipped behind the steering wheel.

The poor woman looked as cold as Corelli felt. "Sorry to keep you so long, Ms. Connors, but we needed to wait for the bodies to be retrieved before speaking to you."

"There was more than one?"

"Two." Corelli waited a second for that to sink in. "Girls. Around eight or nine."

Corelli wasn't sure whether Connors shivered from the cold or the news. "Oh, my God, two girls. I thought it was a woman but you know there were waves and her hair was floating and her face was blurry so at first I wasn't even sure it was a person until I saw the hand waving. What happened? How did they get there?"

"We'll find out. Tell us about this morning. Why were you on the pier so early on such a cold morning? What made you stop and look at the water?"

"I'm a writer. I walk every morning to get my blood flowing and to mull over ideas for my current story. I had a great idea this morning. Usually I stop and make notes but the wind and sleet made that impossible so I decided to think through the idea instead. Anyway, I was gazing out into the water, not really seeing it but trying to imagine where the idea would take the story. Then a gust of wind made me close my eyes and when I opened them I thought I saw a woman in the water. She kept dipping and disappearing so I decided she must be an illusion and went back to my thoughts. When I looked again she was still there. It took me a few minutes to realize she wasn't moving and that all I was seeing was her head and occasionally an arm was thrown up. So I called 911."

"Was anyone else on the pier?"

"Not that I noticed. On a day like today not many people walk out that far. Neither would I normally but I was so involved in my plot, I didn't notice how far I'd gone."

"Did you leave the pier to call?"

"I was freezing but I thought I might not be able to find her again if I left, so I waited to point her out to the police."

It was obvious she hadn't murdered the girls, so there was no need to hold her any longer. "Thank you, Ms. Connors. We'll get back to you if we have more questions. Can we drop you somewhere?"

"My apartment is just a few blocks from here."

After they dropped Connors off, Corelli moved to the front seat. Parker sat with the car in neutral. "What's next?"

"A gigantic cup of coffee. Stop at the café near the station. When we get back we need to check whether the girls were reported missing. And then—"

The ring of Parker's phone cut her off. "Ndep," Parker mouthed the Medical Legal Investigator's name. "Thanks. We're on our way." She broke the connection. "Ndep undressed the girls as soon as they arrived and found something she thinks we should see."

"Okay. After we pick up coffee head to the morgue."

Parker tapped the steering wheel, gazed at the street in front of them and made no move to put the car in gear. Just as Corelli was about to object, Parker shifted to face her. "We're close to your apartment. Should I run you home so you can change into dry clothes first?"

Corelli glared at her. She'd had the same thought but how dare Parker assume she needed special treatment? She controlled the urge to scream but couldn't contain the anger in her voice. "No, Mommy, I don't think so."

Parker threw up her hands. "Sorry, I didn't mean to be considerate." She put the car in drive and turned toward the coffee shop.

The frosty atmosphere in the car made the outside temperature seem pleasant. Corelli knew she needed to get a handle on her emotions. Seeing those two little ones triggered a memory of finding an Afghani woman and her three young daughters raped and slaughtered because the woman's husband fought against the Taliban. Parker didn't need to be attacked for something she had nothing to do with and for being…for caring.

She hated to show weakness. But she also hated that her nastiness made Parker afraid to suggest something that would make her feel better and protect her. She was soaked to her skin and the last thing she needed was a bad cold or even worse, pneumonia. Parker knew she wasn't completely healed from her gunshot wounds and would probably silently celebrate her being sensible for a change. "You're right. We're close to my apartment. I think I'd better change into dry clothing and put on a warmer coat."

Instead of the smart-assed comment or raised eyebrows Corelli half expected, Parker turned in the direction of her apartment. "My pants are soaked from the knee down. I think I might have some jeans still at your place from when I was staying over to care for you so I'll change too."

A half hour later they were back in the car. "Coffee then the morgue?"

CHAPTER TWO

Parking on First Avenue near the building that housed the City of New York's Office of the Chief Medical Examiner and the Manhattan morgue was a bitch so Parker threw their official sign on the dashboard and double-parked. They dropped the remains of their coffee into a bin before entering the building and waited in the busy reception area at the front desk for someone to escort them in. An assistant greeted them and led them back to the autopsy area. He handed them gowns and masks and waited until they put on the protective gear before opening the door to the room. Grim faced, Gloria Ndep looked up from the computer as they entered. The girls lay side by side on steel tables. Naked they looked even smaller and more fragile than they had when pulled from the river.

Ndep moved to stand between the tables. "When I undressed them I was, as we usually do, noting and photographing scars, bruises and any marks that might be a clue to who the deceased is or how they died. I want you to look at this." She parted the blonde's legs, then did the same for the dark-haired girl. Both had extensive bruising on their upper thighs. "I'll know after the autopsy but I'm almost positive we'll find vaginal and anal tearing."

Corelli glanced at Parker and could see her struggling for control. She pushed back her own sadness and reached for professional distance. "What are we looking at?" She wanted to hear Ndep say it.

"I believe the girls were sexually abused, not just once, but multiple times." She turned the blonde over, displaying her back and buttocks. She ran her fingers over the extensive scars. "These scars are healed but they appear to be the result of a whip and we can assume that it was used on her more than once."

Corelli rubbed her eyes. She didn't want to see this but she forced herself to look. "And the other girl?"

Ndep turned over the dark-haired one. "She seems to have escaped being whipped."

"Different Johns, different tastes?" Parker didn't attempt to hide her anger.

Ndep gazed at Parker a few seconds before answering. "Yes, Detective Parker, it appears that way. One other thing…" Ndep lifted the foot of the dark-haired girl and pointed to a raw spot on her heel and then displayed the same raw spot on the blond girl's heel. She gently lowered both legs to the table. "The same mark in the same area on both right heels is too uniform to be fish nibbling. I'd guess someone used a knife postmortem to slice off something, probably tattoos." She stepped away from the bodies to retrieve a metal tray. "I found these sewn into the hem of the darker one's dress." She extended the tray. "I've already checked; there are no fingerprints. You can touch them."

Corelli picked up the small medal saint, the kind you would wear on a chain, and an American Flag pin, the kind that lots of politicians wore. This looked like an expensive one. "The saint may be hers. She could have found the flag. Or stolen it. Maybe we're looking for a pedophile politician or one of the many other phony patriots who seem to dominate the news these days."

"You think a politician did this?" Parker asked.

"It wouldn't be the first time. And given the vile politicians crawling out from under slimy rocks these days, I wouldn't rule it out." Corelli put the medal and pin back in the tray. "One girl showing signs of abuse like this could be attributed to a single sexual predator. I may be wrong but my gut says that two obviously unrelated girls abused like this indicates it's someone providing girls for sex. If their heels *were* tattooed, it indicates an organized effort. And a lot more girls involved."

"I'm afraid you're right. Good luck finding the bastards." Ndep walked them out of the room. "The autopsies are scheduled for tomorrow afternoon. I expect we'll confirm strangulation as the cause of death."

They discarded their gear and bid her goodbye.

They were silent until they were driving across town. "So what do you think is our next step, Parker?"

"Check to see whether any other girls have turned up dead?"

"Answering a question with a question. Surely you can do better than that, Ms. Former ADA."

"Sorry."

"Shit Parker, I know it's been a couple of months but do I have to give you the apologizing speech again? Pussy-footing around an answer irritates me. Acting like you don't know what you're doing irritates me. Apologies irritate me the most. Just answer the freakin' question with a little confidence." Corelli blew out a breath. "Jeez-us. If you'd been this namby-pamby when I was bleeding out, I wouldn't have made it here to give you this lecture. So suck it up. You damn well know what to do."

"Wow. And here I was thinking that nearly two months away had helped your PTSD. I'd almost forgotten how nasty you can be. It only took a day and a half for you to start attacking me and three times in less than three hours is a bit much, even for you."

"I don't have PTSD. If I did, you would have driven me to suicide already."

"You do have PTSD. I was outside your hospital room day and night while you were there and in your apartment a number of days and nights before I went back to work. I heard your screams. I know you have nightmares. I know you don't sleep. It's nothing to be ashamed of. It's the result of honorably serving your country and your city."

Her rage ignited and as it flamed higher, her voice rose. "You don't know a damned thing about me, Parker, about how honorably I served or whether or not I sleep. I will not tolerate this bullshit. If you continue, I'll find someone else to work with me."

"Don't scream at me." Parker pulled into a bus zone and turned to Corelli. "PTSD is brought on by stress and dealing with two murdered girls about the same age as your niece is definitely stressful in my book. I was hoping you would talk to Gil Gilardi about the PTSD but I guess you managed to fool her like you fool almost everyone except me."

"What do you know about Gil Gilardi?" Corelli snarled. "I sure hope you didn't float your PTSD theory to her."

"I beg your pardon. I've protected your privacy so far, so why would I talk to the department psychologist about your mental state when I was there to talk about shooting someone and saving...stopping your bleeding?"

"You're obsessed with the idea of me having PTSD so why wouldn't you? And to answer your question, I didn't talk about anything other than getting shot and shooting someone, exactly what I needed to talk about to get cleared for the job. Gilardi tried to get me to continue in therapy privately and you know, Parker, I actually wondered whether you'd planted the seed."

"I'm done with this conversation. I think we both could use some quiet time." Parker started the car and pulled into traffic.

Corelli opened her mouth to have the last word and thought better of it. She gazed out the window trying to breath the way Dr. Gilardi had demonstrated. She wasn't sure if she got it right, but just focusing on something other than her rage helped calm her. Maybe she needed to think about Gilardi's suggestion that she do yoga to ease her alleged PTSD. They passed the next five minutes in silence.

"Now tell, don't ask me. What the hell would you do next, Parker?"

Parker glanced at her, then looked back at the street. She paused so long that Corelli wondered whether she'd finally pushed too far. "One. Approach Missing Persons and Special Victims about the girls. Two. Search the FBI database for other children who have turned up dead with similar heel marks. Three. Follow up on that religious medal. Maybe ask Father Bart if he recognizes it. Four. Send inquires to nearby departments in New York, Connecticut, Pennsylvania and New Jersey. Five. Try to trace the clothing. That's all I come up with now."

"Good. I'd add asking vice whether there are any brothels in the city specializing in children. Or, if any of the online sex sites are offering children."

"Child sex trafficking?" Parker sounded surprised.

Corelli breathed deeply trying to control her impatience. Parker didn't want to accept it. Well, she didn't want to see it either but they needed to deal with what they had, not what they wished they had. "As I said, two girls about the same age, who don't appear to be related, probably sexually assaulted more than once, beaten, strangled, heels shaved and tossed in the river? It seems like a good possibility. Either that or there's a serial child kidnapper-rapist and murderer with a heel fetish out there that we haven't heard about. Take your pick."

The grim set of Parker's mouth indicated she got it. They drove back to the station in silence.

CHAPTER THREE

It was another snowy, sleety, icy, wet day. The good news: they'd spent the day in the warm stationhouse making calls and doing research on computers. The bad news: they'd spent the day in the warm stationhouse making calls and doing research on computers and they'd made absolutely no progress on the investigation into the death of the two girls.

There hadn't been a missing person report filed for either girl. Plenty of kids had been murdered around the country but none of them could be tied to the two girls. Father Bart had confirmed that the religious medal was the Virgin of Guadalupe, which, like the girl's coloring and features, pointed to a possible Mexican connection but that led nowhere. The clothing turned out to be inexpensive so the labels were no help and vice had no leads on a brothel with children or online sex sites offering them. Since coming home from Afghanistan being trapped inside was intolerable for Corelli but walking outside on the snow and ice was risky. Falling would make her look weak, and worse, might set back her recovery. She hated being afraid. Add to that their lack of progress and she was unable to control her rage, causing her to dump on Parker again. Happily, Parker was fighting back but the tension wasn't doing either of them any good.

In the uneasy silence of the car as Parker drove her home, Corelli knew she was on the edge. Her usual coping mechanisms, attacking her punching bag and a long soak in her hot tub, hadn't helped last night. Running usually relaxed her but her leg wasn't strong enough yet. She'd never felt so out of control, never felt so afraid she'd explode and hurt somebody. It didn't help that her brain was replaying conflated images of her niece Gabriella, the two girls in the morgue and the girls in Afghanistan. She closed her eyes and rested her head against the car seat.

"Try yoga." Dr. Gil Gilardi threw out the suggestion after she confirmed she only slept two or three hours a night.

"You're kidding right?" She glared at the therapist who seemed to be doing her best Buddha imitation. "No way. I run and box and lift weights. I don't need to do that…pretentious, make believe exercise. Why would you even suggest it?"

Gil ignored the condescension in her voice. "Because a lot of veterans find it helps with post-traumatic stress. I can recommend classes taught by veterans for veterans."

"I don't have PTSD. But even if I did, I find it hard to believe twisting myself into a pretzel would help."

"You're probably right about that but these classes concentrate on breathing to control anger and promote less aggressive behavior." She wrote something on a pad and handed it to Corelli. "In case you decide to do something about your PTSD."

Corelli gasped. Her eyes popped open.

Parker glanced from the road. "You all right?"

"Yeah."

She must have dozed off. How weird was it that her mind replayed the conversation she'd had with Gilardi right before she'd approved her return to the job? Despite what she said to Parker and Gilardi, Corelli knew she had PTSD but addressing it would let feelings loose she'd rather not deal with. Hopefully, time would cure her. The dreams had continued during her two months of sick leave but she'd remained calm. Now, three days back on the job and she was in a rage. Before she was shot, she was mostly able to control the rage but when it seeped out she'd unloaded it on Parker. Yet Parker had kept her secret. Today she'd been harsh with Watson and Dietz. She thought Captain Winfry suspected she was hiding something, maybe even suspected PTSD, and if her erratic behavior came to his attention he might put her on medical leave again.

She glanced at Parker. She was strong and loyal. A good detective. She had saved her from bleeding out, had not left the hospital until she was out of danger and had helped care for her during her recovery. She deserved to be treated better.

Therapy wasn't an option. Though she was never sure whether to call Marnie her partner or lover or girlfriend, Corelli was sure she wasn't ready to deal with Marnie's death and the other scars of the Iraq and Afghanistan wars. But she had to do something different before she went crazy or worse—hurt someone. It was worth a shot. She dug in her wallet and found the slip of paper— Yoga for Warriors. The name was intriguing. "Do you have time to wait for me to get some stuff from my apartment, then drop me off downtown, near Franklin Street? It's personal."

"Sure, no problem."

Corelli changed quickly into her warmest sweats, a Henley, a sweatshirt, warm socks and sneakers, pulled on her down coat, then took the elevator to the street. As she exited the building Parker jumped out of the car, weapon drawn, eyes scanning the street. She slid into the passenger seat and when Parker started the car, gave her the address. She could feel Parker's interest but she didn't ask where she was going or why.

"Goodnight, Parker, see you in the morning." Parker was standing in the cold, on guard as usual, but didn't respond. Corelli took the elevator to the third-floor studio. She reached for the glass door then pulled back. This was stupid. Yoga is for yuppies. Before she could turn away a barefoot woman with close-cropped, salt-and-pepper hair, wearing a tank top and soft pants the color of fatigues smiled and waved her in. The woman's muscular build, tattoos and the air of command that made Corelli want to salute, signaled a veteran. Shit. Caught. Corelli straightened her shoulders and entered.

The woman greeted her with an outstretched hand. "I'm Billy Magarelli, a veteran of both Iraq and Afghanistan and the owner of the studio. Welcome."

"Chiara Corelli." She ordinarily wouldn't share but the woman held her gaze expectantly. "Also a veteran of Iraq and Afghanistan."

Magarelli's handshake was firm, her gaze was direct, and she seemed to see Corelli's unease. "Try a couple of sessions. Yoga can help if you can get into it. All our instructors are veterans who served in a warzone so we understand the kinds of problems veterans are dealing with. It's a safe environment." She glanced at the clock on the wall. "I'm teaching a beginners' class in fifteen minutes. If you decide to stay, hang your coat in the locker room, pay at the desk and wait here for me."

Corelli sat on the bench in front of an empty locker. She could walk out and never come back but she'd come because she was feeling out of control and dumping on Parker again. That wasn't right. That wasn't her or at least it wasn't who she used to be before Afghanistan and the three months undercover that followed. Leaving wouldn't alleviate the rage, wouldn't keep her from spewing her anger at Parker. She hated how it made her feel. She could tolerate almost anything for an hour so why not give it a try? She stuffed her gloves into her pockets, hung her coat and scarf, and threw in her sweatshirt. She returned to the reception area, paid for the class, and while she waited, observed the men and women entering. All sizes, all colors, some in suits, others more casual, some with tattoos, some with visible injuries, and some like her with hidden injuries. They were all obviously military. Though she didn't know them, these people, the survivors of the disastrous and demoralizing Iraq and Afghanistan wars, would understand her experience. Maybe yoga *would* help. She relaxed. Apparently three different classes were starting at the same time but Magarelli had pegged her as a beginner and came to bring her into the room where the class was being held.

"Get a mat, a couple of weights and a wooden block, then find a spot on the floor. The way this works is, I model the pose and then everyone does it to the best of their ability. Don't worry if you can't do it at first, or if it's not exact or if you can't hold it as long as the others. That comes with experience." She waited until Corelli was sitting on her mat. "Is it all right if I touch your body to correct a pose? I'll always tell you before I do."

"I think I'll be okay if you warn me."

"Do you have any injuries I should avoid?"

She hadn't thought about the bullet wounds. "I do have some wounds that are still healing." She indicated her leg and shoulder and arm.

"Don't worry, I'm careful." Magarelli smiled. "I have no desire to be slugged." She glanced at the clock then clapped her hands to get everyone's attention. "We have a new member tonight. Her name is Corelli." After allowing time for the smiles, nods and some grunted greetings, Magarelli demonstrated the first pose and then moved around correcting people. As promised, she always warned before touching. Much of the class was devoted to breathing. And Magarelli spent a lot of time with her while the more experienced students held the poses.

At the end of the hour Magarelli guided them through a relaxation exercise and then ended the class. Corelli had worked up a good sweat so she appreciated the cool down. While she put on her socks and shoes, the young vet who'd been next to her during the class did the same, except one of her shoes was part of a prosthetic leg. "Hi. Corelli, right? I'm Sarah. First time?"

Sarah looked too young to be a wounded vet, but there she was, leg in hand, a chopper and U.S.M.C. tattooed on the upper thigh of the same leg.

"Yes, did it show?"

The girl smiled. "Nah. Well maybe a little, but we all start from where we are. Did you like it?"

Good question. Her body felt good. "It was different than I expected but I feel relaxed which doesn't happen that much these days."

Sarah smiled. "I know what you mean." She rolled to her good leg and got to her feet. "See you next time."

Corelli returned her mat, block and weights to their respective piles, observing that most of the people leaving said, "Goodnight, Major," to Magarelli. So that answered that question.

"How did it go for you, Corelli?"

She turned to face Magarelli. "Okay. I didn't expect it to be so vigorous."

"We've all been through boot camp so no wimpy yoga for us. Will I see you again?"

"I'm not sure."

Magarelli smiled. "Let me give you our schedule in case you want to try a few more classes before deciding." They walked out to the desk together. The major handed her a pamphlet and met her eyes. "I've been where you are, Corelli, most of us have. Yoga can help. It's a lot better than drugs, alcohol or suicide and it makes talk therapy easier. Come back."

Chiara was moved by the compassion in her eyes. "I'll think about it."

The major stepped back and saluted. Corelli returned the salute automatically. Magarelli smiled. "Think hard, soldier." Corelli watched her walk to her next class then headed for the locker room.

Out on the street, she looked around to get her bearings and was surprised to see Parker leaning against the car. "What are you doing here, Parker?"

"You know the rules, Corelli. I pick you up in the morning. I drop you off at night. So I'm waiting to drive you home."

Corelli shook her head but she was too tired to argue. Actually she was tired physically, not mentally, and she was looking forward to a long soak in her tub and a glass of wine. It was kind of nice to just get in the car and relax. "Okay, so drive."

Corelli was pretty sure she saw Parker smile before starting the car.

At Corelli's apartment, Parker followed her usual routine, stepping out of the car with her gun drawn, scanning for possible attackers, and watching until Corelli was safely in the elevator with the doors closed.

Home at last Corelli turned up the heat in the huge industrial vat that served as her tub and attended to the two kittens attacking her legs while complaining about her starving them. The monsters taken care of, she lit some candles, heated leftovers, poured a glass of cabernet, stripped and slid into the water. The kittens followed and strolled around the edge of the tub, butted her head and purred in her ear. After a few minutes they settled on the shelf she'd cleared for them and slept. The lights of New Jersey blinked across the dark Hudson River as she sipped and nibbled and considered the yoga class.

The major was attractive in a butch sort of way but that wasn't what interested Corelli. According to the pamphlet, Magarelli was a psychiatrist. She'd served in Iraq and Afghanistan and yoga had helped her deal with her issues so she started the yoga studio to help other veterans. While they hadn't talked specifics, Chiara sensed her nightmares and anger issues wouldn't surprise Magarelli. And she had to admit that after the yoga her body was pleasantly tired instead of tense and fidgety. If the major, a veteran of the same wars who could understand her experiences in a way that no one in her life did believed yoga could help tame her demons maybe she should pay attention. She yawned.

CHAPTER FOUR

The call came at one thirty in the morning. Though she'd managed to sleep almost three straight hours without a nightmare for the first time in forever, the dreams showed up eventually so she was already awake, sitting up in bed with her two kittens curled on her lap, reading a mystery to the comforting vibration of their purrs. "Corelli."

Captain Winfry didn't waste any time on pleasantries. "You've been summoned to a murder scene on the Upper East Side. Parker will pick you up in twenty minutes or so. She has the location."

Homicides on the East Side weren't usually their responsibility. And the captain's job didn't ordinarily involve calling out investigative teams in the middle of the night, or in his words, summoning them. "Summoned? By who? And why?"

"Broderick. According to him, it's a highly sensitive situation. He'll be there when you arrive. I'm told you get any resources you need. Good luck with this one, Corelli. I don't know why only you can handle it, but orders are orders. Unfortunately it sounds like you and Parker are being tossed into the frying pan. I'll do what I can. Keep me posted."

So much for the slow re-entry recommended by the department shrink and her surgeon. Her third day back on the job after almost two months and Broderick tosses her another hot potato. Though to be honest, another day trapped in the office trying to get a lead on the deaths of the two girls might push her over the edge. She was sure to get some action on this one. The case belonged in Captain Benson's precinct and she doubted he'd requested her as the lead. She smiled, imagining his fury at having yet another case yanked from his control and given to her.

She gently lifted the kittens, trying not to wake them so she wouldn't have to hear their pathetic cries for breakfast at this way too early hour. After washing and dressing she removed her Glock 26 from the safe, loaded it, set the safety and slid it into the sheath on her ankle. Next she retrieved her Glock 19, loaded a clip, checked the safety and eased it into the waist holster. It still felt strange to be retrieving them from the safe.

Before she was shot she'd slept with her weapon on her pillow every night. But when she was discharged from the hospital, she was too weak to be alone and fearing she would inadvertently shoot one of her care team in the throes of a nightmare, she'd asked Parker to buy her a gun safe. Since her three sisters, her nephew and her more-than-friend, not-yet-lover Brett were still in and out checking on her, she'd continued to use it now that she was back on the job.

Upstairs she started a pot of coffee then washed the cats' dishes. She knew the kittens would eat as soon as they woke up but she had no idea when she'd be back so she put out food and clean water. While she waited for the coffee to brew, she walked around the apartment still trying to get used to the weight of the two guns. She debated whether to take her cane. She'd pretty much weaned herself off it but her balance wasn't good when she was tired. She'd almost fallen on the pier the other day and judging by the howling wind and the rat-a-tat-tat of sleet hitting the windows, today was likely to be another treacherous day for walking. She chewed her lip. She didn't want to fall on her ass in front of anyone, but the cane made her look weak. As soon as the coffeemaker beeped, she filled two travel cups and turned the pot off. She'd learned her lesson about dressing for this weather so she slipped into her down coat, pulled on her woolen cap, wrapped the scarf around her neck and checked her pockets for her gloves. Ready for whatever the weather gods threw at her she went down the elevator to wait for Parker. Screw the cane. Parker would be there.

It was dark and cold and the wind whipping off the nearby Hudson River was icy and biting. Corelli narrowed her eyes and peered into the darkness through the windows in her lobby. As she suspected, Parker was waiting just beyond the illumination of the streetlight, alert for threats, ready to ward off an attack. Corelli let it go for now but she and Parker needed to have a talk soon. Many of their colleagues had shown up at the hospital as a show of support and since her return the crowds jeering and turning their backs on her and the obvious hatred hadn't reappeared. "Morning, Parker."

"Morning. Happy third day back on the job."

"Maybe." Corelli leaned in, put Parker's coffee in the cup holder and got into the car.

Parker grabbed the coffee as soon as she closed her door. "Hits the spot."

Corelli snapped her seatbelt. "Did they give you anything beside the address?"

"Only that it's sensitive." Parker started the car. "You ready for this?"

"It'll probably not be the quiet, boring day I envisioned yesterday." Corelli laughed. "But holding my nose and jumping in seems to be a consistent theme for my first days back on the job. First time it was going undercover, then walking the gauntlet, now this, which sounds like it could be a career-breaking case."

"Any ideas?" Parker drove the half block to West Street and turned right, heading uptown. Even the highway was half asleep at this hour.

Corelli sipped her coffee. Being cocooned in the warm, silent car in the semi-dark was almost pleasant, but reality would intrude soon enough. "It must be really bad if Broderick is meeting us there. But we'll know soon enough."

Parker pulled up in front of a building the width of three brownstones on Seventy-Fourth Street between Fifth and Madison. It was the only house with lights on inside and out. The rest of the block was dark and quiet. Not a police car, ambulance or CSU vehicle in sight.

Weapons drawn, they got out of the car. Corelli scanned the area. "Where the hell is Broderick?"

They pivoted toward a sudden flash of light on the other side of the street and two men exited a car with their hands in the air. "It's us, Chief Broderick and Commissioner Neil."

Shit. Police Commissioner George Neil. This must really be bad for the commissioner, a civilian, to be here in the middle of the night. They holstered their guns and moved to the men. "Good morning. Have you met my partner, Detective P.J. Parker, Commissioner?"

"Yes. We met at the hospital when you were in surgery. Thank you both for coming so quickly. I'll let the chief explain."

Chief Broderick blew on his hands. "Take a look at the scene first then we'll talk. When you're finished come out to the car and we'll discuss how to proceed. That house. The door is open. Crime scene is on the far end of the second floor. Take your time."

Corelli started toward the house then stopped. "Chief, can I assume no one has cleared the house?"

He flushed. "Uh, no I didn't clear."

"And did either of you touch anything in the room?" She shouldn't have to worry about the brass contaminating the crime scene but experience had shown that they were the worst offenders. They seemed to think they were so important that the rules didn't apply to them.

"We stood in the doorway," Commissioner Neil said.

They stopped at their vehicle to stuff nitrile gloves and paper booties in their coat pockets and then walked up the steps. "Put your phone flashlight on, Parker, so we can get a good look at the door and the lock."

"The door hasn't been forced and the lock looks fine." Parker shut off her flashlight, pocketed the phone, and pulled on a pair of gloves. Corelli did the same.

They stopped in the vestibule to put on paper booties, drew their guns and entered. Music drifted down from somewhere in the house. They moved through the lower floor, clearing a large messy kitchen with commercial appliances, an elevator, a bedroom, a large pantry, a walk-in freezer, a refrigerated wine cabinet, a laundry room, and a living room with a sofa, easy chairs, side tables, lamps and a TV. The sliding glass doors to the backyard and all the windows were secured.

"We'll clear top down." Corelli ignored the elevator and started up the staircase. The music was louder as they approached the second floor but diminished again as they continued up to the top floor. One by one they cleared the bedrooms, beds neatly made, no one in the closets or under the beds or behind the shower curtains in their en suite bathrooms. The last bedroom and its bathroom were as pristine as the others except the bed was stripped down to sheets, the room had no closet and the tall dresser wasn't flush against the wall like in the other rooms. Something was off. Corelli stared at what looked like the outline of a doorway above the dresser. Was that the closet? A secret room?

She waved Parker closer, mimed moving the dresser, and they easily swung it out of the way. Standing on either side of the now exposed door, they locked eyes for a second, then Parker turned the knob and slowly pulled the door open. Gun at the ready, Corelli stared into the closet. It was clear no one was hiding behind the empty hangers or on the empty shelves, but the incongruity of the anal neatness of the bedrooms, bathrooms and closets they'd cleared, and the messy pile of what appeared to be the missing blanket and comforter on the floor, drew Corelli's eye. Was that a foot? She knelt and slowly lifted the blankets, exposing three naked girls probably between six and ten years old, curled together. More girls, more abuse. She swallowed. She had a job to do. She glanced at Parker, not surprised at the shock on her face. The girls seemed to be in a deep sleep, maybe drugged. She sniffed, trying to identify the smell. "Light," she whispered.

Parker turned on her flashlight app.

The leg of the closest girl looked sticky. She touched the spot and sniffed her finger. Fuck. She wanted to scream. Instead, she carefully scanned the girls for obvious injuries, covered them, then stepped out of the closet.

Parker closed the door gently.

Her mind was racing and she could see Parker trying to arrange the facts into a reasonable scenario. "There's no blood and I didn't see any external injuries but they were recently sexually abused. They smelled of sex. I don't know who is dead downstairs but this definitely complicates things." Corelli tossed her gloves in the basket in the bathroom and pulled on a clean pair.

Parker seemed frozen. "What should we do with them?" She whispered but the pain and anger in her voice were loud and clear.

Corelli touched Parker's shoulder to get her attention. "For now, we let them sleep. They should be okay for the hour or so we need to clear the rest of the house and take a look at the main act, or at least what the brass thought was the main act when they called us. Once we have a better idea of what we're dealing with we can figure out how to proceed." She glanced at the closet door. "You okay with that?"

Parker straightened her shoulders. "Yes." They headed for the stairs.

Down on the third floor, they cleared a large comfortable looking living room, an office, a bathroom, a gym, and the master bedroom suite. All appeared normal. Back on the parlor floor, the music was louder. The first room they entered was a formal library, with book-lined walls and a ladder that went around the room, a fireplace, a huge desk, a sofa, a couple of easy chairs, a dry bar with a small refrigerator, an array of alcoholic and non-alcoholic beverages, glasses, and an empty ice bucket. The next room was a recording studio, one half obviously for the singer or group recording and the other half with an impressive array of recording equipment for the technicians. The next room appeared to be a practice room with a piano, a drum set, a desk, and a number of music stands and chairs stacked against one wall. Three framed gold albums hung on the wall, all awarded to Amari DeAndre.

"Looks like the house belongs to a popular singer. I hope she's not the one who's dead." Corelli only recognized DeAndre's name because her sister, Simone, and her nephew Nicky, were wild about the popular singer and her group, Night Walkers. The two twenty-year-olds were part of her care team and when she was too weak to be alone, they often stayed overnight to help her and entertained themselves by singing and dancing to DeAndre's music. "Interesting. The latest gold record is from six years ago, but I'm pretty sure one of her recent albums went gold. Maybe it gets boring after a while."

They continued down the hall then stopped short. Parker used her phone flashlight so they could examine what looked like a pile of vomit with a footprint going in the direction they were headed.

A few steps more brought them to the scene of the crime. They stared into the large room from the doorway, trying not to breathe while trying to absorb what was in front of them. It was hard to know whether to look first at the message CHILD ABUSERS MUST DIE scrawled in what appeared to be blood on the mirrored wall or at the three naked men lying in puddles of their own blood and excrement. Corelli felt a headache coming on. She put her hands to her temples, then became aware again of the music.

Even after a large travel mug of coffee, the music was too loud for this time of the morning and she was finding it impossible to concentrate on the implications of the message and the men and the girls. She pulled her gaze from the dead men and looked for a stereo or radio to turn off. It took a minute for her to spot the small device. "Music off," she commanded. Amused at herself she thought maybe if she said, "Beam me up, Scotty," she could go back to bed and leave this mess for someone else. But the music command didn't work so no beaming up. The crime scene and all its messy fallout was hers. She was seriously considering going in to smash the damned thing or at the least unplug it when Parker issued a command with an unfamiliar name and the music stopped. They were in blessed silence.

Corelli blew out a breath. "Thank you, Parker. You have one of those things?"

"No. But Jessie does."

Corelli turned her attention back to the bloody tableau. A dark-haired man with fashionable dark stubble on his face lay on the floor in front of a bed, a light-skinned black man was draped over the edge of a bed and the third, a blonde, was half off the large sofa at the far end of the room. All three were on their backs, face up. Maybe they were starting to stand before they were shot or maybe the force of the bullets jerked them off the beds and sofa. With all the blood it was hard to tell for sure from the doorway, but it appeared that they were each shot multiple times.

One of the men was immediately recognizable. *Oh yeah, beam me up, Scotty.* She knew it was going to be bad but this was as bad as it could get. "The blond is Harry Stanerd, the Republican Senate Majority Leader. The other is reverend somebody or other." She turned to Parker. "Any idea?"

Parker grimaced. "That's the Reverend William Dumayne from the mega church up in Harlem."

Corelli drew a blank on the third victim. "What about the guy who needs a shave?"

Parker stared at the body for a few seconds. "I'm pretty sure that's Jake Blecker, a Republican billionaire, big in music, TV and movie stuff. Has a reputation as a playboy."

Corelli blew out a breath. "What a fucking mess. Now we know why all the secrecy. And Broderick and Neil don't even know about the kids. This one's not a hot potato. It's a handful of live wires. No use both of us going down. You want off the case?"

Parker snorted. "Still the martyr, I see." She looked away. "I'm interested in finding out who killed these three, but I want on the case to get justice for those kids." She hesitated. "Do you think this is connected in some way to our two floaters?"

Corelli's eyes widened. "Good question. Maybe."

Parker waved her hand indicating the three bodies. "So, what are we supposed to do with this?"

It was obvious that Parker was upset and angry about the sexual abuse but Corelli sensed she shouldn't offer support. If she was honest, she was upset and angry too. And what could anyone say about this that would make it better? "We solve it. If you're in, let's see what we see. You start."

Parker opened her notebook and readied her pen.

Corelli held up a hand. "Describe the scene but don't mention the lack of clothing or the children. I don't want their presence to get out."

Parker tapped her pen on her notebook. "So no naked, no sex. Got it." She scanned the room. "It's not likely any of them would have let the killer in while naked, so maybe the killer had a key or they were expecting someone and left the front door open. Given the message on the mirror, it's likely the killer caught them raping the girls. This wasn't a dispassionate killer. It appears the shooter kept his finger on the trigger, which leads me to believe he or she killed in anger and it was meant to be a massacre." She closed her eyes and took a deep breath. "The good news is that although they appear to have been sexually abused before the murderer got rid of these slime bags, the children are alive."

Corelli mostly agreed with Parker but she had a slightly different perspective. "In the scenario in my head, there are at least two killers. Since the rapists' shirts, jackets, pants, shoes and socks are all neatly folded in the corner and the girls' clothing is tossed nearby, I assume the men were naked and in the act of raping the children when the killers arrived. One of the killers takes the children upstairs to protect them. Either the remaining killer shoots them or he waits until his accomplice returns and they both shoot them."

Corelli gazed at Parker. "What do you think?"

Parker seemed lost in thought for a few minutes. "It works for me. It explains why the men were naked and why the children were hidden."

Corelli turned her attention back to the men. "The easiest and safest bet for us would be to do what we were brought in to do: investigate this as the political murder of three important men. Since these murders were seen as a political hot potato by the brass, it's likely we'll be asked to cover up that message and the fact that children were in the house, children who were sexually abused."

"You wouldn't agree to ignore the sexual abuse of the children, right?"

Corelli narrowed her eyes and glared. "The bullets hit my body, not my brain, Parker. You should know by now I won't ignore it. I have lots of questions that take me away from the easy and safe. For one, where is the Majority Leader's security detail? And how did the killers know they wouldn't be around? Was he the target and everyone else collateral damage? Where did these children come from? Who brought them here? One man with a child could be explained easily because you can buy anything on the web these days. I doubt this was the first time these three high-profile men met to have sex with little girls." She waved her hand around. "Look at this room. Multiple beds, a sofa, cameras and racks of costumes. And that mirror... This is set up for sex and porn. These three men having sex with three children in the same room makes me think of a sick sex club, and perhaps a sex trafficking ring that provides children to rich, perverted men."

"Whoa." Parker lifted her gaze from her notebook. She looked past the dead men to take in the room itself.

Corelli waited for Parker to complete her examination. "It's just a theory. But if the goal was to eliminate these three men, they could have been killed in many other places. Instead, they were murdered here in this room while naked, with three naked, probably sexually abused children in the house and a message accusing them of child abuse scrawled on the mirror, circumstances sure to create an embarrassing scandal for their families, party, and church."

Parker made notes. "Would a trafficking ring call attention to itself by murdering prominent members?"

"They'd probably expect a cover-up but they could still use it as leverage against others. The fact that Commissioner Neil is here on the scene makes me wonder whether he'll try to get us to cover up the sex aspects of the murder."

Pen in midair, Parker met Corelli's eyes. "The chief may have different reasons but my guess is he probably won't like our approach either."

Corelli didn't miss Parker's use of *our* rather than *your*. "Probably not. But if they want a cover-up, they can get other detectives. This will be tough and dirty." She couldn't resist poking Parker. "Maybe a career killer. Still with me?"

"Damn it, Corelli, you're not the only one with a strong moral compass. I'm in. Either way."

"Since you keep accusing me of having a death wish, Parker, I want to be sure you're ready to run toward the gunfire with me." Corelli didn't give her a chance to respond. "We need EMTs we trust to deal with the girls, so I'm going to call Julia Morgan and Allegra Thompson. Hopefully, they're on duty tonight. I'm pretty sure they'll be willing to do what we need and protect the girls. You call Greene, and ask her to get here ASAP, but don't tell her why. I'm assigning her to stay with the girls." With a last look at the bloody scene, they went downstairs to make their calls.

Corelli paced as she filled Julia in on what she needed and the necessity of discretion. Parker was off the phone and waiting when Corelli turned her thumb up and grinned. "They're on board. Hopefully they won't back out when they see what we're dealing with. Let's go break the news to Broderick and Neil. If they want us to stay on the case we'll need to get a team here right away."

They crossed the street and slid into the backseat of the car. The two men shifted to face them. The motor was running and the warmth felt good.

"What's your take?" Broderick asked the question but Neil's eyes were on her. He was a civilian and wouldn't ordinarily have been privy to such a messy crime scene. Was it anxiety?

"A senator, a millionaire and a reverend. Sounds like the start of a joke. But it's far from that. All three naked, all shot to death. And a message in blood that says 'Child Abusers Must Die.' And to prove the truth of the message, we found three naked little girls hidden in a closet on the top floor. We believe they were raped by those three fine gentlemen tonight."

"Shit."

That reaction from Broderick, who made a point of not cursing after his children were born, warmed Corelli's heart. Neil looked queasy. Maybe they wouldn't want to block the investigation.

"How old? And did they say they were abused tonight?" Broderick asked.

"Somewhere between six and ten years old. They didn't say anything because they were in a very deep sleep, probably drugged, but I could see what appeared to be semen and I could smell sex on them."

Neil rolled down the window. Broderick looked ready to run. This could be a career killer for him as well.

Corelli gave them a few seconds to think about the implications of the children being on the scene. "EMTs, friends of mine, are going to take them to a hospital where they trust the staff to check them out physically without asking too many questions. They'll do rape kits and tests to determine whether they were drugged. Hopefully DNA will confirm that the three men were the abusers."

"Damn." Broderick was on a cursing binge tonight. "Are you sure your friends will keep this below the radar until we figure out how to deal with the girls?"

"We won't sweep this under the rug." She wanted him to know the score upfront. "If that's what you want you'll need another team."

"Nobody is asking you to do a cover-up." Commissioner Neil took control. "I asked for the best because I wanted a thorough, honest and discreet investigation. I'd like to hear your thoughts on the murder."

Impressed, Corelli focused on Neil. "We're thinking about a couple of scenarios. The simple one is that these three men were habitual child abusers working alone and two people wanting revenge—parents, former victims, or do-gooders—got wind of it, figured out they'd be here tonight and showed up to murder them. The message on the mirror and the fact the girls were obviously moved to safety before the men were killed point to this scenario.

"Another scenario is that the men were involved with a child sex trafficking ring and were punished for not following the rules. Think about it. Any of these three could have been gunned down on the streets or at home and the murders would have been attributed to politics or crazies. But instead, they were murdered together in the middle of what appears to be an orgy with children. It's repulsive and will ruin their reputations when it gets out. The setup of the room, the costumes and the professional cameras which are probably used to produce porn sold by the ring, support this scenario."

"Theories are just assumptions." Broderick frowned. "I say it's political or maybe a robbery and the abuse is a side issue. We need to be careful."

Corelli expected Broderick to want to take the easy path but she realized his choosing to downplay the abuse meant he was seriously freaked. Or seriously compromised. She hoped it was the former. "In my book, sir, child abuse is never a side issue. We didn't see any signs of a break-in. And no sign of robbery. It appears they didn't touch any of the expensive recording equipment or the valuable paintings I recognized. From the gold records hanging on the wall, it appears that Amari DeAndre may own the house but until the owner or her representative confirms missing valuables, I'm assuming it wasn't robbery.

"Of course, we'll have to determine whether there are currently any political issues important enough to warrant killing a senator and anyone who happened to be with him. But yesterday two girls around the same age as these three were pulled out of the Hudson. Bruising indicated both were repeatedly abused and it appears they were strangled."

She met Broderick's eyes. "Until I find proof of some other motive, my working hypothesis is that the murders are related to the child sexual abuse and a child sex trafficking ring may be involved."

Broderick glanced at Neil. "What do you think, Commissioner?"

"When I asked who was the best detective to handle something as sensitive as the murder of three prominent men, you said Corelli. I say as long as she can do it discreetly, we let her do her job and follow her instincts."

Broderick cleared his throat. "I don't know, Commissioner. If it gets out that we suspect these men were involved in child sex trafficking, we could all be—"

"I have no intention of covering this up, Chief. Whether it was a ring or not, if they were using children they deserve to be exposed. And if it is a trafficking ring, we need to find the leaders and send them all to hell…or at least to jail." Neil turned to Corelli and Parker sitting in the backseat. "Corelli, you're in charge. To the extent possible, do a by-the-book investigation but do whatever is necessary to protect those girls. But let's keep the lid on the sexual abuse until we find the killers and have enough to go public. Report to Chief Broderick and Captain Winfry, as usual, but we'll all meet two evenings a week in my office. My assistant will coordinate so the times are convenient for everyone. Also, I want both of you to have my cell number." He dictated the number and watched them key it into their contacts. "Don't wait for meetings. Call me if you need something. Now tell us how you'll run the investigation and keep the details private."

She shot a look at Broderick. He avoided her eyes. He'd just had his knuckles rapped by his boss. He'd recommended her to lead the investigation because he knew she could handle it, yet, as always, a part of him wanted to play it safe. She wasn't at all sympathetic. If he hadn't figured out by now that she would always follow the evidence, he didn't deserve to be chief.

"To start, we'll bring in handpicked detectives from our precinct and people Parker and I trust, people like Gloria Ndep, an MLI from the Medical Examiner's office and Lou Bullard, the CSU supervisor. We'll ask them to bring people they trust so we can prevent or at least minimize information leaking. Two EMTs I trust are on the way. After getting the girls checked out at the hospital, they'll transport them to a safe place, someplace other than the foster care system, where we can protect them. And to reduce the possibility of leaks and maintain control of information about the case, we may withhold certain information and reports initially. Finally, I'll disclose the names of the three men at a press conference later today. That's as far as I've been able to plan." She turned to Broderick. "Can you clear things with the Medical Examiner and the head of CSU? I need cell numbers for Ndep and Bullard."

"I have Ndep's cell." Parker waved her phone. "She stopped by a few times when you were in the hospital and gave me her number in case we needed anything."

Was Parker blushing? Hard to tell in this light. "Get her on the phone and let me talk to her." As Corelli watched Parker type in Ndep's name it occurred to her that she probably had Bullard's number in her own contact list.

"Sorry to wake you, Gloria. Detective Corelli wants to speak to you so I'm giving her my phone."

Corelli stepped out of the car to speak to Ndep. "We have three bodies and a politically sensitive situation. I trust your discretion and your investigative skills so I want you to be responsible for the scene and overseeing body transport. But this case will be more like a raging fire than a hot potato and we may get blowback, so tell me now if you'd rather not be involved. If you're in, I need you here as quickly as possible so we can start to process the scene."

She could hear Ndep moving around. It sounded like she was opening drawers. "Count me in, Detective."

"Parker will give you the details." She handed the phone to Parker, then pulled her own phone out of her pocket. She did have Bullard's number. She woke him. He was immediately alert. She explained the need for secrecy and people who could be trusted, and though he and his people were less likely to be in the line of fire, she explained the potential danger. He didn't hesitate. He would have a trusted CSU team including the photographer she wanted there, as soon as possible.

Next she called Winfry to update him and to request Detectives Watkins, Greene, Dietz, Kim and Forlini, plus officers Hernandez, Shaunton, Twilliger and Dugan be assigned to the case and told to report immediately.

Corelli and Parker got back in the car. "We were able to contact Ndep and Bullard." Corelli looked at her two superiors. "We need to get ahead of this thing. Parker and I will take care of breaking the news to the Blecker and Dumayne families. Can you arrange for someone in Washington to break the news to the senator's family? And I suppose someone in the senate and/or the Attorney General's office should also be notified."

Broderick dug into the briefcase at his side, removed a pad and made notes. "I'll take care of that."

"If you can, find out why the Majority Leader's security detail isn't with him."

Broderick's eyebrows shot up. "Good question." He made another note.

"Also, could you have your office schedule the press conference for tonight so we can announce the deaths of these three upstanding men? Sorry, I don't mean to be snarky," Corelli said.

"No need to apologize," Neil said. "You'll be there?"

"Unless you'd rather do it." She looked at Broderick. "Can you justify assigning the case to me?"

"Sure. High-profile victims, hero detective with mucho experience, high solve rate, et cetera. I don't think many people will be surprised. You should be there."

"All right. I suggest we give them the bare minimum right now."

"Do you need anything else from us?" Broderick said.

"Yes. The name of the person who found them." It had to be someone with connections who had Commissioner Neil's personal phone number, someone who probably hoped to have this hushed up. Otherwise, why not call 911 and get an immediate response?

"Senator Parker," Broderick said.

Corelli ignored Parker's quick intake of breath but Broderick didn't. "Sorry, I wasn't thinking when I told Winfry to call both of you out. Investigating her uncle could create a conflict for Detective Parker and may compromise the integrity of the investigation."

Corelli glanced at Parker. "You selected us, me and Parker, to lead this investigation because it's sensitive and needs careful handling. So trust that we'll do it right. Where is the senator? We need to interview him while everything is fresh in his mind."

Broderick cleared his throat. "He was upset so I let him go home."

Corelli stared at him. His apparent discomfort made it clear that he remembered enough about crime scene investigation to know that witnesses should be retained at the scene, especially the person who found the bodies. Unbelievable. But blowing up at him wouldn't change the fact that he'd released the major witness and it might result in her being pulled from the case. As messy as this one would be, it was preferable to being trapped behind a desk. She released the air in her lungs and switched her attention to the commissioner.

"Okay. I assume the senator called you, Commissioner. What time? How did he sound? What did he say?"

"The call woke me but I couldn't get to the phone fast enough." Neil checked his phone. "The missed call was at eleven fifty-nine. I called him back immediately." He stared into space for a few seconds. "He was out of breath, like he'd been running, and agitated. He said he'd come for a late meeting and found the three men dead in an embarrassing situation, that it was bloody, horrible and needed to be handled carefully. He wanted to go home but I told him to wait for us. I called the chief and he drove in from Brooklyn and picked me up. We met the senator on the corner of Madison and Seventy-Fourth just about twelve forty-five. He directed us to the house and waited in the car while we went inside to see for ourselves. When we returned, the chief and I discussed who was the best detective to handle such a sensitive case, then the chief called Winfry to get you and Detective Parker here."

So Senator Parker was present when Broderick recommended her. "Did the senator object to having me be the lead on the case?"

"He didn't object," Neil said, "but he mentioned you might be antagonistic toward him because he's been critical of you at times."

"I assure you, Commissioner, his attention-getting ploys won't affect my investigation." She turned to Broderick. "Did the senator explain why he was here? And what he did when he found the men?"

"Stanerd asked to meet with him. He said the door was open and he went upstairs as instructed. He was shocked, then realized they might not be dead so he checked each of their carotid arteries. He was trying to decide what to do when he heard voices from upstairs and ran out thinking it might be the killers." He met her eyes. "He was pretty shaken and I had no reason to doubt he was telling the truth."

She wanted to slap him for bowing down to power and status. Men like Senator Parker lie and do terrible things every day, as the crime scene proved. "Standard procedure as you know is to hold the witness for questioning at the scene when everything is fresh. We should have checked his hands and clothing for gunshot residue."

"He didn't have a gun," Broderick said. "And he was really rattled. You can question him at home later."

Brass seemed to forget every rule of investigation the minute they got promoted. But maybe he'd done one thing right this time. "You searched him?"

"Well, no. But he was empty-handed." Broderick flushed.

She didn't bother to respond because if she did, she'd probably be suspended. "When you talk to Stanerd's people can you find out why he wanted to meet with the senator?" Corelli sniffed. "One last question. Did either of you throw up in that house tonight?"

"No." The men answered at the same time. "To tell the truth, I was afraid I would," Neil admitted.

"It's a vomit-worthy scene, Commissioner." Corelli had never dealt directly with Neil but she liked the sense of honesty and integrity she was detecting. "Which one of you stepped in it?"

"Is that what I'm smelling?" Broderick lifted one foot and then the other. "Me." He extended his left foot.

Once again she bit her tongue. Broderick was aware they were walking into a crime scene and he should have been vigilant. "Give me your shoe."

He gave her the stink eye but he knew they'd have to give it to forensics. He slipped the shoe into the evidence bag Parker held out. Corelli smirked and handed him a paper bootie. She opened the car door. "We'll be in touch later."

"Sounds like a plan," Neil said. Broderick grunted, seeming to agree, but he didn't look happy.

CHAPTER FIVE

Crossing the street to the house after Neil and Broderick drove away, Parker stuck her arm out to stop Corelli. "Two people approaching on the right."

Corelli's hand went to her Glock. She squinted, trying to make them out in the still-dark early morning. She relaxed as they emerged from the tree-lined part of the street. "It's the EMTs."

Parker dropped her weapon to her side but didn't holster it.

Corelli introduced Parker to Julia Morgan and Allegra Thompson and the four women filed into the downstairs living room of the house.

"I'm impressed. How did you manage to get here so fast?"

"We were cruising so we were fairly close," Julia said. "What's with all the cloak and dagger stuff, Chiara?"

Early in their relationship Marnie had introduced her to Julia and Allegra and they'd become close friends. Seeing them right after she returned from Afghanistan and dealing with their feelings about Marnie's death on top of her own guilt and pain had been excruciating. It had been a relief to go undercover a week later because she was forced to withdraw from everyone, including her sisters, in order to stay in role. But even after she was no longer undercover, she'd made excuses to avoid getting together with them. Nevertheless, they had rushed to the hospital as soon as they heard she was shot and had continued to visit her there and at home. They were good friends and it was easier now that she was no longer so raw. "Before I say anything, I need your word you won't reveal what you see here tonight, even if you decide you don't want to be involved."

"That bad?" It was Allegra who spoke this time.

"Yeah, that bad."

Allegra was not easily deterred. "Will our friendship be harmed if we say we don't want in on it?"

"Saying no will definitely not affect our friendship but not keeping it secret will."

"What do you think, Julia?" Allegra looked to her partner.

"It sounds scary but Chiara wouldn't ask if it wasn't important. Either way we'll keep it secret."

Allegra put a hand on Corelli's shoulder. "I guess we're in, kiddo. Let's do this."

She trusted these two women and she'd been almost certain she could depend on them. But still she felt an easing of the tension. "Great."

Corelli removed the booties and gloves from her coat pocket and dropped her coat on a chair. She turned to Parker. "Stay on the door to let our people in and have them wait here. As soon as Hernandez, Shaunton, Dugan or Twilliger arrives, post them on the door with instructions to have everyone except Greene and Serena Lopez wait down here until we can brief them. I'll take Julia and Allegra upstairs and get started. Join us as soon as you can."

Corelli had decided to let the EMTs see the crime scene so they would understand the need to protect the girls. Under normal circumstances the EMTs would be the first responders on the scene with a goal of saving lives, not protecting evidence. But this was far from normal and since Senator Parker had already walked through, she wanted to minimize additional traffic. At the top of the stairs she waited while Julia and Allegra put on shoe covers then warned them about the vomit and led them to the doorway.

"Oh, my," Julia gasped. Allegra put a hand on her arm. "Like any other emergency call, honey."

"Is this the reason for the secrecy? Three naked big shots and a pretty clear message on the mirror? Looks like you're going to have your hands full with this one, Chiara. But what do you need from us?" Julia asked.

"There's more. The names of these three will be released this evening, but the state they're in, the message, and most of all, what I'm about to show you needs to be kept between us. Still with me?"

"Whoa. The murder of three super high-profile dudes who maybe are child abusers isn't the whole secret?" Julia put her hands on her hips. "What else?"

"It's best if you see for yourselves. Come."

Corelli led the two EMTs to the fourth floor and stopped outside the bedroom. "What I want to show you is in the closet. That dresser was blocking the door when we found them. Be quiet when I open the door."

All this stair climbing was hard on her wounded leg. She'd tried to cover the limp but Allegra was right behind her and must have noticed. "You sit."

Before Corelli could protest, Allegra turned the knob and slowly opened the door. The EMTs gasped. The girls were still cuddled together but they'd thrown off the blankets and their little naked bodies were exposed.

"Oh, my God, is this what I think it is?" Julia asked, her voice a whisper. She and Allegra knelt to get closer to the girls. They sniffed. After a few seconds they raised their heads, locked eyes and seemed to come to some silent agreement. They stood, closed the closet door and faced Corelli. "Bastards." Julia made no attempt to control her anger. "What do you need from us?"

"Take them to a hospital, have them examined and treated for any injuries, and get rape kits done. We'll make up some names for you to use."

"That's no problem. Have you given any thought to what happens after we finish up at the hospital? Do you want ACS involved?"

"No. The girls may know something that will help us and whoever murdered those guys may be looking for them. That means they could be in danger. I want them together someplace safe where I can be sure they'll get loving care and the help they're going to need, not in the foster care system."

Julia patted Corelli's thigh. "Get real, Chiara. Where is this happy fairyland? Somewhere over the rainbow?"

"Yeah, I know." Corelli took a deep breath. "There's only one place I can think of that meets those requirements but it might put my sister Gianna and her family in danger." She thought about the danger again, glanced at the closet door and thought about those helpless children. Gianna would want to help. "I hope I don't regret this. Give me a moment and I'll call her and ask."

Allegra touched her arm before she could make the call. "It's a lot to ask. Are you sure, Chiara?"

"No, but I don't see any other option." She'd forgotten it was still the middle of the night and of course, she woke Marco. A sleepy Gianna was asking if something was wrong in the background. After a brief overview and an explanation of the danger involved, he said it was up to Gianna and passed her the phone. Corelli repeated what she'd told Marco and answered the many questions Gianna asked. She held her breath while Gianna conferred with Marco. "It sounds like those poor girls don't have many options. Marco and I trust you will keep us safe so we'll take the girls. But it occurs to me that even without lights or sirens the ambulance in front of our house will bring our neighbors out and call attention to the girls. Why don't I meet them at Maimonides Bay Parkway Pediatric Center? Ambulances are in and out all the time so we could transfer the girls to my car without anyone noticing."

"Just a second, Gianna." Corelli relayed Gianna's suggestion to Julia and Allegra. They agreed it would be much better to transfer the girls away from prying eyes, no matter how innocent. "Okay, Gianna, they'll meet you at the Pediatric Center."

"Have Julia call me when they're on the way and I'll be there when they arrive. Tell them to look for the blue Volvo and the lady in the red hat and scarf. Be careful, sweetie, this sounds like it could be dangerous for you and P.J. too."

Parker and Greene arrived in time to overhear Corelli's conversation with Gianna. Parker and Gianna had become close when Corelli was in the hospital and recuperating at home so she expected some blowback from Parker at putting Gianna in danger. But Parker's reaction surprised her.

"Gianna will take good care of them. Let's make sure we take good care of her *and* them."

"My thoughts exactly, Parker. That's why Greene is here. She'll stay with the girls until they've adjusted to Gianna. Then we'll rotate female officers to guard the house."

Julia lightly punched Corelli's shoulder. "Good maternal instincts, Corelli."

Corelli hip checked Julia. "Yeah, I'm a veritable tit. If it wasn't so freaking cold I'd plant plainclothes officers nearby, but a van with a couple of officers in front of the house will have to do. Working on the premise that the fewer who know, the safer the girls will be, the officers will only be told an important witness is in the house. Shall we get started?"

While Julia and Allegra huddled to discuss which hospital's forensic nursing staff would ask the fewest questions, expedite the girls through the process, do the rape kits, and be discreet, Corelli entered the closet. She pulled out the iPhone Brett, her friend-not-yet-lover, had given her while she was recuperating so they could FaceTime when they couldn't be together. At first she'd refused the gift, but the twenty-year-olds in her life, her younger sister Simone and her nephew Nicky, had convinced her of the benefits of the iPhone and the first time she and Brett used FaceTime she was sold. While Parker sketched the scene, Corelli took pictures from as many angles as she could get in the relatively tight space.

"Serena Lopez is here," Parker whispered.

Corelli had trusted the photographer enough to call her to the crime scene and she'd decided to trust her to do this. She backed out of the closet, closed the door so they wouldn't wake the girls, and after she and Parker moved the chest in front of the door again, they introduced Lopez to the EMTs and briefed her. "Lopez is going to video and photograph the room, then discovering the girls, then you examining them, so let's move into hall."

Lopez started videoing from the doorway, taking in the whole room, then focusing on the chest and above it. She stepped back to capture Parker and Corelli moving the chest aside and opening the door, then moved closer to video the inside of the closet, especially the clump of blankets on the floor. She switched to her still camera to take photographs as well. "Okay, let's see them." She videoed Corelli pulling the blankets back and then gazed at the three girls for almost a minute before moving her camera to her eye again. The two EMTs and the three detectives watched her repeat the photos Corelli had snapped. When she finished, she backed out. Corelli signaled Greene and the EMTs. "Lopez will video you as you examine the girls, so don't rush it." She faced the five women. "Ready?"

Seeing five nods, she opened the closet door. "Okay, Greene, pick one up and hold her while Julia and Allegra do a quick scan for any obvious injuries. Allow time for the pictures."

Greene knelt and gently disentangled the girls' limbs, lifted one, then backed out. Parker closed the door.

The photographer videoed and the three detectives watched as the EMTs examined the girl, lifting her arms and legs, studying her genitals, turning her over and scrutinizing her backside and the backs of her legs. The girl made small sounds of protest and seemed to struggle to wake up as the EMTs touched her, but Greene stroked her, murmuring sweet words, and she fell back asleep. Greene placed her on the bed. "Do we have clothing?"

Corelli shook her head. "It's part of the murder scene so forensics will need it."

"Can we see her right heel?" Parker asked.

"Sure." Julia gently lifted the girl's foot.

Parker sucked in air. A combination of eight letters and numbers was tattooed on the heel.

"Good catch, Parker." Corelli snapped a picture. "Let's check the other two as well."

They repeated the routine with the other two girls. Their heels had similar tattoos.

When the third girl was asleep on the bed, everyone was quiet. Julia blew out a breath but spoke with the video camera in mind. "You were right, Detective Corelli, they not only smell of sex but the three of them are sticky with what is probably semen. It definitely appears they were used sexually tonight. And judging by the abrasions in their genital and anal areas, I would guess this was not the first time. I'm also guessing they were drugged earlier, probably to make them compliant."

Corelli signaled Lopez and she lowered the camera. Grim faced, Julia gazed at the detectives. "Get the bastards."

Parker stared at the three girls on the bed, her face pale, her lips a thin line. "If those three downstairs weren't already dead, I'd kill them."

This time Corelli did touch Parker lightly on the arm. "I think we all feel the same." She looked at the EMTs. "Which hospital are you taking them to?"

It was Allegra who answered. "Bellevue is our best bet. The three of us will each carry a child out to the ambulance parked around the corner. We'll head downtown without sirens and get our friends, the forensic nurses, to take care of the girls and keep it close to the vest. That may take hours and if you give me your sister's cell, I'll call her to get the address of the Pediatric Center when we're on the way."

Chiara dictated Gianna's cell phone number.

Greene went to the closet then looked to Corelli. "We probably shouldn't use these blankets."

"You're right," Corelli said. "Forensics will want to examine them. We cleared a linen closet in the hall when we arrived. I think there were extra blankets. If not strip the other beds."

When each of the girls was snug in a blanket in the arms of the woman who would carry her out to the ambulance, Julia turned to Corelli. "Let us know if you need anything else."

"I will." Corelli hugged Julia and then Allegra from behind. "Thank you for stepping up to help." She put a hand up to stop them from leaving. "Parker, go down ahead of us, send Hernandez and Shaunton into the kitchen with the others who have arrived and close the connecting door so no one will see the girls being carried out."

Parker left the room and Corelli turned to the three women, each with a child in her arms. "Julia, the chain of evidence would be best preserved if Greene signs for the kits and brings them directly to the lab for testing. Can you take her there before going to Brooklyn?"

"No problem. It's close to the hospital."

Parker texted *all clear.*

"Lopez, you can wait for me on the second floor while I escort these ladies out." Corelli walked the three women with the girls down the stairs and out the door and watched Julia, Allegra and Greene disappear into the darkness with their precious bundles. Rubbing her hands together, then wrapping her arms around herself to try to warm up, she returned to the second floor. Before they entered the murder scene, Corelli checked in with Lopez. "How are you doing?"

Lopez dabbed her eyes with a tissue. "Seeing those girls and hearing what Julia said, hit me hard."

Corelli got it. Hearing about these things was one thing, but seeing the girls just after they'd been raped, seeing the semen and bruises, was gut-wrenching. If the adults couldn't bear it, couldn't make sense of it, how were these little girls, who should only be worried about their toys and learning to read, to understand it? Corelli clasped Lopez's arm. "We're all struggling to get our heads around this. The best thing we can do for these girls and others like them is our jobs. We need to get the perverts who hurt them and put them away somewhere where they can learn what being raped feels like. Unfortunately, the three men you're about to see are dead so we won't have the satisfaction of sending them to prison. Are you able to continue?"

Lopez picked up her camera bag, then straightened her shoulders. "Whenever you're ready."

Corelli stood in the doorway next to the photographer and sensed her struggle to maintain the professional distance needed to do this job. Lopez's gaze bounced from the bloody message to the naked men and back, then shifted to take in the mirrored wall, the beds, the cameras and the child-sized costumes. When Lopez gasped and cursed softly, Corelli figured she got that tonight wasn't the first time this room was used to rape children. "It makes me sick to imagine those poor little things with these men. I'm a religious person and I'm supposed to forgive, not hate, but God help me I agree with whoever wrote that message." She shook her head as if to clear her thoughts, then put her video camera to her eye and filmed. When she'd captured the room, Lopez switched to her still camera and documented the scene from every angle.

A pale Lopez slowly packed up her equipment. "I'll wait downstairs for the ME and the forensic team to arrive, but I'm thinking if I develop these and the ones of the children in the office, I'm not sure how long they'll stay secret."

"Do you have another option?"

Lopez tucked a stray lock of hair back into her ponytail. "I could do them in my darkroom at home so there would be no official record until you decide to put them in the files."

"That would be ideal if you're willing to do it." She handed Lopez a card. "My cell number is on here. Call me when you're done and we'll make arrangements for you to bring the pictures and the video to my apartment."

Corelli clasped her shoulder. "I know this is hard, Lopez, and I appreciate your willingness to deal with it my way. I swear I will do my best to find whoever is trafficking these children and make them all pay."

"I know you will."

CHAPTER SIX

Ndep, the Medical Legal Investigator, arrived before Lopez and Corelli went downstairs. She'd come in from Queens and had run into a repaving crew that slowed her down to less than a crawl. Despite being woken in the middle of the night and being aggravated by the delay, the stately dark-skinned woman was as usual composed, confident and ready for work. She quickly donned protective gear and stood in the doorway to the scene of the slaughter. Her gaze slowly swept the room, stopping for a time on each of the three naked victims. She whistled. "Am I right we have a nasty senator, a publicity-seeking reverend and a wealthy playboy? Naked?"

"Correct."

Ndep studied the message written in blood on the mirror. "Is what the message indicates these men were doing the reason for all the secrecy?" She didn't raise her voice or lose her composure but the fire in her eyes and the iciness of her voice communicated controlled rage. "I would never have volunteered if I had known the job involved protecting the reputations of people like this." She waved her hand, indicating the three dead men.

Parker joined them. Always sensitive, she picked up the tension. "Sorry if I'm interrupting."

"I assure you, Ndep, I don't do cover-ups. You're here because you're a talented investigator and because you can be trusted to be discreet. There are things about the case you don't know yet. If you can't give us the benefit of the doubt, you might as well leave now." Corelli paused to give Ndep a moment to decide. "If you're going to stay, tell me what you see."

Ndep looked from Corelli to Parker then to Corelli again. Apparently deciding to trust, her gaze shifted to the room, taking in the beds and the sofa, the piles of neatly folded men's clothing, the little dresses tossed haphazardly in a corner, the walls and the ceiling. She stepped into the room, knelt next to each of the bodies, moved to the table in the corner that contained bottles of scotch, Bourbon, vodka, Pepsi and seven glasses. She sniffed the six that contained liquid. Corelli and Parker watched from the doorway. "It appears that these fine gentlemen have been involved in an orgy of a sexual nature. The message in blood points to the possibility of children being involved as does the presence of girls' clothing and soda in three glasses. Yet, there are no children here. Where are they?" She gazed at Corelli and Parker and getting no answer, turned back to the scene.

"No marks on the walls, indicating missing paintings and the rather expensive looking cameras and lighting equipment are still here. Have you had time to determine whether anything was stolen from the rest of the house?"

"I'm not sure we'd be able to tell," Corelli said, "but there was nothing obvious like a safe blown open or drawers pulled out or stuff thrown around. We'll have to wait until we can get the owner of the house or her caretaker to check."

Ndep's eyes widened. "The owner is a woman, not any of these... men?"

"The singer Amari DeAndre may be the owner," Corelli said.

"Interesting." Ndep walked back to the doorway. "The number of bullet holes I can see in each of the men leads me to believe that this was an emotional killing rather than a hit. Those are my observations until I examine them." She took out her notebook and began to sketch the scene.

Corelli put a hand over Ndep's pad, forcing her to look up. "We want to keep their nakedness, indications of sex, the message and any mention of children quiet for now."

Ndep glanced at Parker. "I thought you weren't going to bury this." She waved her hand indicating the scene.

Corelli knew she had to get Ndep and the others she'd chosen on board with this approach if they were going to solve this case and bring down the trafficking ring she was almost certain was behind this. "I'm not. We'll announce their names at a press conference tonight but nothing about them being naked or any sexual activities. If it looks like we're trying to protect the men's reputations, the killers will think we've overlooked things."

"Things?"

Parker touched Ndep's arm. "We want to find the murderer, not protect the reputations of these men. But right now we believe what we're seeing here is just the surface scum, and we want to root out the entire organism, flush out the whole system."

"Okay." Ndep blew out a breath. "But I need to know what organism we're talking about before I leave here or there's no secrecy." She focused on her sketch.

Corelli suppressed a grin. Parker was more eloquent than she had been and it tickled Corelli that she'd stepped in to convince Ndep. She observed the two women sketching side by side. Could they be more than friends? They would make a gorgeous couple. But wasn't there something going on between Parker and Watkins when Parker started working with her?

Twenty minutes later, Ndep put her pad down. "So let's get on with it." Lopez stepped into the room to photograph her examinations. Ndep knelt and examined the front of Senator Stanerd's body, counted the bullet wounds and scrutinized his penis and his thighs. She straightened. "There are traces of what appears to be semen, so it's likely he's had recent intercourse." Her eyes went to the message again.

Even though she'd been positive about the sexual activity, the rage bubbled in Corelli's stomach.

Ndep signaled Parker and together they turned Stanerd over. She checked for exit wounds and took his temperature anally. "He most likely died of gunshot wounds. Of course, we'll confirm that during the autopsy."

They followed the same procedure with Reverend Dumayne and Jake Blecker and came to the same conclusions, multiple gunshot wounds and signs of recent sexual activity. Ndep pointed out the tattoo on Blecker's ass, a heart with an arrow through it and the words, "young love is best."

"Time of death?"

Ndep looked at the iPad where she'd entered each man's temperature and other information and fiddled with it a moment. "Best guesstimate is between eight p.m. and midnight last night."

Corelli pointed to the folded clothes. "Can you go through their things?"

Ndep picked up a neatly folded pair of pants and went through the pockets. She passed a wallet to Corelli, and placed a phone, keys, gum, condoms, and a handkerchief, in the evidence bag Parker held for her.

"Should we listen to his phone messages?" Parker asked.

Corelli shook her head. The messages weren't going away and they needed to get through this crime scene. "Leave the phones for the team."

Corelli opened the wallet. "Reverend Dumayne had two credit cards, a New York driver's license, two hundred dollars, a Metro card and several business cards identifying him as the senior pastor of the Harlem Calvary Church of Christ." She dropped the wallet in the evidence bag.

No wallet in the next pair of pants, so Ndep searched the matching jacket, handed a wallet to Corelli and dropped keys, some change, a cell phone, a business card, half a package of cigarettes, five condoms, and a handkerchief into the evidence bag Parker held for her.

"The senator's wallet contains three hundred and fifty dollars, every credit card ever issued, a driver's license and his senate identification card." She slipped the wallet into the bag Parker extended.

They followed the same procedure with Jake Blecker. His wallet contained one thousand dollars, five credit cards, and a Florida driver's license. He also had a silver cigarette case filled with rolled marijuana joints and a bottle of pills. Ndep spilled several pills into her hand. "Looks like roofies but we'll test."

Parker copied the home addresses for Dumayne and Blecker from their driver's licenses. Blecker had a Palm Beach address so they'd have to ask the Palm Beach police to notify his family. The wallet went into the evidence bag.

Ndep summarized their findings. "So unless the killers were after something in another part of the house and had no interest in cash or credit cards, we can probably rule out robbery. But what aren't you telling me about what happened tonight? What's this about an organism?" Her eyes went to the message on the mirror. "Did you find children here?"

Wanting to limit the number of people who knew about the children Corelli had considered not bringing Ndep on board, but the woman was fierce and she would be a strong ally in figuring this out. "Before we get to that, is it possible to hold off transporting the bodies to the morgue until we start the press conference this evening? That way we won't have to worry about anyone leaking the names before we make the announcement."

"I can arrange that. I assume you want Dr. Blockman to do all the autopsies?"

"Yes, I trust Archie to keep his findings confidential."

Ndep made a note. "Now about the sex."

Corelli needed to sit so she led Ndep and Parker to the library. When they were seated she focused on Ndep. "We found three naked girls, probably six to ten years old. They're the ones we're trying to protect, not those," she waved a hand, "men." I don't have to tell you how important it is to match the semen found on the girls to the men. Also, the three girls have tattoos on their right heels, confirming your theory about our two floaters earlier in the week and leading us to conclude that case and this one are connected to child sex trafficking. Keeping a lid on it will allow us time to investigate without alerting the trafficking operation and avoid a media frenzy. Besides me and Parker, only Commissioner Neil, Chief Broderick, the EMTs, Serena Lopez, Detective Greene and you, know the girls were found here. And even fewer know where they're being hidden. Nothing will be said about them publicly until we feel they're safe."

Ndep dipped her head. "I'm honored you trust me with this. Hearing about the three girls is upsetting but at least they're alive and perhaps they can help you get the men behind this. I won't include anything about them in my reports since they weren't in the crime scene. I will mention the semen but I'll withhold my report until you tell me to release it. Let me know if I can do anything to help." Ndep stood. "If you don't need me for anything else, I'll get some body bags from my car."

Corelli met her eyes. "Thank you. I appreciate your willingness to come out in the middle of the night. And your confidence in us."

"You've earned it." Ndep smiled.

"We've got this Corelli." Parker pushed her out of the way and she and Ndep hefted the men into the body bags. Once all three were zipped they discussed moving them to another room until Ndep retrieved them later but they decided the techs could work around them so they left the body bags in place at the scene.

Corelli and Parker followed Ndep down the stairs. "Let me know the time of the press conference and I'll come by for the bodies," Ndep said as she walked out. Corelli and Parker turned into the downstairs area to brief the CSU and the detectives about why they were here, what they would see, the importance of secrecy, and her plan of action. When all had signed on they trooped up to the crime scene and let the CSU team get started with Detective Ron Watkins overseeing them.

She asked Dietz to come to the library with her and Parker so they could talk about the support she needed. He and Parker made notes as Corelli spoke.

"Broderick is taking care of Washington, informing Stanerd's family and appropriate organizations. Parker and I will notify the Blecker and Dumayne families. Since Blecker has a Palm Beach address I'll ask the police department to notify and search. But we'll need a team to search Dumayne's home and another for his office at the church plus techies to remove and search his computers in both places. We'll probably need to secure the church office to search their paper files for anything incriminating. Parker will call you when we leave the Dumayne residence so the team can meet us at the church."

Dietz looked up. "What are we looking for? Money, porn, things like that?"

"Yeah, things like that. And coded files. Don't ask. I don't really know what I mean. Just tell them to be on alert for anything that looks strange." She paused to give him time to jot a note. "Also, I need to know who owns this building, how to contact Amari DeAndre and what is Jake Blecker's New York City address, if he has one."

"How the hell do you spell Amari whatshisname and who is he?"

"*She* is a very popular singer. Parker will give you the spelling of her name. Anything I missed, Parker?"

"Shouldn't we send our people to Washington and Palm Beach to search? And what about warrants?"

"Good questions. Let's get somebody on warrants. What do you think about sending our people out to Washington and Palm Beach?"

Dietz tapped his pen on his pad as he considered the question. "Yeah, it would be best to have our detectives on site and maybe our techs too but I doubt we'll have much access to Washington. I'll get Forlini and Kim on drawing up the warrants."

"Okay. Coordinate with Broderick's office about Washington. I'll give you a contact in Palm Beach after I talk to them. That's all I have for now. Talk to Captain Winfry about resources."

By the time she got to the right person in the Palm Beach police department, discussed the murder and what she needed them to do, it was after seven a.m.

Leaving Watkins to work with the CSU, she and Parker went to break the news to Reverend Dumayne's widow. Never a pleasant chore, but even more difficult when the man was a child rapist.

CHAPTER SEVEN

Dumayne's house was a well-cared for Harlem brownstone in a neighborhood of well-cared for brownstones on East 123rd Street between Malcolm X and Adam Clayton Powell, Jr. Boulevards. Corelli had been in some nice neighborhoods in Harlem but never this particular street. Even though the many trees were barren, the block was pretty and peaceful. She imagined it would be lovely in spring. "Nice house in a nice neighborhood but somehow I'd have put a guy who hung with the rich and powerful in a fancy Upper East Side brownstone."

Parker walked around the car and stood next to her. "Being the pastor of a mega church pays big bucks but I guess you have to keep your ostentatiousness down or people get nervous that you're richer than them and don't give as much."

Corelli glanced at her. "How much do you know about the church? Are you a parishioner?"

Parker rolled her eyes. "Damn, Corelli, don't assume all black people are churchgoers. I only know what I read in the papers. It's huge and he's the face of the church, a media darling."

Corelli raised her hands in front of her. "Sorry. That *was* racist. I don't know that much about your private life, Parker, so since you recognized him I thought maybe you attended his church."

"Have you ever asked about my life outside of work?"

Had she? She thought so but maybe she was so self-involved and intent on proving she didn't need Parker to protect her that she hadn't. What an asshole. Parker had saved her life and she'd been there during her recovery. And she couldn't recall making an effort to have a real conversation. My sisters, my nephew, and the woman I'm in…the woman I'm attracted to, have all made real connections to Parker while I've held myself apart from her. Apart from everyone, actually, in varying degrees. Is that the PTSD? I need to do better. "Only when things like connecting with your birth father come up. I'm sorry, Parker. I'm an ass."

Parker looked stunned. Clearly she hadn't expected Corelli to cop to the charge. "Yes, you are an ass and you're missing out on hearing about my exciting life in the hour or two that I have between work and sleeping."

Ah, a little humor is good. "So, you take the lead with Dumayne's wife."

Parker studied her. "Because you assume his wife is black?"

Shit. Was Parker getting PC all of a sudden? Corelli shook her head. "Duh, Parker. I don't know whether she's black. Do you? And, by the way, being the same race, religion, sexual preference or political party of the victim doesn't make it any easier to break this kind of news. If I'm not mistaken, an ADA never has to inform the family of the death of a loved one, so in my opinion, you need the experience. Unless you think it will be too hard."

Parker ignored the sarcasm in Corelli's voice. "Sorry. You're right. I'm assuming just like you were. I'll do it." Parker squared her shoulders. "Feel free to step in if I'm screwing up."

"I always feel free. But I'm sure you'll be fine."

Parker rang the bell. While they waited, Corelli pointed to the camera trained on the door from the edge of the building. Parker removed her hat and held her shield and ID up to the camera. Had they had threats or was the camera just a precaution taken by the wealthy living amongst the not so wealthy and not very far from the poor?

The woman who opened the door was a tall, slender, stunningly beautiful light-skinned black woman. Definitely not your typical preacher's wife. Not even seven thirty in the morning and not a strand of her lustrous black hair was out of place, her light makeup was impeccable, and she was dressed in black slacks and a blue silk shirt. Elegant was the word that came to mind. Parker vaguely remembered seeing pictures of the handsome reverend with his bride. But was she a model? Or an actress?"

The woman appeared puzzled. "How can I help you?"

"Detectives Parker and Corelli to see Mrs. Dumayne." They extended their shields and IDs.

The woman's gaze bounced from their IDs to their faces. She stiffened. "Is everything all right?"

"Are you Mrs. Dumayne?"

"Please come in." She stepped aside and closed the door behind them. "I am Francine Dumayne. Is William all right?" She led them into a sitting room off the foyer.

Parker ignored the question. "Please sit, Mrs. Dumayne. I have some bad news."

"Is he all right? I've been calling him at the church and on his cell phone since six this morning. He often sleeps at the church when he's busy but he usually calls to let me know." Based on the honey in her voice she wasn't long out of the south.

Parker took a deep breath. "I'm sorry to have to tell you, Reverend Dumayne is dead."

"Dead?" She frowned. "How?"

Parker gave her a minute. "He was murdered along with two other men."

"Murdered?" She seemed to not comprehend. "Was it a robbery at the church?"

"No, it was at a private residence. We're just beginning to investigate so we don't have any information to share yet."

"I don't understand. He said he was meeting with the elders at the church and it might run late. I ate by myself and left a dish out for him in case he was hungry when he got home. I waited until midnight, but then I was falling asleep over my book so I went to bed."

"Was anyone with you?"

"No." She closed her eyes and took a few breaths.

"Can you think of anyone who would want him dead?"

"Everyone loved William."

"Who will be in charge at the church now?"

"I have no idea. His assistant, Reverend Wilkerson, would know." She appeared composed but her hands continued to clench and unclench.

"How long were you married?"

"Almost six months." Her eyes went to the framed wedding picture on the mantel. "I can't believe… Are you sure it's him?"

"We are, though we'll need you to formally identify him at the morgue."

She looked horrified. "I don't know if I…. Can Reverend Wilkerson do it? They were very close."

"We'll ask. How did you meet Reverend Dumayne?"

Her gaze went back to the wedding picture. "About nine months ago he came to preach in Atlanta. Friends invited me to go hear him. I was impressed with his passion and his intelligence. My friends introduced us and we connected." She glanced at the picture again. "We had a whirlwind courtship. He declared his love after just a couple of weeks and he sent flowers and gifts and cards almost every day. He flew to Atlanta frequently so we could spend time together. We went out to all the best places and had dinner with the governor and senators and other important people. I was flattered and overwhelmed and caught up in his passion. Three months after we met, we married."

"Were you happy?"

She seemed surprised by the question and thought for a moment before answering. "I've been lonely. William is always busy with the church, writing sermons, meeting with people and doing his political things so I don't see much of him. We rarely go out. And I haven't made any friends. When I go to church on Sunday, I feel as if I'm on display so I shy away from contact. Mrs. Wilkerson has been friendly. She took me to her book club, but I'm twenty-four and the women in it are all in their fifties and sixties. When I lived in Atlanta I worked as a model so I was busy with that and I had lots of friends. I socialized a lot, went out for dinner and sometimes dancing." She shrugged. "It's been hard to adjust."

"What will you do now?"

She stared at her hands in her lap. "There's nothing for me here. I'll probably go home."

"Did you have contact with anyone last night? A telephone call? A food delivery?"

"No. It was just me and my book, like most nights." Her eyes filled and the tears overflowed. She reached for a tissue. "I need some time to take this in so if you don't have any other questions, I'd like to be alone now."

"Just another couple of questions. Do you know if Mr. Dumayne had a will?"

The woman frowned. "He never mentioned one."

"Does he have a home office?"

"It's upstairs, the second door on the right."

"We'd like to look through it, if it's all right with you."

"I guess that would be all right."

"We're expecting several detectives to arrive momentarily. They'll do a thorough search of the office and they'll probably take his computer and some papers with them when they leave." They stood. "We may be back to ask more questions later."

"Please close the door behind you. And when you and the other detectives are done upstairs, just pull the front door closed."

"They'll need you to sign for anything they remove from the house, so I'll tell them to knock on this door." Parker turned. As she pulled the door closed she caught a glimpse of Mrs. Dumayne staring straight ahead.

Parker and Corelli looked through the files in and on his desk and found nothing of interest. Twenty minutes later, two detectives showed up. They briefed the detectives and headed out to their car.

"What do you think of her?" Corelli asked.

"She's gorgeous and has a lot of dignity. Though she did shed some tears, she didn't seem all that broken up. She never said directly that she wasn't happy but it sounded to me as if she'd been caught up in the attention and the wooing and regretted marrying him. When I turned to close the door as we left, I could swear I saw a smile on her face."

Corelli hadn't detected any deep emotion in Mrs. Dumayne and it had occurred to her that perhaps the woman was relieved. "I missed the smile but it doesn't surprise me. A girl of twenty-four married to a man twenty-five years older, who may have married her as a cover for his sexual proclivities and as arm candy rather than for love or passion. Besides, it sounds like he isolated her."

Parker started the car. "She seems pretty naïve so I doubt she bought an automatic weapon, surprised the three men and killed them all before they could move. On the other hand, she doesn't have an alibi and we don't know whom she knows or what she knew. To the church?"

"Yeah. I'd like to catch Reverend Wilkerson before the troops arrive so he's off guard."

CHAPTER EIGHT

The modern wood and glass building stood out like a shark in a fish tank in this neighborhood of abandoned factories and run-down tenements. The front door to the church was locked so they circled toward the rear where two polite young men in leather coats stopped them. Both had a hand in a pocket and she assumed they were packing. Right now Corelli's priority was to get to Wilkerson, but she made a mental note to follow up later. They flashed their badges and were about to be escorted through a side door into the church offices when a man, probably in his late sixties, breathing heavily, rushed up to them. "What's going on, James?" He directed his question to one of the men.

"These two detectives come to see you," said the young man.

"Detectives?" He pulled a handkerchief out of his coat pocket and wiped his brow. "Why?"

"I'm Detective Corelli and this is Detective Parker. We need to speak privately."

He looked at the cards they handed him, then at the two young men lingering nearby and making no attempt to hide their interest in hearing why the detectives were here. "Yes, of course. Let's go into the office."

They followed him in. The huge space was divided by a row of wooden file cabinets. One side contained a glass-enclosed conference room with a long table, plush upholstered chairs, a credenza, and bookcases, all in the same gleaming cherry wood as the file cabinets. On the other side a woman sat at a desk focused on a computer. Behind her were four closed doors and in front of her six easy chairs grouped together around a coffee table. The woman looked up as they entered.

"Oh, Gladiola, I didn't expect you in so early. Um, Gladiola is the church secretary. I'll be meeting with," he glanced at their cards, "Detectives Corelli and Parker. Please hold my calls."

The secretary had a mane of wild brown hair with bold blond streaks, big brown eyes and bright red lips. She was wearing a flamboyant multi-colored dress that showed off her curves and accentuated her bulges. Her gold hoop earrings matched the golden tones of her skin. Her gaze tracked them even as she lifted her phone and texted.

They followed Wilkerson into the office. He carefully hung his coat on the back of the door, then wiped his face again with the crumpled handkerchief in his fist before sitting behind his desk. "Sorry I'm running late this morning." He indicated the two chairs in front of his desk. "Please sit and tell me what I can do for you?"

Corelli didn't miss a beat. "Can you explain the hierarchy of the church?" He looked surprised but complied. "The Reverend William Dumayne is the senior pastor. There are six church elders that advise and assist him. I'm the senior elder and I work full time as the assistant pastor. I'm responsible for the day-to-day operations of the church and William, Reverend Dumayne, is primarily responsible for fundraising and parishioner recruitment. He and I meet with the elders monthly to discuss church business and finances."

"How many members do you have?" Corelli expected him to balk at revealing the number. "Do they tithe or pay some kind of dues to belong and attend services?"

He glanced at his wristwatch. "Reverend Dumayne can answer those questions. He should be here soon." He stared at the door as if willing it to open, glanced at his watch again, tapped his fingers on the desk, then stood. Apparently he'd come to a decision. "I'm sorry this is William's bailiwick. If you take a seat outside, I'll make sure he speaks to you as soon as he arrives."

They remained seated. He looked uncomfortable. She guessed people usually obeyed his polite orders. It was clear she wouldn't get more information without telling him. "Mr. Wilkerson—"

"Actually, it's reverend. I'm the only ordained elder." He stood straighter.

"Reverend Wilkerson, I'm sorry to be the bearer of bad news but Reverend Dumayne was found dead this morning."

"Oh, dear Lord." He stared at her for a second before dropping into his chair. "Why didn't...?"

He seemed remarkably controlled but she knew everyone handled bad news in his or her own way. "Why didn't what, Reverend?"

He seemed lost in thought and for a minute she thought he hadn't heard or understood but then he focused. "Why didn't Francine call me to tell me he had died?"

"Because he didn't die at home. And because we broke the news of his death to Mrs. Dumayne right before we came here." Interesting that his first thought wasn't to ask how he died or to express sorrow. Wilkerson was the subordinate of a younger man. Perhaps there was some resentment.

He straightened the folders on his desk. "Was it an accident?"

Corelli wasn't ready to answer his questions. "When did you last see him and do you know whether he had plans last night?"

"He looked in before he left last night around six p.m. to say he was going out to dinner with Senator Stanerd and Mr. Blecker and might be in late today."

So Dumayne lied to his wife about meeting with the elders last night. "Was he friends with Senator Stanerd and Mr. Blecker? Do you know them?"

"He spent a lot of time with Mr. Blecker, who is a major supporter of our youth programs. Senator Stanerd occasionally attends services so I've met them both here at the church but I wouldn't claim to know either."

"What kind of youth programs does the church sponsor?"

He sat back and tented his hands, clearly comfortable with this question. "There are different programs for different age groups. We have day care for children three months to twelve years old. For three- to five-year-olds we have a pre-kindergarten program. We also have tennis, baseball and swimming programs for different age groups. And we're about to start a music program."

"Who will take over the church now?"

He rubbed his temples. "Since he's much younger than all of us elders, we thought we had time so we discussed succession but never put a plan in place. As the only other ordained minister it would be logical for me to take over in an emergency. We've been trying to recruit someone younger than me to work as his second in command, someone who could energize our flock the way William does. But we haven't found anyone we could agree on."

"Where were you between eight and midnight last night?"

The change of subject seemed to shake him. "Is that when he was killed?"

Corelli gazed at him hoping to make him nervous. "Why do you assume he was killed rather than died of a heart attack?"

"You can't possibly think I had anything to do with his death."

"Reverend, those are not optional questions." Her voice was hard.

He looked like he wasn't going to answer but then gave in. "If he died naturally it wouldn't matter where I was so I assumed he was killed." His eyes went to the door of his office. "Gladiola and I worked late on financial reports. She left about ten and I stayed until about eleven, then I went home. My wife was asleep when I arrived around midnight."

"Do you live in walking distance or do you drive?"

"I live in the Bronx so I drive. The church leases a car for me."

She gave him a minute to ponder the situation then switched back to her financial questions. "How many members do you have and do they tithe or pay some kind of dues?"

Now that he was in charge he was more forthcoming. "We're at nearly seven thousand members now. Some tithe a percentage of their annual income and some contribute a suggested annual fee. And, praise the Lord, we have a few contributors like Mr. Blecker who give enormous sums."

"Are all of the church's records, financial and otherwise, stored here physically or on computer?"

"Yes. Everything is here."

"A team of detectives will arrive momentarily to interview the staff and look at the books and records of the church. We'll remove equipment if we deem it necessary. The church offices will be off-limits to everyone until we're finished with our examination. We'll have a twenty-four-hour police presence here to ensure it's secure."

He picked up a pencil and began to tap it on his desk. "That seems excessive. What exactly are you looking for? Reverend Dumayne was the face of the church but I can easily answer your questions and direct you to anything you'd like to see." He retrieved his wrinkled handkerchief from his pocket and wiped his brow.

Back to sweating. "I'm sorry, Mr. Wilkerson, we have to follow our normal procedures. We need access to everything."

His eyes darted to Parker as if hoping she would say something different. Seeing no help there, he sighed. "As soon as you leave, I'll call an emergency meeting of the elders and discuss it with them. I'm sure we can allow some access."

Corelli stood and placed her hands on his desk. She leaned in closer. "We're not asking for permission, Reverend. We have a warrant, which my detectives will bring with them. And, just so you know, you won't have access to the office until we're done. Unless you're meeting with the police, you'll have to meet in the church." She heard the rumble of her people in the reception area. "They're here." She turned to leave. Parker stood.

Wilkerson also stood. "Wait." He put out a hand. "You haven't told me how Reverend Dumayne died."

Corelli turned in order to see his face. "He was murdered."

Wilkerson swallowed. "Murdered? Sweet Jesus. Where?"

"Jake Blecker's house." Corelli gave him a moment to absorb the news. "Reverend."

He looked at her.

"My people are here. We need you and your secretary to assist them and answer questions. I know this is a lot to ask, but I'd like you both to stay the rest of the day and come back tomorrow and every day as long as we need you. This will speed up our examination and give you control of the office sooner."

"Yes, of course."

"Good. Ask your secretary to come in so I can inform her of Reverend Dumayne's death."

Gladiola confirmed Wilkerson's alibi. She took the death in stride, saying the right words but not showing any real emotion. Corelli was getting the impression that Reverend Dumayne was not beloved or even liked. So far, neither his wife, nor his assistant pastor, nor his secretary seemed particularly upset by his death.

Dietz was in the waiting room with a group of detectives, some Corelli knew, others she didn't. Corelli introduced Dietz to Reverend Wilkerson and Gladiola Foster and after a brief discussion, Dietz assigned two detectives to work with Wilkerson, two to delve into Dumayne's office, four to go through the file cabinets and two to work with Ms. Foster.

Corelli approached Foster's desk. "Before you get started I'd like the name of the security agency that the church uses."

The woman looked baffled. "I'm sorry, Detective, I don't know what you mean."

Corelli pointed to the door. "There are armed guards patrolling the grounds. I want to know which security company you hire them from."

"Armed?" Foster shook her head. "We don't use a security company. Reverend Dumayne hires them. We have twelve on staff now for round-the-clock coverage."

"Thank you." Corelli pulled Dietz aside. "The guards outside are packing. Get a list from Foster and run the names. I want to interview them to determine whether they and the guns are legal and to assess what they know about the goings-on inside the church. Coordinate with Parker on the schedule."

"Gotcha. Here's the info you asked for on that DeAndre woman and an article about her that might interest you." He handed Corelli a slip of paper with the address and telephone number for Amari DeAndre and a printout of an article.

"Is she in New York City?"

He scratched his head. "Her manager gave us that number. I assumed she was here."

"Thanks, Dietz. We'll see you later."

CHAPTER NINE

In the car she scanned the article, then checked the time on her phone. "I don't think it's too early to visit Ms. Amari DeAndre." She entered the number Dietz had provided into her phone.

"Amari here."

"Ms. DeAndre, this is NYPD Detective Chiara Corelli. I have a few questions for you. Are you at your Central Park West address?"

"Yes, I am. My manager told me to expect your call and I'm happy to help but to be frank, I've been wracking my brain trying to figure out what this is about."

"We'll be there in a few minutes. I'll explain when we see you."

At DeAndre's brownstone facing Central Park, Corelli rang the bell. At first glance the woman who opened the door appeared to be a friend or assistant but the intensity of her gaze and her hypervigilance suggested otherwise. A glimpse of a holster under her jacket confirmed it. "Detectives Corelli and Parker to see Ms. DeAndre. She's expecting us." They displayed their shields and IDs.

After carefully examining their IDs, the woman extended her hand. "Kelly Dexter, Ms. DeAndre's bodyguard. Please come in." The English accent didn't surprise Corelli. She knew female bodyguards were popular in England for the royals as well as for wealthy foreigners whose wives and daughters were forbidden contact with men.

Dexter led them through the house. It wasn't as large or as fancy as the mansion where the murder took place but the part they saw was homey and warm, filled with concert posters, paintings, masks, instruments and art objects, the kind of place Corelli imagined a successful young musician would occupy. They entered a sunlit room fitted with a sofa, a couple of easy chairs, a piano and a guitar on a stand. Other guitars and instruments were hung on the walls along with several gold records. DeAndre was seated in what looked like a comfortable chair next to a table with a lit candle, an open notebook and a pen on it. She was humming and strumming a guitar. Corelli assumed the candle was the source of the pleasant aroma that filled her senses. The singer looked up.

DeAndre stood as Dexter introduced them. Tall and willowy, barefoot, wearing jeans, a long-sleeve blue T-shirt and no makeup, she looked younger than her publicity photos and even more breathtakingly beautiful. Her mane of black hair was pulled back into a ponytail and her large blue eyes darted between the detectives. "Please sit. The coffee is fresh and we can make tea or if you'd prefer, get you water."

"We're fine, thanks." Corelli answered for both of them.

Amari sat and leaned forward. "So how can I help you?"

"Do you own the mansion at 4 East Seventy-Fourth Street in Manhattan?"

DeAndre glanced at her bodyguard. "I do not. This is my house."

"Do you know Reverend Dumayne, Senator Harry Stanerd, or Jake Blecker?"

"I've been introduced to Reverend Dumayne a couple of times but I wouldn't say I know him. I've never met the senator." There was a brief silence. "Jake Blecker is my former manager. May I ask what's going on?"

"Just a few more questions. What is your relationship to Mr. Blecker?"

More silence. Her lovely olive skinned darkened. "He helped me get my start. We used to be...um, friends but we had a falling out several years ago."

"What happened?"

"Why do you need to know?" She sounded distressed.

"Let's put that question aside for now. Is there anything you can tell us about Jake Blecker? His address in New York City? Who his friends are? Does he have a family?"

They listened to DeAndre's labored breathing for a long minute. "He owns and lives in that mansion on Seventy-Fourth Street. I thought he and Marianne Phillips were married but I read recently they weren't but they had a falling-out. I don't know his friends now, but he used to be involved with a lot of wealthy and powerful men."

"I was intrigued to see some of your gold records on his wall, in a room that looked to be part of a recording studio. How did that come about?"

DeAndre fidgeted, then stood and started to pace. Hand shaking, she yanked a tissue from a box on the coffee table, patted her eyes, then continued pacing, leaving a trail of fluffy particles as she shredded the tissue.

Corelli and Parker exchanged a glance. Corelli chanced a guess at the cause of her distress and hoping to calm her, moved toward DeAndre with her hand out. Dexter was between them in a flash. So much for the relaxed bodyguard.

Corelli put her hands up. "I mean no harm. I intended to reassure Ms. DeAndre."

DeAndre stopped pacing and grasped Dexter's shoulders from behind. "It's all right, Kelly."

The bodyguard stepped aside.

Corelli moved closer. "May I call you Amari?"

"Yes."

"I've been out of commission for a few months and two twenty-year-olds, my sister and my nephew, spent a lot of time taking care of me. They're both huge fans and because of them I've listened to a lot of your music. To be frank, from time to time I wondered about your lyrics. Do I remember correctly that it was Mr. Blecker who discovered you and gave you your start?"

"Yes."

"How old were you when you met him?"

"Eleven."

"Were you molested by Mr. Blecker?" Corelli spoke softly.

DeAndre seemed to have trouble taking in air. Her gaze went to Dexter, as if looking for help. Her shoulders shook. Corelli caught her as she started to go down. Parker and Dexter rushed to help her stand. They moved her to the sofa. Dexter put a protective hand on the girl's shoulder. Parker held the cup of tea the young woman had been drinking to her lips and met Corelli's eyes over the girl's head. Corelli responded with a quick nod.

"Amari." Parker's voice was just above a whisper. "Look at me." The girl slowly raised her eyes to Parker. "He's dead. You don't have to be afraid anymore."

Corelli observed the two women. Dexter showed no emotion. Amari seemed stunned.

"D-d-dead? How? He just..." She covered her face as her body shuddered with sobs.

Corelli gave her a moment to deal with the news. "He was murdered last night, Amari. He can't hurt you anymore. What you were about to say? What did he just do?"

Amari's sobs turned to sniffles. Then she sat up and dried her eyes on her sleeve. She gazed at her hands clasped tightly in her lap. "He left a message last week when I was still on tour that he had a big deal lined up and the guy wanted to meet me. When I walked away from him seven years ago, he told me he wasn't done with me, that I owed him. I ignored the call but I'm pretty sure he was offering sex with me as a bargaining chip."

Dexter knelt in front of the singer and took her hand. "You don't have to talk about this, Ami." She looked up at Corelli. "How did he die?"

"Shot in his mansion."

Amari gasped. "Good. I hope the bastard suffered."

Dexter stood but kept hold of Amari's hand. "So why is it necessary to have Ms. DeAndre relive unpleasant memories?"

Corelli hesitated. "I'd like to speak freely. Can we agree that whatever is said here will go no further?"

"That works two ways, Detective." Dexter spoke for Amari. "Anything that Amari says must be confidential unless she agrees it can be made public."

Dexter seemed more protective of Amari and spoke for her in a way that went beyond her role as bodyguard. Were they in a relationship? "We have indications that Mr. Blecker was a child abuser and perhaps a child sex trafficker. I'd like to expose him and anyone involved in order to root out the scum involved in abusing children, but I need something solid to move on."

"Just what do you need?" Again it was the bodyguard who spoke.

"I'd like to know how Ms. DeAndre got involved with him, did he abuse her, for how long, were other men involved and who, and anything she knows that might help us figure out if he was a trafficker."

DeAndre's olive complexion became alabaster and she seemed to have trouble breathing.

"I know this is difficult—"

"I can't." Amari sobbed. "Not now."

Dexter stepped between Corelli and Amari. "Okay, that's it. Ms. DeAndre is doing a benefit tonight and a concert tomorrow. She can't deal with this right now. You'll have to come back another time. Be sure to call first."

"Sorry to upset you, Ms. DeAndre. We will be back and I hope you'll be willing to work with us then." Corelli moved toward the door but turned at the last minute. "Can you tell me where you both were last night?"

Dexter answered. "We were here. We took the redeye from California and got in about six a.m. yesterday morning. We spent the day relaxing and we both were in bed by ten o'clock."

"Amari?" Corelli asked.

"Yes. We just took it easy so I could be rested for the benefit tonight."

"Can anybody vouch for you?"

"You mean other than each other?" Dexter responded again. "Not really. Nan, the housekeeper, lives here but she took some time off while we were on tour and won't be back until tomorrow. We ordered food that was delivered about seven thirty last night but after that it was just the two of us."

"And how long have the two of you been together?"

The bodyguard and the singer locked eyes but once again Dexter answered. "I've worked for Ms. DeAndre for close to five years."

"Thank you. Sorry to bother you."

"Detective Corelli, wait." They turned toward Amari who had moved to the desk by the window. "What are the names of your sister and nephew?"

Corelli frowned. "Simone and Nicky. Why?"

"Just a second." Amari picked up a Sharpie and wrote on something. She handed Corelli two CDs. The one for Simone said, *I sing for you*, and the one for Nicky said, *With a song in my heart*. Both were signed, *love, Amari*. She smiled shyly. "I'm thrilled they were able to make a fan of you. If it's okay with you, I'll leave two tickets to tomorrow's Radio City concert at the box office for them. Are they both Corelli?"

"No, my nephew is a Gianelli. It's a generous offer but I can't accept any gifts."

"Please let me do this. I don't expect special treatment." Amari wrote the names down. "Is Nicky related to Joseph Gianelli?"

Corelli stiffened. "Joseph is his father. How do you know him?"

"I've only met him a few times but his firm, Gianelli Trucking, packs and transports the instruments and other equipment for my band when we're on tour. They're terrific. They always arrive on time and everything is always in working order."

"His company is in Brooklyn. How did you come to hire him?"

"I'm not sure. He's been with me almost from the start. Either Jake or his assistant Ernesto must have set it up. When I broke with Jake I hired a new manager, a new bodyguard, a new agent, and a new PR firm. Gianelli was the one service I didn't change."

"Why is that?"

Amari handed Corelli a postcard with the information about the concert. "Jake controlled and profited from all aspects of my career so changing those people and companies allowed me full control and full profit from anything I did from the time I left him. Of course, he still makes money from the albums I released when I was under contract with him. Anyway, I was happy with Gianelli's service. My new accounting firm found no indication that he was kicking back to Jake and confirmed his rates were competitive so I've continued to work with him."

Could this case get any more complicated? She opened her wallet and pulled out two twenties. "I appreciate the offer, Amari. They'll be thrilled with the CDs but I'll only take them if you let me pay you. And I definitely can't accept the comps for the concert. But after this case is over I hope you'll let me bring Simone and Nicky around to meet you." She placed the twenties on the table. "We'll be on our way but we'll be back at the end of the week."

Dexter led them to the door. "Thank you for waiting to get her story, Detective. It tears her apart to even think about it and she really needs to be focused in order to put herself out there the way she does at every concert."

Once they were in the car, Corelli put her head in her hands and groaned. "Can this case get any more fucked-up? Your uncle. My brother-in-law. In a city of eight and a half million people you'd think we could catch a case that doesn't involve anyone we know."

CHAPTER TEN

The crime scene unit was still at work when Corelli and Parker returned to the mansion on Seventy-Fourth Street. Corelli wasn't expecting any big revelations but you never knew. If they were detectives in a TV show, the killer would have left a clear fingerprint in the message on the mirror and the murder would be solved. But each time she entered the scene, the message smacked her in the gut, reminding her this was real life.

Watkins was on his knees as they came into the crime scene. He shook a bag he was holding. "We just found a shell casing under the sofa." He stood. "Bullard and I are just about finished with evidence collection in here. The rest of the CSU team is working its way through the house."

Not a fingerprint but good news, nonetheless. Especially if they were able to find the gun. A professional would have collected all the casings so another indication it wasn't a professional hit or maybe they'd used a throwaway and didn't care.

"Have you checked the cushions on the sofa and the chair?" Parker's question surprised the two men.

"Obviously there's blood." Bullard gestured to the cushions. "Do you expect us to find something else?"

Parker bit her lip, then shot a glance at Corelli. "Semen."

Watkins' eyes went to the message on the mirror. "Holy shit, you think the victims had sex here?" Watkins looked at Corelli but she remained silent, letting Parker take the initiative. "With children?"

Parker's gaze flicked to Corelli again. "We found three children about six to ten years old in a closet on the fourth floor, and they showed signs of recent sexual activity, as did the men." She unzipped one of the body bags.

This time it was Bullard who responded. "Holy shit is right. Is that Senator whatshisname? Naked? I assume this is not to be shared in reports and only on a need to know basis with the team?"

"Right. Lopez obviously knows," Parker said. "And yes, it is Stanerd. The others are Reverend William Dumayne and Jake Blecker, both also naked. We'll be releasing their names later at a press conference, so after that, revealing their identities will be all right but anything related to sex and the three girls should be limited to reports meant for our eyes, not those for general distribution."

This was the first time Parker had stepped out of her trainee role to act as the partner she was. Corelli suspected anger at the abuse of the girls was firing her up but whatever the reason, she had taken a giant step by not asking permission. "We'll be in the library down the hall, if you need us. And Bullard, let us know when the team gets up to the bedrooms on the fourth floor."

They left the two men discussing whether to take the cushions or just the covers.

They started by examining the huge wall unit with file drawers in the bottom half and bookshelves almost to the ceiling. Leaving the books on the higher shelves for others, they flipped through those they could reach. As she thumbed through book after book of pornography Corelli's stomach churned. A glance at Parker confirmed she was distressed as well. Realizing this wasn't doing either of them any good, Corelli decided to leave the task for others who could be more dispassionate. "I've seen enough. If we had any question that Blecker was a child abuser, his huge collection of porn would have pointed us in that direction. It's sickening. Let's leave it for the Special Victims Unit to go through."

Parker's hands were shaking, and as she attempted to replace the book she was holding, she knocked several others off the shelf. Corelli picked up a couple to re-shelve but Parker put an arm out to stop her. She removed more books from that shelf and the shelves under and above it. She turned to Corelli. "Do you see what I see?"

Corelli squinted at the wall behind the exposed shelves. It was barely visible. "A button. I'll bet there's a mechanism to move these shelves out of the way." Corelli pressed the button, then stepped back. A motor engaged and four shelves and the cabinets under them swung away from the wall, exposing the door of a safe about five feet tall. "Good catch, Parker. Call Dietz to get someone here to open the safe. Also, we'll need Lopez down here to record what we find. After you make the calls, go through the file drawers. I'll move the shelves back to hide the safe and replace the books, before I start on the desk."

They went through files for an hour and a half before Lopez arrived. "I hope you haven't found any more..." She glanced over her shoulder before dropping her voice. "...children."

Corelli smiled. "Nah, just a safe. Sorry to call you back but we need a video record of it being opened and of us removing the contents." Lopez took out her camera and snapped pictures of the room.

"Corelli." The three women turned toward the door. Officer Shaunton had a short, stocky, bald man with her. "Paulie Massetti, the safecracker you ordered." She walked away, grinning.

The three women stared at Massetti.

"Um, that's NYPD Detective Paulie Massetti, from robbery. Safes are my area of expertise."

Corelli was glad he clarified that he was a cop. For a second she wondered whether NYPD would send a criminal.

His gaze swept the room. "Where is it?"

Corelli introduced Lopez and Parker. "Lopez is going to film every step so we covered it again. Okay, Parker demonstrate finding the safe." Corelli watched Massetti as Parker knocked over a couple of books, then pressed the button she'd exposed. His eyes widened as a large section of the bookcase swung aside to reveal the safe.

"Good find, ladies, um, Detectives. Shall I?" He directed his question to Corelli.

"Yes, please do."

He removed a pen and pad from his bag and rolled up his sleeves before moving to the safe. Lopez trained the video camera on him. "Nice setup. Professional." He played with the dial. "It's high-end, tough to crack." He turned to Corelli. "Don't worry, I can blow it if I can't get it open."

In less than twenty minutes he had broken the code. He grinned, made sure the door was disengaged but left it for them to open. He stepped back and handed her the slip of paper he'd jotted the combination on as he worked. "You might need this later, but I think I'm done here."

"Good job, thanks." Corelli said. She and Parker moved to the safe. Lopez began to video. Parker pulled the door open and an interior light flashed on. They peered in. It was much wider than the door, at least five feet wide with floor to ceiling shelves on all sides. Corelli grabbed a handful of passports. She shuffled through the stack. "All with photos of Jake Blecker, some in his name from countries like Saudi Arabia, Brazil, Egypt, England, Germany, and France and some US with different names, some other countries with different names." She displayed each of them so Lopez could capture the information on video, then put them in an evidence bag and set it aside.

She pulled out a stack of CDs and examined them. "There are hundreds, at least, of these CDs labeled Top Notch Movies, and judging by the names on the labels, they're porn. There are also hundreds of thumb drives labeled in the same way. These will be viewed and their contents confirmed." She signaled Lopez to move in closer to show the stacks of CDs and thumb drives.

She pulled out several bricks of hundred-dollar bills. "Stacks of cash." She leaned in to do a quick count. "I estimate three to five million dollars and several million Euros." They placed the money in evidence bags used for large items.

Parker entered the safe and came out with four small black pouches. One pouch at a time she poured the contents out on the desk and counted. "Fifty diamonds in each pouch, two hundred diamonds, value to be determined."

They carried out thirty-one accordion style folders each labeled with NYC and a year and placed them on the desk. Corelli opened the one on top and slid the contents out. The three women gasped. Pictures of girls of all ages being assaulted by men whose faces weren't shown, some with the girls dressed and posed. She looked at the backs of the pictures hoping for a name or two, but each had two sets of numbers written on them plus NYC and a date. They would have to study the pictures to try to identify the victims and the rapists and attempt to break the code, but not now. Corelli had Lopez video a couple of the photos front and back, then enough photos to show the contents of the envelope. They did that with the next thirty accordion folders. Lopez was pale but kept the video going. Parker looked ready to vomit but Corelli knew better than to offer them a break.

"Boss, we're starting on the fourth floor." She turned toward Watkins. His eyes widened. "A safe?"

She wrinkled her nose. "Filled with porn and other goodies that you'll get a chance to sift through later. Have the team go ahead with all the rooms except the one with the dresser pulled away from the wall. We'll need just you and Bullard for that. Let us know when everyone else is gone and we'll come up."

She pulled out multiple piles of papers including the deed to the house, various contracts and agreements, all of which would have to be examined in detail. She reached in and pulled out two notebooks. One had a list of numbers and initials similar to the tattoos on the girls' heels. She thumbed through page after page. It looked like several hundred victims. Hopefully, the next book would have the corresponding names. But it was another book of different codes with ruled columns following a like and dislike column, and a last date of service column, likely the rapists. She scoured the safe looking for the names that went with the codes but there was nothing. She ran her hand over the bottom, top and sides of the shelves and found a key taped under the bottom shelf. A safe deposit box. Damn. This could be at a bank anywhere in the world. She blew out a breath, displayed the key so Lopez could video it, then slid it into an evidence bag. They dragged out file boxes filled with folders that someone would have to go through at the stationhouse. Finally the safe was empty and the three of them sat to take a break.

"That's it for today, Lopez. Thanks. And just so you know, Bullard and Watkins are the only ones who know the names of the victims, the state of their bodies and that we found the girls here."

When they were called to the fourth floor, she led Bullard to the closet and described how they'd found the girls. He fingerprinted the chest of drawers and the door then knelt inside the closet to bag the blankets. "We'll test these for semen," Bullard said as he picked up something that fell out of the blankets. He held it up. An earring. A diamond or pearl stud or something gold wouldn't have surprised Corelli, but a three-inch shiny plastic or paper-mache earring in tropical colors—turquoise, pink and yellow—did. Very interesting. "Do you think you can get a print from it?"

"Maybe. And if we're lucky, we might get DNA from the part that clips on the ear."

By four o'clock in the afternoon the CSU had finished with all four floors. Hernandez and Shaunton would remain on the door until Ndep came to transport the bodies to the morgue. After that their overnight replacements would show up—with instructions to allow no one in the house.

Hoping to surprise the senator and throw him off guard, she'd had Watkins call to set up the interview. Now, as she and Parker grabbed a quick bite with Watkins in a coffee shop near Senator Parker's Manhattan office, Corelli briefed him.

CHAPTER ELEVEN

Senator Aloysius T. Parker was standing at the window, his back to them, engaged in a heated conversation on his cell phone. He turned at the sound of his assistant closing the door.

Corelli had only seen him ranting on TV. In person, he was taller and fitter than she'd imagined but no less arrogant or condescending. He was handsome, with the same fine features and coloring that made Parker beautiful, but if he shared his niece's humanity and caring he hid it well. Dressed impeccably in what appeared to be expensive tailored clothing, he projected confidence and the air of superiority and entitlement she associated with privileged white men. You would never guess he'd grown up on welfare with an abusive, alcoholic mother. He took his time ending the call but his gaze never left the three detectives. "I thought I was being interviewed by a Detective Watkins."

Watkins stepped forward. "That's me."

The senator shifted his gaze to Parker. "Isn't there some rule about police not interviewing relatives, Penelope?"

Corelli didn't give Parker a chance to respond. "Detective Parker is training under my supervision and she'll only be observing. Detective Watkins and I will interview you."

"Given our history I would prefer to speak with Detective Watkins alone."

She wasn't surprised by his unwillingness to speak to her but she'd never figured out the source of the intense antagonism he demonstrated toward her. They'd never met before today, yet he attacked her as a racist in press conferences and on TV at every opportunity. Of course he never offered proof. Not surprising since there was none. She wouldn't claim to be free of racism. Marnie hadn't been shy about pointing it out wherever she saw it. And, in some sense it came with the job, but she tried to be aware and deal with everyone fairly. But his attacks weren't limited to accusations of racism. Most recently when she'd brought down the leader of a ring of dirty cops, he defended the man and hinted she was the crooked one. And when she was wounded in the line of duty, he implied she'd stepped in front of the bullets for the publicity. "As you know, Senator, this is a very sensitive investigation and since you found the bodies, you're an important witness. So you can talk to me here or you can talk to me at the stationhouse, but you will talk to me. My goal is to get the information I need from you, and if possible, to eliminate you as a suspect."

"Suspect?" His complexion darkened. He turned toward his desk. "I'm going to call the commissioner."

"We'll wait. But Commissioner Neil put me in charge so I will interview you. The only question is here or the stationhouse?"

"I won't be railroaded by you, Corelli."

"If you know anything about me, Senator, you know *I* don't rush to judgment. But if you refuse to talk to me, I'll assume you have something to hide."

He stomped to his desk, pushed some papers around, glared at Parker and then at Watkins. "Is it necessary for them to be in the room?"

"It is." Like most bullies he was losing steam when confronted.

"Let's get this over with. I understand you'll announce their names tonight and I have an enormous number of tasks to complete before I head back to Washington to deal with this situation in the Senate." He sat in the huge leather executive chair behind his desk and waved them into the chairs facing him.

Corelli and Watkins moved forward. Parker remained in place, leaning against the wall near the door. Hoping to irritate the senator, Corelli took her time settling in the chair. "What time did you arrive at the scene of the murder?"

He stared at his hands. "I'm not sure."

"Come on, Senator. You're used to a tight schedule so I assume you know exactly when you arrived. Where were you before and what time did you discover the bodies?"

He glared at her but once again he caved. "I was supposed to arrive at ten but I was running late and didn't get to the midtown fundraising dinner in my honor until nine thirty. About ten-twenty Stanerd called to ask where I was and I told him the earliest I could get there was eleven thirty. But the dinner broke up sooner than I expected and I was able to extract myself fairly quickly. When we got to Seventy-Fourth Street I told my driver not to wait, I'd grab a taxi after the meeting. He said, 'It's ten fifty-five now. What time should I pick you up in the morning?' I got out of the car and went right into the house so I probably found them about five or ten minutes later."

Good, the fundraiser and the driver were easily verifiable. "Why were you meeting with them and why so late?"

"I'm a senator. I work whatever hours are necessary." He made no attempt to hide the sneer in his voice.

Slick. Answer without answering. "Of course you do, Senator. But why did you go to that house to meet those three men at that time last night?"

"I thought I was meeting Majority Leader Stanerd, not the three of them. And it was so late because Stanerd insisted he needed to see me immediately about something important and private before he returned to Washington in the morning. He determined where to meet. The first time I was free all day was after the fundraiser."

Corelli tried to place his accent. The few times she'd seen him on TV he'd been vicious, angry and ranting, and some of those times attacking her, so she'd never really listened to him. He didn't sound like the New Yorker or welfare kid from Harlem that he was. His accent was posh, upper-class American like the image he cultivated. "What was so important?"

"He didn't say but he was trying to get me on board with the president's latest hare-brained proposal so I assumed it was that." His eyes glazed over for a few seconds and he seemed to remember something.

Corelli met his eyes. At least they agreed the president was off the wall. "Why meet in New York City when you both spend most of your time in Washington?"

"I don't know. He insisted we meet there." He looked away and straightened the folders on his desk. "I'm sure you understand that comment about the president and all of this conversation is not for public consumption."

Good. She'd made him uncomfortable but that wasn't her goal. She needed him to be relaxed enough to cooperate. "As you well know, there are those in the department that do leak information, but Detective Parker, Detective Watkins and I would never leak to the press or to anyone. And I assure you, given the sensitivity of this investigation, all the information we gather will be protected." She waited for him to raise his eyes. "As I said earlier, we're here to learn what you know about the murders and to clear you as a possible suspect, not to do political harm." He didn't comment so she plunged in. "How did you get in? Tell us what you did and saw."

He took a few seconds to gather his thoughts. "Speaker Stanerd said the front door would be unlocked and they would be on the second floor. I let myself in. The music was so loud I thought a party was going on and I'd entered the wrong house. I stepped outside and verified it was number four. Once I was assured I was in the right place, I followed his instructions to walk up the stairs and go to the last room on the left." He closed his eyes as if wanting to blot out the image. "I was annoyed at Stanerd for insisting we meet so late so I stomped up the stairs and down the hall. I stopped short in the doorway and grabbed the doorjamb to keep from falling over. The stench was overwhelming. I gagged. And it took a few minutes for my brain to comprehend what I was seeing. Three men I knew, dead. Naked. I felt as if I'd stepped into a horror movie. I couldn't move.

"Eventually I forced myself to go in and confirm they were dead. I was just getting ready to call 911 when I heard a noise from upstairs. It could only be the killer. I ran out of the house and turned toward Madison Avenue, figuring it would be well lit and I'd be able to get a cab. But I was so out of breath I ducked into the small yard in front of a dark house about halfway down the block. I stood against the house in the shadows trembling, trying to catch my breath. I was in shock. I couldn't think clearly. I must have been there fifteen or twenty minutes before I calmed and concluded that calling 911 was the best course of action. Right before I turned to walk to Madison, two men ran out of Blecker's house and walked quickly in the opposite direction, toward Fifth Avenue. I shudder to think what would have happened had I encountered the killers." He removed a handkerchief from a rear pocket and wiped the sweat, and maybe tears, from his now pale face. His gaze moved from one to the other of the three detectives. "I've never been so close to killers, never seen people slaughtered like… I don't know how you do it." He rubbed his eyes as if wanting to wipe the images away.

She let him sit with that thought and those images. Maybe he'd see the NYPD in a more positive light now. "You said you gagged. Did you throw up?"

"No. I was able to control myself."

If not him, it had to be one of the killers who vomited. "What did the people who exited the house look like?"

"It was dark so I couldn't see any detail." He closed his eyes. "There was difference in height. One was taller. The shorter one had a hard time walking fast. Sorry, that's all I remember."

"Are you sure they were men?"

He seemed puzzled by the question. "I assumed they were. But..." His eyes raked Parker then returned to Corelli. "The way you and Penelope dress you could certainly pass for men in the dark. So, I'd have to say I'm not sure."

"Can you describe the scene?"

He blinked and looked out the window. Just when she decided he was going to balk, he turned his gaze on her. "As I said, it was bloody, very bloody." He blew out a breath. "All three were totally naked." His gaze went to the window again. "Covered in blood." He wrinkled his nose. "And excrement."

"Did you notice anything else in the room?"

"Isn't that enough?" He sounded incredulous.

"Was there blood anywhere else, say the walls, the mirror, the ceiling?"

He closed his eyes. "When I looked up from...the bodies, I saw my reflection in the mirror. I remember thinking it was weird that I looked so normal while three men were dead at my feet. I wouldn't swear to it but there may have been some blood splashes on the mirror and the walls. I didn't look at the ceiling."

"Did you touch anything?"

"No. Yes, of course, I touched their necks. I don't think I touched anything else but I wouldn't swear to it."

"At what point did you call Commission Neil?"

"It took me some time to stop shaking and think clearly after the killers left, but once I reached Madison Avenue there was traffic and it was brighter so I calmed down. I started to dial 911 but then I realized it would be a public relations disaster if that publicity hound Captain Benson and officers from his precinct were involved, so I called Commissioner Neil hoping he could figure out a way to control the situation."

Corelli assumed "control the situation" meant cover it up. If so he was in for a surprise. "Did you know the other two men?"

"I'd sat on a few committees with Reverend Dumayne and we'd had dinner several times. I occasionally attended services at his church."

"What about Jake Blecker?"

The look of distaste that flickered across his face was covered so quickly by his bland politician's façade, Corelli almost thought she hadn't seen it. He carefully straightened some pens on his desk seeming to buy time before answering.

"I met Jake Blecker many times over the years but I wouldn't say we were friends." He hesitated. "I didn't care for him. There was something, I don't know, crass about him, yet he was always in the company of men I thought would have better options for friends."

"Can you be more specific about his...crassness?"

Without answering he stood and keeping his back to them, walked to the window and gazed out. They waited. "He brought up sex often and talked about women—senators, waitresses, girls—inappropriately, in my opinion."

Corelli was sure he knew something. "Nothing more specific?"

"I've heard rumors that he was involved in a sex ring of some sort, but there are lots of rumors, most unfounded, so I chalked it up to someone trying to explain his preoccupation with sex."

"Can you remember who passed the rumor on to you?"

He laughed and turned to face them. "Are you kidding? Congressional gossips are at work twenty-four-seven. It could have been almost anyone from the president down to the guy in the coffee shop."

She doubted he talked to the guy in the coffee shop. "Do you think Reverend Dumayne and Speaker Stanerd were involved in some nefarious sex thing with Mr. Blecker?"

"Good question," he said almost to himself. He returned to his desk. "I keep trying to put the image of them naked out of my mind but it certainly appears that way."

"Can you think of a reason for the three of them to be at Blecker's mansion?"

"Other than the obvious, sex, they would have been there because Blecker was a large donor to the church and probably Stanerd's campaign. And as I said, Blecker has cultivated friends in Washington and in high society in general. Personally, I can't fathom being friends with a man like that. I never saw his charm but then I'm considered stodgy, straight-laced, old-fashioned and uptight by many in those circles."

He glanced at the expensive Rolex on his wrist, probably signaling that a powerful and busy man like him needed to end the interview.

"Commissioner Neil's phone shows he received your call at eleven fifty-nine. What were you doing between eleven and eleven fifty-nine?"

"One thing I wasn't doing was keeping a minute by minute diary about what I was doing. I was in shock, Detective. I don't know how long I was in that room or how long I stood outside trying to gain control."

There it was again. Control. Being in control was important to him. She wasn't satisfied that required almost an hour but she'd pushed enough for a first interview.

"Because I know you're busy I won't ask you to come down to the station to complete a written statement, but before you leave for Washington, write down everything you've told us and anything else you recollect about the evening. Sign and date it and have your secretary messenger it to me at the address on my card." She walked to the desk and handed him her card. "And while you're in Washington, note anyone who mentions a possible Blecker sex ring and be alert for anything related to the murders."

"You want me to spy on my colleagues?"

"Not spy, help us with the investigation. Until we figure out who killed them and whether other senators might be in danger, we need to have eyes and ears in the senate. You're the most likely person to do that." His face darkened, apparently not happy to stoop to help them, but she rushed on before he could protest. "The killers were still there when you arrived, so it's possible you were also a target. Perhaps if you'd arrived when you were expected, you would have been killed as well."

He looked down his nose at her. "I assure you, I would have been fully clothed. You think I might be a target?"

"Truthfully, I don't know but it *is* possible. Better safe than sorry so I'm planning to ask the Capitol Police to provide round the clock security for you. I hope you won't fight me on that."

"I won't fight it. But how can you justify—"

"I'll have to brief the Capitol Police on the murders and it's likely they'll want to be involved to some extent so they'll be aware of the danger to you."

"My current driver is ex-NYPD so I should be safe."

"We'll talk to him and check him out but a team on you would be safer, if that's all right with you."

He stared at her as if assessing her trustworthiness. "Whatever you think is best."

With his confident, arrogant mask back in place, Corelli couldn't sense what he was feeling as his gaze settled on Parker still standing near the door.

The senator's voice pulled her back from her thoughts. "Do you have any suspects, any idea of why they were killed?"

"We have some theories but nothing solid and nothing I can share with you. But I intend to find out, Senator. We'll keep your name out of it, so I expect you to respect the investigation and not discuss anything you saw or anything you learn with anyone but one of us."

"Good. That's good. I knew you were the right one for the investigation."

"What do you mean?"

"When Neil and I spoke, I suggested you as the lead detective."

Not exactly what Neil and Broderick said. "Why? You hate me."

He had the grace to look embarrassed. "I knew you would consider all angles and do what was necessary to find the murderers. I hadn't thought I might be a target but that makes me sure you're the right detective to handle it since if you allow me to be killed, it will look like revenge." He put his hand up to stop her from speaking. "I'm sure that's not true but we both know the press would jump on that angle. And now I must get to work. Good luck finding the killers." He stood, indicating the meeting was over. Somehow he had signaled his assistant because the door behind them opened. "And please keep me posted."

CHAPTER TWELVE

With just enough time to touch base with Winfry at the stationhouse before heading to One Police Plaza for the press conference, they left Watkins to take a taxi to Seventy-Fourth Street to retrieve his car. Luckily they were close to the East River Drive. Traffic was slow but that was as good as it got in rush hour Manhattan.

"What does it mean that the senator didn't mention seeing the children or the vomit or the message on the mirror?" Corelli threw the question out to Parker.

Parker swerved into the left lane to avoid the car in front of her. "You'd think drivers could think ahead a second and get into the turn lane before the turn. As for the senator, I can see him being so spooked that he thought he heard a noise. And if we assume the killers were still in the house, they probably had already moved the girls and were incensed enough to go back and write the message. Maybe touching the blood caused the vomiting." She shrugged. "Just playing devil's advocate."

"That's part of your job," Corelli laughed. "I guess it's possible but something seems off to me."

Parker tapped her fingers on the steering wheel. "Me too. And it seems less and less like the work of a trafficking gang. Can we assume the noise he claimed to have heard was the killers moving the chest of drawers in front of the closet?"

"Given how loud the music was I'm not sure he could have heard a jackhammer upstairs," Corelli said. "And I'm not buying his explanation of why it took him almost fifty minutes to call Neil. If he was as freaked as he says he was, wouldn't he have gone with his first instinct to call 911 to get the police there? Instead he called the commissioner to, in his words, control the situation?"

"Stumbling on a scene like that would shake anyone, even a professional. And we know everybody reacts differently to stress," Parker said.

Was Parker defending the senator or just being her usual non-judgmental self? "So any feelings about the interview with Senator Daddy?" *Damn, she hadn't meant to be provocative.*

Parker glanced at her. "Senator Uncle, remember?" She turned her attention back to the street. "I spent my life, at least the time I lived with them, fighting him. I was too engaged to have any distance. Watching him from the outside today solidified my opinion that he's a pompous asshole trying to be whiter than white." She stopped talking and focused on zigzagging around a bottleneck on Seventh Avenue. "But I have to hand it to him. He pulls it off. He used to throw his superiority in my face. I don't know how many times I was subjected to the story of the brilliant black kid from Harlem who went to Yale undergrad on scholarships and felt like an outcast. And how halfway through his first semester, he realized he was smarter and the difference between him and them was how they dressed and how they spoke and how they occupied space in the world. He worked two jobs and often missed meals so he could save money to buy clothes in the expensive stores they shopped in. At the same time, he picked one of the popular white boys as his model and practiced speaking, laughing and moving like him. By his sophomore year he was speaking out in class more and offering his white role model and his white friends help with assignments. Sometime in his junior year, he was absorbed into that group of rich white boys. The lesson I was supposed to learn was they never noticed him when he felt inadequate and invisible, but when he dressed and spoke like them, they accepted him as a social equal."

Corelli didn't comment. Parker was rarely forthcoming about her family background and she didn't want to interrupt.

"He seemed to be telling the truth today but I don't trust him. He's an actor. He's good at zeroing in on the feelings and needs of people and using that knowledge to his advantage. The most authentic moment today was when you told him he might be a target. But even that has to be regarded with suspicion in my opinion."

Corelli agreed. He was a good actor. She would go along and see how things played out. "Do you believe he asked for me to head up the investigation?"

Parker glanced at her. "Feeling like the chosen one?" She laughed. "He knows how to do that. Sounded like the commissioner and the chief discussed it in front of him and he figured he could use you to his advantage. But I would guess he thinks it will confuse you and you won't look so hard at him." She laughed again. "But he doesn't have the vaguest idea of who you are, who he's up against."

"Should I take that as a compliment?"

"You definitely should."

Corelli didn't respond but she felt good that Parker thought she was a tough opponent for the senator. "His comment that Blecker was always in the company of men he thought would have better options, made me realize we've talked to people who knew Dumayne but so far we haven't found anyone close to Blecker. I'll make an appeal through the press later but I'll bet there are lots of articles about Jake and his powerful friends. Before we leave the station let's ask Dietz to do some research and set up some interviews."

Parker swung the car into a spot in the station's lot. She put her hand on Corelli's arm to keep her from getting out and surveyed the police standing outside. "All right, let's go."

"We need to talk about this. The crowds no longer show up and I don't think I'm in any danger from the ones who still turn their backs."

"It's true a lot of police came to the hospital, some visited you at home, and feelings seemed to calm while you were out of commission, but, trust me, there are still a lot of unhappy police out there looking for a weak spot. I say, 'not on my watch.' So humor me a while longer."

As Corelli followed her out of the car, she considered the request. It's a given that every police officer has to trust her partner to watch her back. After she'd exposed the group of dirty cops known as Righteous Partners, she was ostracized and threatened by her colleagues and it was hard to know whom to trust. The chief selected Parker, a new detective unconnected to other police, to work with her. Parker not only watched her back but kept her flashbacks and PTSD secret. And, she reminded herself, saved her life. Parker was annoying because she was more vigilant than most and needing a guard made Corelli feel weak. But that was her pride talking, wasn't it? She trusted Parker. It wouldn't hurt to keep things the way they were for now. "Okay."

Parker stopped short, stared at her, then turned toward the stationhouse, her lips twitching.

"Sit." Captain Winfry waved them in. "So what's all the secrecy about?"

Relaxing for the first time since the early morning call, Corelli sat with her legs extended and described the scene, what they were doing to keep it under wraps, and what they'd done so far, in detail.

Winfry seemed stunned. "Jeez...us. I knew it was bad but this is even worse than I expected." He rubbed his jaw. "You'll need to be on your toes. I'll assign the floaters to someone else so you can focus."

Parker didn't hesitate. "The two cases are connected, sir. The other day Corelli suggested that two seemingly unrelated girls murdered and dumped might indicate a child trafficking or prostitution ring. It seems too much of a coincidence that we now have three living, probably trafficked children with tattoos on their heels, the same area sliced off our drowned girls."

Winfry frowned. "Why would traffickers kill their moneymakers?"

"Good question," Parker said. "They appear to have been strangled so it wasn't accidental." She stared out the window running through possibilities. Her eyes widened. "Damn, they were beaten, raped and strangled. Maybe they were the victims in snuff movies. Child porn combining murder with sexual violence would probably be a huge moneymaker."

Interesting theory. Parker wasn't just a new detective she was also a former Assistant District Attorney so why should Corelli feel so proud of her response? But she did.

"Shit." Winfry looked ready to throw up. "This whole thing is beyond disgusting. Are you two up to it?" He made eye contact with Parker, then Corelli.

"We are." Corelli answered for them both. "We're determined to get these bastards. And unless we find something that says otherwise I agree the two cases belong together."

"Fine. You have what you need?"

"Everything but a clue."

Winfry's eye's widened. Parker stared at her.

"What? Why are you looking at me like that?"

Winfry and Parker exchanged a look. Winfry grinned. "Did you just make a joke, Corelli?"

The press conference went as expected. The announcement of the three victims was followed by stunned silence for a few seconds until the reporters caught up and threw out lots of questions they couldn't or wouldn't answer. But Corelli took the opportunity to ask the friends and family of Jake Blecker to come forward to assist with the investigation.

When they were alone with Neil and Broderick, Corelli informed them that Senator Stanerd's protection team had contacted her. "They wanted to take over the case but I blew them off and told them to call you, Commissioner, if they wanted to escalate the request."

No surprise. Broderick thought letting them have the case was a good idea. Commission Neil on the other hand, asked for her opinion. "Do you think they'll pursue the child trafficking aspect of the murders?"

Corelli held his gaze. "I think they'll bury it."

The commissioner chewed his lip. "I'll handle them. Unless the president orders us to turn it over, we'll keep it. I'm confident you and your team will get to the bottom of it."

"Yessir." Corelli relaxed.

"Speaking of Stanerd," Broderick said, "his office indicated that his trip to New York and his meeting with Senator Parker were not on his calendar and neither his family nor his staff knew about the trip or a meeting with Senator Parker."

"If no one knew he was here I'd say he was in the wrong place at the right time, not the target." Corelli stood. "That simplifies the investigation somewhat. The killer was probably after Dumayne or Blecker or maybe both. But I'm not sure how the secret meeting with the senator fits."

Parker followed Corelli out but they didn't speak until they were in the car. Parker snapped her seatbelt into place then turned to Corelli. "The chief didn't look too happy."

"Yeah, he likes to play it safe these days, though he used to agree that doing the right thing was the right thing." Corelli couldn't help giving Parker a poke. "You haven't changed your mind, have you?"

Parker gave her a dirty look. Corelli grinned and fastened her seatbelt.

Parker's phone pinged and she retrieved it from her coat pocket. "It's Jessie. Captain Isaacs. He says if we're interested in some background info on Reverend Dumayne, he's at Hattie's. What do you think?"

Corelli tensed. Her heart raced. Jessie and Marnie were unlikely friends, but he'd taken her under his wing when she was fresh out of the academy and they'd forged a solid friendship. The last time she'd been to Hattie's Harlem Inn was the night before she and Marnie left for Afghanistan. Flooded with memories of that night, she closed her eyes picturing Marnie, head thrown back, laughing at something Jessie said. And dancing. Marnie loved to dance and she was mesmerizing when she was into it. Her body...

"If you'd rather, we can meet tomorrow to hear what he has to say." Parker had picked up her reluctance.

Corelli took a few calming breaths. If she was ever going to be with Brett, it was time to start confronting her memories. "No, it's fine. Let's go."

CHAPTER THIRTEEN

As usual, Hattie's was jumping with a mostly Black crowd. It was one of the only places that still offered live music and dancing seven nights a week and it hadn't changed at all in the almost two years since she'd been here—or probably, the hundred years before that. Marnie used to joke that if they somehow sucked out the smell of fried food and beer, the building would collapse. No doubt she was right.

Isaacs waved from a booth in what was the closest thing to a quiet corner in Hattie's. She felt Parker's interest as he pulled her into an affectionate hug and greeted her like the old friend she was. "Chiara, you look awful."

A pang of loss shot through her. He always greeted the two of them like that. She forced a smile and gave the usual reply. "I feel good, though."

He switched his attention to Parker and Corelli slid into the booth. She struggled to push back the memories and contain the sadness and grief triggered by being here and being with one of Marnie's best friends. Breathe, commanded the voice of therapist Gil Gilardi, as clear as if she was sitting across the table.

Parker's voice brought Corelli back to the bar. "I'm sorry, what did you say?"

"Would you like a drink?"

A glass of wine would be wonderful but better not to drink when she was feeling so vulnerable. "A seltzer and lime would be great."

Jessie sat on the other side of the booth and studied her. He and Annie had visited her in the hospital and at home while she was still recuperating from being shot, but Brett had been there and they hadn't talked about Marnie. "So how are you, really?"

She knew what he meant. She was sure her being here awakened the same memories for him. "I miss her every day, Jess, but I'm hanging in there."

He reached across the table and grasped her hand. "I remember sitting here about two years ago and hearing you and Marnie repeat a promise that if one of you died in Afghanistan the survivor would mourn then move on to live and love. Marnie would be spitting fire to hear you were just hanging in there."

Corelli laughed. "Yeah, she would be hugely pissed." She blinked back a tear. "But I don't know how to let her go."

"I saw you once in the hospital and once at home with your friend Brett. And I thought I picked up a pretty strong vibe between you."

Corelli reddened. "There is but thinking about anyone else feels like cheating on Marnie. I'll get to it in a while."

Isaacs laughed. "I hate to repeat myself but need I remind you that Marnie would kick your ass if she heard you say you're planning to do it sometime, someday, whenever."

She looked down at their hands. "Give me a break, Jess."

"Give yourself a break, Chiara." He squeezed her hand and she looked up. "I miss her too. I realize it's harder for you but she really would want you to be happy. We face danger every day in our jobs and none of us knows how much time we have. You need to move on. Now. Not in the future."

Parker cleared her throat as she neared the table. They both looked up. Isaacs let go of Corelli's hand. "You promised Marnie, right at this table."

Parker put their drinks on the table and sat next to Corelli. She looked from Corelli to Isaacs and back to Corelli. "So you two are friends?"

"We are." Corelli looked at Isaacs. "But I'm assuming we weren't invited here for a reunion. What do you have for us, Jess?"

"I guess we'll skip dancing tonight." He laughed that deep rumble of his. "I saw the press conference earlier and I was surprised to see you assigned to a case that belongs to Benson's precinct and could be a career killer. I can't help but wonder, Chiara, whether you're suicidal or somebody high up is trying to get rid of you."

"Parker would probably say I'm suicidal. And no doubt plenty of police would be happy to see me go down. But Commissioner Neil and Chief Broderick called us both in on the case. We could have said no but we didn't."

He eyed the two of them. "Other than concern for the two of you, I have a couple of things but nothing substantial. I don't know how this fits but there are rumors Dumayne was into child pornography and maybe more. Someone told someone they were fixing his computer and saw a ton of files buried under innocuous names. I haven't been able to verify it."

"We have his home and office computers and twenty-four-hour guards on the office. I'm sure we'll find everything there is to find. You have anything else?"

"More rumors." He sipped his drink. "My wife's friend, who's a member of Dumayne's church, is upset about rumors accusing him of abusing girls. Annie dragged me to services there a few times to see whether I picked up anything concrete but I didn't. It all looks good. At least on the surface."

Corelli studied him. "And you believe the rumors?"

He rubbed his chin as he considered the question. "It's the combination of rumors. In my experience, unless it's a smear campaign, rumors like this are often based on truth."

Corelli and Parker exchanged a glance. Corelli didn't hesitate. Isaacs was one of the good guys and completely trustworthy. She told him what they'd found.

"So you think the girls were there for… Geez, I hate even saying it…sex?"

He gazed at Parker as he spoke. Corelli could see he was checking in but she didn't know why. Unless? If the senator had abused Parker as a child, she had to assume Parker knew it was relative to the case and would have said something. Otherwise, it was irrelevant. If Parker wanted to share with her, she would.

Corelli waited for his gaze to shift to her before responding. "We're sure they'd already been abused and pretty sure it wasn't the first time."

"Fuckers." Isaacs jerked up out of the booth. "I need something stronger than beer. Anyone else?"

They both declined. Parker peeled the label off her beer and Corelli twisted the plastic stirrer that came with her drink.

"It's not what you think." Parker spoke softly.

Corelli faced Parker. "And what makes you think you know what I'm thinking."

"Because I know how tuned in to people you are and I know you saw Jessie checking in with me about the sexual abuse. It's not relevant. It wasn't my uncle."

Corelli waited for Parker to elaborate but apparently that was all she was going to get tonight. "The case is likely to bring up memories. You're sure it won't interfere with your decision making?"

Parker didn't hesitate. "Yes."

"Then I'm okay with it too. Thanks for letting me know, it's one less thing to worry about. But I expect you to tell me if that changes."

Isaacs slid into the booth with a large glass of something amber. "Sorry, I want to kill guys who do that to children."

"You're not alone." Corelli reached across the table and covered his hand.

"There is something else," Isaacs said. "An old friend, Ben Fine, an FBI agent in the New York City office, called me after he saw the press conference. He'll be back in town in the next day or so and wants to meet with you."

She'd get a runaround from Stanerd's protection while they tried to cover up their part in his death so an insider who could be trusted would be a great help. "You vouch for him?"

"Ben and I grew up together. I'd trust him with my life." Isaacs relaxed and leaned back. "In fact I did. He was my partner when he was with the NYPD."

"Why is he interested?" Corelli asked.

He sipped his drink. "I honestly don't know. He saw the press conference and called to ask whether you could be trusted or were the kind of cop who would be involved in a cover-up. Talk to him. Judge for yourself."

She also would trust Jess with her life but it wasn't just herself she had to worry about, it was also the people she'd pulled into the middle of this mess. "It's not that I don't trust your judgment, Jess, but as you mentioned, this investigation could be a career killer for me and Parker and for the others we've involved." Parker had been silent but she had a stake in this too. "What do you think, Parker?"

Parker straightened. "At the very least, we need eyes on information that only the FBI has. I say we meet with Fine and see what he has to offer."

Corelli was pleased. More and more, Parker was stating her opinion without hemming and hawing. And she was right. They needed access to the information in Washington. And an FBI agent had access to a lot of data they wouldn't normally see or even know existed. "Set it up as soon as you can, Jess."

He saluted. "Aye, aye, captain. It's best to keep the meeting out of view so I suggest we meet here in the late evening, tomorrow or the next night, whenever he arrives."

"Thanks, Jess." She yawned. "Sorry. We've been awake nearly twenty-four hours and I know my bodyguard," she elbowed Parker, "won't let me take a taxi so I think it's time for us to go. Let Parker know when it's set."

CHAPTER FOURTEEN

When she arrived home, Corelli dealt with her screaming kittens, grabbed a quick bite and then luxuriated in her industrial vat bathtub with a cup of mint tea, trying to relax enough to get a little sleep. Her body responded but her mind was on high speed, reviewing the case so far, thinking about the young wife of the Reverend Dumayne, Senator Parker, and the possibility they'd find a lead to a child trafficking ring. Mostly though, she thought about the three little girls. When she talked to Gianna earlier in the evening, Gianna laughed and said she felt like a crook when the ambulance pulled up next to her car in the Pediatric Center's parking lot and they quickly transferred the girls and Greene to her car. On the way home, Allegra and Julia had followed a little way behind her in the ambulance and when she and Greene opened the car doors to move the girls into the house, they turned on the ambulance lights and sirens and slowly drove past hoping to draw all eyes away from the girls.

As you would expect, she said, the girls are frightened and withdrawn, but they'd connected with Gabriella and seemed to feel safe doing whatever she was doing. And that helped her bathe them, put them into Gabriella's pajamas and get them to eat.

Recognizing that sitting in the tub wasn't having the desired effect, Corelli dried off and did her physical therapy exercises, not an easy thing with the kittens crawling over her. She thought about calling Brett but remembered she was on a plane from the west coast. So instead of Brett's throaty voice and the warm vibe she exuded, she'd have to settle for the fictional crime in her mystery to divert her mind. The sleeping kittens were curled together on her pillow but even in their sleep it only took a few minutes for them to drape themselves over her. They really were a comfort. She'd been kidding herself thinking she would take them to a shelter but that wasn't an option anymore. It was time to name them. Soothed by the soft kitten snores, she yawned. Instead of reaching for her book, she turned off the light and slid under the covers. She'd fallen asleep quickly, but the nightmares woke her as usual a little more than three hours later and she'd spent the rest of the night reading and dozing.

At five a.m. she slipped away from the kittens, showered, dressed and went upstairs to make coffee. The buzzer indicated someone was coming up in the elevator. She glanced at the clock, five thirty. Only one person with a key visited at this hour. The elevator door slid open and Brett Cummings looking beautiful, even at five thirty in the morning, strode across the room and wrapped her arms around Chiara. "Good morning. I got back from Vancouver late last night. I'm sorry I haven't been able to check in with you since you went back to work. Did they put you right to work?"

She sank into Brett's strong arms and closed her eyes, enjoying her warmth and her caring, letting herself feel the strength of their connection. "I'll say. We caught a real doozy." *Marnie.* The guilt edged in, making her anxious. "Do I smell fresh bagels?"

Sensitive to Chiara's moods, Brett pulled away. "Trade you a cup of coffee for a bagel."

"You got it." She turned to pour, remembering Jessie's words, hearing Marnie's laugh and her voice saying the promise out loud. *I will mourn, but not forever. I will not forget but I will let myself love again without guilt.* Marnie would want her to be happy. Brett made her happy so why was she still holding her at arm's length? Brett had confessed her attraction soon after they met. She understood Chiara was still mourning Marnie and had pledged to wait as long as necessary.

After the shooting, Brett had spent as much time with her as she could, given her responsibilities as CEO of a brokerage firm badly in need of a cultural overhaul. Brett, Gianna, Parker, Simone, Nicky and Patrizia had been her main overnight caregivers. She and Brett had slept together many nights, though given their agreement to be friends Brett was always outside the covers. But they'd spent a great deal of time talking and getting to know each other. Brett, like her other caregivers, had witnessed her nightmares and her inability to sleep more than a few hours, though sometimes with Brett on the bed she was able to fall back to sleep for a few more hours.

The instant she saw her for the very first time Chiara felt an electric connection to Brett, and now, when she let herself feel it, she knew she was in love with her. She loved Brett's playfulness, her sense of humor, her intelligence, her beauty and her integrity. Chiara of all people knew how you could lose someone you love in a second, yet she was doing this, she was keeping them apart when it was clear they were meant to be together. Marnie would most definitely be pissed. Maybe it *was* time to do something.

She handed Brett the coffee and Brett handed her a plate with her favorite—an onion bagel with scallion cream cheese. They sat opposite each other at the table and talked while Chiara ate and the kittens climbed over the two of them.

Brett sipped her coffee. "I talked to Gianna in the limo on my way back from the airport last night. She insisted she was fine, but she sounded stressed. Do you know what's going on?"

"I'm afraid that's my fault. I involved her in my current case. She's caring for...um a couple of witnesses. It would be better if you didn't go there right now." The murder of the three men was public so she could talk freely about them and what they represented, but she needed to think about how much, if anything, to say about the girls.

Brett took her hand and looked into her eyes. "What aren't you telling me, sweetheart? I'm pretty sure you wouldn't involve Gianna and her family in a normal case." She should have known Brett would see right through her.

She held Brett's gaze. "You're right. But I can't tell you. I'm sorry."

Brett moved around the table to hug Chiara from behind. "Don't be sorry. I know you're doing your job. It sounds dangerous. Please be careful. I can't lose you before I even have you."

She stood and held Brett. "You do have me. I promise I'll do whatever I can to come all the way." She kissed Brett's lips lightly and stepped away.

Brett touched her lips and smiled. "I'm here whenever you're ready. But now I need to go into the office." She pointed to the bagel bag. "There's one for Parker, too."

Corelli was ready and waiting in the lobby when Parker arrived, as instructed, at eight rather than their usual six thirty a.m. She hoped Parker had gotten some extra sleep.

Parker stood outside the car, gun drawn, scanning the area. Once Corelli was in the car, Parker holstered her gun and got back in.

Corelli handed her a mug of coffee and the bag. "The bagel is from Brett."

Parker grinned. "She dropped in?"

"Who else visits at five thirty in the morning?"

Parker took a bite of the bagel and followed up with a swig of coffee. "Where to?"

"Let's head to Gianna's house. I want to get there before Leslie Court, the psychiatrist, so we don't interrupt her work and frighten the girls more than they are already. This morning she's mainly going to assess the girls and establish some trust. She'll leave the specific questions for another day when they seem comfortable with her."

Parker glanced at Corelli before snapping her eyes back to the road. "And you're okay with that."

Corelli stared out the windshield. "Of course I want to wring every bit of information out of them immediately but I'll wait until it won't be so traumatic for them. Based on the hospital findings, we know they were definitely sexually assaulted so that gives us enough to continue down the path we're on. Hopefully, Dr. Court, or maybe Gianna, can learn whether they're local or imported from somewhere else."

Corelli's PI friend, Tess Cantrell, gun in hand answered the door to Gianna's house. "Everything is quiet. They're in the kitchen."

"Thanks for stepping up to help, Tess." Corelli clasped her shoulder. "We're expecting Dr. Leslie Court, a psychiatrist, in about a half hour."

They dropped their coats off in the hall closet and walked to the back of the house. Gianna was at the table with the three girls and Gabby, all dressed in what were probably Gabby's pajamas. And Gabby, bless her, was chattering away, asking the girls questions and encouraging them to eat the pancakes Gianna had made. Gabby jumped up and threw her arms around Corelli. "Auntie Chiara." She hugged Parker then sat down and attacked her pancakes.

Gianna hugged Corelli. "Girls, this is my sister Chiara and my friend P.J. They're policewomen and will make sure you're safe." They girls averted their eyes. "Chiara and P.J., this is Maria, Crissy, and Teresa." She pointed to each girl as she said their name.

Chiara smiled. "Good morning, Gabby, Maria, Crissy and Teresa. I hope you're enjoying those delicious looking pancakes." Teresa looked up while the other two snuck a look, but only Gabby said anything. "My favorite."

Gianna caught Corelli's eye. "I'll be right out in the hall. Just call if you need me."

Gianna spoke in a whisper. "The poor things are terrified but they connected with Gabriella so I'm keeping her home from school today. My heart breaks when I think about what they've been through." She brushed the tears from her eyes. "Sorry. Anyway, when they got here they ate some soup and toast, then Greene and I put the three of them in a warm tub. When Gabriella asked to get in with them, they relaxed a little and I was able to wash them and put them in pajamas. I think Gabby makes them feel safe so I moved a mattress into her room and they slept there. Me too."

Corelli pulled her sister into a hug. "Thank you. I knew you were the right person to take care of them. Have they said anything other than their names?"

"No, but I haven't pushed. Come inside and have pancakes with them, I'm sure they'll feel more comfortable with you if they see Gabby relate to you."

Gabby was her usual ebullient self, thrilled that her friend P.J. and her Aunt Chiara were having breakfast with them. She peppered them with questions and chattered about school and the Nancy Drew book she was reading. When she slowed down, Corelli and Parker asked her questions. It didn't take too long for the girls to get curious and begin to warm up. Corelli was tempted to question them but she knew it would be better for the psychiatrist to do it so she let Gabby control the conversation flow.

The doorbell rang. Parker excused herself and went to escort the psychiatrist to the kitchen. She introduced Dr. Leslie Court as Leslie, a friend.

Probably in her early thirties, the blue-eyed blond psychiatrist smiled and joined them at the table. She accepted a cup of coffee and laughed easily as she answered Gabriella's many questions about where she lived, was she Auntie Chiara's friend, and so on. Her warm smile, soft voice and gentle presence seemed to relax the children and it wasn't long before they actually ventured to look at her. When Gianna admonished Gabriella to let someone else talk for a change, there was a moment of silence before Leslie directed a question to the girls. "Well, I now know Gabriella," she patted Gabby's hand, "but I'm sorry I don't remember your names." She picked up her coffee and sipped. "Would you remind me?" She gazed at the three and smiled to encourage them.

Corelli caught Gianna's eye and tilted her head toward Gabriella. Gianna moved behind her daughter and placed her hands on her shoulders, ready to silence her if necessary. Gabby looked up at her mother but didn't comment. Seconds passed before a small voice whispered. "I'm Crissy."

Leslie smiled "Hi, Crissy, I'm Leslie, pleased to meet you." She extended her hand. Crissy hesitated, then touched her and quickly pulled away.

"And what about you two?" Leslie switched her gaze to the other two girls.

Maria looked at Gianna. The older woman smiled and touched the girl's shoulder lightly. "You can tell her, sweetie. She's our friend."

The girl turned back to Leslie. "I'm Maria and this is my sister, Teresa." She put a protective arm over the younger girl.

Corelli thought her heart would break. She couldn't look at any of the adults for fear of the tears escaping.

Leslie leaned in close. "I'm so happy to meet you Maria and Teresa." She extended her hand again and waited for the girls to touch her. It was brief but they touched her hand.

"I have to leave in a few minutes," Leslie said. "But I'll be back tomorrow with some games so we can play together. Would that be all right, Crissy, Maria, Teresa and Gabriella?"

Of course, Gabby responded immediately with an enthusiastic yes. The other three hesitated, looked at Gianna, and seeing her smile, offered whispered agreement.

"Good, I'll see you tomorrow."

Corelli followed the psychiatrist out of the room. "What do you think, Dr. Court?"

"Please, call me Leslie. Gianna and Gabriella have done a great job bonding with them in a short while and they seem to feel safe. That's important. My gut feeling is the girls will be receptive. Does your sister have a husband, sons?"

"She does but when I told Gianna and Marco about the girls, they thought it would be best if they didn't have to deal with any males so Marco and Giancarlo are sleeping at my parents' house."

"I think it would be helpful if they could stay away for a while."

"Gianna will do whatever is necessary to help the girls. Should she keep Gabriella home from school again tomorrow?"

Leslie grinned. "What a gift. Gabriella is so vibrant and trusting. Having her there will help me establish trust with the girls. So if

Gianna is willing, yes. Have you learned anything else about who the girls are and how they came to be abused?"

"No, but we will. It will help if you can get their last names and where they come from, if they know."

The psychiatrist studied Corelli. "You think they're trafficked?"

"It's possible and we'll be pursuing that and any other angle we come up with. I hope you understand you can't discuss this situation, the girls, this address or anything that you learn about the case with anyone but me or Detective Parker. The girls may be in danger, which means my sister and niece may be in danger. And you may end up in danger as well."

The psychiatrist narrowed her eyes. "Dr. Gilardi explained all of this in excruciating detail when she asked me to get in involved. You must trust Gil since you asked her to find someone to work with the children so I assume I can discuss them with her if I need a professional to bounce ideas off."

"Yes, of course." At the door, Corelli greeted Charleen Greene who had replaced Tess Cantrell. Tess would come back tonight when Greene went off shift.

Corelli went back into the kitchen where the four girls were coloring while Parker and Gianna were doing the dishes. "I'm leaving a credit card on the table so you can order some pajamas and clothing for the girls. Get everything they need." She hugged Gianna from behind. "Leslie said you're doing a great job. How are you holding up?"

Gianna swiveled in the embrace and faced her sister. "I'm fine. It was tricky last night getting the girls to let me bathe them and put them in pajamas. Francesca and Gabriella were really a big help. And, as you see," she tilted her head toward the table, "my rambunctious Gabriella has opened her heart to them. And Francesca got up to help me when the girls woke up crying several times overnight. What did Leslie have to say?"

"She thought being here without any men around was helping. Am I pushing it to ask that Marco and Giancarlo stay away another couple of days? And that Gabriella misses another day of school?"

Gianna hugged her. "Push as hard as you like, Chiara. I'll do whatever I can to help the girls."

"Does Francesca know she's not to mention the girls to anyone?" She worried that the twelve-year-old would need to talk to feel important.

"She does. And she won't. I didn't go into any detail about why the girls are here but she's thrilled to be involved in a clandestine operation with her Auntie Chiara."

CHAPTER FIFTEEN

Driving from Bensonhurst to the stationhouse, Corelli voiced something she'd obsessed about overnight. "We need to tell Dietz, Kim, and Forlini about the girls and the child abuse angle. Operating with half the facts could result in the teams missing something important, and having to censor our thoughts and speech when making assignments could hamstring the investigation, but we won't tell them where the girls are."

Parker glanced at Corelli then quickly looked back at the road. "We know they're trustworthy and it will motivate them to work even harder to get the bastards. Besides, it would be awkward lying to them even if it's by omission."

Back at the station, someone manning the tip line handed Corelli a tip sheet. An anonymous call had come in at six this morning. The voice was muffled so it wasn't clear if it was a man or a woman. The message was specifically to be given to Detective Corelli. "Girls in upstairs bedroom on Seventy-Fourth Street."

She passed the message to Parker. "Hiding them, then worrying they might not be found are the actions of a feeling human being, not a cold-hearted killer. This strengthens the argument against the traffickers as the killers."

Parker frowned. "Sounds like he didn't see any mention of the girls and got worried they'd starve to death."

Corelli took the note back and read it again. "Yeah, it appears that way."

To ensure what she had to say was only heard by Dietz, Kim and Forlini, Corelli and Parker met with them in an interview room. She told them about the men being naked with traces of what appeared to be semen on them and the presence of three sexually abused girls.

Kim broke the silence. "Are they in foster care?"

"For now they are safe and being taken care of outside the system. Besides me, Parker, Greene and Watkins, you three are the only investigators aware they exist. We need to keep it that way. We believe the men were involved with a child sex trafficking ring and the girls may be in danger." She locked eyes with each of them in turn. "Okay, let's get to work."

Dietz, Parker and Corelli settled at the conference table with Watkins. Dietz pulled a stack of papers toward him. "We got people on Dumayne's home and office computers and on Blecker's computers. Palm Beach removed Blecker's computers from the house but didn't find a safe. They'll get back to us about our guys searching the house but they agreed to let us send someone to check the computers."

"The West Palm Beach Chief of Detectives promised full cooperation. Let him know it's crucial that our guys locate the safe because we expect to find it filled with child porn. Also, ask whether they have anything on Blecker." Corelli waited for Dietz to look up from his notes before continuing. "Get approval from robbery to send Detective Paulie Massetti with one of our own guys. Massetti knows where the safe was hidden in the NYC house so he'll know what to look for, and he can crack it when he finds it. Be sure we have a video recording of everything so send a CSU photographer. Has Blecker's wife, or should I say companion, cooperated?"

"Her name is Marianne. She doesn't live in the Palm Beach house. We're still trying to locate her." Dietz pointed his pen at Watkins. "Go."

"We identified a number of Blecker's big shot friends and of the three who were willing to talk to me, two claimed not to know much about his life. The third, Roger Horn, a hedge fund manager, said they were close. Amongst other things included in my report, he said one night after a lot of drinks Marianne confided that she was fighting Jake and Dumayne for control of a jointly owned business. When he asked for details she refused to say anything more about it except that he and she would be in danger if word got out. She swore him to secrecy before stumbling out of the bar. He had no idea what business she was talking about."

"Interesting. Can you follow up with Blecker's attorney? And Dumayne's as well?"

"Will do." Watkins smoothed the papers in front of him. "On other fronts, as we expected Washington won't give us access to the senator's home or office, or any of his computers for security reasons. And Kim and Forlini have been overseeing the canvassing of the Blecker and Dumayne neighbors. Tell us what you have, Forlini."

"Yeah, ten or fifteen minutes before midnight on the night of the murders, one of Blecker's neighbors, a Mrs. Vera Rumford, thought she heard noise from the yard in front of her brownstone and went to make sure her door was locked. She saw a tall, well-dressed black guy facing the street. She thought he dumped some papers in her garbage can but she wasn't sure. She went to get her cell to call 911 but by the time she got back to the window he was gone. No one else saw or heard anything."

That confirms that piece of Senator Parker's story. Corelli watched Parker and Watkins make notes. Joey Forlini was always thorough but she had to ask. "Has anyone checked the garbage bins in front of her house?"

"We did," Forlini said. "But we missed the regular five thirty a.m. pickup yesterday and those cans and the others along the street were empty. Do you think it's worth digging through the garbage at the dump?"

"It would be nice to know what he had, if anything, but I don't think it's worth the manpower."

Forlini pointed at Hei-ki Young Kim. "So one of Dumayne's neighbors usually walks her dog before the ten o'clock news and says she saw Mrs. Dumayne leave her house around nine thirty the night of the murder. She's seen her out walking several times and each time she's been picked up by someone in a car."

Parker leaned forward. "Did she see who picked her up?"

"No, she couldn't see the driver." Kim took a swig of water from the bottle on the table in front of her. "Assuming she's still doing it, I'll watch her to see if we can get a plate number."

Dietz jumped back in. "So the MTA said Stanerd's Metro Card hasn't been used since October." He cleared his throat. "And we're still waiting for the phone records for the three men."

"Put some pressure on the phone companies, Dietz. Watkins, did you check out Senator Parker's driver?"

"Yes. As you thought, Mack Sullivan is not in great shape. He's overweight, a heavy smoker, and I believe, a heavy drinker. He confirmed the senator's story."

She looked around the table. "Anything else?"

"Yeah." Dietz glanced around the office. "Where the hell is Greene? I need her to do some research but I haven't seen her all day or yesterday, for that matter."

"She's with the girls. Ask the captain for someone to do the research. We get everything we need on this one."

"We located the safe deposit box at JP Morgan Chase," Dietz said. "Me and Watkins checked it out. It contained three passports for Blecker and three for Marianne Phillips plus tons of cash in dollars and Euros and a bag of diamonds."

Corelli swallowed her disappointment. She'd hoped to find what they needed to break the codes to identify the children and the rapists. "Thanks, Dietz."

Parker pointed to her wrist to indicate it was time to go. Old habits. Of course Parker didn't wear a watch. "We're meeting with the chief and the commissioner this evening so I'd appreciate some bullet points on anything you guys think we should bring up or anything we need. We'll be back later. Let's go, Parker."

They headed off to Corelli's apartment with enough time to eat some of the many leftovers her sisters dropped off a couple of times a week, before Joseph Gianelli, her brother-in-law, arrived. She'd called him after leaving DeAndre's house and arranged to meet him here so as not to alarm her sister Patrizia. Her request to meet privately had surprised him but he readily agreed to come to her apartment.

Corelli was waiting when he stepped off the elevator. They embraced. He greeted her in Italian and asked how she was feeling. Then he noticed Parker and switched to English to greet her. They settled with coffee in one of the many sitting areas in the huge loft.

He waited a few seconds before jumping right in. "I'm intrigued by all the secrecy, Chiara. I hope Nicky isn't in any kind of trouble. How can I help you?" He still had an accent but his English had improved tremendously in the twenty-something years since he and Patrizia had married.

"I'm interested in a customer of yours. Amari DeAndre. She says you transport all her equipment and instruments when she's on tour and have been doing it for years. She speaks highly of your company but I'm interested in how you came to get that account. I imagine it must be very lucrative."

"It is lucrative. I've been doing it for about ten years now. I believe it was Ms. DeAndre's first big tour and the transport company they'd hired was having trouble making the schedule, had damaged some equipment, and had misplaced or stolen a guitar. They needed a dependable replacement to step in immediately. My friend, Ernesto, a guy I grew up with in Italy, contacted me out of the blue and offered me the job if I thought I could handle it. The catch was I would need to have a truck in Chicago the next day. When he told me what it paid, I didn't hesitate. I was still in start-up mode, with only a few trucks doing small jobs. This was the big time. I said yes, rented a truck in Chicago and flew there with Vinnie, my best driver. I was able to hire one of the men from the other company since they were laid off. It took me and Vinnie a couple of moves to learn the ropes, and after a month I let the original guy go because he was lazy and not interested in doing a good job. I brought out another one of my best men and hired a new guy. The four of us did the job together for another month before I felt comfortable enough to leave them to it. I flew home and they finished the tour. I was able to parlay that job into many others that allowed me to build the business to what it is today."

Parker took advantage of his pause. "What's Ernesto's full name? And do you know where he is or how to get in touch with him?"

Joseph turned to Parker. "Servino. I haven't seen him in a few years so I have no idea where he is but I can give you his cell number. Maybe it's still active." Parker waited while he scrolled through his phone then wrote down the number he rattled off.

Joseph put his phone on the coffee table. "Are these questions related to the murder of his boss, Jake Blecker?"

Corelli gazed at her brother-in-law. He seemed relaxed, as usual. She prayed he wasn't involved. "How well did you know Blecker?"

He laughed. "I never met the man. Ernesto said he was a weird guy but he paid well. Back then Ernesto was planning to leave as soon as he had enough money to go back to Sicily and live the good life. But the last time we spoke it sounded like he was addicted to the good life here in the US and planned to stay and work with Blecker."

"Why did Ernesto throw the DeAndre job your way? Did he think you were a big company with a large fleet? Did he ask for a kickback?"

Joseph shook his head. "We grew up together. I paid his airfare from Sicily, I paid for him to take English classes, I supported him until he could get a job." He grinned. "When he got his first paycheck he took me out to celebrate. We both got drunk and he had what we thought was a brilliant idea, that we get matching tattoos." Joseph lifted his pant leg and exposed his calf so they could see the small but elaborate design that incorporated the American flag and the map of Italy. Chiara had seen the tattoo many times over the years but she never knew the story behind it. "Patrizia went nuts when she saw it and was ready to throw me out. After that Ernesto felt he owed me even more. He saw the job as an opportunity to pay me back for what I'd done for him. And it did."

"Did he ever share anything about his boss, his likes and dislikes or anything?"

"He said they traveled a lot, that Blecker had friends in high places, things like that, but nothing personal. He did tell me that Mr. Blecker had plucked Ms. DeAndre off the street and was making her a star. And I guess he did because even I know her music."

Corelli put a hand on his knee. "Joseph, we think Jake Blecker and maybe Ernesto Servino were involved in some pretty disgusting sexual shit with children. I'll find out one way or another but I'd much prefer hearing directly from you. Are you or have you ever been involved in any other dealings with either of them?"

"I swear, Chiara, only transporting Ms. DeAndre's equipment. After Ernesto set that up I only saw him for a drink once or twice a year but it's been at least four years since I heard from him. I did hear something disgusting about Blecker, but the guy who said it was drunk so I didn't believe it. I never heard anything bad about Jake Blecker from Ernesto."

"What did you hear and who did you hear it from?"

He thought for a few seconds. "Last Christmas one of my large corporate clients hosted a party for their vendors at Trilago, a popular bar downtown." He hesitated and smiled at her. "I know you mostly see the mean-spirited side of your sister Patrizia, the controlling side, but she can be a lot of fun and very outgoing when it's just the two of us. Anyway, we had a ball dining and dancing and socializing at that party. Right before we left, around midnight, I went to the men's room and while I was in the toilet, I overheard two drunks talking at the urinals. They couldn't see me so they probably thought they were alone."

"What did they say?"

"They were making a bet about who would be the first to seduce one of the college interns working at the company. A third guy came in and joined them at the urinal as they were discussing how young the girls were and which one would," he blushed, "fuck one of the girls on his desk first. The third guy said something like, 'if you're willing to pay, I can get you pussy as young as you want.' One of the drunks said, 'I'm done with drug-crazed pimps and drug-crazed prostitutes.' The third guy said, 'Jake Blecker is an important man with important friends and the kids are fresh. But you'd better not repeat his name to anybody or you'll be in big trouble. Let me know when you want to buy.' He left and they followed. I was ready to throttle them but I figured they were drunk and bragging the way some men do. But the third guy sounded sober."

"Did you recognize the third guy?"

He shook his head. "I was in the stall so I just heard their voices but they seemed to know him so maybe they were coworkers."

"Thanks, Joseph. Call me immediately if you think of anything else." She picked up the CDs Amari had given her. "Listen, would you give these to Nicky? He and Simone are crazy about Amari's music and she signed a CD for each of them."

He looked at the signed CDs. "Oh. I didn't know or I could have…." His shoulders dropped. His eyes filled. "I guess there's a lot I don't know about my son." Sadness leaked in every word.

Before she was shot Corelli had discovered her nephew was gay and hiding it from everyone except Simone. She'd talked to him and promised she'd go with him when he came out to his parents. One afternoon soon after she got out of the hospital, Simone, Nicky, Patrizia and Joseph were her only visitors and Nicky had bravely faced his parents. Patrizia and Joseph were stunned. They didn't understand but they rallied to let Nicky know they loved him. It was a relief. Given Patrizia's unhappiness with Corelli's lesbianism, she and Nicky both expected a harsh attack, not love, from Patrizia. "How are you feeling about Nicky's being gay? Have you two talked?"

He rubbed his chin. "I don't know how, Chiara. In Sicily my father didn't pay attention to me or my brothers, except when we did something wrong. And I guess I'm the same. I've concentrated on growing the business and left the children to your sister. I rarely spend time alone with any of them and sometimes I feel like an outsider in my own family. At family gatherings I feel jealous of Marco because he seems so close to Giancarlo and the girls. You know."

She did know. Was the difference geography, education or personality? Gianna's husband Marco grew up in Milan, a cosmopolitan city, in a well-to-do, educated family. Both his parents were doctors and he went to college and medical school. Now he did biomedical research at Rockefeller University in New York City, but whether it was Gianna never letting him off the hook on childcare or his natural instinct, he was very much involved with his children. Joseph, on the other hand, grew up poor in a small town in Sicily where the old way was the way things were done. Education was a luxury he didn't have but he'd focused his attention and his energy on building his business into the successful company it was today. And, though Patrizia was only a few years older than Gianna, she believed the old way was the right way, the children were the mother's responsibility and the father was not to be bothered.

Joseph didn't expect an answer to his question. "This thing with Nicky, finding out he's been afraid to tell us something so important, made me realize that I've missed a lot. If I'd been around more maybe he wouldn't be gay."

Seeing him struggle to understand Nicky, Corelli felt new respect for her brother-in-law. In their extended family mild-mannered Joseph had always been a silent figure dwarfed by his wife's angry, controlling personality. "Being around more wouldn't have made him straight, Joseph, but it would have made for a better, stronger relationship with your firstborn. The important thing is that you want to get closer to him now. It's not too late."

"What can I say to him?"

"Why don't you talk to Father Bart to get some perspective on the issue." Brett's brother, a priest, had met the Corelli clan in the hospital, and like Brett, had been absorbed into the extended family. "Since his sister is a lesbian I'm sure he has some thoughts he could share. Then spend time with Nicky, either alone or with me as a buffer if you prefer. Patrizia looms large in his life so it would be good for him to spend time alone with you. It might be awkward at first but it will get easier. He's curious about your business. And I'm sure he'll be thrilled that you know Amari. Use the CD as an icebreaker and discuss your connection to her. Think about it, Joseph. I know it's something you both want."

"Thank you, Chiara. Father Bart is easy to talk to. And using the CD as a starting point is a great idea. Maybe I'll ask him to spend a day at the office with me." He turned to Parker. "Sorry to involve you in the family drama, P.J., but I think of you as a part of the family."

Parker bowed her head. "I'm honored you trust me with your feelings, Joseph."

Corelli walked him to the elevator, pulled him into a hug, and grinned. "I'm glad you reminded me that Patrizia has a fun side.

Though she's been gentle and caring since I was shot, I'd forgotten how playful and full of life she was when you two got together."

"Almost losing you has changed her, so enjoy the new her." He kissed her cheek and stepped into the elevator.

"That was intense," Parker said. "He always seemed so macho... No, I think reserved is a better description, but he really made himself vulnerable today. That bodes well for Nicky." She stood. "He seemed to be telling the truth about not being involved with Blecker but the conversation he overheard in the bathroom was...upsetting. Too bad he couldn't give us the guy's name. Any ideas on how to figure out who the contact was?"

Corelli walked over to the window trying to tamp down the rage that bubbled up as it had when Joseph described how casually the men discussed abusing children. She felt trapped. She knew the stress of dealing with the abuse exaggerated the PTSD and the PTSD exaggerated the rage. She feared if she tried to deal with the PTSD in therapy she might explode and hurt Dr. Gilardi. But if she didn't deal with it and Marnie's death, she'd never be able to have a completely open, loving relationship with Brett. Breathe, she reminded herself. She took in air and processed it as she'd learned the other day. After a few minutes, she calmed a little. Maybe she needed another yoga session. She turned from the window. It was clear that Parker had observed her struggle. Happily, she didn't comment. Some day she might acknowledge to Parker that she was right about the PTSD. But not today. "Yeah, I agree. Joseph wasn't involved with the abuse. My only thought on figuring out who was pimping for Blecker is to send a couple of guys to nose around Trilago." Corelli went into the kitchen and took two bottles of water out of the fridge. She tossed one to Parker. "Drink up then let's head back into the station again for a couple of hours. We need some fresh leads. Hopefully something new has come up."

Trying to be discreet, they sat at their desks and searched the two books they'd found in Blecker's safe for the codes tattooed on the heels of the three girls. Line after line, page after page of precisely written codes was hard on the eyes, so after about forty minutes, Corelli was relieved to hear Parker's soft, "Got one."

It took another half hour to find the codes tattooed on the other two girls. Seeing the X's next to some of the codes sent a shiver up Corelli's spine. These were probably murdered. "Parker," she spoke softly, "call Ndep and ask if her research has turned up other children's bodies with tattoos, or as with our two Jane Does, their heels shaved."

Parker left the room to make the call. Corelli stared at the codes. Any information the three girls could provide might be the key to this code. She opened the other book. She was convinced these were codes for the men involved. Now all she needed was to find the two matching books with the actual names. Her phone rang. "Corelli."

"Hi, it's Joseph. I think the third guy was managing the event. As I was driving home this afternoon, I kept hearing his voice saying, 'Welcome, and let me know if you need anything.' I hope that helps. He had an accent, maybe English or Australian. Hard for me to tell."

"That's great Joseph. Who was the client that hosted the party?"

"Mathews and Macrady, a large financial services firm. We do all their moves. Do you want the name of my contact there?"

"Yes." She wrote down the name and number. "Thanks, Joseph." Parker was looking at her when she ended the call. "Joseph thought the voice he heard in the men's room belonged to the person managing the event at Trilago but he didn't know whether he worked for the bar or the host company. I'll ask Dietz to follow up."

Corelli went to the conference room. Dietz looked up when she sat across from him. He handed her a large sealed envelope marked confidential. "This was hand delivered from the ME's office about ten minutes ago."

She handed Dietz the slip of paper with the information Joseph had provided. "Contact this guy to get the name of the person who managed their Christmas party at Trilago last year and bring him in. I want to interview him."

She smiled as she unsealed the envelope. She had no idea Dietz could be so discreet. She was sure he was dying to know where the girls were, who had given her the tip about this guy, and what the autopsy reports said—but he didn't ask. She opened the envelope and Dietz went over to talk to Forlini.

Parker entered the conference room and sat next to her. "Ndep hasn't come up with anything yet. She sent the autopsy reports over a little while ago."

Corelli tapped the papers in front of her. "Got them." She passed one of the autopsy reports to Parker.

Parker finished first. "Confirms Stanerd had sex before being shot four times. Nothing much else except they submitted a drug screen and are testing his DNA."

"Same for Dumayne." Corelli did a quick scan of the third report. "And for Blecker, except six bullets." She slid the three reports back into the envelope.

After reviewing the points the team had prepared for their meeting at One Police Plaza, Dietz handed Corelli a thin stack of folders and a sheet of paper listing the names and times of the church security guards they would be meeting with tomorrow.

CHAPTER SIXTEEN

Corelli was in a lousy mood. The meeting with Neil and Broderick was frustrating. They seemed to expect miracles. She could forgive Neil but Broderick should've known better. Thank god for Captain Winfry. He understood what an investigation like this required and helped her and Parker steer the discussion so it remained productive. Maybe she'd made a mistake by not insisting Neil and Broderick go in the house to see the abused girls. Maybe then they would've understood how small and fragile they were, that it would take time to get them to talk about what happened to them.

Add to that her internal battle about what she needed to do to let go of Marnie and move closer to Brett. She'd made and unmade the decision about therapy so many times today that she had no idea whether she'd decided to call Dr. Gilardi or not. And, the damn weather. The icy downpour had continued without interruption all day and she had again let her pride get in the way of her health. Each time Parker offered to drop her off at the door of their destination, she had foolishly insisted she would stay in the car while Parker found a spot. So, for probably the tenth time today, she was wet and chilled. For a change the overheated bar felt welcoming rather than stifling.

Sitting across the table from Captain Jessie Isaacs for the second time in as many nights, waiting for FBI Agent Fine to put in an appearance, she pushed her half-eaten bowl of gumbo aside and glanced at her phone. He was more than an hour late.

Jessie put his huge paw over her hand. "It was only an estimate, Chiara. He'll be here as soon as he can get away from his meeting."

She needed a distraction. "So tell me, how did you meet Parker, Jess?"

"I don't think—"

"It's all right, Jessie, she knows part of my story," Parker grinned at him, "and you know how much you love to tell your part."

Why had she asked this question? She'd expected Parker to object. Was asking Jess to expose Parker's personal life another aspect of her dumping her anger and discomfit on Parker? "Wait. I'm sorry. I was out of line asking that. Let's talk about the shitty weather."

"I don't mind," Parker said. "You know some of my story so you might as well know all of it."

Corelli was humbled. Despite her constant baiting, Parker trusted her. Since the shooting and Parker's display of…friendship, partner concern, support, or whatever, she'd tried not to dump on her but she wasn't doing a good job. Maybe Parker understood. "You're really okay with it?"

"I am, but let me warn you, Jess likes to tell the story like it's happening right now and do the voices. I don't remember the details so I have to trust he's telling the truth."

Jessie held his hands as if swearing on a bible. "I promise to tell the truth and just the truth, so help me God." He grinned. "So I was just out of the academy, in my first week walking my beat in Harlem, looking for trouble. And I spotted it. A tiny bare-assed kid with legs sticking out of a trashcan, kicking like crazy, obviously stuck. "Need help, I asked?"

"'Get me out of this fucking thing!'" Jess did his best to imitate a child. "The voice was muffled but not the annoyance."

"'I'm gonna grab you so don't punch me.' The legs stopped thrashing. 'Don't touch me, just tip the can over.'"

"I'm a police officer, I won't hurt you."

"'Shit a cop.' Activity inside the can indicated panic mode. 'Go away.'"

"I'm afraid you'll suffocate. How you gonna get out?"

"'When the garbage truck comes they'll dump me on the sidewalk.'"

"While she was still, I grabbed her around the waist and pulled her out. Believe me, she came out kicking and swinging, her little legs pumping as if she was running a race. I held her away from me as she punched and kicked. Finally, when she was tired, she pulled her pants up and looked me in the eye. 'You gonna take me to jail?'"

"Nah. What were you looking for?"

"'Sometimes people throw away pizza crusts or parts of sandwiches.'"

"I put her down but I held onto her shoulder. Come on, I'm gonna buy you something to eat. How about a burger?"

"'Is this a police trap?'"

"I was just going to eat so I thought maybe you'd like something."

"'Can I have fries too?'"

"Sure."

"I'm Jessie, what's your name?" He glanced at Parker before continuing.

"'Precious Jewel.'"

Corelli didn't react but she felt Parker tense up. If she remembered correctly, Parker had been with her mother until she was three years old, so her mother gave her the name that indicated she was loved. She'd been taken in by her aunt. Why was she looking for food in garbage cans?

Jessie grinned, clearly loving this story. "I almost laughed at the ferocious wild peanut with a name like that. 'I'm gonna call you P.J., is that okay?'"

"'Why?'"

"''Cause Precious Jewel is too long and you're too fast. You'll be around the corner before I finish saying it."

"Her toothy smile was white against her dirty face and I knew I'd said the right thing. She let me lead her to a coffee shop and that was the beginning of our unlikely friendship. She was almost six years old, filthy and smelly, not just from the garbage. She looked like she hadn't bathed in a month, her clothes were too big and foul, her hair looked like it had never been cut and it was so dirty and tangled that I didn't worry about anything living in there. We got into a routine of eating dinner together every night, sometimes lunch and breakfast too, if she was around."

He signaled the waitress for another round. "Even back then I knew it wasn't a good idea for a single guy to take a little girl home and bathe her but I wanted to get her cleaned up. Then one day on patrol,

I was walking past the beauty parlor where the young woman I'd been flirting with for weeks worked. She smiled and waved. I was thrilled that she'd noticed me. I fantasized about asking her out but I knew I wouldn't because I was shy and I was sure she'd say no. But later when P.J. and I were eating dinner I had an idea. The next morning I stopped in the beauty shop and introduced myself to Annie Mackay, who as it turned out, was the owner of the salon."

After we chatted for a while Annie turned the conversation to P.J. "'I've noticed you buying the Parker girl dinner. Actually, lots of folks have noticed. What are you up to?'"

"I'm up to feeding her. She shouldn't have to dig in garbage pails to find something to eat."

"'I agree. Some of us have tried to help but she'd never let anybody near her.' She filled me in on P.J.'s background—mother dead, lived with her addict aunt, also dead, and was now with her alcoholic grandmother. And then she said, 'That child needs a good scrubbing, a haircut, and some clean clothes that fit.' We were silent while I worked up the nerve to ask, but then at the same time I said, 'Would you?' she said, 'Could you get her to let me help?'"

"Anyway to make a long story short, after having dinner with me and Annie for a week or so, Ms. P.J. agreed to go to Annie's apartment above the beauty parlor for a bath and a haircut. She screamed and yelled the whole time. But underneath all that hair and the dirt and grime was this cute little girl. The three of us got in the habit of having dinner together in Annie's apartment above the shop. When we realized P.J. wasn't in school, I paid her grandmother to go with me and got her enrolled in kindergarten. Somehow her alcoholic grandmother managed to keep track of the social worker's home visits and made sure P.J. was washed, had a scarf on her head and wore the one dress she owned, so the child support checks would continue. But P.J. spent most nights at Annie's apartment so she was fed, bathed and always had clean clothes. We were surprised when we realized she already knew how to read so we got her books and taught her to write.

"When P.J. was almost eight, Annie and I married and decided we would adopt her if we could. Once we convinced her grandmother she would get more money on welfare than she was receiving for child support, she agreed to let us adopt so I contacted the social worker assigned to her case. It turned out before we could go ahead with the adoption we had to have all relatives sign off. Enter Aloysius T. Parker. As long as nobody knew she was his niece he'd had no problem leaving her on the streets—hungry, dirty, and uneducated. But he couldn't bear to have her adopted by two people who loved her. Needless to say he won the court battle but the judge wasn't happy with him so we won the right to have her overnight one night a week, some weekends, and some weeks during summer vacations. In reality, he and his wife were happy to let us have her as often as we wanted. I think P.J. will agree, she got a topnotch education from them, but all her love came from Annie and me." His expression as he looked at Parker said it all.

Corelli was stunned. She'd never read Parker's file but none of this would have been in there anyway. She'd met Parker's biological father but she didn't know anything about her mother except she was murdered when Parker was three years old. She didn't know what to say. "Thank you both," she looked at Parker then back at Jess, "for sharing that story with me." She took a deep breath, knowing that if she said anything else she'd expose her emotional response to the story and embarrass Parker.

Jessie to the rescue. He stood as a white guy in a soaked trench coat moved toward their table. His hair was plastered to his head and he was passing a handkerchief over his dripping face. Clearly it was still raining. Any doubts that this was Jessie's friend went out the window when he pulled the slender man into one of his bear hugs. "Benny." He pulled Fine down next to him, facing the two detectives. "Detective Chiara Corelli and Detective P.J. Parker, Special Agent Ben Fine."

"Sorry for keeping you waiting." Fine shrugged out of his coat. "My meeting went way over and the rain made it almost impossible to get a cab, especially one willing to take me to Harlem. Add to that the street flooding that slowed everything down." He waved the waitress over. "Anybody need another?" Jessie was the only taker. "Two bourbons on the rocks, put it on his tab." He pointed to Jessie.

Once his drink appeared, he took another swipe at his face, stuffed his handkerchief in his pocket and turned his attention to Corelli. "So you've got quite a hot potato. Tell me what you have so far."

Already pissed about being kept waiting and irritated by his entitled FBI attitude, she half stood, placed her hands on the table, and leaned into his face. "You know, Fine, I've been in places where mothers couldn't trust their sons wouldn't kill them, where anyone from a two-year-old to a ninety-year-old grandma could be a lethal weapon sent to blow me up and every road was an actual minefield designed to kill me and others like me. And then I came home to my safe place and found that the people I'd trusted to watch my back, my friends of many years, had turned into money-grubbing murderers who wouldn't hesitate to kill me or any cop who got in their way. So

I'm not big on trusting strangers. Jessie says you can be trusted but you're going to have to give me something before I share anything about this investigation. If not, I'll finish my..." She looked at her glass not sure what she was drinking tonight.

"Seltzer," Parker said.

Her gaze went to Parker. "Yeah, my seltzer, and go home."

He put his hands in the air as if surrendering. "Sorry. I try not to be your run-of-the-mill, asshole FBI agent but assholeness is ingrained at the academy so if I'm not careful, I slip into the role. Sit. Let's start over."

She eased back into the booth.

"I asked Jessie to set up this meeting because we've had Blecker on our radar for possible child sex trafficking for quite a while. So when we noticed he and Stanerd spending a lot of time together, we began to focus on the senator as well." He grinned. "And coincidently around that time Stanerd's house was broken into. Nothing important was taken but somehow all his computer files got copied to a secret FBI server. We found lots of porn."

"Only porn? No connection to trafficking?"

Fine met Corelli's eyes. "Is that what you think is involved in this case?"

Corelli didn't blink. "Do you have anything solid on the trafficking?"

Fine huffed out a breath and turned to Jessie.

Jessie laughed. "Don't look at me. I told you she was tough. Stop playing footsy and put your damn cards on the table."

Fine tapped his glass as he considered how much to say. "This is all off the record. The Capitol Police would like to bury the senator's murder since it makes them look bad. The FBI is backing off as well."

"So do you have solid proof on the trafficking?" Corelli followed Fine's gaze as he scanned the room. It was late. The crowd was thinning as tonight's band packed up. Clearly, despite his disclaimer, Fine *was* just a run-of-the-mill, no-share FBI agent. Jessie was usually right on about people but his old friend was a disappointment. At least to her. She stood. "Nice to meet you, Agent Fine. Let's go, Parker."

"Don't," Fine said in a voice that sounded like a command.

Corelli laughed. "Really? Don't is all you've got?" She slid out of the booth. "Give me or Jessie a call when you want to talk. Goodnight, Jess." She pulled her coat off the wall hook and walked toward the door, Parker on her heels. Both their phones pinged as they were about to exit. Texts from Jessie. *He's ready to share.*

Corelli stopped. "What do ya think, Parker?"

"Jessie says he's a good guy. I say we give him another chance." They sat again.

Fine was uncomfortable. "Sorry. We raided some massage parlors in West Palm Beach and rescued twelve girls six to thirteen years old. They were held in groups of four in separate places so they only knew the girls in their group, yet their stories are remarkably similar. Several of the older girls identified Blecker as the man who beat and raped them and took pictures while they were forced to have sex with other men. Stanerd and some other big shits were also fingered."

Now they were getting somewhere. "And you haven't brought charges against Blecker and Stanerd because?"

A flash of anger slipped past Fine's blank FBI face. "We were warned that unless we had absolute undisputable proof, and the girls weren't considered that, there would be no prosecutions and our jobs might be in danger because these guys travel in high circles." He chugged the rest of his bourbon and brought the glass down hard. Jessie signaled the waitress to bring Fine a refill. "I have three grown daughters and four granddaughters and when I think of those freaks…" He took a deep breath. "I'm sorry they're dead. I wanted to expose them, to see them writhe in shame, and put them in a prison where they'd learn everything they never knew about rape."

"Get in line. So you have porn on Stanerd's computer and these girls who point to him and Blecker. Any idea how they get the girls into the country?"

"No. We've identified people like Marianne Phillips and Ernesto Servino who are involved, but we haven't been allowed to interview them."

"We're told Phillips doesn't live in Palm Beach. Do you have an address for her?"

"She travels a lot but our most recent information is that she lives in an apartment on Fifth Avenue overlooking Central Park. I'll have to call you with the address. That's what I have. Your turn."

She still wasn't sure how much she wanted to share with the FBI but she'd give him some stuff. "One more question. What is the FBI going to do now that Blecker and Stanerd are dead?"

"My best guess is nothing."

Just as she thought. "So why are you interested in what we have?"

"The FBI may want to do nothing, but I can't let this go. I think the two of them were just the tip of the iceberg and if that's true, their deaths aren't the end of it. I can't do anything directly but I'd like to work in the background to help your investigation."

"Just you? Not your team?"

"Just me for now. If I involve anyone else, it's more likely to get out. I can feed you information without calling attention to myself. And though it's not a condition, if you find anything that is broader than New York City and requires FBI involvement, I hope you'll bring it to me."

Corelli checked in with Jessie and Parker. Both dipped their heads slightly which she took as approval. She was still cautious but she was inclined to include him. "Okay, so we have a credible witness, someone who has nothing to gain by coming forward, who we think was one of Blecker's victims. She's reluctant so we have to go back to her to get the story. Also when we searched the safe at Blecker's New York City mansion, we found thousands of pornographic photos and videos of children who look to be as young as one year old and up to about fifteen, each carefully labeled with a code that we think identifies the child and the man or men involved. Blecker also sold porn and has a huge distribution network." She drank the rest of her warm diluted seltzer. "Finally, the night of the murder we found three girls between six and ten years old, drugged and hidden in a closet in Blecker's mansion. They appeared to have been used sexually, and not just that night. Only a few people know about the girls. If it gets out, I'll know it came from you."

"Fuck." Fine slammed his hand on the table. "I've seen the porn but hearing that makes me want to kill somebody. How do you control the rage?"

"Not very well. But we believe there were two killers and the murders were connected to the abuse of children but maybe not to the child sex trafficking ring, so we're focusing our anger on finding the killers and the thread we need to unravel the trafficking operation."

Fine pushed his hands through his hair. "Jesus, I get you don't fully trust me so I'm grateful you've shared this. Do you have any leads on the killers? And why do you believe it wasn't the operation getting rid of them?"

"We believe if the child traffickers wanted to send a message, they would've killed the men and the girls while the rapes were occurring or at least taken the children with them. Also, someone called the next day to make sure we'd found the girls in the closet. Not exactly trafficker behavior."

Fine tapped his fingers on his glass while he considered her theory. "I agree. What do you need from me?"

Corelli relaxed. Maybe involving him was the right call. "Get us anything you can on trafficking and porno sales. Also, have you heard anything about why Stanerd's protection was nowhere to be found? Anything else you have would be welcomed."

"Will do. According to Stanerd's security he didn't tell them he was leaving town. How do you think Dumayne fits? Innocent bystander?"

Corelli laughed. "Not so innocent. He had child porn on his computers, and like the other two, he had semen on his genital area. So guilty in my book." She stretched. "And now I have to go home and get some beauty sleep. Let me know when you have something. Go through Jessie if it's safer for you."

They ran through the rain and jumped into the car. Parker headed downtown. "So what do you think, Parker? Was it a mistake to bring him in?"

"We said we wanted an ally in the FBI and I think we have one. And he seems willing to follow rather than lead."

"For the good of the investigation I hope we made the right call. But I'm not convinced the FBI ever follows. Time will tell."

CHAPTER SEVENTEEN

Corelli and Parker arrived at Harlem Calvary Church of Christ at seven thirty a.m. and relieved the two officers who'd spent the night there. Then, as the detectives assigned to search the files drifted in, Corelli and Parker met with them briefly to get a sense of what they were finding. All the computers in the office had been taken to the station where the experts would break the code on the many encrypted files they'd found. They'd also found a safe deposit box key taped under a drawer in Dumayne's desk. The detectives planned to spend the day going through the paper files in all the offices, Ms. Foster's desk and the many file cabinets. They hoped to be done by the end of the day or early tomorrow.

The key reminded Corelli of Blecker's safe and she wondered about Dumayne. If he was in it with Blecker, he must also have had cash and passports hidden for a quick getaway. She spoke to the supervising detective. "Before you leave check the entire office for a hidden safe."

Dietz had scheduled Gladiola Foster as the first interview of the day and she bustled in right at eight, cheerfully greeted everyone, hung her coat in a closet and started a pot of coffee. She moved to her desk. "Is it all right if I listen to messages before we start?"

"Go right ahead." Corelli hadn't really paid much attention to the secretary yesterday but Foster looked younger than the thirty-five years Dietz had noted in the sheet he'd prepared on her.

Foster played the three messages from members of the church who'd called asking if there would be a service this Sunday and noted their names and phone numbers. "Would you like coffee, Detectives?" she asked when she looked up.

"No thanks," Corelli responded for both of them from the doorway to Dumayne's office.

Coffee in hand, Foster followed them into the office and joined them at the conference table. Parker took the lead. "Ms. Foster, the church has twelve guards with twelve unregistered guns. At least that's how many we've turned up so far. Are there more and how did you obtain them?"

Foster made no attempt to hide her irritation. "I already told that other detective that I never saw any paperwork for gun permits or had any discussions with Reverend Dumayne or anyone about guns. In fact, I didn't know the guards carried guns. The church has been open for four years and we've never had a problem so I don't understand why he felt the need." She picked up her coffee. "Maybe it made him feel important." Parker did not miss the anger in that muttered comment.

After gentle but persistent questioning by Parker and considerable dancing around the questions by the secretary, she caved. "I shouldn't talk bad about the dead but he was not a nice man. I really disliked him and he didn't like me much either."

Parker asked questions from multiple angles to tease out the reason for her intense dislike. "He thought he was the only person with a brain. And he wanted to fire me because I'm loyal to Reverend Wilkerson."

Parker spoke softly. "I hear in your voice that it was something worse than that."

Foster had confronted Parker's questions head on but that gentle suggestion seemed to rattle her and her gaze slid from Parker's face down to her own tightly clasped hands. She appeared to be waging an internal battle. Minutes later she looked up. "Last week, I was filing some financial reports he had been working with and four pictures of him having sex with children slipped out of the folder. I was shocked. They were disgusting. He was disgusting." Tears filled her eyes. "He didn't deserve to be called reverend."

"What did you do with the pictures?"

"My first impulse was to burn them but I decided the church elders needed to know so I gave them to Reverend Wilkerson. We were both so embarrassed we couldn't even look at each other the rest of the day. He said he'd take care of it."

Parker must have recognized something in Foster's demeanor because her voice was gentle but she put it out there. "You were abused as a child weren't you, Gladiola?"

Foster's eyes were wild, her breathing sped up and she appeared ready to bolt but Parker's next words seemed to calm her. "So many of us were."

It was personal but it wasn't. Parker hadn't confessed anything and *us* could mean women in general but acknowledging that it was common for girls to be abused took away some of the shame that so many victims felt.

Foster locked onto Parker's eyes. "Yes. By the pastor of my church."

They were silent, giving Foster the space to cry. "How did you know?"

Parker spoke softly. "I sensed your pain, and given the number of girls who are abused, it was a safe guess." She touched Foster's hand. "Don't worry, your secret is safe with us."

Foster smiled through her tears. Parker changed the subject and when Foster seemed in control, thanked her for trusting them, gave her permission to leave and asked her to send Reverend Wilkerson in to speak to them.

As the door to the office closed, Corelli turned to Parker. "Nice. You politely edged her into a corner so she had no choice but to reveal what she knew and admit her own abuse. Now we know Wilkerson knew of Dumayne's interest in sex with children."

Wilkerson knocked and walked in. "You had a question?"

"We did," Corelli said. "It seems you left out an important bit of information the last time we spoke."

He clasped his hands in front of him and gazed at her. "I don't think so."

"Really? You don't think that pictures of Dumayne having sex with little girls are important to our murder investigation?"

His gaze flitted around the room as if searching for an exit and eventually settled on the table in front of Corelli. He looked like a little boy about to be punished. "I, uh, I was so shocked by the murder that I completely forgot about them."

Corelli moved close to him forcing him to look at her face. "Please give the pictures to Detective Dietz and send in the first of the guards waiting to be interviewed." She made no effort to hide her disgust.

Parker introduced herself and Corelli to Darnell Mason, the guard, and waved him into a seat at the conference table. She'd expected a rag tag gang but Mason was clean-shaven, his hair was trimmed and he was neatly dressed in khakis, a shirt, tie and jacket. Corelli pulled his file from the stack Dietz had provided. They'd turned up nothing on Mason. He had no record. She scanned the single sheet of basic information like his address, start date, and salary and the one-page letter of recommendation from Thomas Harris, one of the elders of the church. Mason was a security supervisor but had only been employed by Dumayne for five months.

Corelli looked up at the thirty-six-year-old. "Where were you between six and midnight the night Reverend Dumayne was murdered?"

He seemed surprised by the question. "I picked up a pizza after work and was home alone, reading. I don't have many friends in the city yet so I didn't see or talk to anyone. I was in bed by eleven."

Corelli observed him for a few seconds but he seemed relaxed. "How did you come to be employed at the church, Mr. Mason?"

"I moved to New York from Atlanta about six months ago. A member of my church gave me the name of his cousin, Mr. Harris. When we met, I said I was looking for work and he introduced me to the reverend." His voice was soft and he had a distinct southern accent.

Corelli made a few notes. "I see you're a supervisor. How did that happen? And what does the job entail?"

"I'm former military and I worked in security in Atlanta so Reverend Dumayne thought I could teach the security staff, make them more disciplined." He waited a few seconds and getting no comment, continued. "The job includes training, scheduling, acting as personal protection for the reverend and driving him or his wife."

Corelli gazed at the polite, neatly dressed, seemingly self-possessed man sitting in front of her. "Are you licensed to carry a gun?"

He looked uneasy. "I was in Atlanta. Not in New York. The reverend said he had approval for the team to carry while our licenses were in process."

Corelli made a note. "Did you or any of your staff fill out any paperwork or have fingerprints taken?"

He looked down at his hands. "I didn't. I can't speak for the others. When I asked about it, the reverend said it was being taken care of."

Corelli decided to get to the point. "When you drove the reverend, did he ever have children with him or pick up children?"

"No." He shifted in his chair. "But I have heard rumors. One of the newer staff mentioned someone hinted about transporting children for him."

"I see." Corelli waited until he looked up at her. "What do you think he was doing with those children?"

He paled. "It made me think of child abuse."

Corelli leaned in. "Did you question Reverend Dumayne or report it to your friend the elder or the police?"

His eyes filled. "I sure wouldn't go along with something like that. But it was only a rumor, ma'am. And most of these guards are immature boys so it could have been a total fabrication to make someone seem important. If I'd been able to confirm it, I would have done something about it."

"Any questions, Detective Parker?" Corelli asked.

Parker stood. "Not right now."

Corelli stood. "You can go for now, Mr. Mason, but I may have other questions after interviewing the remaining staff. You've been warned to stay in the city so don't go anywhere."

Parker escorted Mason to the door and called in the other guard supervisor. "Mr. Johnson, we're ready for you."

T'Wayne Johnson, thirty-one years old, was full of himself. Dressed in tight black jeans tucked into black boots, a tight black T-shirt, and a black leather jacket, he sauntered in, blatantly eyeing Parker with hungry eyes. She stood between him and the table, staring at him. His fingers twitched. His eyes darted from one side to the other, trying to avoid looking at her, but the short distance between them and the intensity of her gaze gave him no choice. In the total silence it seemed like forever but it was only a couple of minutes before his complexion darkened and his gaze dropped to floor. Corelli repressed a grin.

"Sit," Parker ordered, treating him like the dog he seemed to be. She stepped aside and sat at the table. She rarely used her ADA interrogation voice but she addressed Johnson as if he was on the witness stand. "How did you come to work at the church, T'Wayne?"

He sat up straight. "Um, my uncle is an elder here and he introduced me to Reverend Dumayne."

Parker fired another question at him. "Were you aware you were violating the law by carrying an unlicensed gun and that you're liable to be arrested?"

The look of panic on his face was priceless. "No. I thought it was licensed. I would never—"

"So you thought that despite the strict gun carry laws of New York State that you were licensed without being fingerprinted or filling out any paperwork? Don't tell me you were so dumb."

He squirmed. Parker had cornered him. If he said, "Yes he thought so," he looked dumb, something his ego probably couldn't handle, but if he said, "No, he knew that wasn't how it worked," he would be admitting he knew he was violating the law. "I...the Reverend—"

"So you were willing to do illegal things for Reverend Dumayne?"

He glanced at Corelli, probably looking to be rescued.

Corelli figured this was a good time for the good cop to appear. "So what was it you did for the reverend? We need specifics."

His gaze settled on her. "I, you know, supervise the guards, with Darnell."

Corelli waited calmly. Parker glared.

"And, we, uh, protect the church, do odd jobs around the reverend's house. Some of us drive the reverend when he goes out and protect him. We drive his wife places and deliver things for him, stuff like that. Know what I'm sayin'?"

Corelli smiled and he seemed to relax. "Did you ever deliver children for him?"

His jaw dropped. "Children?"

"Yes, children." Corelli leaned forward and enunciated each word. "Did. You. Ever. Deliver. Children?"

He swiped his arm across his forehead. She assumed he was sweating. His discomfort confirmed her feeling that he was a follower and would do anything to bask in the glow of Dumayne's light. She'd bet he was a bully. He pushed his chair back. "I know my rights. I don't have to talk to you."

Parker appeared ready to spring.

Corelli laughed. "You think you're special? From what we heard he used you just like the others."

"Others?" He looked confused. "But he said I was the only one he trusted."

Corelli stood and loomed over him. "Trusted to do what? If you lie, I'll drag your ass into a cell so fast you'll think Scotty beamed you up. And I'm sure you've heard how popular sexy studs like you are in prison."

He paled and tears filled his eyes. She had no sympathy for him. Guys like him gave no thought to the terror and pain of the children. Guys like him only thought about themselves, about power and money. He whispered something.

"Speak up. And be specific." Despite Corelli's attempt to control her growing rage, it came through loud and clear.

He jumped at the harshness in her voice. A tear dribbled down. "I drove children places sometimes and picked them up too."

"Where did you pick up the children?" She was in his face, practically growling.

He leaned away but fear seemed to work as a motivator. "It's different every time. Reverend Dumayne gives me an address, a street corner somewhere in the city, even Queens, the Bronx, Brooklyn, or Staten Island, where I meet a van that brings the children. They transfer them into our car and I drive them to a house or an apartment. Then we do the same thing in reverse when they're done."

She slapped her hand on the table in front of him. "Were the children awake or asleep when you picked them up? How did they act?"

He responded quickly. "They were usually awake but quiet when I got them but they were asleep when they were done. One of the van drivers told me the men gave them roofies so they would cooperate."

Parker tossed a question from the other side of the room. "You said you picked up the girls when they were done. Done with what? T'Wayne, do you know what the children were there for?"

Corelli knew Parker's intervention was basically a time out for her. She needed to back off, breathe and get back in control before she beat the bastard to death. She walked to the window, leaving it to Parker to squeeze what they could from him.

He'd relaxed when Parker stepped in but now she loomed over him. Her face looked as if it had been chipped from a block of ice, cold, hard and sharp. His eyes widened and he was breathing as if he was at the end of a marathon. "Done with…done with the men touching them and loving them."

"You mean raping them, don't you?" Parker spat the question out.

"N-n-n-o. Reverend Dumayne said kids liked it."

Parker stepped back. "And simpleton that you are, you believed that? Of course, they had to be drugged to endure it. You enabled the rape of multiple children, T'Wayne. You were an accessory to rape. That's a felony. Your only hope is to tell us whatever you know. Do you understand?"

Sweat dripped from his nose.

Parker gave him a few seconds to worry about the next question, then dropped it on him. "Where are the children kept?"

He put his hands in front of him as if warding off an attack. "I don't know. I only meet the van on the street."

Parker eyed him and apparently decided he was telling the truth. "Okay, give us the names or the addresses of the men involved."

"Reverend Dumayne is the only one I know. The van driver gives me a slip of paper with the delivery address and I have to give it back to him on the return trip. I don't know no names."

"When was the last time you delivered children? And where?"

He rubbed his eyes. "Two nights ago. I don't remember the number but it was Seventy-Fourth Street by Fifth Avenue. I could show you." He hung his head. "I'm sorry."

Right. Sorry he was caught, not sorry for hurting innocent children but now we know how the girls got there. "What time?"

"I was supposed to be there at nine but I got turned around in Staten Island and ended up on the New Jersey Turnpike going south. Then I got lost in New Jersey so I was more than an hour late. I think it was about ten thirty."

"What did you do when you got to the house?"

He didn't look at her. "I rang the bell. Reverend Dumayne opened the door. He was really pissed by me being so late. He said he'd deal with me later and took the girls in the house with him."

"And what time did you pick up the girls that night?"

"The reverend never called me so I figured they slept over like they do sometimes."

"And was it Reverend Dumayne who told you to toss the dead bodies of those two little girls in the Hudson River?"

"Wwwhat?" He jumped up. "I never saw no dead girls."

Though each answer brought her the information they needed, Parker felt her the rage building. She took a deep breath and removed the Miranda warning from her bag. She locked eyes with Corelli for a second.

Corelli tilted her head slightly.

Parker read Miranda and had him sign each statement as required. "Stand up," she commanded.

She pulled his arms behind his back, cuffed him, and marched him out of the room.

In the ten minutes it took Parker to arrange transport to the stationhouse, Corelli did some of the breathing exercises she'd learned at yoga and calmed down.

Parker was grinning when she returned to the room. "That was fun."

Corelli tipped an imaginary hat. "And you got the first solid information on the abuse aspect of the murders."

Parker flushed. "Before I bring in another guard, I'm thinking T'Wayne is a city boy and probably needed help to drive around the boroughs. Though it didn't seem to help him in Staten Island, I'm going to ask Dietz to have someone check the GPS on his phone."

"Good idea," Corelli said. "Have the GPSs on all their phones checked and a list of addresses compiled." She laughed. "But in T'Wayne's defense, he's not the first person to get lost in Staten Island."

During the interviews with the remaining ten church security staff, they identified two more guards involved with transporting children but the only new information they gathered was that they occasionally communicated with the van driver on their cells. Parker immediately called Dietz and asked him to compile a list of calls to and from the phones of Johnson and the two other guards involved.

When Parker escorted the last guy out, Corelli stretched. She'd stood, paced, done some breathing exercises and had even gone outside for breaks to get some air between interviews. Being cooped up was not something she dealt with gracefully. Hearing the three ragtag guards talk casually about the children they transported and shrug off the experiences they imagined those children had, set off the rage that had been hot and ready since the beginning of this case. She'd flashed back to Iraq again. Thankfully, Parker, always sensitive to her, suggested breaks periodically so she didn't lose control. But she was on edge. Maybe she'd try yoga again tonight.

CHAPTER EIGHTEEN

They were putting on their coats after interviewing the last guard when the supervising detective came in grinning. "Good call, Corelli. We found a wall safe behind a painting in the conference room. It contained the paperwork for a safe deposit box at a midtown bank, several passports for Dumayne and a shitload of cash. I sent it all down to Dietz."

"Thanks." Her phone rang. "Corelli."

"Hi, this is Officer Twilliger. I'm assigned to the, um, house on Seventy-Fourth Street and we have a Marianne Blecker here who says this is her house. Should we let her in?"

She smiled, remembering the extremely tall Twilliger swooping in like some giant bird to save her when she was attacked by a crazed media mob on her last case. "Absolutely not. Keep her with you. We'll be there in less than fifteen minutes." Corelli grinned at Parker. "Marianne Phillips is at Seventy-Fourth Street claiming it's her house and insisting she needs to go in. Sirens and lights, please."

Eleven minutes later they pulled up in front of the mansion. Corelli took a deep breath. Parker, of course, noticed. "Do you want me to take this one?"

Corelli got out of the car. Did she? She was exhausted, not always good when she needed to be alert and patient. "I'll start. Feel free to jump in if you think…even if I'm not about to kill her."

The attractive middle-aged woman chatting amiably with the two officers in the entryway to the mansion shattered Corelli's mental picture of Marianne Phillips. She was far from young bitchy eye candy. Her blond hair was tastefully highlighted and styled, her nails beautifully manicured, and her clothing designer. She exuded confidence and sophistication. But nothing about her communicated sorrow or that she was mourning the loss of her dead lover.

"Mrs. Blecker," Twilliger said, "Detectives Corelli and Parker." He pointed to each as he introduced them.

The background information Dietz had given Corelli indicated that though Phillips and Blecker had been together nineteen years they'd never married. Since she'd never taken his name it was strange she was using it now that he was dead.

"Thanks, Twilliger. Please unlock the door." He did as she asked, and when he stepped away Corelli turned to invite Phillips to follow her. The self-satisfied look was only on Phillips's face for a second but Corelli didn't miss it. Aha, Phillips thought she was getting access to the house.

Inside Phillips turned toward the stairs but Corelli grabbed her arm and Parker moved between her and the stairs. "We'll talk in the sitting room down here."

Phillips didn't move. She looked from Corelli to Parker. "Talk? Really." The condescension in those two words came through loud and clear. "I just stopped by to pick up a few of my things."

Given what she knew about their relationship Corelli didn't buy that Phillips still had anything of importance at his house. More likely she'd expected to get into the safe. "Why don't you tell me what you need and I'll send an officer up to retrieve it for you?"

Phillips sighed. "What did you want to talk about?"

Corelli followed her into the sitting room and sat opposite her. Parker leaned against the doorjamb. Neither detective spoke. Phillips looked from one to the other. "I don't have all day. If you don't want to talk, I'll just go upstairs and get my belongings." She shifted forward as if to stand.

The imperious Marianne Phillips did not surprise Corelli. "So what *belongings* do you need to get?"

"I don't think that's any of your business." Her face darkened. "For the last time, what did you want to talk about?"

A quick transformation from warm, gentle society lady to angry condescending bitch. Now they were getting somewhere. Corelli leaned forward. "Just so you know, in a murder investigation everything is my business. And the officers are here because this is still an active crime scene." She waited for Phillips to absorb that information. "According to Mr. Blecker's attorney, you and Mr. Blecker never married. And you've been in acrimonious negotiations for more than a year. What were you fighting over?"

"That's none of your business."

"His attorney also reported that Mr. Blecker had all your belongings shipped to your Fifth Avenue apartment and had the locks and alarm passwords changed at all of his houses, specifically to keep you out."

Phillips offered a gotcha smile. "I didn't realize he'd changed the codes and locks. But I'm Jake's heir so I have every right to be here." She stood. "If you'll excuse me, I need to call a locksmith and the alarm company."

Corelli remained sitting. "I guess no one told you he changed his will?"

Phillips sank back into the sofa. "Jake was a bastard but I don't believe he cut me out of his will."

"Call his lawyer if you like." Corelli sat back. "We'll wait."

Phillips' eyes blazed and her face morphed into a hard, twisted version of the woman who'd greeted them earlier. "That fucker. I'd kill him again, if he wasn't already dead."

Well, at least they agreed on that. Corelli allowed her to stew in the acid of her greed and hatred before continuing. "What do you mean, kill him again?"

"Just what I said. If he wasn't dead, I'd kill him," Phillips said, every word dripping with rage. "Last month the fucker offered to settle for a measly one hundred thousand dollars a month and the half of his estate I would get when he died. How stupid was I to have trusted the sleazy bastard?"

If she hadn't figured out that a man who would sell children for sex was not someone to trust, Ms. Phillips deserved what she didn't get. "Where were you Tuesday night between eight and midnight?" Corelli threw the question out, hoping to catch her off balance.

"Tuesday? I don't re…right. Ernesto, Jake's former right-hand man, and I had dinner at my apartment."

"Ernesto Servino? Do you have a recent cell number for him?"

"Yes." Phillips dictated a phone number.

"How long were you together that evening?" Phillips' makeup made it difficult to see the blush but the color creeping up her neck gave her away. Her gaze shifted to the wall behind Corelli. "He lives with me." She met Corelli's eyes. "And, yes, we're involved. And no, he's not the reason Jake and I separated. Actually, that was because Jake was fooling around with younger women and was no longer interested in someone near his age."

Corelli waited a beat or two. "How young?"

Phillips frowned. "He's dead. That's history."

She was sure Phillips knew about the children. So far they hadn't found anything in the safe to incriminate her but they were still sifting through the pictures and documents, so it was possible they'd turn up something. "How young were the girls and how involved were you in procuring them for him?"

"Procuring?" She glanced at the door as if calculating her chance of escaping. "The girls were, I don't know, eighteen or twenty, way too young for him and made him look ridiculous. And then he wanted me to act like I didn't know he was cheating while he was parading his bimbos around town. I refused. That's why we separated."

Was it possible to live with a child abuser for nineteen years in a house with a room that seemed to be set up for abuse and not have some involvement in his activities? Not likely. "Are you claiming you were unaware Mr. Blecker was having sex with children as young as six years old and trafficking them as well?"

Phillips gasped. "How dare you?" She stood. "If you want to continue this insulting conversation, you'll have to call my attorney." She slipped into her coat. "You should be spending your time finding his killer, not making unfounded accusations, slandering a man who can't defend himself." She started for the door but Parker blocked her.

It was probably a mistake to ask that question without any proof. Now having her attorney there when they interviewed her again would make it difficult to get the information they needed about Blecker's sex business. They'd have to dig up some proof before they interviewed her again. Corelli stood. "What's your attorney's name and number?"

"Laney Gold." Phillips spelled the first name, opened her phone and read out her number. Her smile was more a snarl as she stormed out.

Parker jotted down the information, then sat across from Corelli. "Well, that went well."

Corelli sighed. "Yeah, I probably shouldn't have pushed her but she brought it up and I couldn't resist probing. I have to keep reminding myself that we're investigating the murders of the three men, and the child abuse only matters if it was the reason they were killed."

Parker leaned forward, elbows on her knees. "So are we doing a cover-up now?"

Parker wasn't confronting, just reminding her. Corelli stood and took a couple of deep breaths. "Sorry, it's the exhaustion talking. My brain is fried. Of course, it matters. One way or another, child abuse appears to be the motive for these murders and we'll pursue the murders and the abuse at the same time. I'm frustrated because I blew it with Phillips. We need concrete evidence before approaching her again. Or anyone."

CHAPTER NINETEEN

Corelli glanced at the paper she'd removed from her jacket pocket. "I'm going ask you to drop me downtown again if you don't mind, but first I need to get a few things from my apartment."

"I don't mind as long as you don't complain when I wait for you."

"You don't give up do you?" Corelli groaned. "All right it's a deal."

Halfway through the yoga session, Corelli started to relax and feel warm. Once again, the major spent a lot of time with her, adjusting positions after asking permission to touch and correcting her breathing. But it wasn't just her, the major worked personally with each of the twelve men and women in the class.

At the end of the class, Corelli returned her mat, block and weights and picked up her towel to leave but the major stopped her. "Since you're back, I'm guessing the yoga helped."

She draped her towel around her neck. "Yeah, I wasn't breathing exactly right but it still helped."

"Did it help with the therapy?"

"I'm not in therapy."

"Shit, Corelli, do the therapy. There's no reason to feel everything I know you're feeling, the nightmares, the sleepless nights, the sweats, and the rage eating away at you. No reason at all. I can make a referral if you need a recommendation for a good therapist."

Damn. Add the major to the list of people pushing her to go to therapy. Corelli used the breathing skill she'd worked on earlier. "I've got a good therapist. I just have to make the call. I'm pretty sure I will. Soon."

"If you'd rather not do one-on-one therapy another option is a PTSD group with other female military. The VA has them and I run some if you're interested."

The major threw an arm over Corelli's shoulder and walked her to the locker room. "I'm sorry. I don't mean to preach, but you know, been there done that. The combination of the yoga with the therapy can speed things up. Let yourself feel good. Life is too short. See you soon, I hope." She threw a casual salute and went into her next class.

As she pushed through the glass door, Parker jumped out of the car idling in front of the building, immediately alert for threats that Corelli was sure weren't there. She shifted her gym bag to her shoulder and pulled her collar up against the biting wind before approaching the car. "So?"

Parker straightened. "So what?"

"What do ya think? How do I look?"

Parker glanced away. "You look fine. Why?"

"Come on, Parker, you're a detective. I know you investigated to make sure I was safe and figured out I was taking a yoga class at Yoga for Warriors. So how do I look?"

"I confess I checked. All the testosterone emanating from the female and male warriors I encountered convinced me you were safe in there." Parker studied Corelli. "You have some color in your face. You seem tired but relaxed and more...I don't know, energetic. Shall we go?"

In the car, Parker turned to Corelli. "It's a good first step. How do you feel?"

Happy not to get Parker's PTSD lecture, Corelli answered truthfully. "Hopeful."

"Good." Parker headed uptown to Corelli's apartment building in the Meatpacking District of Manhattan.

Corelli cleared her throat. "Um, Parker, I requested your mom's murder file but I haven't read it yet. I'm thinking maybe I'm being intrusive."

Parker looked at her for a second before turning back to the street. "Why do you want to read it?"

"I got the impression from you and Jess that not a lot was done to solve it. I thought maybe I'd see something the detectives missed."

"So not just curiosity? A desire to help?"

"Yeah, it bugs me."

"I looked at it when I became an assistant district attorney but what did I know? Read away. And thanks for asking."

"Great. Come up and have dinner. If you haven't OD'd on Italian yet we can eat more of the food Simone dropped off the other night and talk about the case." Corelli surprised herself but if Parker was surprised she didn't show it.

"Sure."

Corelli's phone beeped. An incoming text from Brett.

Are U Home? I'll bring dinner if ok

She responded. *On the way. Parker joining us*

Brett texted immediately. *Gr8. I have Thai and Chinese and Japanese. Enuf 4 an army. C U soon*

"It's Brett. She's on the way with a ton of food. Are you up for having dinner with the two of us and not discussing the case?"

Parker's gaze jumped from the road to Corelli. "Would you rather be alone with her?"

Parker had connected with Brett from their first meeting and they'd gotten tight while Chiara was in the hospital and when she was recuperating at home. She knew they would enjoy the chance to hang out and it would ease the pressure of being alone with Brett and pretending all she wanted was friendship. "Stay. She'll probably sleep over so we'll have plenty of alone time when I wake us both up later."

"If you're sure, I'd love to."

"I'm sure."

Parker found a spot in front of the building. The wind was fierce but the lobby was close. They entered the waiting elevator. "The nightmares haven't gotten better?"

She punched Parker's arm lightly. "Is this your new strategy? Bring up my alleged PTSD when I can't walk away?"

Parker grinned. "I hadn't planned it but if it works, I'll remember it. Seriously though, no wonder you're exhausted, not sleeping is dangerous for your health. Have you given more thought to seeing Dr. Gilardi to work on your...your nightmares?"

The downside of recuperating at home attended by those close to her, rather than in a rehab center, was anyone who stayed the night with her knew that after a couple of hours sleep her nightmares woke her up, often screaming, and she rarely got back to sleep again. She knew the nagging came out of caring for her. "Even Major Magarelli, the yoga instructor, is on my back about therapy. I'm getting close."

As soon as they stepped into the apartment, Corelli was attacked by her kittens. She shrugged her coat off, knelt to pet them, then picked them up and carried them to their dishes. "I need to name these guys."

While she fed them, Parker set the table. "Are you finally admitting you're keeping them?"

They both turned as the elevator door slid open and a beaming Brett strode in carrying three large bags of food and her briefcase. Their eyes locked and a frisson of excitement shot through Corelli's body. It happened every single time. Brett placed her briefcase on the floor near the elevator and the food on the table, hugged Parker and then after Corelli tossed the empty cat food can into the garbage, pulled her into a tight hug and kissed her lightly on the lips. "I smell eau di cat tuna. Thank God it's not on your breath." Laughing, she moved to the table to help Parker unpack the many containers of food she'd brought. Corelli watched for a moment, charmed by Brett's graceful and fluid movements, fascinated by how she connected through touch, and amazed at the light she brought with her into every situation. She shook her head. She was definitely enamored. She carried three beers and three glasses to the table.

Brett was her usual vibrant self, entertaining them with stories about her employees and clients and getting Parker to talk about herself as an ADA. And she got Corelli to talk about her yoga class. They laughed a lot, something both Corelli and Parker needed with the stress of this case.

At ten thirty Parker offered to clean up but Corelli sent her on her way. After they'd packed away the leftovers and loaded the dishwasher, Brett settled down to do some work she'd brought from the office and Corelli brought out the file Dietz had given her earlier. They worked side by side, stoically allowing the kittens to dash over and around them until they tired themselves out and fell asleep in Corelli's lap. She was careful to keep her files away from Brett. Parker had agreed she could read her mom's file but that didn't necessarily include letting Brett see it.

The case was nearly thirty years old and it was clear the detectives hadn't spent too much time on the death of the young black woman. Tasha Parker was almost twenty-two and on welfare. She and her three-year-old daughter Precious Jewel lived in a small studio apartment in a building in the projects that was a haven for drug dealers and drug addicts. She'd been dead anywhere from three to five days before neighbors became concerned that she hadn't been seen outside with her daughter and got the super to open the door. She was beaten and shot and left in a puddle of blood on the floor. Her well-cared for little girl was found sitting next to her, holding her death-swollen hand. All around the child were banana peels, boxes of cereal and bottles of milk she had obviously taken out of the refrigerator. The body was covered with flies. The three-year-old was talking, but when they asked who hurt her mommy, all she could tell them was, "The man was angry." She didn't know his name. They were unable to find any identification or any money.

When the social worker arrived to take the girl to a foster family, she asked the little girl's name. The policewoman said they didn't know and the child piped up, "I'm Precious Jewel Parker." With her full name the police were able to locate her grandmother and her aunt.

Judging by the number of library books found in the apartment, Tasha appeared to be a reader and the note in the file from a librarian in the neighborhood library confirmed that. She'd heard about the murder and someone said the police didn't know the name of the victim. She said if the police had followed up on the library books, she could have identified her. According to the librarian, the young woman was quiet and respectful. She brought her daughter, who was already reading, to the library almost every day and read with the girl until she fell asleep. Then Tasha read herself.

Several things were clear from the file. First, the detectives had done nothing to find her killer. They decided a drug dealer killed her over money even though there was no mention of drugs found in the apartment and nothing else indicated drugs were involved. Second, if they'd done even a minimal investigation, they could have easily identified her from the lease she signed or the library books. Third, evidence had been gathered and stored but not tested.

Corelli put a note in the folder instructing Dietz to have the evidence tested and returned the file to her case. Brett was still working so Corelli let her mind wander. From what Randall Young, Parker's birth father, had said, Tasha, Parker's mother, was an excellent student intent on becoming a lawyer. They planned to get married when he completed boot camp but Tasha's alcoholic mother had withheld his letters and had stolen the ones Tasha left for the mailman so they each thought the other had found someone else. Parker's grandmother had actually recently confirmed that she did that. Corelli couldn't imagine a mother being that spiteful but there it was.

Deep in thought Corelli didn't feel the cushion next to her depress under Brett's weight. But the warmth of Brett's breath and the brush of her lips on Corelli's temple got her attention. "Finished?"

"Uh-huh." Brett put an arm around Corelli's waist and pulled her around for a kiss. Corelli responded and deepened the kiss. This "friends only" thing she'd sworn Brett to was getting harder and harder for Corelli. They'd somehow slipped into kissing. Who was she kidding? Brett had honored their agreement but she had initiated the kissing. Now she was having difficulty keeping her hands off Brett. She reluctantly pulled away. Though it was the right thing to do, the loss of the physical connection made her sad.

Brett shifted to the end of the sofa with her back against the arm and swung one leg up. "Come here, sweetheart. Let me hold you."

Corelli moved her legs on to the sofa, slid closer to Brett, and when she felt Brett's breasts against her back, relaxed into the embrace. Brett swung her other leg up and wrapped her arms around Chiara. Cocooned by Brett's body, Chiara leaned her head back on Brett's shoulder, enjoying the renewed physical connection, and the sounds of Brett's soft breaths. Brett kissed Chiara's cheek. "Want to talk about what's bothering you?"

Corelli had been so focused on the guilt of loving again and on keeping her distance from Brett, that she hadn't allowed herself to fully accept the love Brett offered without demands. When she was honest with herself, she could admit she was deeply in love with Brett. On the occasions she allowed herself to feel, she burned with that love, burned to make love to Brett, but she wanted more. She wanted the touching, the sharing of everyday life and its problems and triumphs, the comfort of knowing she was loved. And she wanted to be fully committed, not halfway between Brett and Marnie. She resolved again to deal with her demons and her guilt about moving on from Marnie.

She squeezed Brett's arm. "I'm thinking about how good it feels to be with you, to have your arms around me." Not being open and honest was the best way to kill a relationship. Time to let Brett in. "But I'm bothered by the case we're working." She twisted to see Brett's face. "I trust you to keep anything I say about the case confidential."

"Of course." Brett kissed her forehead. "It's important for both of us to trust we can discuss everything and anything, no matter how sensitive or horrible, without worry."

She took a breath and launched into talking about the children, the sexual abuse, the men, the possible sex trafficking. She didn't expect Brett to have answers but sometimes just talking about a case helped and sometimes a civilian's questions could help view the case from a different angle or trigger new leads.

The joy of having found another perfect lover filled Corelli. First Marnie, now Brett. They were very different yet shared so many wonderful qualities and miraculously she'd found them both and they both loved her. How did she get so lucky?

CHAPTER TWENTY

While Parker was out of the room taking a phone call, Corelli slid Tasha's murder file and the note she'd written over to Dietz. "Parker knows I'm looking at the case but I want to protect her privacy so could you take care of it yourself?" He could sometimes be too talkative but she trusted him on this because he and Parker were pals and he wouldn't want to hurt her.

He skimmed the note. "Will do."

By the time Parker returned they were back to discussing the reports.

"Sorry," Parker said. "That was Kelly Dexter, DeAndre's bodyguard. Amari would like to meet with us today, if possible. I told her we could be there in about an hour. I hope that's all right."

Something had shifted with Parker. She was taking more and more responsibility and Corelli liked it. The former ADA was intelligent and organized and had what it took to be a great homicide detective. All she needed was more homicide experience and that's why they were working together. "Perfect. If we're lucky DeAndre will give us something to rattle Phillips."

As Parker negotiated the heavy Tenth Avenue traffic, Corelli asked. "Did Dexter say why today? Are they leaving on tour?"

"Apparently since we met with DeAndre, she's been anxious and agitated when she's not performing," Parker said. "This morning she realized now that Blecker is dead, she could talk about it without fear of reprisal. She wants to get it off her chest."

A woman with gray braids, a friendly smile, a warm vibe, wearing a colorful caftan opened the door of DeAndre's Central Park West brownstone. "You must be the detectives. I'm Nan, Amari's housekeeper. Come in, she's waiting for you in her sunroom."

The housekeeper shut the door. "Follow me."

"Before you take us to Ms. DeAndre," Parker said, "I'd like to know your last name and where you were Tuesday night?"

Nan frowned and leaned against the door. "Can I ask why?"

Parker smiled. "I'll explain but I need the answers to my questions first."

"My last name is Fredericks. I've spent the last two weeks in Woodstock with my son and his family, helping out after the birth of my third grandchild. Your turn, Detective."

"Thank you. We're investigating the death of Ms. DeAndre's former manager, Jake Blecker, and the questions are routine. So how did you come to work for Ms. DeAndre?"

"Why don't you ask her that question?" She led them to the sunlit room where they'd met with the singer during their last visit.

Pale, with dark circles under her tired eyes, Amari rose from the sofa to greet them. She waved them into the club chairs facing the sofa, settled on the sofa in the Lotus pose, then reached for her guitar. Corelli admired her flexibility and ease in assuming the yoga cross-legged position, something she wasn't sure she'd ever accomplish. DeAndre clutched the guitar to her chest like a child embracing her favorite doll for comfort. She looked young and fragile. Corelli trusted Parker's own experience as a victim of abuse would ensure she would be sensitive to DeAndre's fears and reluctance to talk about Blecker's abuse. She was also confident the former ADA wouldn't allow the musician's pain to keep her from pressing for the details they needed.

Dexter was standing in front of the window behind them, facing Amari. Not only was Corelli uncomfortable with someone, especially an armed someone, behind her, but she also didn't want Dexter in a position to signal DeAndre while they were questioning her. Parker spoke before she could comment. "I'm sure Ms. DeAndre will be more comfortable with you sitting nearby, Ms. Dexter. Please have a seat on the sofa."

The bodyguard hesitated but then moved to the middle cushion on the sofa, next to Amari and touched her knee as if to reassure her.

Parker gave them a moment. "Ms. DeAndre, thank you for inviting us back to talk about your relationship with Jake Blecker. I'd like to record our discussion. We'll do our best to keep it confidential."

De Andre glanced at Kelly Dexter but didn't wait for her response. "I'm used to being recorded when I'm interviewed so that would be okay as long as I get a copy within a day."

Parker and Corelli had discussed this on the drive here. "No problem, provided you keep the interview confidential."

"Where should I start?" DeAndre's anxiety was evident.

Corelli kept her eyes on the couple seated on the sofa while Parker began the questioning. "You said you met Mr. Blecker when you were eleven years old. Tell us how that came about."

Corelli could almost see DeAndre going back in time, digging into her memory. "It would never have happened, at least not the way it did, if my grandmother hadn't died." Her hand ran up and down the neck of her guitar. "You see my mom died giving birth to me and my father blamed me for her death. From the arguments I heard growing up, he would have given me up for adoption if his mom, my grandmother, hadn't intervened. She raised me. And loved me. And encouraged me. She bought me my first guitar, encouraged me to sing and write music and got me into a special school for musically gifted children." Her gaze went to a battered instrument hanging on the wall and a soft smile flickered on her lips. "He was around sometimes but the older I got, the more I looked like my mom and if I walked into a room, he walked out." She wiped the tears filling her eyes. "Sorry. It still hurts."

Corelli could feel her anger percolating. Self-indulgent bastard. What kind of monster is so cruel to the daughter he created with the woman he supposedly loved? Her hands fisted. She wanted to beat the son of a bitch senseless.

Parker cleared her throat and Corelli realized she must have made a sound or movement that gave her away. She sat back and attempted to relax. The ebb and flow of her anger was exhausting.

"And then a couple of months before I turned eleven my grandmother had a massive heart attack and died instantly. I was… alone, lost. Grandma had two friends in the building who knew the score and they basically adopted me. I had dinner with one of them every night, they made me breakfast and lunch, helped with my homework, washed my clothes, cleaned the house, and got money from him to take me shopping for clothing and shoes. They came to my school events and cheered me on. I had just turned eleven when I overheard him telling one of them he couldn't cope. He'd decided to put me up for adoption. She offered to take me in but he said he wanted me somewhere he didn't have to see me every day. Neither of the women could afford to leave their low rent apartments. I was terrified."

She started to shake. Tears streamed down her face. Kelly put an arm around her and when she stopped shaking, Kelly got up and pulled four bottles of water out of the small refrigerator on the other side of the room. She handed one to Amari, placed one in front of each of the detectives, and opened one for herself as she sat again.

"Not long after that, I was the lead in a musical at school. When I was singing I was in a happy place and I think that came through when I was on stage. Jake and Marianne showed up at the last performance. I don't know how he heard about me but he had. And he'd come to see for himself. He talked to my teacher and the principal and they introduced him to the two neighbors who were there with me. They gave his card to my dad."

"Of course I wasn't privy to the negotiations but my beloved dad signed away his rights to me. Marianne and Jake became my guardians and my dad was paid ten thousand dollars each year until I turned eighteen. The good news is that he got screwed. By the time I was fourteen I was selling millions of records and earning more from concerts, TV shows and merchandise than I'm sure he could ever imagine. The bad news is that I lived with Jake and Marianne." She stood. "I need a bathroom break."

When DeAndre left the room, Parker turned her attention to the bodyguard. "Ms. Dexter, I was wondering how you came to work for Ms. DeAndre."

Dexter stood and stretched. "As part of Amari's cleaning out traces of Blecker's control of her life, she asked her new manager to find her a new personal bodyguard. The manager selected me and three other women she thought were suitable and arranged for each of us to meet with Amari. Aside from training and experience the most important requirement for a personal bodyguard is chemistry with the client. If you don't like each other it will be impossible to spend so much time together in close quarters." She grinned. "We clicked and she hired me."

Amari returned, did a couple of bends and stretches, picked up her guitar, then sat on the sofa again. "I'm ready when you are."

After everyone was seated again, Parker leaned forward. "I'm sympathetic, Ms. DeAndre. I was abused as a child and then taken in by relatives who fed and clothed and educated me but didn't want me. I was lucky, though. Another couple did want me and while they couldn't adopt me, I was their daughter in all the ways that counted. I've only recently been able to talk about this so I know how hard it is."

Corelli was surprised and pleased that Parker was putting herself out there in order to connect with DeAndre and she could see how the admission moved the young woman. The widening of Dexter's eyes was the only sign of her surprise.

"Thank you for sharing that, Detective Parker. It helps to know I'm not the only one." She strummed her guitar. "So. The first four months in my new home were okay, a little awkward living with people I didn't know, but okay. Nothing much changed. I went to the same school, driven and picked up by Ernesto. During the summer I continued with the same vocal, guitar and dance classes, and afterward I would hang out with my friends or visit with the two neighbor ladies. Then Ernesto or a car service would pick me up and bring me back to Manhattan. Many nights Jake and Marianne went out and I ate dinner alone but I was never alone in the house. Either Ernesto or Veronica, who also lived there, stayed with me. But then right before school started in September, Marianne told me they were going to homeschool me and while I was reeling from that announcement, Jake said I was ready to move to the next level and he'd hired top professional singing, guitar and dance teachers to prepare me to perform and put out an album next year. Needless to say I was freaked out.

"There was no landline in the house and I didn't have a cell phone. I was totally isolated and kept so busy I never had time to visit friends. The teachers he brought in were great. I could feel myself growing and my self-confidence zoomed. But I was never alone with any of my teachers. Ernesto or Marianne or Veronica sat in on every class. The homeschooling was okay. Marianne and Veronica were responsible for separate subjects in the curriculum and they made them interesting but I like learning so I didn't need much pushing.

"While all these changes were taking place, Jake was getting more and more affectionate, touching me, squeezing my ass, kissing my forehead and sometimes my lips. I started locking the bathroom in my room because he would walk in without knocking. Then Ernesto or Marianne would give me a drink or cigarettes or something to bring up to him while he was in his bathroom, sometimes on the toilet, sometimes in the bath or shower. And when I'd had a particularly good rehearsal he'd get into bed with me and tell me how wonderful I was, how great I was going to be, all the time running his hands over my body.

"My dad had never touched me that I could remember. I thought this was how dads were with their daughters. I felt good that Jake liked me but I was confused because his touching made me uncomfortable. On one of those great nights he came to my room in his underwear and got into bed with me. When he started kissing and touching me all over I tried to squirm away but he held me down and raped me. I screamed in pain and continued to scream until he covered my mouth with his hand. The other three adults were in the house but no one came. He said, 'Just relax and enjoy it. Show me how much you appreciate everything I'm doing for you. I'm going to make you a star.'

"When he finished he got up and left me crying. A little while later Marianne came in and took me in her arms. 'I'm sorry he hurt you sweetheart, but he loves you and that's how he shows his love.' She put me in the bathtub and soothed me, then had me drink a glass of warm milk that, in hindsight, I believe was drugged. I slept. The next day Ernesto, who had always joked and teased and talked to me, wouldn't look at me and avoided being in the same room. Not only had I been violated, I had lost the only somewhat caring person in my life."

"My daytime activity schedule continued as normal— homeschooling, voice, and guitar or dance practice—but my nights became a nightmare. A couple of months later it got even worse. Some nights he and one or two other men raped me while they took pictures. Sometimes other girls around my age were raped at the same time in the same room. Marianne took care of us until the men were ready. Some of the girls didn't speak English and Marianne was mean to them, shoving the soda we had to drink at them and yelling at them to drink. The morning after those nights I was sticky and sore when I woke up. The only thing I could remember clearly was sitting with several other girls drinking soda, no one talking, everyone avoiding looking at anyone.

"Jake warned me over and over that if I told anyone he would have my friends and their families killed and hand me over to a pimp. He even took me to meet some prostitutes and made me watch their pimp rape and beat one of them so I'd see for myself what that meant. When I turned fifteen Jake lost interest in sex with me but there were still other men. It wasn't until my first record went gold a few months later and my concerts started bringing in a great deal of money that the abuse stopped. And I pretended it had never happened." She put her head on Dexter's shoulder and closed her eyes. Dexter rubbed Amari's arm for a moment and when Amari lifted her head, the bodyguard jumped up to get another round of water from the fridge.

Parker waited for DeAndre to finish her water before posing the next question. "So you were his biggest star and as your guardian, I imagine he had made sure you were tied into him legally. How did you get away?"

For the first time since they arrived, DeAndre smiled. "I was sixteen when my second record went gold. My third album had wrapped and would be released soon. I was at the top of the charts and touring nonstop, bringing in millions. One day on the tour bus I was semi-dozing when it occurred to me that I had some power and I needed to do some research to figure out how I could use it. Ostensibly because of my age, I was never without my bodyguard and a watcher, and on that leg of the trip Veronica was the watcher. Luckily she wasn't down my throat like Marianne so I started reading the trades to find out who managed the stars and which law firms represented them. Then I researched them online to figure out who was connected to The Blecker Corporation, his recording company. It took me months to compile the information and identify a powerhouse law firm that I hoped could stand up to Jake. Not only did it discreetly represent huge entertainment stars and corporations, but it also had a highly regarded woman partner who apparently had never lost a case and dedicated lots of pro bono time to women's issues. Research done, I had to figure out a way to contact them without anyone knowing. I was sure Jake had access to my cell so I needed a burner phone and I needed someone to buy it for me.

"Vinnie, the manager of the Gianelli trucking team, had been with me since they took over transporting our equipment and I was pretty sure I could trust him. So the morning after we wrapped in Miami, while they were packing our equipment, I pretended there was a problem with the amp he was holding and whispered that I needed to talk privately with him. He leaned over the amp as if checking it. 'Tell me what you need, Amari. Don't look at Veronica. Now point to the amp as if you're explaining something, I'll move so she can't see your face, then tell me.'"

"I kept my eyes on his face. 'Can I trust you?'"

"'As far as I'm concerned, you're my boss. I'll do whatever you need.'"

"We bent over the amp with our backs to Veronica. 'I need a phone that's not controlled by Jake Blecker so I can have some privacy. I think they're called burner phones. Will you buy me one with the most minutes you can get? I can't give you money right now but I'll pay you for it. I need it when we get to New Orleans.'"

"'Don't worry. I got your back. You know, we all see more than they think. I'll slip it into your backup guitar case so open it when you're alone.'"

"You're a lifesaver, Vinnie."

"He blushed. 'Tell it to Joey. Maybe he'll give me a raise.'"

"It took a while but one afternoon Veronica wasn't feeling well and went to take a nap. I called the law firm and spoke to Stella Fortunato, the attorney, for about fifteen minutes. I liked her a lot. Once she confirmed I was interested in working with her, she suggested we FaceTime late at night when I could speak freely. She promised me our talks would be confidential. And that's what we did. Over the course of several nights we spent hours talking. I told her everything—even the abuse—and what I wanted. I didn't have copies of contracts or agreements but since I was a minor, she said she'd get what she could from the courts. Her plan was to file for emancipation to terminate their guardianship and then file a demand for all contracts and legal agreements related to me. But she decided it was important to prepare an attack without my name or any information leaking, so as her minions researched issues and she discussed the problems with her partners and other attorneys in her firm, she was the only one who knew my name. She didn't write it down anywhere. And though we discussed billing rates, she didn't bill until we settled things. I'm happy to say Stella was successful in her effort to liberate me. Once I had control, I cleaned house."

Parker smiled. "You were a very resourceful and brave young woman. And Blecker let you go without going public?"

DeAndre grinned. "I *was* resourceful. It was all cloak and dagger for a while but it worked out in the end. Stella threatened to bring charges against Jake and Marianne for the child abuse and prosecute him for stealing from me, which, of course, he was doing. But Jake always had to have the last word. After we settled he reminded me he had pictures of me having sex with a lot of men. That's why he felt he could trade me for a business deal and I would have no choice but to go along. But I talked to Stella after he called last week and we agreed she would prepare a child abuse, rape case against him. At this point, he has—had—more to lose than me."

Dexter pulled back. "I didn't know that."

DeAndre patted her arm. "Sorry, Kell, it got lost in the rush to fly back and then we heard he was dead and it was no longer an issue."

"Are we done?" Dexter asked Parker.

Corelli shifted her gaze from Dexter to Parker, not surprised to find her studying Dexter. Parker turned back to DeAndre. "I'd appreciate it if you could hang in for a few more minutes. You seem to allege that Marianne Phillips abetted Mr. Blecker's raping you during the years between your eleventh and fifteenth birthday and that she was also involved in providing you and other girls to other men for sex?"

"Yes, she was involved in both. And, sometimes when Jake raped me she was in bed with us and they had sex too. Other than that, her role was to soothe me and keep me singing. After a while I caught onto the fact that she and Veronica were his assistants, not my friends."

"Was Ernesto Servino involved?"

DeAndre sighed. "Ernesto was always nice and respectful to me but he was involved. His bedroom was down the hall from mine. He had to have heard me screaming. And he was the one who brought the girls to the house and I guess he drove them away after but I was always drugged so I didn't see him."

"We need Veronica's last name."

"It sounded Russian but I never really knew it." DeAndre looked sad. "She died from a brain tumor a few years ago. She and Marianne were nice to me but I'll never forgive them for what they did."

"That's understandable," Parker said. "Last questions for today. Do you know the names of any of the men he forced you and the other girls to have sex with? Do you know where the other girls came from? And finally, we'll be interviewing Marianne Phillips later today. I'd like to tell her we have a witness who will testify to her involvement in the sexual abuse of multiple children. I won't mention your name unless I have to but it may come to that."

"I don't know the names of most of the men but over the years I've recognized a television news guy, a movie star and a senator." DeAndre waited while Parker wrote down their names. "I might recognize others if you have pictures." She shifted forward, her eyes cold, her jaw tight. "As for Marianne, please feel free to use my name. I'll happily testify against her."

Parker clicked off the recorder and pocketed it, then stood. DeAndre rose from the couch and moved so she was face to face with Parker. "Thank you, Detective Parker, I was dreading talking about this but knowing you understand the pain and shame I feel, made it so much easier. Before today I'd only shared this with Kelly and Stella Fortunato, my attorney. Knowing he's dead makes it less scary but it's hard not to feel I did something wrong."

"I get that," Parker said. "The victims feel the shame, as if they were the criminals and unfortunately, that's how the courts and the press often present them. We appreciate your willingness to testify if necessary, Ms. DeAndre."

"Hey, please call me, Amari." She turned to Corelli. "So did your niece and nephew like the CDs?"

"Actually, it's my younger sister and nephew. They're the same age. And they were thrilled to get them. Thanks, again, Amari. I'm sorry but I have two more questions."

"Okay."

"In your liberation from Blecker, did you sign any papers prohibiting you from bringing charges against him and his wife?"

"I think I did, but as I recall, it was only Jake. You can call my attorney to be sure." She picked up her phone and read off Stella Fortunato's telephone number.

"Thanks. Final question. We asked Nan Fredericks how she came to work for you and she suggested we ask you. So I'm asking."

"That's an easy one. Once I was free I went back to Queens looking for friends. Nan, one of the neighbors in my Queens building who fed me and took care of me after my grandmother died, was still living in the building. Nan led me to Mary, the other woman who looked after me. She was living in an appalling nursing home in Queens and Nan helped me find her a much nicer place with excellent care. And then I asked Nan to work for me, so she does some cooking and oversees a cleaning crew and the gardening people. As you can probably guess, I believe in payback. Both good and bad."

CHAPTER TWENTY-ONE

As they stood on the steps of DeAndre's brownstone facing Central Park, Corelli marveled at the beauty of the snow-covered paths and the trees dripping snow and ice in the park. She shivered and pulled on the warm gloves Brett had bought her. In prior winters, she'd been perfectly happy in her leather coat. But neither the weather nor her body's reaction to it was something she could control. She was feeling the cold more because of her injuries but it was definitely wetter, icier and snowier than usual and it wasn't even Thanksgiving yet. As annoying as it was, she'd rather wear the bulky clothing than get sick and be confined to the apartment again. Brett's offer of a sailing vacation in the Caribbean was looking better and better. Maybe when this case was over.

She relaxed into the warmth of the car as they headed downtown, happy that Parker had immediately turned the heat to high. "That was a great interview, Parker. You immediately established trust, asked the right questions and got her to agree to testify if we need her. Since you made the choice to put your own abuse out there, I'm assuming you're okay with it." She pulled her gloves off. "You know this interview could be exactly what we need to get a bead on the group behind the sex trafficking."

Parker kept her eyes on the street. "You're definitely thinking organized sex trafficking?"

"It's clear from what Amari said that they were involved in it. Don't you think?"

Parker focused on the traffic, obviously formulating her response. "DeAndre confirmed it for me too. Blecker was bringing in foreign girls when she was eleven or twelve, long before Dumayne was on the scene. And it appears he was still doing it all these years later. That implies a widespread, ongoing organization."

"Yeah. Hopefully we can squeeze Phillips and Servino to get the information we need about his trafficking connections."

"It's only been a couple of days and I'm sure we'd have heard if the girls revealed anything important," Parker said, "but now would be a good time to swing over to the West Side Highway to go to Gianna's house if you want to check on them."

"Do it. I want to see for myself how they're doing and get a feel for the likelihood of learning anything from them."

The door to the brownstone opened before they knocked. Charleen Greene stepped back so they could enter. She'd drawn her weapon but kept it pointed down and close to her side. "Good morning."

"Morning. Any problems?" Corelli asked. Greene looked tired. This case was stressing all of them.

"All quiet." Greene holstered her weapon. "They're in the kitchen. It's learning time."

"Learning time?"

"Yes, Chiara." They spun around at the sound of Gianna's voice behind them. "The girls have never been to school so I'm teaching them to read and write. And Gabriella and Francesca are helping." She hugged Corelli, then Parker. "Right now they're drawing. Dr. Court thought drawing would help them express what they're feeling so I alternate coloring and drawing."

"How are they? And how are you holding up? You look exhausted."

Gianna pushed her hair behind her ears. "According to Dr. Court, the girls are resilient and are doing okay given what they've been through. She thinks they're too young to be much help to you and if they know anything it will trickle out over time." Her smile was sad. "I'm tired. One or all of the girls wake up crying two or three times a night so I'm up with them. Sometimes it takes a while before they fall asleep again. Francesca has been helping, but she has to get up for school so I try not to wake her unless all three are crying. Gabriella and Francesca are back in school so except for the hour or so Dr. Court is here, I'm alone with the three of them all day."

Maybe she'd made a mistake asking her sister to take responsibility for the girls. "I'm sorry, Gianna. I didn't think it through." Corelli wrapped her arms around her sister. "I'll have them moved to a group home where there are staff to take care of them."

Gianna pulled away and glared. "Absolutely not. They're starting to trust me and I would never forgive myself for sending them somewhere they don't get love and comfort. And we both know group homes are understaffed and they'd probably be left to cry alone in the dark."

Corelli couldn't argue with that since it was one of the reasons she'd brought them to Gianna in the first place. "What about hiring a couple of people to help you? They wouldn't have to live in, just be here either overnight or during the day so you can get some uninterrupted sleep. Any ideas?" Corelli looked from Gianna to Parker to Greene.

"What about Simone?" Parker suggested. "She's good with the little ones. And Nicky. He's good with his younger brothers and sisters too." She looked uncomfortable. "It means putting more of the family in danger but it also means no strangers in the house."

Corelli wanted to punch her for mentioning them. But she was right. It would be easier to get Gianna to accept Simone and Nicky rather than strangers and they were already providing protection so two more wouldn't matter. Besides, having family members go in and out or stay over wouldn't raise any eyebrows in the neighborhood. It was a good idea.

"That's brilliant, P.J." Gianna looked to Corelli. "Dr. Court said I could begin to reintroduce Marco and Giancarlo but I think Nicky would be even better to start with because of his experience with his siblings. I think the girls would feel comfortable with him. He and Simone could sleep here or go home depending on how they feel. Would you trust them to keep it secret?"

"I trust them but we'll have to brief them. Parker, see if they're available to meet us when we're done here." She eyed Gianna. "Tell them to bring whatever they'll need to stay over tonight but don't let on they'll be staying here rather than at my place."

"Come. Say hello to the girls." Gianna took her arm and led her into the kitchen.

Since it was Saturday Gabriella was coloring with the girls and Francesca was supervising but her eyelids were drooping. They definitely needed help.

Gabriella glanced up as they entered. "Auntie Chiara." She jumped up and hugged Corelli. Francesca yawned and waved. The three girls watched with interest.

"Hey, everyone. Are you having fun?"

Corelli didn't expect anyone but Gabriella to answer so she was surprised to hear Crissy's, "Yes."

"Good." She smiled and moved behind the girls to look at their drawings. Crissy had drawn an airplane with two figures, a girl and a woman, flying through a dark gray sky. There was a house with no windows on the ground, a tree without leaves and black earth. "Have you flown in an airplane, Crissy?" She smiled and kept her voice soft for fear of upsetting the girl.

The child turned to gaze at Corelli, then lifted her tiny shoulders indicating she didn't know. Corelli felt herself drawn into the big, brown, sad eyes but not sure her touch would be welcomed, she fought the impulse to hug her and focused on the drawing instead.

"Well, this is a nice picture. Thank you for showing it to me." She glanced at the papers in front of the other girls. Teresa had multicolored scribbles while Maria had drawn ten or twelve small dark figures with a big sun shining over them. Corelli pointed to the figures. "Who are these people, Maria?"

The girl glanced down at the picture then looked up. "I don't know."

Could Dr. Court interpret the drawings? Did Crissy's plane trip come from experience? And who did Maria's figures represent? She'd hoped they would be able to work with the police artist to come up with a sketch of their keepers or provide some clues to where they were kept, but she could see that wasn't possible. She sighed. She'd got what she came for. The poor things deserved some happiness and she hoped Gianna and Dr. Court could comfort them and help them feel safe. She complimented each of the girls, including Gabriella, on their drawings, and hugged Francesca and Gianna before she and Parker who had slipped into the room said their goodbyes.

Parker had arranged to meet Simone and Nicky at a pastry shop near Corelli's parents' restaurant. Their faces went from cheerful to sickly as she explained that the girls had been sexually abused and Gianna was taking care of them until they could resolve the case and find their parents. She explained the need for secrecy, told them about the around-the-clock protection, and gave them each the option of helping or not. They had a million questions and she answered what she could without giving them too much information. They both agreed. They'd both stay tonight and most nights to relieve Gianna. And they would be here as much as possible during the day, depending on their classes and schoolwork.

While Simone and Nicky called home, Corelli answered a call from her friend Darla North, the WNYN reporter. When she clicked off, Corelli stood and stretched. "Darla stopped by to see us at the station and left a packet of articles she collected when she interviewed Dumayne several months ago. She thought we might see something she missed."

"Yippee, something else to read." Parker grabbed her coat. "Kidding. I'll meet you at the car." Without waiting for a reply, Parker slipped into her coat and strolled away.

Corelli and the kids pulled on their own warm clothing and followed. It was only a block or so to the car but all three of them moaned in appreciation as they slid into the warmth. Parker smiled and headed to Gianna's house. The kids were not their usual chatty selves. Corelli wondered if asking them to deal with abused children was too much. But when they got out of the car Simone hugged her. "Thank you for trusting us, Chiara. We'll do anything we can to help." Nicky waited for Simone to step back and then pulled her into a tight hug. "What Simone said, Auntie." He kissed her cheek.

CHAPTER TWENTY-TWO

The streets around the stationhouse were jammed. Cars were parked haphazardly and uniformed officers were hurrying through the cold in the direction of the stationhouse. After circling nearby streets trying to get closer, Parker pulled over two blocks away. "Something must have happened. This is as close as I can get."

Corelli observed the crowd for a moment. "They looked hyped. Let's—" Her phone vibrated in her pocket followed immediately by Parker's phone. Corelli stared at Watkins' text. *McGivens dead. Prison fight. Blue demo, media too.*

Bile rose in her throat. Her ex-partner and friend Jimmy was dead. Regret, mixed with shame and guilt, washed over her. She'd sent him to prison and now he was dead. Images of the many good times they'd shared flashed through her mind—the two of them laughing and horsing around, meals on the job and barbecues in his yard, dinners with her family, coffee breaks at her favorite spot in sight of the Statue of Liberty. She glanced at Parker, her current partner, a loyal and honest cop talking on the phone, figuring out how to protect her in the face of what could be a dangerous walk through the crowd. Her thoughts went back to Jimmy but this time the images that came to mind were of the cruel macho braggart he'd morphed into during the year she was in Afghanistan, the Jimmy who brushed off her grieving for Marnie as if their love hadn't mattered.

Her friend Jimmy had died a long time before today. The Jimmy who died today was a major player in Righteous Partners, the gang of dirty police who stopped at nothing, even killing other police, to protect themselves and their illegal drug activities. He'd set her up to force her to join the group, unaware she was working undercover and had set him up to invite her in. The Jimmy who died today had threatened to kill her sisters and she didn't doubt that he would have killed them and her had she not been able to wield a weapon even stronger than Righteous Partners.

"Captain Winfry suggests we avoid the stationhouse." She followed Parker's gaze to the officers hurrying along the street. Happily they hadn't been noticed. "I guess I was right," Parker said. "Not all the anger toward you disappeared when you were shot. And some of our brethren in blue still believe you should be ostracized or worse for getting rid of dirty cops."

"You *were* right." Corelli gazed at the angry faces hurrying to attack her. "But they'll be here later and tomorrow and who knows how long, so I'm going in. But you don't—"

"Don't pull that martyr stuff on me again, Corelli. I hate to repeat myself but where you go, I go, and I go there when you go there. Anyway since we have no idea what their intentions are some of the team are coming to walk us in."

They both jumped at the knock on the window. "And speak of the devils, here are our escorts. Ready?"

Corelli was moved. It wasn't just Watkins, Kim, Dietz, Forlini and other team members who had come to escort her through the crowd it was also six or seven other officers and detectives from the station. Walking in the middle of the group, she wasn't noticed until they got close. Then the crowd pushed and shoved at her escorts and chanted, "Murderer. Traitor. Lock Corelli up."

She estimated there were a couple hundred of them. The scarves and hats everyone was wearing to protect against the cold weather made it hard to see faces but she could see the hate in their eyes. Not for the first time she wondered why these officers who had sworn to protect and defend hated her for doing just that. They couldn't all be criminals. Was it mob mentality? Or was there something ugly just beneath the surface of people who otherwise seemed normal?

As they entered the building, Captain Winfry strode toward them with a bullhorn in his hand. "Sorry, Corelli, it happened so fast I didn't have a chance to clear them out." They moved aside and he exited.

She turned to her escorts. "Thank you for your support guys." She got lots of pats as everyone went back to their jobs. Once they were in the team conference room she faced Watkins. "What happened?"

Watkins had worked with her and McGivens and had always thought Jimmy was a racist bully. She'd come to agree with that assessment when she was undercover. It was clear he discounted her relationship with Marnie because she was African-American and that his so-called joking with Watkins and others had the underpinnings of racism that she couldn't or maybe didn't want to see at the time.

"It was quintessential Jimmy," Watkins said. "Apparently he was always needling and challenging the guy who ran things in their cellblock. This wasn't their first fight, but this time Jimmy allegedly pulled a knife and they were wrestling for it when he got stabbed."

"A Jimmy power play." Her sadness surprised her but not the anger.

Captain Winfry walked in as she, Dietz and Parker settled around the table. "Okay, they're being moved across the street behind barricades and that's where they'll be as long as they come here. It's so cold I don't think they'll be there long tonight. But you two," he looked from Corelli to Parker, "need to be extra careful. I'm putting a car on both your buildings. And one behind you tonight and the next day or so depending on how this goes." He raised his hand. "This is not up for discussion, Corelli. It's an order."

"Yessir."

He looked confused. "Right. Good." He strode out of the room and they burst out laughing.

Dietz punched her shoulder. "You really flummoxed him. He was all set to battle with you."

"Keep 'em guessing I say. So what have you got, Dietz?"

Somebody inside must have tipped off the mob of police milling around in the cold that she was leaving, because with her scarf concealing half her face and her hat covering her forehead, she was sure even her mother wouldn't recognize her. Yet as soon as she opened the door, the chants started and with a roar the crowd broke through the barricades. Pinned in the bright light of TV cameras she instinctively shielded her eyes from the flashbulbs and backed away. Parker's hands on her shoulders grounded her. "Look at the people," Parker said softly, reminding her that staring at the flashing lights was a sure path to a flashback.

Police with hate filled eyes loomed behind the screaming media. She wanted to talk to them to make them understand that good cops needed to root out the bad, but she knew their hatred had nothing to do with the truth. No, the hatred was something else, something she couldn't put her finger on.

Captain Winfry appeared with his megaphone, ready to disburse the mob but she had concluded she needed to face the questions or the media would hound her. "I might as well answer their questions now, Captain, or they'll chase me."

He spoke into the megaphone, "Detective Corelli will answer a few questions but when I say we're done, I expect all of you to leave immediately."

She stared into the crowd. She wasn't surprised to see Andrew Baron, from Channel 43, front and center. He was always trying to hit her where she was vulnerable. And what better way for him to show what a great reporter he was than putting her on the spot about Jimmy's death? A sudden flurry of activity caught her attention and that of the media. The crowd parted, TV cameras spun and lights flashed as Carol, Jimmy's wife, and their two daughters made their way to Baron. She should have known they'd do everything possible to use Jimmy's death against her. It was painful but inevitable.

But she wasn't alone. The whole murder team had come out to stand behind her. Parker was at her left side in protector mode, one hand touching Corelli, the other on her weapon inside her coat, and sharp eyes scanning the crowd for danger. Watkins and Dietz flanked her right side, equally alert and protective. The others fanned out behind them.

Corelli forced herself to hold Carol's gaze. She respected the woman for defending her husband, though he didn't deserve it.

Unable to hide the smirk on his face, Baron placed a hand on Carol's shoulder. "Detective Corelli, your former partner and friend, James McGivens, was murdered in prison today. His grieving wife, Carol, and his two daughters," he pointed as if she didn't know who they were, "want to know how you feel knowing you were the one to put him in harm's way."

She didn't flinch from Carol's gaze. "I'm sorry for his death." She felt Parker's hand on her back as she always did when they were somewhere where flashing lights and loud noises could trigger a flashback, but her connection with Carol was so intense the lights barely registered. She took a few seconds to breathe and spoke directly to her. "Jimmy, Carol, and I were close friends when I left for Afghanistan. By the time I returned a year later, Jimmy was a leader in Righteous Partners, the ring of dirty police that worked for a drug czar, selling drugs, doing his dirty work, murdering other drug dealers and their wives and children, and anyone else who got in the way of their criminal enterprise. Including Police Officer Vanessa Forrest." There was a gasp. Carol looked shocked. Since there hadn't been a trial, most people didn't know the full extent of the group's depravity and fewer still knew Forrest was Captain Winfry's daughter. She held Carol's gaze for a few more seconds then focused on Baron. "I exposed Righteous Partners. They all pled guilty, which is why Jimmy and the others went to jail. But I'm very clear, Andrew, it was Jimmy's choice to be a leader in an organization that carelessly murdered innocent people with bullets and drugs that put him in prison. Not me. It was his choice to antagonize rather than get along with other prisoners that put him in harm's way. Not me." Baron turned and whispered to Carol.

Corelli steeled herself for Carol's attack. But Carol shook her head, turned and disappeared into the crowd with her two daughters.

Corelli watched her go, wondering whether Carol had heard what she said. She hadn't killed Jimmy.

Parker poked her and whispered. "Jody Timmons asked whether you're going to attend Jimmy's funeral."

She snapped back. "I'm still reeling from the news of his death, Jody. I really haven't thought that far ahead."

Winfry stepped up. "Okay, everyone, time to clear out."

The area darkened as lights were turned off and officers herded everyone back beyond the barricades.

"Sorry about that," Winfry said. He had his own grief and he got how hard it was for her to have Carol's accusing and sorrow-filled eyes glaring at her while in front of a pack of reporters and cameras.

She shivered, suddenly aware of the cold.

CHAPTER TWENTY-THREE

Though she never doubted it, Captain Winfry was true to his word. The cars had trailed them last night and this morning on the way to the station. Given it was another record-breaking cold day and today's swirling snowfall was rapidly covering everything and everybody with a coat of white, she didn't expect the small group of protestors and few members of the media who greeted them, to last the morning. Sometimes this freaking weather was your friend.

Dietz was humming when they settled at the conference table to begin the morning review. Hopefully, that meant good news. He rubbed his hands together. "Let's go, Watkins."

"Good job with the impromptu press conference last night, boss." Watkins sipped his coffee. "So I interviewed all the elders at the church. A couple said outright, and others hinted, that Dumayne and Wilkerson were locked in a power struggle. Dumayne was planning on pushing Wilkerson out as soon as they hired a younger man to take over his administrative duties but Wilkerson found a reason to reject every candidate they interviewed. He'd lost the battle over his wife's position. She used to run all the church's community programs but Dumayne moved her aside and put an inexperienced man in charge.

But he's been fighting to keep Gladiola Foster, the secretary, who is loyal to him. And his own job."

"A little different than the story Parker and I heard from Wilkerson. Did you get any sense how the elders feel about him taking over as senior pastor?"

"Mostly they're supportive but they still want a fiery younger pastor under him to pull in parishioners and money." Watkins grinned. "I'm taking bets that Wilkerson will want to re-interview some of those he rejected."

Could Wilkerson, his wife and Foster find it in their hearts, or guts, to murder someone over a job? Could the pictures of Dumayne having sex with little girls be repulsive enough to tip them toward killing Dumayne? Even if it was enough, why would they do it at Blecker's mansion? Did they know about Blecker? Was he also a target? Of course, walking in on him and the other two men having sex with the children would have been justification for killing all three perverts. "Parker and I will take another run at the three of them. Do we have copies of the pictures Foster found?"

Dietz wrinkled his nose. "I haven't looked at any of it myself, but let's ask the expert. Maynard, got a sec?"

"For you, Dietz baby, I always have a second." At least five-ten, with broad shoulders that pegged her as a swimmer, Maynard's bushy hair fought confinement in a bun, and her sparkling eyes and wide smile radiated humor. She strode to the conference table, glanced at Corelli but her gaze lingered on Parker. "Hey, P.J." Parker's color heightened. She sort of half waved but didn't comment.

Dietz did the introductions. "Detective Debbie Maynard, this is Detective Chiara Corelli. Maynard and the two sitting with her are on loan from the Special Victims Unit. They're examining the porn."

"Detective," Corelli said, "have you come across the photos showing Dumayne having sex with children?"

"You mean the four turned over by somebody at the church? Let me get them." She walked back to her desk and returned with an open file and read from a sheet of paper. "Apparently the secretary at the church found them on Dumayne's desk and gave them to Reverend Wilkerson and he gave them to us." She passed the photos to Corelli.

She understood why Dietz hadn't looked at them and if she had a choice, she wouldn't either. The bastard was naked on a bed in a different position with a different girl in each photo. The oldest child couldn't have been more that ten. The photos could definitely be a motive for murder. She handed the photos to Parker. "Thanks, Maynard. Can we get copies? Have you found anything of interest so far?"

"Yeah. Each photo has a couple of codes written on the back but I haven't found what the codes mean. A couple of the men have identifiable tattoos on various parts of the bodies—one on his ass, one on his bicep and a couple have them on their calves. Two men are wearing recognizable rings. All the pictures so far seem to be taken in the same room. Usually the men's faces aren't visible but I found a couple where someone snapped the photographer taking pictures and the rapist's face appears to be reflected in his glasses. We'll do some enlargement and enhancement and hopefully we'll get something useful. That's it so far but we have a shitload of printed pictures to go through and tons on the computers. I've requested more help and I'd appreciate it if you could push it from your end."

As Maynard threw out her observations, Parker made notes. And Corelli thought about tattoos. The girls were tattooed. The men's tattoos and the rings could help identify them but she needed to narrow their focus. They were already investigating a triple murder and child abuse/child trafficking, so it was the murderers and the traffickers, not the johns she was after right now. But she didn't want to discourage Maynard. "Thanks. I'd appreciate copies of the pictures with tattoos and rings. And of course whatever you find in the enlargements you're doing."

"Absolutely. Nice to finally meet you." Maynard sashayed to her desk, glanced back at Parker and then focused on her computer screen.

"I think you have an admirer." Corelli spoke softly so only Parker could hear.

Parker kept her eyes on her notebook. "I'll add her to the list."

Corelli's burst of laughter caught Maynard's attention and she gazed at them for a few seconds before turning back to the photographs in front of her.

Parker hadn't said Maynard wasn't her type. Watkins flirted heavily with Parker during the Winter case, but she seemed to hold him at arm's length. Was it Watkins or men that didn't interest her? Damn. Since when did she care about Parker's sexual preferences? "Where are the autopsy reports? Didn't one of our vics have a tattoo? Maybe we can tie him to the porn."

Parker found the envelope with the autopsy reports. It turned out that Blecker had a tattoo on his buttocks, a heart with an arrow with the words "Young Love is Best" going through it. She made a couple of copies of the tattoo and walked one over to Maynard. "One of our vics had this on his buttocks. Please separate any photos with him in them."

Maynard grinned. She held Parker's hand just a couple of seconds longer than necessary as she accepted the copy. "Sure, sweetie. For you, anything."

"Thanks, sweetie," Parker said, the sarcasm a sharp contrast to Maynard's honeyed tone.

Standing nearby talking to Kim, Corelli observed the interaction with amusement, then turned her attention back to the work at hand. "Yo, Dietz. Let's get back to work. Anything else?"

He hustled back to the table. "Yup. While you two were having fun, I was making sure things are moving along."

"I, for one, am glad you're working to keep us organized," Corelli said. "What else?"

Dietz thumbed through a stack of reports and passed one to her and one to Parker. "Kim interviewed Lester Harwell, Blecker's attorney. He said it was a strange situation. He and Phillips' attorney were negotiating a deal between them but neither attorney had any idea what they were fighting over. It wasn't alimony because they never married. In Harwell's opinion, Phillips was totally out of control. She went into a crazed rage after he locked her out of their houses and threatened to expose Blecker in the newspapers. He laughed at the threat and said it would damage her more than him and she dropped it." He read silently for a few seconds.

"Harwell also said Phillips was practically foaming at the mouth when Blecker offered to settle for one hundred thousand dollars a month and half his estate upon his death. Phillips said the money was barely enough to scrape by on but maybe she'd settle and then kill him to get the rest of what she was owed. Apparently Blecker took that threat seriously and two days before he was murdered he signed a new will cutting her out."

"Yeah, Harwell told Parker about the new will when she called to ask who inherits his estate. Marianne was shocked when I mentioned Blecker had changed his will so it appears he never told her. I'd say she had a really good motive for killing Blecker."

"A couple more things. The guy who hosted that party at Trilago quit his job a couple of months ago and went back to Australia. No forwarding address." Dietz glanced at the clock on the wall. "We got the cell records for Dumayne and his drivers and the phone company is helping us locate the house where the girls are kept. Also, three of the drivers called Ernesto Servino quite often." He straightened the pile of reports. "And you might be interested in the messages we found on Dumayne's home answering machine. Blecker left a message around lunchtime the day of the murder. Mrs. Dumayne's mother left several messages for her on that same machine later that night, during the time Mrs. Dumayne claimed she was at home." He handed Corelli the transcripts.

'William. Jake here. We have a guest tonight so your guy will be picking up three kittens, not two. Unless your wife is ready, we don't have a sitter to keep them busy until we're ready to fuck them, so have them delivered around nine so we can be finished before our esteemed late-night guest shows up. Oh shit. I thought this was your cell.'

"Hi Francine, it's Mom at ten p.m. Just calling to chat.
"Hi honey, it's eleven p.m. Are you okay?
"Hi, honey, it's eleven thirty. It's unlike you to be out at night.
"Has William finally taken you out?"

Corelli read the messages and handed the papers to Parker. "Blecker's message confirms the use of someone to care for the girls while waiting to be raped, which supports DeAndre's story. Is DeAndre's statement enough to bring Marianne Phillips in?"

Parker tossed the transcript to Dietz. "Definitely."

"Give me her lawyer's number." Corelli keyed the number as Parker read it off. A secretary answered but she was put right through to Laney Gold, the attorney.

"Detective Corelli, Marianne said you might call," Gold said, when she picked up. "I assumed this is related to Jake Blecker's murder and since I'm not a criminal defense attorney I've set Marianne up with a law school friend. I'm not sure whether he's available on such short notice. When do you want to meet?"

"As soon as possible but no later than tomorrow. I believe Ms. Phillips has crucial information and her reluctance to talk to us is interfering with our investigation. Have her or her attorney call Detective Dietz to set up an appointment for today or tomorrow. If she doesn't show, we'll pick her up and hold her." She ended the call and turned to Dietz. "Marianne Phillips—"

Dietz put a hand up. "Got it. I'll text when it's arranged."

She waited for him to make a note for himself. "Have they found any folders with lists of names and codes on the computers?"

Dietz shook his head. "Lots of porn on Dumayne's home computer, some on the church computers. We did find that the Dumayne brownstone and the Wilkerson's apartment are owned by the church. Nothing but porn so far on Blecker's computers." He stood. "Are we done here?"

"We are." Corelli stretched and yawned. "So, Parker, it looks like we need to talk to Mrs. Dumayne again. Someday we'll have a case where all the witnesses tell us the truth the first time we ask."

"Dream on." Parker stood. "You know, watching those kids drawing yesterday got me thinking. What do you think about putting T'Wayne Johnson and the other two church security guys with a police artist, see if they can come up with a reasonable likeness of the guy who transported the girls."

Was Parker a mind reader? She'd thought the same thing earlier but it had slipped her mind. "Great idea. Hey, Dietz."

CHAPTER TWENTY-FOUR

Mrs. Dumayne answered the door, barefoot, wearing jeans, a T-shirt and no makeup, yet she managed to look as beautiful and elegant as the last time they'd seen her. Today, though, she looked relaxed. She stared a few seconds as if trying to place them. "Oh, hi. Please come in."

She led them to the room they'd been in the last time. "I'm sorry, I don't remember your names." She leaned in as if trying to read their IDs.

"Detective Corelli. And this is Detective Parker. We'd like to go over a few things about your husband's death with you."

"I don't know what I can tell you but I'll do what I can to help."

Corelli liked this young woman and hoped she wasn't the killer but she would do her job and eliminate or arrest her. "You told us you have no friends here in New York City, yet a neighbor claims you meet someone with a car several times a week. Who is it you're meeting?"

Dumayne managed to control her voice but the loss of color in her face gave her away. "She's a busybody."

"How do you know the neighbor is a woman?"

She looked Corelli in the eye. "Because I've seen her walking her dog and I thought she was following me. In any case, I'm alone all day and I like to take a walk in the evenings to make it bearable. And if I did get into a car, it's nobody's business but mine." She looked like she might cry. "Did William hire her to spy on me?"

"Not that we're aware of. She said she was worried because you didn't know your way around the city and might get hurt."

She shook her head. "Walking outside didn't hurt me. William hurt me by bringing me here under false pretenses, then ignoring me. I feel free and alive when I'm outside."

"What do you mean he brought you here under false pretenses?"

Dumayne seemed to struggle to find the words. "He... He wooed me and made me feel desired and loved and then once we were married he insisted we look at dirty pictures before we had sex. It was disgusting. He was disgusting. I've been thinking of leaving him."

Corelli spoke in what she hoped was a soothing voice. "What kind of dirty pictures?"

The young woman reddened. "It's too horrible to talk about."

Before Corelli could insist, Dumayne stood. "He kept them in the bedroom. I'll bring them down to you."

It took her just a couple of minutes to hand the porn to Corelli. As she expected, it was two different sets of men and women in bed together while the men were raping little girls. The bastard was probably trying to desensitize her so he could bring a girl into their bed. She passed the photos to Parker, then closed her eyes and took a couple of yoga breaths, trying to clear the images from her head. When she looked up, Mrs. Dumayne was watching her.

"I saw by your face that it disgusts you too. But you don't seem surprised."

Should she tell her? It would probably come out eventually and she already knew half the story. "Pictures of him having sex with little girls were found on his desk at the church."

"Oh." It sounded as if the young woman had been punched in the stomach. Tears streamed down her face. "Those poor girls."

Corelli hesitated but seeing she was still listening, continued. "And there's extensive porn of men with children on his home and church computers. Did he ever try to get you to bring a child into bed with you?"

"No. I would have been out of here immediately. The porn was enough for me. I was ready to leave him but my mom said a lot of men like porn and I should be sure before doing anything. I thought about it and I'd decided to leave him."

"Speaking of your mom, she left several messages for you Tuesday night, when you said you were home all night."

"I know. I had my cell off because I was upset and I didn't feel like talking."

"The messages were left on the answering machine in his office. The first was at ten p.m. and the last at eleven thirty p.m. You said you were home all night yet you didn't pick up the phone for your mother. I'll ask again. Where were you from eight o'clock to midnight Tuesday night?"

"The landline is in his office and even if I hear it ringing, I ignore it."

Corelli was losing patience with her evasiveness. "Answer the question, please."

She blushed. "I went out a little after nine with a friend but... they...he remembered another engagement so I was home by ten. I spent the rest of the night reading. My cell phone was off."

"He?"

"Someone from Atlanta. A friend. Believe me I'm not having an affair. William was enough to deal with. But I'd rather not share his name."

Corelli considered whether to push but decided they'd get the name another way. "We talked to Mr. Dumayne's attorney. He made a will after you were married. You'll inherit quite a bit of money."

Dumayne looked like she might be sick. "I don't want anything of his. I'll give it all to a charity for abused children."

Corelli stared until the young woman squirmed. "So if it wasn't the money, why did you kill him?"

"What?" The color drained from her face. She sat straighter. "He disgusted me. I felt abandoned and used, and at times I wished he was dead, but I never once thought of killing him. I was going to leave him. I even bought a plane ticket." She thrust her phone at Corelli. "Here, you'll see I bought it two weeks ago."

Corelli pushed the phone away. The ticket could be part of her alibi. "Thank you, Mrs. Dumayne. Please don't leave New York City until we complete our investigation. We'll see ourselves out."

"Please call me Francine. And I'll be changing my name back to Waters as soon as I can."

"She's either a good actress or she's telling the truth," Corelli said. "But I'd like to know who she's meeting so I'm going to put someone on her."

"She certainly didn't hide her feelings but I don't see her as a murderer. I think we should have the Atlanta police interview her mother." Parker put the key in but didn't turn the car on. "And speaking of Atlanta, it occurred to me that Darnell Mason and Francine Dumayne came here from Atlanta about the same time. Maybe they knew each other from there. And Mason said he sometimes drove Dumayne and his wife so we know they had contact."

Corelli snapped her seatbelt into place. "Hmm. Do you see them as the killers?"

"I don't. But it's an interesting coincidence. Perhaps she was meeting him." Parker started the car. "To the church?"

"They're holding services today, the first time without Dumayne, and Wilkerson is officiating so he'll be tied up for a while." Corelli turned the heater down. "But Foster is waiting for us."

The parking lot was only about a third full, not a good omen for the church's future. But maybe word about the resumption of services hadn't gotten out. The security guards were still patrolling outside. "Parker, have Dietz ask the precinct in this area to do spot checks on the guards to be sure they're not packing again."

They didn't expect to find Darnell Mason hanging over Gladiola Foster, who was sitting at her desk, dressed in what appeared to be Sunday finery, including a hat. And clearly, he hadn't expected them. He jerked up, almost knocking her hat off and she pulled back with a small yelp. Her earring danced as he backed away from the desk. They both looked guilty. Foster recovered first. "Detectives, nice to see you again. Darnell and I were just going over payroll." She glanced at him. "Are we done, Darnell?"

"Yes ma'am. I'll be going. See you, Detectives."

"How can I help you?" Foster seemed chipper today. Was it because Dumayne was out of the picture? They sat. Corelli waited for Parker to take out her notebook and pen before starting. "Where were you Tuesday night between eight and midnight?"

"Tuesday? Oh, the night Reverend Dumayne was murdered? I thought I already told you Reverend Wilkerson and I worked late to complete the financial reports. We ordered pizza around nine. I left around ten and I was home by ten thirty."

Was her answer too pat or was it just that she was organized and noticed the time? "Can anyone verify your presence from ten thirty on?"

"No. I live alone."

"How did you come to work for Reverend Dumayne?"

She looked into the distance, smiled, then met Corelli's eyes. "I've worked with Reverend Wilkerson since I was nineteen. He asked me to come with him when he joined the staff here. At that time,

Reverend Dumayne had his own assistant but she didn't work out so he fired her and I took over both jobs."

"What was it like working for Dumayne?"

Corelli gazed at the secretary, watching her discomfort grow in the silence, knowing human nature would force most people to fill it. After twirling the pen for a minute, Foster looked up. "Like I said last time I made the best of it but he wasn't nice. He was full of himself and thought he was smarter than everyone. He didn't listen and acted as if I couldn't possibly understand the intricacies of managing a church when I've been doing the job since I was a teenager."

"How did you feel when you found those pictures of Reverend Dumayne with little girls?"

Foster's breath hitched, she sat up straighter, but this time she didn't hesitate. "Repulsed. I almost threw up. He was supposed to be a man of God, which didn't mean he was perfect, but to do something like that to innocents... I was enraged. I could have..." She stopped. Took a breath. "How would you feel if you picked up a folder and pictures of your chief naked having sex with little girls fell out? How would any normal person feel?"

Once again Corelli remained silent until it was clear Foster had said all she wanted to say on the topic. "Why did you bring them to Reverend Wilkerson?"

"He's the assistant pastor. He needed to know. We'd heard rumors about porn but this was beyond porn. This was, I don't know, is it rape when a grown man has sex with a child?"

Recognizing it as a rhetorical question, Corelli continued. "How did Reverend Wilkerson react?"

"Like any moral person, like a man of God, he was outraged." Foster made no attempt to hide her pride in the man. "After all, Reverend Dumayne's actions could destroy the church, everything we've accomplished."

One way or another the truth always oozed out. Sure the pictures were upsetting, repulsive. But these two so-called people of God weren't worried about the harm to the children. They were worried about the reputation of their church, their livelihoods. Was it enough to compel them to murder three men? "What did the two of you do with the pictures?"

For the first time Foster looked unsure. "We, uh, talked it over, Reverend Wilkerson discussed it with his wife Oline, and we all agreed to think about it before telling anyone."

Corelli fanned out the pictures in front of Foster and made no attempt to hide her anger. "These pictures couldn't be any clearer. He raped four little girls. What was it you needed to think about?"

Foster rolled her chair away from the desk as if she feared the pictures. "You know, should we tell the elders, should we confront Reverend Dumayne, how should we handle it?"

Parker cleared her throat, a signal to Corelli to control herself. And she was right. She needed this witness to talk and yelling at her would discourage that. Corelli softened her voice. "I understand you were upset, but did you consider going to the police? Or was protecting the church the priority?"

"We did think about the police but then Reverend Wilkerson thought we might be able to use the pictures to control Rev—" Foster stopped short. Her gaze skidded around the room. "I'm sorry, it's so upsetting to talk about. What I meant was, to get help for Reverend Dumayne."

Corelli decided to change the subject. "How did you find out that Reverend Dumayne was trying to get rid of you and Reverend Wilkerson?"

Dropping the discussion of the pictures seemed to relax Foster and she answered without hesitating. "One of the elders told Reverend Wilkerson in confidence and he told me."

"Wow. Then you found the pictures and the power shifted. Now you could control Dumayne. Did he agree to do your bidding?"

"No. There wasn't time to—" Foster's eyes widened as she realized what she'd just admitted. Her jaw tightened, her eyes narrowed but she managed to maintain control. "I don't like what you're implying, Detective, but this has all been so trying I can hardly think straight. I'm unable to continue right now."

Corelli smiled. "That's okay." She scooped up the pictures. "We'll just wait here for Reverend Wilkerson."

CHAPTER TWENTY-FIVE

Corelli flicked her eyes between her phone messages and Foster, who was focused on the door that led directly into the rear of the church. She'd clearly said more than she intended and no doubt would have gone to warn Wilkerson if they'd left her alone. Instead she sat there doing nothing, probably willing Wilkerson to stay away.

Fortunately the secretary didn't have the power to send mental messages, and twenty minutes later a beaming Wilkerson burst through the door. Foster jumped up. One look at her face and he slowed, then glanced from her to the two detectives. "Is something wrong?"

Corelli stepped between them to break their contact. "Not at all. We're just filling in some missing information." She looked at the phone in her hand. "But we're running a little late so I'd appreciate it if we could go right into your office." Wilkerson cast a worried look at Foster but entered his office. They followed and Parker closed the door.

"Please sit," he said, waving them to the chairs facing his desk. "How can I help?"

Preaching seemed to agree with him. He seemed taller, much more energetic than during their last visit. Corelli smiled. "I take it your first sermon went well."

"It did. The congregation was receptive. They loved my sermon and seemed thrilled with having me take over as the pastor. They cheered and clapped when it was announced. Everyone congratulated me and a number of people said it was wonderful to have a real preacher in charge." Gone was the humble assistant, replaced now by a man puffed up with pride.

Corelli hoped his wife was with him so they could kill two birds with the proverbial stone. "I assume Mrs. Wilkerson was at the service. Is she here at the church?"

"Of course she was there but she went home when I came into the office. She thought I was wonderful too." Was pride a sin in this religion?

While Wilkerson was taking a celebratory victory lap in his head, Corelli popped the question. "So, what did you think when Ms. Foster showed you these pictures of Dumayne having sex with children?" She placed the pictures, one at a time, on the desk in front of him. His gaze flicked from the pictures to the door and back.

He frowned. "I was shocked. Absolutely shocked."

"You'd heard rumors that he liked porn. Why did the pictures matter?"

"Rumors. But this was proof. What a disgusting man, having sex with little girls. He was morally bankrupt, unfit to lead this, or any church. And he wasn't even a properly trained minister like I am."

Were his arrogance and his attitude always there, hidden under the humble presentation? She shouldn't be surprised. People were layered and sometimes when you peeled away the image they projected to the world, the layers exposed were violent and filled with hate. And sometimes the exposed layers appeared peaceful but were filled with arrogance and self-glorification.

"What did you do about the pictures?" Corelli shot back. "Did you go to the police? The church elders?"

He didn't respond. She could almost hear his brain processing alternatives to the two actions she presented but it appeared he couldn't. At least that's what his rigid posture and darkening complexion indicated to her.

Corelli stood and leaned over his desk. "Or did you decide to blackmail the man who had removed your wife from her position and was working on getting rid of you and Gladiola Foster?"

He looked down to avoid her gaze but quickly looked up. "I didn't blackmail him. I was trying to figure out how best to handle the pictures without harming the church. And yes, how best to ensure I ended up as the pastor. But his being murdered solved the problem."

"You were willing to let him get away with raping little girls so you could become the pastor of this church?"

"No. I needed to make sure I had the support of the elders, then they and I would figure out how to handle the pictures. We probably would have gone to the police."

"Really? You expect me to believe you would have exposed him and jeopardized the church's reputation?"

"I guess we'll never know, will we?" His smile left no doubt he felt he'd outsmarted her. "I was planning to go to the police but he was murdered before I could. That's not a crime, is it?"

"Pretty convenient that he was murdered just after you found those pictures, wasn't it?"

"The pictures were enough to get me what I wanted. There was no need to murder him." He stood. "If you don't mind, I have to plan a celebratory funeral for Reverend Dumayne so we can have the service when his body is released."

Corelli slipped the pictures into the envelope. When they broke this case, she'd make sure the media knew all about Dumayne's sex life and the sham of a celebratory funeral would expose this church as the money-grabbing machine it was. She flashed an inauthentic smile. "Let us know if you want some enlargements for the service."

That wiped the smile off his face.

"It's like his inner asshole was released with Dumayne out of the picture," Parker said as they buckled their seatbelts.

Corelli removed her gloves and loosened her scarf. "Yeah. I'm thinking he realized blackmail would solve the immediate problem of Dumayne trying to clean house of all traces of him but it wouldn't get him control of the church. And judging from the transformation after getting it, I would say he wanted it badly enough to murder for it. What's your thinking, Ms. ADA?"

"Feeling he deserved to be the leader of the church could be a motive for murder if he wanted it badly enough. And he's arrogant enough to convince himself he was killing Dumayne for moral reasons. But we need more information about opportunity and means. Let's start with his whereabouts at the time of the murders. Want to visit Mrs. Wilkerson?"

"Let me text Dietz for their address." Sitting in the car waiting for the address, Parker lifted her chin in the direction of the parking lot. "Foster is getting in the car with Mason. Do you think they have something going?"

"They sure looked guilty when we walked in on them." She watched Foster lean over and kiss his cheek.

Dietz's text came in and they headed to the Bronx.

CHAPTER TWENTY-SIX

The Wilkersons lived in a decent middle-class neighborhood in the Bronx. And like the Dumaynes' Upper East Side brownstone, the Wilkerson apartment was a perk of working for the church. However, the borderline rundown building was a considerable step down from the senior pastor's residence.

They found parking about a block away. It had stopped snowing but the sky was dark and heavy with the threat of more to come. Corelli slammed the car door, then hunched against the wind as they retraced their route to Wilkerson's building. Up close it was even more dilapidated than it had appeared from the car. "I wonder whose decision it was to treat the second in command as a second-class citizen? I'd guess the radical difference in accommodations was a sore point for Wilkerson." Corelli pressed the buzzer for the Wilkersons' apartment.

A woman responded. "Who's there?"

"Is this Mrs. Wilkerson?" Parker said.

"It is. Who's there?" She seemed out of breath.

"Detectives Parker and Corelli. We'd like to chat with you about Reverend Dumayne."

"Chat?" Corelli mouthed, as the door to the building buzzed.

Parker grinned. "You have to talk their language."

Corelli elbowed her lightly. "Okay, so you handle the chatting for this interview."

When the elevator door opened on the fifth floor, a woman, presumably Mrs. Wilkerson, waved from the doorway of her apartment, a little way down the hall. The apartment itself was large, six rooms she said, and appeared well-maintained. The architectural details included an arched doorway between the living and dining rooms, intricate moldings and a patterned ceiling. It was lovely. Both rooms had a wall of windows with small leaded panes that gave a church-like feel and a bright airiness. Assuming the other rooms were similar, this would not be a bad place to live— unless of course, you were comparing it to a four-story brownstone located in a pretty Manhattan neighborhood, convenient to your job.

Corelli moved to the wall of photographs. You could learn a lot about people from the pictures they chose to display. In the earliest pictures, the couple looked to be in their twenties and were wearing what appeared to be Sunday finery. There were several of Wilkerson in an army uniform, a few in his clerical garb, and various others with the two of them over the years. She faced Mrs. Wilkerson. "Was Reverend Wilkerson an army chaplain?"

Her hand jumped to her throat. She glanced at the pictures. "No. He was called to the ministry after he left the service." She smiled. "Please have a seat." She waved to the sofa at the center of the comfortably furnished living room. "Can I get you tea or coffee?"

"We're fine thank you," Parker answered for both of them.

Was Mrs. Wilkerson nervous or was the nonstop fluttering of her hands, fluffing of pillows, brushing the arm of the chair she was seated in, and smoothing of her hair just her normal state of being? Once they were all seated her movements slowed. "What did you want to chat about?"

Parker smiled. "I'm sure you know it's important in a murder investigation to confirm the whereabouts of everyone who knew the deceased on the night of the murder."

Her hand went to her throat again. "Yes, of course."

Parker leaned toward her. "So can you tell us where you were and what you were doing last Tuesday between eight and midnight?"

"Tuesdays are book club night. We start at seven and go until ten and it usually takes another half hour for everyone to clear out. This week we met at Dorlie Hynes's house and she asked me to stay after the meeting to help her with a knitting problem. Between chatting and fixing her problem, I didn't get home until a few minutes after midnight."

"Please spell Ms. Hynes's name and give us her address." Parker waited as Corelli wrote down the information Wilkerson dictated. "Can Mr. Wilkerson confirm the time you arrived?"

She frowned. "He wasn't home when I got here. I called him to let him know I would be late but he didn't answer so I left a message. I wasn't concerned because he doesn't always remember to turn his phone on. He came home after I was in bed, about one a.m."

"Did he tell you where he was?"

"I didn't ask."

Parker spoke softly. "Why did Reverend Dumayne put Bernardo Sanchez in your position as director of the church youth activities?"

Wilkerson was aflutter again, hands in action. She shifted in her chair, dug in a pocket for a handkerchief and blew her nose. "I noticed that some of the children got agitated or started crying whenever Reverend Dumayne came into the room so I asked him if he had done something to upset them. He said I was crazy. He didn't want to answer my questions and he didn't want me to talk to the children, so he brought in a crony of his and pushed me aside. He's been telling people he thinks I have dementia."

"What do you think was going on?"

Her gaze shifted from Parker to Corelli and back to Parker. "Probably some sort of abuse but I haven't figured out how he managed it. Nelson and I tried to talk to the elders but he's stacked the group with supporters so they ignored what I said."

"What did you think of Reverend Dumayne?"

Wilkerson's laugh was harsh. "He was a despicable person, manipulative and out for himself. Children don't react the way they did to him for no reason. I'm sure he was abusing them. I never thought I'd say this about any human being but I'm glad he's dead. Whoever killed him did a service to humanity. I hope he burns in hell."

"What was your reaction when Mr. Wilkerson showed you the pictures Ms. Foster found of Reverend Dumayne having sex with little girls?"

"Sweet Jesus." Her voice went up an octave. "Nelson didn't show me any pictures, but why bother? I knew Dumayne was an abomination. Better he took them right to the police."

"Is that what you would have done?"

"Of course."

"Thank you, Mrs. Wilkerson. We'll let ourselves out."

CHAPTER TWENTY-SEVEN

Corelli raised the heater. "If her alibi holds, Mrs. Wilkerson isn't involved. And it seems that Mr. Wilkerson lied to us about the time he got home and to Foster about discussing the pictures with his wife."

Parker focused on avoiding icy spots and occasional piles of snow in the streets, proof that the complaints about streets in the Bronx not being ploughed as well or as frequently as those in Manhattan were true.

In the silence, Corelli replayed the interview with Mrs. Wilkerson. "I was surprised Wilkerson was in the military. Did we confirm Mason's military service?"

"I think we just checked the security guys for priors but Mason said he was ex-military when we interviewed him," Parker said. "What are you thinking?"

"The killer was controlled, not many wild shots, so an experienced shooter. What better place to learn than the military? Wilkerson would have received weapons training in the military. But that would have been a number of years ago. Mason, on the other hand, is thirty-six and probably served in Iraq or Afghanistan or both."

Parker interrupted Corelli's musing. "Where to?"

Corelli stared out the side window, considering the question. She needed some peace and quiet to organize the information they had so far. They had so many balls in the air at the station that it was impossible to find a quiet space. She dug her wallet out and looked at the yoga schedule. "Let's go to my apartment and try to figure out where we are. I'd like to make a class at Yoga for Warriors in a couple of hours and I'd appreciate a lift there. Brett may come by for dinner, and if you're free, you could join us."

"Your apartment is good. Since it's going to be an early night, I may have plans for dinner. I'll let you know after yoga. You and Brett are spending a lot of time together. That's great."

"Yeah. She's wonderful. It's good to connect and laugh. Is there anyone in your life that you enjoy spending time with?" Damn. Though she wanted to keep her nose out of Parker's business, let her tell her what she wanted her to know when she was ready, she couldn't seem to stop asking intrusive questions.

Parker's hands tightened on the steering wheel. "Sure. I also enjoy being with Brett. Not as much as you do, obviously. And I have other people I hang out with when we're not working." Her gaze briefly shifted to Corelli. She took a deep breath and continued. "I told Ndep I'd call her for dinner when I had a free night but she may be busy."

They were at Corelli's building but there were no free parking spots so Corelli used her remote to open the garage door. Parker pulled into one of Corelli's spots near the elevator. Her Harley and the one she'd bought for Marnie were under tarps in the adjacent parking spaces. Hopefully, she'd be able to ride in the spring.

As they rode up to her floor, Corelli cleared her throat. "Sorry, Parker, I didn't mean to pry."

Parker shrugged. "It's okay. Since I spend so much time with you and Brett and your family, I figured I could be more forthcoming."

While Parker set up the coffee pot and put out dishes, silverware, mugs and napkins, Corelli rummaged in the refrigerator for something to eat. She pulled out ham, salami, prosciutto, provolone and Swiss cheese, mustard, mayonnaise, lettuce and hot peppers. She sliced some tomatoes and onions then added them, bread and a bowl of cut fresh fruit to the table before sitting down.

They ate quickly, cleaned up and refilled their coffees. With Parker's assistance Corelli retrieved her aluminum flipchart easel, a fresh flipchart pad, and a box of colored markers from the closet. They set up the easel in front of the sofa in one of the loft's seating areas.

"So where do we start?" Parker asked as she picked up a marker.

Corelli thought for a minute. "Let's list suspects. I'll start. Senator Parker."

Parker's hand hung midair in front of the whiteboard. She looked over her shoulder at Corelli. "You really think he killed them? Would he have access to a gun?"

"Feeling protective of dear old uncle Aloysius?" Corelli grinned. "We both know the killer often reports the murder thinking it will make him look innocent. We don't have a motive or any evidence that he did it or has a gun, and we may have some evidence that says he didn't do it, but let's identify all possible suspects."

Parker wrote her uncle's name on the board and then added Reverend Wilkerson. "He certainly had a motive, he was in the military so he has the means, and he had opportunity. Gladiola left at ten so he had time to drive there, kill them and still be home by one a.m."

Corelli sipped her coffee and thought about Wilkerson as the killer. "But if the senator's story about two people running out of the house was true, who would have been with him?"

"Unless her alibi checks out, I would guess his wife, though Gladiola Foster is a good bet too. Both women are smaller than Wilkerson so that fits the senator's description," Parker said. "Both have motive and opportunity and either could have moved the girls upstairs while he shot the men." Parker added both women to the list.

Corelli stared out the window. "Although we confiscated twelve illegal weapons, who knows how many they have hidden at the church? So unregistered guns would probably be readily available to Wilkerson. Darnell Mason intrigues me. He seems too innocent in the middle of those people. He's ex-military and appears to have a relationship with Foster. He probably has access to the guns and no alibi for the time of the murders but I don't see a motive unless he loves Foster so much he'd kill for her."

Parker added Mason to the list. "What about Amari DeAndre? It seems like Blecker was trying to pull her into something sexual to benefit his business. That would be a strong motive to get rid of him. Plus she doesn't really have an alibi. Would she have any contacts that could get her an unregistered gun?"

Corelli stood, retrieved the coffee pot and refilled both their cups. "She said she asked her attorney to prepare a child abuse case against Blecker. We can check and if it's true, why murder him?" She stared at the list. "Actually, my money would be on Kelley Dexter, DeAndre's bodyguard. It's pretty clear she's in love with DeAndre. She's very protective and ex-military, plus she didn't know Amari was preparing to take on Blecker publically. I would bet *she* has a couple of throwaway guns stashed somewhere. And she has no alibi."

Parker's hand hovered in front of the whiteboard. "If we're looking for two killers as described by the senator, Dexter and DeAndre would fit the taller and shorter description. Do you think DeAndre has it in her to participate in killing, not just Blecker but two other men?"

Corelli sat and sipped her coffee. "My first inclination was to say no, but if they stumbled on them raping the children, she might have gone along with it. Maybe she brought the girls upstairs while Dexter did the deed?"

Corelli watched Parker jot down the two names. She would be objective but for the sake of her fans she hoped that DeAndre wasn't involved. "Let's add Ms. Marianne Phillips to that list. I would say she has a great deal of rage and a pretty good motive since he cut her out of his will. The missing-in-action Ernesto Servino is her alibi. We don't know how tall he is but he might be the other half of a duo. Maybe his motive is love of Marianne or love of money. We'll have to find out. Anyone we've missed?"

Parker stared into space considering, then refocused. "What about Dumayne's wife. She's admitted she's happy he's dead and still won't admit who she's been secretly meeting with."

"Hmm. I liked that she didn't try to hide how she felt about him. Maybe I'm not the most objective person at this moment but I don't think she has it in her. Running away seems more her style. And I don't mean that as a negative. Getting away from him while she could was probably the healthiest thing she could have done for herself. On the other hand, given the Atlanta connection between her and Mason, she might have paired up with him. Put her on the list and let's see what our stakeout and her mother give us." Corelli leaned back and put her feet on the coffee table. "What are your thoughts on the child trafficking ring now? Do you think they killed them?"

Parker frowned. "I think we've kicked that one to death. As you've said, the girls are valuable product and a link to the gang so it's not likely they'd have left them. And extremely unlikely they'd call to make sure we found them."

"Yet we have two dead girls who appear to be part of the ring so maybe our assumption that the traffickers wouldn't abandon the girls is wrong."

"Playing devil's advocate Corelli? The two dead girls can't talk but the three live ones might be able to identify those involved. Plus, leaving the girls and calling to make sure they're okay doesn't fit my image of these people."

"I agree. So we have suspects with reasons to kill Dumayne and Blecker but not Stanerd. Why?" Corelli said.

"First," Parker ticked off a finger. "Senator Stanerd's calendar didn't include the fact he would be in New York City Tuesday night or that he would be meeting with Senator Parker. Second, according to Ben Fine, Stanerd slipped away without telling anyone, including his security team and his wife, where he would be. Third, he traveled alone from Washington on Amtrak. Fourth, if he was the target, he could have been murdered out on the street somewhere. Why risk a home invasion where there might be lots of people?"

"If the killers were after child abusers, they got a bonus with Stanerd. My money is on Blecker and Dumayne as organizers or part of the trafficking ring but I would bet Stanerd was just a customer. And speaking of customers Blecker has thousands of pictures of various men raping children, a perfect setup for blackmail. It's possible that someone he's been blackmailing decided to end it and the other two were collateral damage."

Parker wrote "Blecker blackmailer?" on the board.

Corelli checked the time on her phone. "I think I'll go contemplate my navel now. Maybe I'll find the answer there. Let me get into my yoga things."

They hit some traffic on the way downtown so Corelli was a few minutes late. She hung her coat and hurried to the yoga room. She froze in the doorway, not sure what was happening. Three of the regulars had a guy down on the ground. Magarelli knelt beside him with a hand on his shoulder speaking softly. Corelli scanned the faces standing nearby and confirmed she was in the right room. Not sure what to do, she closed the door and leaned against it.

"Let him up," Magarelli said. The three men released the guy. He lay there a minute and then sat up looking dazed. Magarelli sat next to him. "We need to support Turk tonight, so no yoga. If you don't want to stay, leave now, but if you're staying, make a circle."

Curious, Corelli made a snap decision and sat along with the rest of the class. Had there been a fight or had Turk had some kind of attack?

Magarelli waited for everyone to settle. She made eye contact with each person, then turned back to Turk. "You want to tell us what happened tonight, Turk?"

He rubbed his hands over his face. "On my way here, I saw a guy who looked just like Corey, my...best friend. He smiled at me and suddenly I was back there, the night Corey pushed me aside and took the bullets meant for me. He died saving my fucking life. I loved him and I had to act like it didn't matter." He broke down, his sobs coming faster than he could hold them back. Corelli closed her eyes, pushing her emotions back and when she opened them Turk was wrapped in a group hug.

After he stopped sobbing, Magarelli looked around the group. "Anyone want to talk about losing a close friend or a lover over there? Remember the rule, what's discussed in these sessions stays in these sessions."

Corelli's mind filled with the image of Marnie, there one moment and gone in a puff of smoke in an instant. Her heart felt ready to explode but she couldn't speak.

Finally, Sarah spoke. "We were on a mission to rescue some guys wounded in a surprise attack. We came under fire and my helicopter was shot down. Everybody was killed but me. I was alive but pinned in the copter. The team sent to rescue us decided to take my leg rather than leave me to the enemy. I don't understand why I lived and they died. They were my best friends." She broke down and the woman next to her pulled her close.

A couple of others spoke about losing friends and then it was silent. Magarelli's gaze went from one person to the next. She hesitated at Corelli, probably reading the pain in her face. Without intending to, Corelli spoke. "My girlfriend and I volunteered to train Afghani police. We planned to be together forever but a couple of weeks into the tour, one of the trainees in Marnie's group showed up wearing an explosives belt. I walked out of the building to watch her work with her group. She smiled and waved, then there was an explosion and she was gone. I saw her die yet I can't seem to let her go." She didn't realize she was sobbing until Sarah and the guy next to her wrapped her in a hug.

Magarelli waited until Corelli stilled. "I too lost someone I loved while we were there." She looked around the room. "No one mentioned guilt. I feel guilty every day that it wasn't me."

One by one those who'd spoken, including Corelli, acknowledged their guilt at being alive.

The door opened and one of the instructors stopped short. "Oh, sorry, I have a class in here in five minutes." He backed out.

Everyone seemed to take a breath. "Everyone okay? I have to arrange for a replacement for my next class but I'd like Turk and anyone else who needs to continue to talk to meet in my office in five minutes." She stood. Slowly the members of the class followed. Corelli considered going but she'd had enough and Parker was waiting.

Magarelli grabbed Corelli as she headed for the door. "You sure you're okay?"

Was she okay? Not by a long shot. "I don't usually talk about seeing Marnie die but I'm good. Does the class often turn into a therapy group?"

"From time to time someone loses it and I can't just ignore it. Class members always have the option to leave. And we don't charge for the class." She put a hand on Corelli's arm. "I'm glad you stayed."

"I'm glad too." Though she was wiped out, she felt calmer, more centered. And she was curious. "Do you still have a therapy practice?"

"I do one-on-ones privately and I run PTSD groups but in a separate office. I try not to mix the two, but as they say, shit happens. You should consider a PTSD group, if not with me, with the VA; they're free either place."

"I'm thinking. Thanks again for tonight."

Parker had the car running and warm when Corelli left the building. Seeming to sense something, she eyed Corelli, but didn't comment. Once they were on their way uptown, Parker spoke. "Dietz texted. Phillips and her attorney will be in at eleven tomorrow. Shall I pick up you at six thirty so we can spend some time reviewing reports?"

"That's fine. I need to text Brett about dinner tonight. Are you staying?"

"No. I'm having dinner with Ndep."

"Enjoy." Corelli took out her phone and texted Brett.

After dinner they cuddled on the sofa with soft jazz playing in the background, Chiara's arms around Brett, her chin resting on Brett's shoulder, talking about the day. "What was Em like?" Chiara felt the surprise in Brett's quick intake of breath. In the almost three months of intense connection since she was shot, Chiara had never asked about Em. Brett seemed to get that it was meant to avoid talking about Marnie and she'd respected the unspoken pact. She'd promised she would wait as long as it took for Chiara to feel free to be with her and she was true to her word. No pressure.

Brett turned to look at Chiara. "Since you asked, I assume you really want to know." She tipped her head back onto Chiara's shoulder and closed her eyes. "She was passionate about learning, about teaching, about living every day in the best way she could. And about me. She was sometimes hilarious and other times extremely serious. She could be stubborn and pigheaded and sweet and forgiving and gentle. She loved sports and the outdoors. She played volleyball and baseball and even though she was short, basketball. She swam, hiked, ran and sailed. She was a terrible cook, mainly because it didn't interest her, but a lover of good food and good wine. She was kind and generous, always there for her students, her friends and her family."

Chiara kissed Brett's temple. "She sounds wonderful. How did you meet?"

Brett smiled at the memory. "At the beginning of my last semester in college the professor scheduled to teach my psychology class was badly injured in a car accident and Em took over. She was dark haired, dark eyed and sultry. One look into her eyes and I was hers forever. She took my breath away. In fact, the very first word she said to me was, 'breathe.' It was the same for her. But she was too ethical to get involved with a student and she kept me at arm's length until I graduated. When we got together she told me it was the hardest thing she'd ever done." She turned to look at Chiara again. "We had ten good years before cancer took her. I miss her every day."

Neither spoke for a few minutes. "Big shoes to fill."

Brett sat up and faced Chiara. She put her hands on Chiara's shoulders. "Don't you dare do that to yourself. Emily was wonderful. But I had the original, why would I want a carbon copy? If you need me to list everything I love about you I will, but just know this, it's you I want. I want all of your flawed, passionate, stubborn, kind and loving wonderfulness." She leaned in and kissed Chiara with a fire she'd always tempered before now. "I know I said I'd wait forever, but my body seems to have a mind of its own. I hope this sudden interest in my ex means you're working on us."

This is what she'd been missing. Her demand that Brett give her time, that they only be friends was keeping them from the relationship they both wanted. Marnie would have walked out if Chiara had tried to put artificial restraints on their relationship. "Wow. I like that." Chiara fanned herself.

Brett looked stricken. "I'm sorry. I overstepped."

Chiara kissed her lightly. "No, you didn't. We need to do more of that. I don't want to be just friends anymore. And I promise I'm working on us."

Brett caressed Chiara's face. "Tell me about Marnie. If you're up to it."

"I'm glad you said you miss Em every day because I miss Marnie every day. I still love her but I feel guilty because I also love you."

There. She'd said the L word.

Brett's eyes filled with tears. They kissed, then held each other. "I love you too, Chiara. It's not a competition. I believe the heart expands to hold as many loves as we are lucky enough to find in our lifetime." She cupped Chiara's face. "Do you compare me to Marnie?"

Chiara took Brett's hands. "No. I don't compare. But some differences and similarities are obvious. For example, Marnie, unlike you, had little patience for what she called my self-indulgent dithering. To her you were in or you were out. I doubt she would have put up with waiting for me. But she was playful like you and she and I laughed a lot, like you and I do. She was passionate about music of all kinds and she loved to dance. I know you enjoy classical music and jazz but I don't know how varied your taste is or whether you like to dance. She was strong and confident and proud and that's how I see you as well. She was bisexual and I was the first woman she was with. You're an out and proud lesbian with a long trail of broken hearts in your past. There are so many things. You're brilliant, quick-witted and intellectually curious. Marnie was also quick-witted and had an innate intelligence combined with street smarts. You're gentle and laid-back while she could be aggressive and in your face, though I think she would have mellowed. And like you she was kind and loving and generous and passionate, both temperamentally and sexually."

Brett squeezed Chiara's hands. "So you think I'm passionate sexually?"

Corelli nuzzled her neck. "I'm banking on it. And I plan to find out for sure when this case is over. I would love a couple of weeks sailing with you in the warm and sunny Caribbean."

Brett laughed. "Do you want to get away with me? Or away from the cold?"

"Well. It is pretty cold this year." Chiara punched her arm lightly. "With you, of course."

Brett yawned. "Oh, sorry, I need to get some sleep. So am I still relegated to the top of the covers?"

Chiara rubbed Brett's shoulders. "Do you think you can control yourself if we snuggle under the covers?"

Brett turned and tickled Chiara. "What about you, Detective. Can you control your urges?"

Chiara laughed and pushed Brett's hands away. "Hmm. Did I mention that like you, Marnie was extremely competitive?"

CHAPTER TWENTY-EIGHT

Parker grinned when Corelli and Brett walked out to meet her at six thirty in the morning. Corelli opened the front and back doors. Brett handed Corelli one of the thermos cups she was holding and slipped into the back. Corelli passed a cup to Parker before getting into the car. "We're dropping Brett at her place before we head into the office."

"You might want to read this on the way down." Parker unfolded a copy of *The Daily Post* and displayed the headline: **A Message in Blood at Scene of Triple Murder.**

"Oh, shit. We have a leak." Corelli held the paper so Brett could see the headline. "This was a bit of evidence we were withholding," she explained. "I'll read the article out loud."

The Daily Post has received an anonymous tip that a message was left for the police at the scene of the murder last week of Senate Majority Leader Harry Stanerd, Reverend William Dumayne and Republican billionaire Jake Blecker.

According to the tipster, the message, *Child Abusers Must Die*, was written in blood on a large mirror in the room where the murders occurred. The police routinely withhold information during an investigation so the *Post* was unable to confirm that such a message was found. But if it was…

Is it an attempt to smear their reputations? Or were they child abusers?

These three upstanding citizens deserve a professional investigation and a quick arrest of those responsible, especially in light of the slanderous nature of the alleged message.

Detective Chiara Corelli seems to be dragging her feet on this case. Perhaps she came back too soon from her sick leave and is not up to a full-blown investigation. Or perhaps her guilt over the death of her former partner, whom she put in the prison where he was murdered, is slowing her down.

Brett leaned forward. "I have to confess I never noticed before we met but it seems that damned rag is always ready to attack you. Is it because you exposed Righteous Partners or was there something else?"

"*The Post* has always attacked the police, especially women officers. A lot of the antagonism toward me in particular derives from Righteous Partners, fueled by Senator Parker's incendiary rhetoric." Though she knew Parker agreed with her, Corelli checked her reaction but seeing none, continued. "It's part of the job. Our last several cases have been high-profile and intense scrutiny comes with them."

The car stopped. Brett touched Parker's shoulder. "Thanks for the ride, P.J." She got out of the car. Corelli lowered the window and Brett leaned in and gave her a quick kiss. "Go get the bad guys. I'll figure out the arrangements." She turned and ran into her building.

"Arrangements?" Parker grinned. "You guys getting married?"

"Hardly. We're going sailing in the warm Caribbean as soon as we solve this case. So let's get on it."

Parker swung north onto West Street, heading to the stationhouse. "Nice article, huh."

Corelli wrinkled her nose. "About what I expect from *The Post*. The question is who leaked it? I don't believe it was one of us. Any ideas?"

Parker tapped her fingers on the steering wheel and considered the question. "Senator Parker claims he didn't see a message on the mirror. If we assume the murderers stopped to write the message after hiding the children, getting it out must be important to them."

Corelli grunted. "Pain in the ass. Now we're going to be hounded by the media demanding information."

As they pulled into the lot at the station, Corelli pointed to the large media contingent waiting along with a small crowd of police protesters across the street. Jimmy would be proud that the protestors were braving the cold to accuse her of his death but she would bet the media was there because of the leak. "And there they are."

"Ready?" Parker had parked and turned off the car. Corelli didn't move. "You all right?"

"Yeah. I was just remembering a documentary I watched about how to deal with dangerous animals you encounter in the woods."

Corelli could see Parker struggling to make sense of her non sequitur. "If you turn and run, the animal will chase you, but if you stand still, make yourself larger and slowly back away, the animal will leave you alone. I'm thinking that's also true of the media."

"Okaaay. So?"

"So, we hold an impromptu press conference outside in the cold like we did the other night, answer a couple of questions then go to work. Hopefully, they'll go away."

Parker matched Corelli's slower pace as they crossed the parking lot to the barricades. The chants got louder, the TV lights blasted on and questions were tossed at them. Corelli held up her hand and waited for quiet. "I'll answer a few questions."

Following the stunned silence a young reporter Corelli didn't know grabbed the moment. "Jen Wiley from New York One. Was a message written on the mirror at the scene of the murder? And are you pursuing the child abuse angle?" She extended her microphone.

"I can assure you we're following any and all leads but I can't comment on the crime scene or any details of the investigation at this time."

"Helen Dugan, Channel 29 News. Will you confirm that the police sometimes withhold information to trap the killer?"

"Thanks, Helen. Depending on the department, the investigators and the circumstances, information only the killer would know might be withheld in order to confirm the right person has been arrested."

She responded to several additional questions before calling on a smirking Andrew Baron. He must have a good gotcha. The Channel 43 reporter brushed his chin-length hair back before asking his question. "Is it true that semen was found on the bodies of the three men?"

Corelli felt Parker tense. She smiled. "Now Andrew, did you make that up or did you bribe someone to release a confidential autopsy report? You've been around long enough to know that even if your supposed inside information was true, I wouldn't comment on evidence in an ongoing murder investigation. Next question." She watched his face flush.

Phillip Melnick from the *Daily Post*, her least favorite reporter, smirked as he thrust his microphone at her. What little bomb did he have for her? "Okay, last question. Mr. Melnick?"

"Do you suspect the three men were murdered *because* they were child abusers? And are you pursuing this angle? Or just covering it up because of who the men were?"

"There will be no cover-up as long as Detective Parker and I are on the case. We will follow the evidence. If it leads to child abuse, you can be sure we'll go there. I'm insulted you feel you have to ask. Or should I say insinuate? Thank you." Questions and chants followed them as they crossed the street to the stationhouse.

When they entered the conference room, the few people already there were standing in front of the TVs watching replays of the interview. The rest of the team slowly wandered in and got down to work. Everyone was putting in extra time. Coffees in hand, Dietz and Watkins joined Corelli and Parker at the conference table.

"Nice job with the media this morning." Dietz held up the newspaper. "I don't believe this leaked from us."

"I don't either," Corelli said. "Get someone over to *The Post* to talk to whoever took the call. Maybe we can squeeze out some information about the caller. Same for Andrew Baron. Try to get the source of his information."

While Dietz made notes, Watkins opened his black leather notebook. "On my way in this morning, I got a call from a detective I know in Chicago. He saw a CNN feature last night about the murder of our three vics that mentioned the message in blood found at our murder scene. Apparently that exact message was written in blood on a wall at one of their murder scenes a month or so ago. The killer was the parent of a child raped by the murdered man and they caught him right away, so we don't have a serial but maybe a copycat. The murder and the message were plastered all over the Chicago media but didn't seem to get much national press."

"Got it," Dietz said, before she could ask. "We'll get in touch with CNN and see how they got the story."

"If it was mostly local coverage, our murderer may have been in Chicago during that timeframe. Do you have the dates? It could help narrow our list of suspects." Corelli turned to Parker. "Ideas?"

"Amari DeAndre comes to mind. She was touring right before the murders. I believe they flew in from California but I'll bet they performed in Chicago. I'll get the tour schedule so we can compare the dates."

"Let me check her website," Watkins said. "You guys go on."

Dietz passed a drawing to Corelli. "This is what the artist, T'Wayne Johnson and the others came up with. Recognize him?"

"No." She handed it to Parker. "You?"

Parker studied the drawing, then shook her head. "We should show it to the other security guards, the church elders, Wilkerson, Foster and Mrs. Dumayne. Oh, and Marianne Phillips and Ernesto Servino."

Dietz pushed an envelope across the table. "We found this under a pile of reports. It's addressed to you and marked confidential, so I didn't open it."

Corelli recognized the envelope. It was the one Darla North had left with articles she'd tracked down in Texas about a guy she thought was Dumayne. "Thanks, I'd forgotten about that." She pulled the envelope closer. "I'll go through it later."

Dietz waved a report. "Special Victims got a tip about a brothel in Queens offering children. It was empty when they raided it but they found a stash of child pornography that Maynard says looks like it was taken in the same room as the pictures she's been sifting through. Neighbors reported seeing lots of children going in and out. Based on the telephone calls we've been looking at, we were zeroing in on that area, so it seems likely that was the house we were looking for."

Damn, they were close. Police leaks and police informants playing on both sides made it difficult to surprise these houses but she wouldn't give up so easily. "It's likely their safe house was nearby so they could move quickly. Keep looking in that area."

CHAPTER TWENTY-NINE

Officer Samantha Dugan poked her head into the conference room. "Marianne Phillips and her attorney are here to see you, Detective Corelli. I put them in interview room two. Ernesto Servino came with them and is asking to see you as well."

"Thanks, Dugan. Put Servino in a separate interview room." She stood. "Ready, Parker?"

Parker gathered her things. "Are you planning to reveal what DeAndre said?"

"Only if we have to. Depending on her attorney, it might be possible to badger her into admitting something incriminating." She turned to Dietz and Watkins. "Sit in if you have the time."

Corelli knocked and opened the door to the interview room. She stopped short at the sight of Louden Warfield III leaning against the wall. The uber criminal defense attorney, known for demolishing police and prosecutors in the courtroom, flashed his killer smile, but that didn't make her feel any better. As usual his crisp, long-sleeve shirt was the exact color of his deep blue eyes, and though he was wearing his immaculately tailored blue suit jacket, his signature red suspenders peeked out. She and Parker had met him on an earlier case and they were on a first-name basis. She liked and respected him but his reputation as a cop killer and a case destroyer was well documented so they'd have to be very careful dealing with him. He extended his neatly manicured hand, exposing elegant gold and diamond cuff links. "Detective Corelli."

Corelli shook his hand. "Mr. Warfield, I can't honestly say I'm happy to see you."

He laughed. "Well, I'm happy to see you healthy and back at work." He extended his hand to Parker. "Detective Parker."

She smiled and shook his hand. Though the last time they'd met he insisted they call him Deni, Parker also kept it formal. "Mr. Warfield."

He waited for Parker and Corelli to sit before taking the chair opposite them. "Given your quick wits you've probably figured out that Ms. Phillips has engaged me as her attorney."

"Yes, we have." Corelli tipped her head toward Phillips. "Glad you could make it."

His presence changed the game. She was almost positive Warfield wouldn't let Phillips answer any questions that implicated her in the child abuse. She glanced at Parker and got a tip of her head, indicating she got it.

"So Detective Corelli," he said in his baritone voice, "my client couldn't explain exactly why we're here today. Can you fill me in on why she would need a criminal defense attorney at her side?"

Phillips looked as if she'd already won just by hiring him. Corelli intended to do her best to wipe that smug look off her face.

"Let's see." Corelli waited while Parker placed her notebook and pen on the table. "During the press conference announcing the murder of Mr. Blecker and two other prominent citizens, I asked for Mr. Blecker's family and friends to come forward to assist us because we had been unable to locate Ms. Phillips. She ignored that request but showed up one day at his mansion, identified herself to the officer on duty as Mrs. Blecker and demanded to go in to retrieve a few of her belongings."

Corelli watch Warfield make a note. "Though I knew they never married, I offered to send an officer to retrieve her belongings. When she refused to say what she needed I pointed out that she and Mr. Blecker had been in contentious negotiations for more than a year, that he had shipped all her belongings to her apartment and that he had changed the locks on all his properties so it would appear she didn't have a right to enter. She repeated the lie that she was his wife and said he had promised her half his estate, so she was calling a locksmith. She didn't know his will had been changed to exclude her and when I mentioned it she went into a rage, saying if he wasn't already dead, she would kill him." She stopped to take a breath. "A billion or two seems like a really good motive for murder to me." Phillips didn't react.

Warfield looked skeptical. "Unless you're accusing my client of murder, I don't understand why she needs a criminal defense attorney."

Corelli held a hand up. "According to Ms. Phillips, she separated from Blecker because he was fooling around with young women. I think the question that got us to this point, the one that led her to state she would only talk to us with her attorney present was…" She turned to Parker. "Please read the question, Detective Parker."

Parker thumbed though her notes. "Are you claiming you were unaware Mr. Blecker was having sex with children as young as six years old and trafficking them as well?"

Phillips sucked in air. Maybe she thought with an attorney present they wouldn't ask the question again.

Warfield opened the folder he'd placed on the table in front of him, scanned a page, and frowned. He looked up at Corelli. "In light of today's news about the *Child Abusers Must Die* message at the scene of the crime, I'm guessing you have some proof that Jake Blecker was having sex with children and was involved in sex trafficking?"

"We do."

He met Corelli's gaze, probably trying to judge her truthfulness. She wasn't above lying when interrogating a suspect, but she wasn't stupid enough to chance it with him. Who knew the release of the message would have positive consequences? Now he had to take the question seriously. She watched him make some notes.

He shifted slightly to look at Phillips, then turned back to Corelli. "Do you have proof that my client knew or was involved in these activities?"

"I need the answer to that question."

Corelli assumed Phillips hadn't told the attorney about the question or whether she was involved. She also assumed Warfield knew Corelli was too smart to lie with him in the room, so if she already had proof, there was no danger in letting Phillips answer— unless his client hadn't been honest with him. But since Corelli didn't say whether or not she had proof, it could be a trap. One of the things that made him a good defense attorney is that he didn't take anything for granted. "I'd like to speak to my client in private please. And," he looked at the mirror, "that means everybody."

Dietz and Captain Winfry joined them in the hall. Dietz handed them each a bottle of water. Winfry narrowed his eyes. "I hope you have proof."

Corelli grinned. "Even I'm not crazy enough to try to bluff Louden Warfield the third."

Twenty minutes later Warfield stuck his head out. "We're ready."

She wasn't sure just how far he would allow the questioning to go but just to be safe she turned to Parker. "Please read Ms. Phillips her Miranda rights."

Warfield must have warned Phillips to expect it because she was stone faced throughout, answered when necessary and signed without comment.

Corelli waited for Phillips to look up. "Detective Parker, would you remind Ms. Phillips of the question that prompted her to call for an attorney. I'd still like an answer."

Parker looked Phillips in the eye, extending the tension, then read the question. "Are you claiming you were unaware Mr. Blecker was having sex with children as young as six years old and trafficking them as well?"

Warfield kept his gaze on Corelli. "You can answer, Marianne."

"Do I have to?"

Warfield turned his steely blues on her. He didn't like to be blindsided by clients. He didn't need to know if they were innocent or guilty but he did require when he asked a direct question that he got a truthful answer. Apparently Marianne didn't get the memo or more likely she thought it only applied to the riff raff, not a rich lady like her. "Let's take another five minutes. And…" He glared at the mirror, "that means everybody. I want privacy."

They walked to the hall again. Dietz was grinning. "Oh boy, this is getting interesting."

Although they actually tried not to listen and couldn't make out the actual words, the gist of the conversation came through loud and clear in the raised voices blasting from the interview room. Fifteen minutes later a grim Warfield called them back in.

"My client will not be answering that question. Are there any other questions?"

"Not at the moment."

Phillips' lip lifted slightly, the beginning of a smile, but she quickly caught herself.

"But we do have some information to share," Corelli said. She waited until Phillips met her gaze. "We have a witness who will testify to Ms. Phillips' involvement in rape and child trafficking activities."

Her eyes wild, Phillips jumped up. "You're lying. There's no one who could testify against me."

"Sit, Marianne," Warfield commanded.

Corelli was confident he'd heard what she heard, not a denial of wrongdoing but a statement that no one could testify to her wrongdoing. His face grim, he met Corelli's eyes. "Who?"

Corelli hesitated a moment, listening to Phillips sucking in air as her anxiety escalated. She had no qualms about letting the bitch suffer, but when Warfield shifted his gaze from her to Phillips and back, then narrowed his eyes, she relented because she wanted to corner Phillips. "Amari DeAndre."

"The singer?" Warfield asked.

The color bled from Phillips' face. She slumped in her chair but then brightened.

"She signed an agreement. She can't testify." She directed the comment to Warfield.

Corelli waited a beat or two before shattering Phillips' bubble. "She can. And she will if necessary."

Warfield sighed. "Since I'm the only one here who doesn't know what's going on, I'd appreciate an explanation. What can Ms. DeAndre testify to and what agreement is my...Ms. Phillips, talking about?"

Phillips started to speak but he put a hand up. "It's a little late for you to fill me in, Marianne. I need the detective to explain what she has that implicates you in child sex abuse and trafficking."

Corelli gave him a moment to cool. She wanted to be sure he focused on what she was about to say. "When she was almost eleven years old Jake Blecker and Ms. Phillips became Ms. DeAndre's legal guardians. A few months later, they isolated her from her school, her friends and the singing, dancing and acting teachers she'd worked with for years by homeschooling her, bringing in new teachers, and ensuring she was never alone with any of them. Soon after, Jake Blecker raped Ms. DeAndre and did so repeatedly until she turned fifteen. Your client knew about it, and in fact, she told DeAndre it meant he loved her. In addition, Ms. Phillips and Mr. Blecker also prostituted Ms. DeAndre and other children to men who paid to rape them. Ms. Phillips was responsible for drugging and keeping DeAndre and the other girls quiet while they waited for the men to be ready to rape them. Ms. Phillips and Mr. Blecker also photographed hundreds of girls and some boys having sex with men whose faces were masked or not shown and sold the pornographic photos and videos."

Warfield was red-faced. Corelli couldn't tell if he was going to throw up or punch his client. She understood the urge to do both. A glance at Parker revealed the same urges. It was hard to think about even though they already knew the story. Phillips also looked like she wanted to vomit but probably for a very different reason.

"Why haven't I read anything about this?" Warfield asked.

"We're just uncovering the facts. I assume you and your client will keep this confidential so as not to interfere in the investigation."

"Of course." He shifted his icy blue eyes to his client. "And it's in Ms. Phillips' interest not to discuss any of this if she has any hope of cutting any kind of a deal with the district attorney's office. But what's this about an agreement?"

"Part of the price of Ms. DeAndre's freedom from Blecker and from his record company was an agreement not to reveal any of what I just told you. According to Stella Fortunato, Ms. DeAndre's attorney, the agreement only pertained to Jake Blecker and now that he's dead, even he's no longer protected. Fortunato said to give her a call if you want to discuss the agreement."

Phillips gasped. "He told me I was protected." She started to cry.

Corelli leaned back, not moved at all by Phillips' plight. They'd had calls about Blecker from people who knew and/or had dealings with him and they'd learned he was a cruel, abusive man who used people and cheated many out of wages and contracted amounts. After nineteen years one would presume Phillips had a realistic view of Jake Blecker's self-centered cruelty, she must have known what he was capable of, but she probably thought she was special.

Despite the flash of distaste she'd seen, Warfield slipped back into attorney mode. Being a criminal defense attorney required a strong stomach. "Are you willing to offer a deal?"

"I'll see if I can get ADA Brooks here today but any deal will depend on the information Ms. Phillips provides. I want a description of the trafficking organization, names and numbers for the traffickers, a description of the porn network and the names of anyone involved in the porn sales. I also want to know where the records for both activities are stored. Ms. Phillips is a flight risk so I'm going to book her. We'll contact you when ADA Brooks is available to meet." She stood.

Corelli waited for him to protest booking Phillips but he ignored it, apparently understanding they would spend a lot of time fighting a battle he would lose. Not only was there little sympathy for sex traffickers, but also, like Blecker, Phillips probably had multiple passports in different names stashed somewhere and was a high flight risk.

Phillips seemed to snap out of her daze. "Wait, you want me to stay in jail? No way. What the fuck am I paying you for, Louden? Do something."

"Sorry, Marianne, you heard the detective. You're a flight risk. We can try to fight it but it's likely you'd spend days in jail while we try to make a case for you not staying. And then lose. If you think you can get better representation, be my guest." He handed her a yellow legal pad and a cheap stick pen from a box he took out of his briefcase. "In the meantime, write down everything and anything you know. The more you have to offer the better the deal we can negotiate."

Corelli and Parker walked out, leaving Warfield to deal with the enraged Phillips.

"Good job," Captain Winfry said.

"Don't forget we got Servino waiting," Dietz said. "There are sandwiches in the conference room courtesy of the captain so stop by and have a bite whenever you finish here."

A few minutes later Warfield joined them in the hall. He blew out a breath. "What a clusterfuck. I always tell clients when I ask a direct question, I want the truth. And still they lie or leave out critical information." He took a deep breath. "Let me know when Natalie Brooks is available and I'll make it my business to be here."

Watkins joined them as they ate. "DeAndre performed in Chicago during the intense media coverage of the murder so presumably she could have seen or read about the message in blood left at that murder scene. But, of course, with the internet and cable news it's possible that even people who weren't in Chicago saw the message." He sipped his coffee. "However, we just got information about taxi usage in the area. The night of the murder Kelly Dexter was picked up by a taxi on Central Park West and dropped off on Fifth Avenue and Seventy-Fourth Street at eleven fifty-three. The taxi in the opposite direction deposited her on Central Park West at twelve twenty-five."

Corelli sat back. "Dexter makes sense. She's former military and no doubt has or knows how to get unregistered guns. She's clearly in love with DeAndre and very protective of her. And Blecker had threatened to force DeAndre to have sex to seal his business deal. I would kill the bastard myself." She threw the second half of her sandwich on the plate. "But I don't really see her being dumb enough to use a credit card to pay for the taxis. What do you think, Parker?"

"If she was angry enough to kill and tired from their redeye flight from California, she might not have been thinking clearly. But the evidence doesn't support her as the killer. The vics were found naked, possibly indicating they were interrupted while raping the girls, but the girls had no blood on them, and as far as we can tell, they didn't witness the murders. So a lone killer leaves open the question of who moved the girls into the closet? And if we believe the senator is innocent and telling the truth, he saw two people leave the house not one, and it's more likely the two people he saw did the deed."

"Let's see what Dexter has to say. She turned to Watkins. "Pick her up."

Dietz plopped down in a chair at the table. "Maynard went out for a walk but she left this for you." He handed her an envelope. "She heard you were interviewing Marianne Phillips so when she found an envelope labeled 'Marianne' in one of the boxes pulled from the safe, she figured you might like to see it. The original is in evidence but she made copies of the pictures for you."

The small manila envelope had Marianne written across it. She undid the clasp and spilled the pictures on the table. Parker and Watkins moved behind her. She felt the bile rise as she thumbed through five pictures, each showing a naked Marianne in bed with Jake Blecker while he was raping a child. She stacked them, slid them into the envelope and then closed the clasp. Parker and Watkins sat again. No one spoke for a few seconds. "Thank Maynard for me, Dietz. I think ADA Brooks will be happy to have these before we start negotiating with Warfield."

"One thing before you go in to talk to Servino," Dietz said. "He's a pretty good match to the sketch we got from Johnson."

CHAPTER THIRTY

Ernesto Servino stood as Corelli and Parker entered the interview room. Since he grew up in Sicily with her brother-in-law, she assumed he'd be short, dark and good-looking like Joseph. So his height, light hair, light eyes and pale skin surprised her even though she, her sister Simone, her nephew Nicky and her late brother Luca, exhibited the same genetic remnants of intermarriage with the Norman conquerors of Sicily. Any traces of Servino's humble beginnings were hidden beneath his fashionable haircut, neatly trimmed mustache and goatee, his finely tailored clothing, and his air of sophistication.

"Chiara." He extended his hand. "Joseph speaks highly of you and it's so good to finally meet you." The nails on his long, slender fingers looked professionally manicured and the large diamond in the ring on his pinky looked expensive.

In Sicily playing the family friend game might give him a get out of jail card. Not in New York City. Not with her. Besides, according to Joseph, they hadn't spoken in years. She ignored his hand and his comment.

"Sit, Mr. Servino," Parker ordered. His head swiveled toward her. He seemed surprised she was in charge but he dropped his hand and his smile and did as she ordered. Only the redness creeping up his neck betrayed his anger at Corelli's treatment. Good, they needed to get underneath that cool, self-satisfied confidence.

Parker stood beside the table looking down at the file in front of her as if reading something, then raised her gaze. "Do you know why you're here, sir?"

Nice touch, Parker. Let him think you respect him even if Chiara, his presumed Sicilian connection, doesn't. Corelli pretended to write something in her open notebook, drawing his gaze to her.

"I presume it has to do with Jake Blecker's death." Even his slight accent added to his worldly air.

"You mean murder, don't you?" His gaze swung back to Parker.

"Yes, his murder. I saw it on the newspaper, I mean the TV."

"If you saw it on TV you must have heard Detective Corelli appeal for assistance with the investigation from anyone who knew Jake Blecker. So why is it that it took almost a week for you to come in?"

"I guess I missed that part." When she didn't respond, he added. "Or I would have come in right away."

"What do you think about Mr. Blecker's murder?"

He seemed confounded by the question. Parker let him sit with it. His gaze wandered around the small room and seemed to settle on the two-way mirror on the wall to his right. "I guess I think it's sad."

"You guess?" She tossed the ball back to Servino. "How many years did you work for the man? And you *think* it's sad?"

"Thirteen." He kept his gaze focused over Corelli's shoulder, avoiding her eyes. "Uh, I am sad. Jake was very good to me. I was just a waiter when we met but he took me in and taught me about the world and how to get along."

"Where were you Tuesday night between eight and midnight?"

"Is that when he was murdered?"

Parker pinned him with her gaze. He tried to push his chair back but it was attached to the floor. "I was with Marianne Phillips at her apartment, having dinner."

"What time did you leave?"

He glanced at Corelli, maybe expecting some help, but she made no comment. "I didn't. I live there with her so we were together from about six o'clock until we went to bed about twelve thirty. After dinner I watched a movie while she took a bath, then we went to bed."

"How long have you been in a relationship with Ms. Phillips?"

He flushed. "About three years."

"So while she was still living with Mr. Blecker?"

"That's correct." He hesitated. "Look, he didn't care. He was done with her. For years they only had sex when…." He caught himself and seemed to search for the right word. "Rarely. Marianne was too much of a woman for him."

"So they only had sex after he raped a child? Is that what you meant to say?" Corelli tossed a picture on the table in front of him. Ernesto visibly recoiled at seeing Marianne in bed with Blecker while he raped a child. He didn't speak.

"Did he teach you how to rape children and then have sex with Marianne? Oh, let's not forget selling the children." Parker's voice was low but she made no attempt to hide her anger.

His gaze jumped to Parker. "I don't know what you're talking about. Their sex life has nothing to do with me. I don't have sex with children and I don't know anything about what Jake, what *they* did with children."

"Really." She paged through her notebook. Maybe you remember this." She held up two fingers on both hands, indication quotes. "'The morning after Jake raped me for the first time, Ernesto who had always joked and teased and talked to me, wouldn't look at me and avoided being in the same room. Not only had I been violated, I had lost the only caring person in my life.'"

He paled but maintained eye contact. "I don't know who or why but someone is playing you, Detective. Better check your sources before making such accusations." He folded his hands on the table.

"Oh, I'm sure of my source. And so are you, Ernesto. You allowed an eleven-year-old girl who trusted you, who thought you were her friend, to be raped that night and countless other nights for the next four years. That's brutal and disgusting but it wasn't just Jake raping her, was it? You and Jake and Marianne were involved in child sex trafficking."

She threw a copy of the sketch on the table. "In fact, you've been identified as the person who delivered children to people who purchased them."

He stared at the sketch. He swallowed but his voice was strong when he spoke. "I'd like to speak to an attorney."

"Come with me." Parker stood and moved toward the door. "You get one call." He stood and followed.

Corelli waited until he was at the door. "By the way, don't waste the call on Marianne. She's being booked as we speak."

He staggered. Parker grabbed him and led him out of the room.

Parker was grinning when she returned. "Nice touch telling him we have Marianne in custody. The person he called will get back to him so I told Dietz to hang on to him."

"C'mon, Parker, let's take a walk to the coffee shop around the corner."

Parker stared. "You want to go outside and walk in the freezing cold to get a cup of coffee?"

"I need to clear my head." She grinned. "I'm sure you'll keep me from falling and I'm not worried about the cold because I'm wearing the brand-new super duper silk thermals that Brett gave me last night. I can't imagine how she came up with that idea." She slipped into her coat.

Parker turned away but couldn't hide her grin. "Me neither but you know Brett is brilliant and she sees all."

"Hmm." Corelli wrapped her scarf around her neck and headed for the door. A few TV vans were parked nearby but no one was behind the barricades. "I guess no one bought them silk thermals, poor things."

CHAPTER THIRTY-ONE

Chilled but refreshed by the cold air, the walk and the coffee, Corelli and Parker entered the interview room where Kelly Dexter was pacing. "Why the hell am I here?" she spat as soon as the door opened. "Don't think I don't know that keeping me waiting in this claustrophobic room is part of the process."

"Please sit, Ms. Dexter. Sorry we couldn't get to you sooner but we've had a very busy day, and as you know, questioning suspects takes what it takes."

Corelli and Parker sat. Corelli put her notebook on the table.

Parker waited until Dexter took the seat opposite them. "Where were you between eight p.m. and midnight last Tuesday, the night Jake Blecker was murdered?"

She glared at Parker. "This is bullshit. I already answered that question. What do you really want?"

Parker took her time answering but Dexter had been special ops in the military and she didn't respond to the silence. "How about the parts you left out?"

"I don't know what you're talking about."

Parker stood. "You think about it. We'll stop by when we have a minute later tonight." Corelli walked to the door.

"Wait. I assume you got the taxi receipts?"

They returned to the table.

Dexter blew out a breath. "Amari told you Blecker called to tell her he wanted her to have sex with some guy. I didn't know she decided to go public with his abuse of her so I went there to warn him to stay away from her."

Parker looked skeptical. "You mean you went there to kill him, don't you?"

"No." Dexter's alarm was palpable. "I only meant to put him on notice that I would kill him if he didn't leave Amari alone. He was a vile bastard. I wouldn't have hesitated to kill him if he'd continued to bother her."

"Why don't you tell us what you really did that night?"

Dexter took a deep breath. "After Amari fell asleep, I slipped out of bed. It was twenty, twenty-five minutes after eleven by the time I got out of the house. With this bloody cold spell getting a taxi is almost impossible but I finally caught one on Central Park West. He crossed the park at Seventy-Second Street, went up Madison, turned on Seventy-Fifth and dropped me off on Fifth Avenue and Seventy-Fourth Street. I had just started walking toward Blecker's house when I saw two figures in dark clothes rushing toward me. I wasn't sure of their intentions so I drew my weapon, darted off the sidewalk and crouched behind a car. Apparently, they hadn't noticed me because they rushed past me, crossed Fifth, got into a car and drove downtown."

"What did they look like?"

"It was dark, scarves covered part of their faces, hats and gloves hid the rest. I thought it was two men until I heard their voices, then I realized it was a woman and a man."

"What else did you notice?"

She rubbed her temples. "The woman was slender and he was practically dragging her because she was lagging behind. I think... I think she may have been wearing heels."

"Did they say anything?"

Dexter closed her eyes. "She said, 'That was horrible.' He said, 'I'm glad I decided not to...' and I didn't hear the rest. He had an American accent of some sort but I can't distinguish them."

"What about the car?"

"It was parked on Fifth right at Seventy-Fourth so I could see the side but not the number plate. It was navy or black, I couldn't tell, but it had a dent in the rear fender on the driver's side."

"What happened after they drove away?"

"I waited a moment and then moved onto the path and walked toward Jake's house. A man rushed out to the sidewalk and jogged in the opposite direction toward Madison Avenue. It crossed my mind that Jake or someone on the block was having a party."

"Did the man come from Blecker's house?"

"No. He was down the block a bit from Jake's."

"Go on."

"I'd brought Amari's key to the house with me so I could scare Jake by walking in unannounced, but the door was wide open and music was coming from somewhere above, confirming my party theory. I was so intent on following the music I almost stepped in a pool of vomit before I got to the room with the three men dead on the floor in pools of blood and excrement. After I got over my shock, I was happy Jake was dead and couldn't hurt Amari anymore. I didn't know the other two men but since they were all bare-assed, I assumed they were perverts too. I thought about searching for the pictures of Amari that he threatened to send to the newspapers if she didn't cooperate, but it's a big house and I didn't want to be caught there so I left."

"Detective Corelli, please read Ms. Dexter her Miranda rights."

Dexter looked from Parker to Corelli. "I didn't kill them."

Corelli removed the rights papers from the folder in front of her but Parker held her hand out to stop her. "Why should we believe you? You had motive, means and opportunity."

"I'm former special ops and I assure you if I'd gone there to kill him I wouldn't have used public transportation and left a trail of receipts and a taxi driver who could identify me. Besides, I wouldn't have used a gun. I'd have grabbed him from behind, described in detail how and why he was going to die, and then I would have slit his throat and watched his terror as the life bled out of him. Maybe I would have stuffed his genitals in his mouth for good measure. But even if I'd gone to kill him that night, once I realized he wasn't alone, I wouldn't have done it. My days of killing strangers in cold blood are behind me."

Parker gazed at Dexter. She believed her and a glance at Corelli confirmed that they were in agreement. "You're a trained observer. What did you see in the room?"

"It was what I didn't see that's been nagging at me. It was obvious they'd had sex and girls' dresses were tossed in a corner so I assumed they'd raped girls before they were murdered. But what had happened to them? As for what I did see…" She closed her eyes and described the scene they'd found except there was no mention of the message in blood. She opened her eyes. "That's it. I left and caught a taxi on Fifth. I'd been gone about an hour and Amari never knew. I didn't kill them. But the scum deserved what they got and more. You can test my gun if you'd like and the one at home in the safe."

"What about your unregistered guns? You must have at least one if you thought you might have to kill him."

"I'm licensed to carry and my three guns are all registered. If I wanted to shoot him, I'd have found a throwaway." She met Parker's gaze. "But as I told you, I'd use a knife to give him a taste of the helplessness and terror the children feel when he's raping them."

The coldness in Dexter's voice chilled Parker. Would she ever feel so passionate about someone that she'd kill to protect her? Is that how Corelli felt about Brett? She blinked, forcing herself to focus. "You left something out, didn't you?"

"That's everything."

"You didn't mention the message."

Dexter grinned. "Oh, that. I couldn't resist. I want the world to know Jake Blecker was a child abuser and put the other bastards who abuse innocent children on notice." She stared at her hands. "I've held Amari many nights when she wakes up from nightmares about her abusers. Hearing about your experience, Detective Parker, helped Amari talk about what those bastards did to her but she's still filled with shame, as if she did something wrong." She blew out a breath. "Anyway, when I dipped that sock in blood and wrote that message on the mirror, I felt like I'd hit the lottery. I was disappointed there was no mention of the message in any of the papers or news reports so I made a couple of calls."

"Sock?"

"Yeah. I used one of their socks and tossed it in a bin on Central Park West. It wouldn't do to have you find my DNA at the murder scene."

"Did you also tip reporters about semen on the men?"

"Nope. Not me."

"Are you aware we could prosecute you for interfering with a crime scene and jeopardizing our investigation?"

"Yeah, though I suppose finding those three upstanding citizens naked in pools of blood means you have bigger fish to fry, as they say."

Parker glanced at Corelli and seeing the tilt of her head, proceeded as she'd intended. "You can go for now but if you breathe another word to the press or anyone about what you saw in that room, we will prosecute."

Parker opened the door and asked Officer Samantha Dugan to escort Dexter out of the stationhouse. She stared after them, then turned to Corelli. "The taxi receipt says she was dropped off at eleven fifty-three. The senator said he saw two people run out of the house before he walked to Madison Avenue and that fits with when she saw them. You know, for a few minutes I wondered whether Dexter was playing us, whether she'd used the credit card to pay for a taxi to throw us off because she would know we would think someone with her background was unlikely to make a stupid mistake like that. Then I realized she had no idea who would be investigating this murder, and if she got one of the 'let's do the easy thing' detectives, she would have provided the evidence to charge her."

"I had the same thought. Ask Dietz to check the CSU reports to confirm a sock was missing from the crime scene."

She watched Parker make a note. "Were you okay with her mentioning you sharing your experience?"

"It made me anxious but I've decided if I want others to talk about it, I have to be open with them. Sexual abuse is the dark, dark secret of our society that rarely gets talked about but many girls and boys are abused every day. Maybe this case will bring some attention to the issue," Parker said from the doorway. "So where does this leave us?"

"Where do you think it leaves us, Detective?"

"Well, *Detective*, in my humble opinion," Parker stretched, "though we would usually use something like the message to filter out the crazy wannabes who claim they did it, Decker wrote it after the killers left so it doesn't matter to the case. Other than raising questions from the media we'd rather not be bothered with right now, I don't think it matters."

Corelli grinned. "Actually, I think Warfield's knowing about the message helped us with Phillips."

CHAPTER THIRTY-TWO

"Hey, boss," Watkins grabbed them as they left the interview room. "The good news is we're getting lots of calls from women who read about the *Child Abusers Must Die* message and say they were abused by Blecker and Phillips and/or Dumayne. The bad news is that we're going to have to interview all of them."

Corelli turned to Parker. "Unintended consequences. And they may matter to the case." She turned back to Watkins. "Can we get more help from the Special Victims Unit?"

"Working on it," Watkins said.

"Unfortunately, I'm going to add to the workload. We need eyes on tapes from cameras on Fifth Avenue going downtown from Seventy-Fifth Street to Fifty-Ninth Street, on Madison Avenue going uptown from Seventy-Second Street, and a few blocks on Seventy-Second Street going east. We're looking for a dark car with a dented rear driver-side fender and two passengers somewhere between eleven-fifty and midnight."

Parker sat at the conference table and cleared the space in front of her by pushing one of the three file boxes toward the other end. Corelli did the same. "Any word from ADA Brooks or from Servino's attorney?" Dietz joined them at the table. "Brooks has been in court all day so I don't expect to hear from her till later. We haven't heard a peep from an attorney for Servino."

Dietz tapped the boxes in front of him. "These boxes contain stuff from Blecker's safe. Watkins and I looked through them this morning trying to figure out who would be best to review the content. Anyway, there's some pretty nasty stuff in here and we thought you and Parker should take a gander."

Parker grunted or maybe she moaned. Corelli felt like banging her head on the table. They had detectives trained to analyze these kinds of files. She closed her eyes and breathed for a moment. Dietz could be dramatic but he was usually on the mark and Watkins was always on the mark. She needed to pay attention. "Where do we start?"

Dietz pulled a hefty mailing envelope out of one of the boxes and placed it in front of her. "Start with this one." Aloysius Parker was scrawled across the large envelope in big bold black letters.

Dietz stood. "Call me and Watkins when you want to talk."

Parker slid her chair closer as Corelli pulled out the stack of papers. The top document looked like a magazine article, with pictures and sidebars. The title jumped off the page: **The Real Senator Aloysius T. Parker**. Parker moved closer and Corelli placed the article between them so they could read it at the same time. It was vicious. It started with his alcoholic mother who prostituted herself, recounted his time in a Harlem gang where he supposedly ruled the neighborhood with an iron fist and murdered a man during a liquor store robbery, it talked about his sister, Tasha, who had an illegitimate daughter and lived on welfare until she was murdered by her drug supplier. It went into great detail about his drug-addicted sister, Tiffany, who prostituted herself and her niece for drugs. It mentioned this same niece living on the street and eating out of garbage cans and his fighting to keep her from being adopted by a loving couple. Then it went into what Parker had told Corelli about his effort to remake himself in the image of white college boys.

There were damning interviews, all anonymous, with people who supposedly had known him in Harlem or in college and law school. Many of the college interviewees ridiculed him and described how he had been used and ridiculed by boys he'd thought were his friends. It hinted that he was involved with drug trafficking and laundering money for Righteous Partners. It also tore apart his career in Washington and attacked his effectiveness as a senator. His marriage was described as a loveless financial transaction between his wife's father and the senator and his activism was derided as racism and political opportunism since he did everything he could to be white. It was a well-written attempt to destroy him. Although she didn't care for the man, Corelli found it hard to read on a human level. When she'd finished, she sat back and waited for Parker to look up.

"So now you know the last bit, about my aunt selling me for drugs." Parker was pale, her voice soft. She pushed the document away and took a deep breath. "He's a self-serving, arrogant, condescending bastard and if even half of this is true, he deserves to be exposed."

Corelli wanted to say something to Parker about her being raped when she was six years old or younger, but Parker had already acknowledged the rape, just not the circumstances, so anything she said about it now would be gratuitous. "As you know, Senator Parker is not my favorite person and though I agree with you, we need to be extremely cautious. Most of the sources are anonymous and I'll bet some of those named don't exist."

She thumbed through the remaining documents in the stack, newspaper and magazine articles about him from the start of his career, a copy of the liquor store murder book, listing suspects, reports from investigators, written statements by people interviewed—most of them anonymous—payments to people for interviews, payments to the author.

She tapped the stack. "Based on these documents, Blecker hired investigators and a writer to produce the article, which I have no doubt he intended to use to blackmail the senator. I think we can assume the senator received a copy and it's what brought him to a late-night meeting at the house of a man he despised. This is a blatant attempt to destroy his life. It strikes me as a motive for murder."

Parker's voice was flat but strong. "It's definitely a motive for murder. I assume he could get a gun but I'm not sure he knows how to shoot."

As much as she hated the man for attacking her, Corelli had never seriously considered him a suspect but this was as good a motive for murder as any she'd ever seen. If the stories about his gangster youth were accurate, the senator might just have the balls to murder in cold blood. They would take their time to figure that out and/or find more evidence. "Good point. Let's look into whether he really was in a gang when he was younger or in a shooting club at college. If he's our killer he must have learned to shoot somehow."

The remaining envelopes in the three boxes contained damning information on some well-known people and others whose names they didn't recognize. All the envelopes, including those for Senator

Stanerd, Reverend Dumayne, and Marianne Phillips, contained incriminating photographs involving sexual abuse of girls. In Phillips' case, there were many pictures of her in bed with Blecker and girls who seem to range in age from six to fourteen and a stack of emails illustrating her roles in the sex trafficking and porn operations. In an email exchange with Blecker and Dumayne dated two days before the murder, Phillips objected to the idea of doing any more snuff movies even though they were a huge moneymaker because it was difficult to judge the amount of pressure on the girls' throats and the one they'd just done had resulted in losing two assets.

"Shit." Corelli handed the email to Parker. "I think this explains what happened to our floaters."

Parker read the email then left the room.

Corelli got up to get a bottle of water. When Parker returned they skimmed Ernesto Servino's file together. It contained records of arrests in Sicily and New York City plus recordings of him pimping children, pictures of him behind the camera photographing child rape scenes, plus e-mails documenting his role in trafficking and selling the porn.

Corelli separated those files plus Senator Parker's file from the others before waving Dietz and Watkins over. "Can we keep these five files locked up?"

"I'll find a place," Dietz said.

"Also, I would guess at least some of the men in those files," she pointed to the boxes, "are being blackmailed by Blecker. We need to interview them, find out about the blackmail and confirm their alibis for the time of the murder. And let's evaluate whether any of them can be charged with criminal activity, especially child abuse. I'd like to get as many of the bastards as we can."

Watkins tossed her a salute. "ADA Brooks is on her way and Warfield just joined Phillips. They're waiting for you."

"Couple more things. Have someone dig up the file on this murder in Harlem." She handed him the sheet from the senator's file. "Someone probably got paid to pass that page to Blecker's people. Find out who signed the file out recently. She stood. "I know I'm burying you guys in work but I'd like to see a copy of Senator Parker's driver's statement. I'm wondering whether he would commit murder for him."

Watkins' eyebrows shot up. "You think he, they killed—"

She patted his shoulder. "You know what they say. Everyone is a suspect until we prove them guilty."

He laughed. "Yeah, they say something like that."

"I heard that, Corelli." They all turned toward ADA Natalie Brooks standing in the doorway with her hands on her hips. "And you don't even look embarrassed." At five-feet-two the fifty-something prosecutor was often underestimated by those who didn't know her, but she was smart and tough and respected because she always strove for unbiased justice. Her warm and witty personality made her a pleasure to work with. Her chin-length, red hair neatly coiffed as usual, her brown eyes intense, she joined them at the table with a big smile. "Sounds like you guys landed a doozy. Isn't it a little soon for you to be back in the hot seat, Corelli? How are you feeling?"

Corelli laughed. "Health wise, I'm good. Case wise, we're all," she waved her hand indicating the entire room, "working our asses off as usual."

Not one to waste time, Brooks dove right in. "Looks like the child abuse angle is out of the bag. Have you made any progress on that? And from Dietz's somewhat cryptic call, I assume Marianne Phillips was involved."

Parker reviewed what they had on Phillips including money as her possible motive for murdering Blecker and then handed Brooks the envelope with the documentation Blecker had put together to blackmail Phillips. They waited while she thumbed through the pages and watched the color drain from her face as she examined the photographs of Phillips with Blecker and girls. She had tears in her eyes when she looked up. "If she knew he had this file it would be an even better motive for murder than money. In any case, it looks like you have enough to put her away for quite a while. Why are you considering a deal?"

Parker glanced at Corelli to confirm she should continue. "We believe she and Blecker were involved in a child sex-trafficking ring and a huge porno sales business. We also believe she can give us what we need to destroy both operations, plus the names of the wealthy and powerful men who participated. And that envelope gives us leverage to give her as little as possible in return."

Brooks slid the pile of papers back into the envelope. "How much fight do you think I can expect from Warfield?"

"She's repeatedly withheld information and lied to him," Parker said. "He's disgusted with her but he'll do his job and try for the best deal he can get."

Brooks turned to Corelli. "Do you agree?"

"Yeah. He'll hold his nose and do his job, but hopefully, he'll also push Phillips to give us everything she knows." Corelli stood. "Ready? Can't keep our guests waiting too long."

"Wait." Parker held up a hand as they started toward the interview room. "Shouldn't we take Phillips' file with us?"

Corelli looked at Brooks. "We've already disclosed that Amari DeAndre will testify against her if we go to trial. Do you think it's a good idea to show all our cards, Natalie?"

"We'll have to turn it over to Warfield at some point if we go to trial. But showing it now could convince her to give us everything she knows and avoid a trial. Maybe we'll get lucky. I'll play it by ear."

CHAPTER THIRTY-THREE

Warfield stood when they entered. "Good to see you again, ADA Brooks."

She and Warfield had faced off in negotiations and court many times and had a healthy respect for one another. "And you, Mr. Warfield."

He tilted his head. "My client, Marianne Phillips."

Brooks let her gaze settle on Phillips. "So what do you have for us, Ms. Phillips?"

"Ms. Phillips has written down what she remembers and I've had copies made for everyone so you can read it before we start." Warfield handed them each a copy.

Phillips' handwriting wasn't the best but Corelli understood enough to realize that the three pages had little of the information she needed to take down the trafficking ring. When the others looked up from the pages of notes, Corelli tossed her copy on the table. "I'm sorry to have bothered you, ADA Brooks. What we have here isn't worth the paper it's written on. Ms. Phillips hasn't given us a damn thing we don't already know. But it doesn't matter. We have enough evidence in that envelope in front of you to send Ms. Phillips away for a very long time. Forget a deal." Phillips and Warfield eyed the envelope.

Warfield put a hand up. He met Corelli's eyes. He knew what she was doing but he also guessed she was telling the truth. "What isn't there that you expected to see?"

"I want to know where to find the files with names, locations, logistics and financial arrangements of the trafficking network which Ms. Phillips worked for and benefited financially from. And the same detail on their porn operation. I want to know who murdered the two girls while making a snuff sex movie and I want to know about Ms. Phillips' role in both operations. Without all of that, forget it."

"Marianne do you have anything to add to what you've written?" Warfield asked.

"I can't add anything because I don't know what she's talking about."

Parker pulled the envelope to her and held it up so attorney and client could see Phillips' name written on it. "This was prepared by Mr. Blecker. We found it in his safe." She tugged a stack of papers out of it, thumbed through them, and then stopped. "This is an email thread between Mr. Blecker and Ms. Phillips discussing the trafficking organization. It's pretty detailed." She read a couple of sentences. This email discusses the death of two girls while making a snuff film and implicates Ms. Phillips in their murder. "And these might be interesting as well." Parker spilled a few photos of Blecker and Phillips in bed with girls on the table. "There are lots more in the envelope."

Warfield didn't attempt to hide his disgust.

"He forced me to do that and to work with him," Phillips said. "If I say anything, they'll have me murdered in jail."

"Who is *they*?" After a moment of silence, Corelli turned toward the door. "Collect the evidence, Parker. We're done." She opened the door.

"Wait," Brooks commanded. Corelli stopped and Brooks turned to Phillips. "Ms. Phillips, if you give us everything, and I mean everything, that you know about this group and your pornography business, and you agree to plead guilty, we may be able to avoid a trial and keep your name out of anything to do with the trafficking." She glanced at Corelli. "Is that all right with you?"

It seemed like a good solution to Corelli. They got Phillips and the information they needed to get the others, but she wasn't sure. She needed former ADA Parker's advice. "What do you think, Parker?"

"If she agrees to cooperate for as long as we need her and we get to sign off on the deal once we see the evidence provided, it would work for us."

"Mr. Warfield?" Brooks threw the ball to him.

"Marianne, in either case you'll probably do substantial jail time, but if you assist with the case, your name will be kept out of the trafficking takedown and I'm sure your cooperation will be taken into consideration at sentencing. Do you want to speak privately or are you ready to proceed?"

Phillips gazed at him, looked at each of the three women and then took a deep breath. "I'm ready. But could I have a cup of coffee and something to eat?"

The tension went out of the room. "Let's take twenty," Brooks said.

When they reconvened, Corelli, Parker and Brooks took turns questioning Phillips and bit by bit, dragged information from her. After four hours during which Warfield only interrupted when he felt it necessary to protect his client's interest or to suggest a break or dinner, he stood. "That's all for tonight. Ms. Phillips is exhausted and so am I. Can we pick this up late tomorrow morning?"

The detectives agreed. Brooks checked her schedule. "Eleven is good for me." Everyone agreed. Parker volunteered to take Phillips to a cell for the night. Phillips looked like she might protest but then her shoulders slumped. "I guess this is my future?"

Warfield looked sympathetic. "I'm afraid so, Marianne. The police got a search warrant and found multiple passports under different names for you and Mr. Servino in your apartment. And since it's likely you have others stored elsewhere, there's no way a judge would grant you bail."

As she walked to the conference room to wait for Parker, Corelli turned on her phone. She had a message from Dietz. "Put the envelope with Phillips' information in the safe." He left the combination.

Lemoine, the detective in charge of the overnight analysis teams, greeted her. "Corelli, Dietz wanted me to point out the safe he got for highly sensitive information." He led her to a chin-high safe in the far corner. "He said you would have the combination."

"Thanks, Lemoine. I'll take it from here." She listened to the message again, entered the combination, and placed the envelope on top of the others.

"I'll meet you outside," Parker said when she arrived at the conference room.

Corelli wished she could close her eyes and be home in her nice warm apartment. But unless she was going to sleep at her desk, putting the heavy winter gear on and walking to the car was her only option for now. She really was starting to long for sunny beaches.

Parker, thankfully, continued to ignore her protestations that she didn't need the car warmed up. "You know Parker, after listening to Phillips talk about Blecker entering names in ledgers that only he saw and used, I'm thinking there has to be another safe in the house. Blecker was smart. He knew if anyone found the safe in the library, they would assume they had everything so keeping the really important stuff separate would protect it and ensure he had what he needed to continue to operate. If he referred to these ledgers frequently, and it sounds like he did, he would want them in a convenient place nearby."

Parker didn't comment until she'd stopped the car in front of Corelli's building. "That makes sense. Should we search ourselves or send a team?"

"We should be there but a team would make the search go faster. I'm thinking the most convenient place for access to the books would be somewhere on the same floor as the library where the big safe is, but I want to search every room. Let's see if we can get Detective Paulie Massetti and a couple of our guys to meet us. Ask Dietz to arrange for Serena Lopez, Massetti, Kim, Forlini, Watkins and one or two others to meet us at Blecker's house at eight tomorrow morning."

Parker pulled out her notebook and jotted down the names. "It seems wicked out there. Do you want me to drive into the garage?"

Corelli felt the rage rise into the throat but she closed her eyes and swallowed it. Parker was trying to take care of her and she was just about to shred her for being kind. Exhaustion was no excuse. She took a couple of yoga breaths. "No thanks. The good news is I have river views. The bad news is I'm close to the river and the wind off it is bitter. I'll just make a dash for it. See you at seven tomorrow. Thanks." She held on to the door as she exited the car, trying to keep the wind from using it to knock her over. She didn't have to look back to know Parker would be out of the car and standing in the street, weapon drawn, to protect her. Parker must be having a good laugh since between her aching leg and exhausted body, dashing was not a word that could be applied to her stumbling gait. She stepped into her lobby, pulled the door closed and turned. Parker was back in the car, but instead of laughing, she was looking straight ahead and talking on the phone.

CHAPTER THIRTY-FOUR

While she was awake in the middle of the night, she thought a lot about the senator as the possible killer. No doubt that article would ruin his career and the life he'd so carefully constructed. But would he murder three men to prevent it from being published? It definitely was a motive but a motive wasn't proof. Then there was the matter of the gun. Assuming he knew where to get one, and assuming he had the article in advance, did he bring the gun to the meeting because he intended to kill Stanerd? The only scenario that made sense was a two-person team, one to kill, one to deal with the girls. Given his aloofness and condescension she doubted the senator had friends or lovers willing to commit murder or act as an accessory to murder for him.

She continued ruminating about the senator while she fought off the kittens, dressed, made coffee and pulled a couple of bagels from the freezer. Having his story about two people leaving the house confirmed by Kelly Dexter supported the theory that those two were the killers.

She handed Parker her usual thermal mug of coffee and the toasted bagel with cream cheese she'd prepared. She wasn't sure when it had become part of their morning routine for them to share coffee and sometimes breakfast in the car, but they did. Parker took a couple of minutes to eat part of the bagel and drink some coffee before heading uptown to Blecker's mansion.

Corelli's mind wandered back to Parker's uncle as the murderer and that led to thoughts of Parker's mother, his murdered sister. What had that twenty-something lawyer who aspired to be superior, to gain wealth and status, thought about his penniless, unmarried sister with a child? Did he see her as a blemish, a weakness that might be used against him? According to Parker's biological father, Randall, Aloysius had ignored his calls and messages when he came back after boot camp to locate Tasha and ask why she'd stopped writing to him. Parker's life would have been very different if Randall had found Tasha and they'd foiled her mother's plan to punish her for having a man who loved her and for wanting a decent life for herself and her daughter. Tasha's killer had spared her three-year-old daughter just as the killer on their case had spared the girls. Would Senator Parker have murdered his sister yet let his niece live?

"You seem deep in thought this morning."

Corelli jerked to attention. "Believe it or not, I've been obsessing about your uncle for the last couple of hours. Do you think Randall could give us some background on him?"

Parker took a moment to consider the question. "Probably. Randall knew him when they were growing up. And Jesse could help too. He can tap into lots of people from the old neighborhood."

Officer Twilliger greeted Corelli and Parker with a huge smile when he opened the door to Blecker's house. He listened attentively and made notes when Corelli gave him the names of the detectives she was expecting and instructed him to call if anyone else showed up.

Serena Lopez was the first to arrive.

"Thanks for coming, Serena." Thinking the irony of storing the book of rapists' names in the room where they were committing their crimes might have appealed to Blecker, Corelli led the way down the hall to the room where the murders had occurred. The stench had lessened but the message in blood was still on the mirror. The mattresses and the sofa cushions had been stripped but blood and other body fluids had seeped through and left dark stains.

Corelli and Parker started with the mirrored wall. It was one huge sheet of glass and they quickly determined, not a likely place for a safe. They removed pictures and smaller mirrors from the other three walls and checked behind them. They were about to start on the floor when the burst of voices told them help had arrived.

Corelli briefed the team, showed them the safe they'd found behind the bookcases, then assigned two detectives to check the floor in the sex room and sent two more teams to start on the living space on the floor above. Since her logic told her the safe was most likely on this floor, she kept Detectives Massetti and Kaminski from the robbery unit with her and Parker.

"The library is the most likely place for a second safe and I think you two," she dipped her head toward Massetti and Kaminski, "should start there. Parker and I will do the recording studio and the practice room. When the guys in the sex room finish, we'll have them move on to the hallway. Any questions?"

"Sounds like a plan," Massetti said as he and Kaminski disappeared into the library.

Corelli and Parker searched the small amount of wall and floor space in the recording studio and carefully examined the equipment but they didn't find a safe or a secret storage area so they moved on to the practice room. It was large but it didn't contain much furniture. They started with the wall that contained Amari DeAndre's gold records. It turned out that the framed records weren't just hanging on the wall. They were locked into rails on the bottom and the sides, making it difficult to remove them. The clear outline of a small safe was visible under the third gold record. Corelli stared at it. "Blecker was a tricky bastard. Let's remove everything from the walls to be sure this is the only one." Just as they exposed another safe in the floor under the piano, Massetti came in. "We found it in the library," he announced, as he entered. He stopped short. "Whoa, what have we here?"

Lopez videoed Massetti and Kaminski opening the three safes and Corelli and Parker placing the contents of each safe in an evidence box labeled to protect the chain of custody. They'd found four books. One contained the codes, names, addresses, banking information, and whether the men who paid to rape the children preferred girls or boys; another had documentation on each of the girls and boys; a third appeared to be a record of transactions with dates, times, locations, men and children involved and prices and the fourth looked like a record of blackmail payments. Each book was placed in a separate evidence bag with separate chain of custody documentation. The safes also contained more cash, several safe deposit box keys, passports and credit cards in various names for Blecker, plus more document-stuffed envelopes clearly meant for blackmail.

Just as they were getting ready to leave, another safe was found in the bedroom on the second floor. Deciding they could go through it quickly, Corelli led her little group of safe crackers and documenters upstairs. The contents, which included financial records, lists of outlets, and buyer details related to the porn operation, were packed into an evidence box. The small, black leather three-ring binder Parker pulled out was placed into its own evidence bag.

It was getting late and Corelli didn't want to keep Warfield and Brooks waiting so she left Watkins in charge while the teams continued checking every room in the house for additional safes. Parker signed for the four boxes and five books they were taking to the stationhouse.

On the way downtown Corelli looked at one of the books. Her breath caught. She shouldn't have been surprised to find a best-selling author, a bishop, CEOs of major corporations, a director in the FBI, a cabinet member, two diplomats, and a few senators and representatives among the names she recognized. But she was. Next she picked up the small, black leather three-ring binder. Her heart skipped as she flipped through it. "Parker." When Parker glanced at her. "This is even bigger than we thought." She showed her the notebook. "It's organized like a huge international corporation. And this is the corporate handbook. It documents the structure, identifies all the locations around the world, and names the leaders and next-level people at every location. It's everything we need to bring down the fucking traffickers. The top level is called the Triumvirate Sexualem Parvulus and is run by three men whose names I don't recognize. The world is broken down into Petit Triumvirates and three people run each. The United States is divided into six of these Petit things. Well, well, well. The leaders of the Northeast United States Petit Triumvirate are Jake Blecker, Marianne Phillips and William Dumayne. They have satellite organizations in all large east coast cities, each with an Operations Manager who actually runs the business. Ernesto Servino is the New York Operations Manager."

Parker's jaw dropped. "I'll be damned. Phillips has been playing us."

Corelli couldn't recall ever hearing Parker swear but she had to admit this discovery and Phillips' attempt to get away with lying about it was astonishing. "This is huge. Way too big for us. The FBI has the resources and the international connections to get it done. But one of the names in here is a big deal in the FBI so if we don't get it to the right people, it will be buried."

"Should we have Jess call Ben Fine?"

"Let's touch base with Jess again to confirm he believes we can trust Fine to break this thing wide open." Corelli closed the book and put it back in its evidence bag. "But we need to be careful. The originals will be held in evidence against Phillips and Servino and who ever else we pick up, so you and I will make copies for the FBI and for us. And we'll also review the books together so we're clear on what they contain in case something leaks and it gets dangerous. Do you have a safe in your apartment?"

In the lot at the stationhouse Parker found a spot close to the front door. "You think it's that dangerous?"

"It could be. A better place for the safe would be Jessie's house so if anything happens..."

Parker's jaw tightened. "Jessie is a good idea as long as it won't endanger Annie or him."

Corelli was pleased that Parker didn't flinch in the face of potential danger if their names were connected to the takedown of a huge and no doubt vicious gang of traffickers. "No one would have to know he has copies in his safe. I'll ask Brett to put copies in the safe in her office."

Parker gazed out the windshield for a second before nodding her agreement. "Shouldn't we involve the chief and the commissioner in the decision? Or should I ask, when should we involve them?"

"Once we've made the copies, reviewed them, put them in safe places and confirmed Ben Fine is trustworthy, we'll meet with Broderick and Neil to show them what we have and tell them our plan." Parker's shoulders dropped, no doubt relieved to not go rogue on turning this over to the FBI. "How about we go finish with Phillips and take care of Servino."

While Parker went in to get a dolly to move the boxes, Corelli thumbed through another of the books. It was a list of the children in order by the codes tattooed on their heels, and contained a name, usually just a first name, a place, probably where they came from, a price for those they'd bought, the name of the source and disposition which given the ages of the earliest entries was probably where they went when they aged out of the children's market. This information could facilitate returning some of the children to their families.

Parker pushed the dolly with the evidence boxes and Corelli carried the five books. The door wasn't far but the pounding wind made progress difficult. Corelli kept her eyes down to avoid icy spots but she looked up when Parker put an arm out to stop her. "They're back."

Corelli followed Parker's gaze to the small group of demonstrators and the equally small media pack across the street. Her stomach tightened. She should have expected them but her excitement about finding the books had pushed it out of her mind. "Tomorrow is Jimmy's funeral. I know it's not safe but I'm thinking of going, not for him, but for his wife and kids."

"Think, Corelli." Parked spun to face her. "Your presence will cause a disturbance, or worse, at the funeral parlor, church or cemetery, wherever you choose to go. You'll be the focus, not Jimmy, and you'll ruin the day of mourning for Carol and his kids. Call Carol and express your condolences. And if she's willing to see you, I'll drive you to see her late some night when no one else is around so you can actually talk."

An officer walked out the door and Corelli pushed past Parker into the warmth of the station. She was freezing. Parker was right. Her guilt had pushed her head up her ass so far she wasn't thinking clearly. It wasn't about her. "You're right. Thanks."

ADA Brooks and Detective Maynard were chatting at the conference table when Corelli and Parker entered. As they approached, Maynard greeted them, smiled at Parker, then sauntered back to her workstation. "Detectives," Brooks said. "I'm early so we can discuss where you want to go with this." She handed each of them several typewritten sheets. "These are the main points from yesterday's discussion with Phillips."

Corelli scanned the pages. "We have proof that she lied to us, that she's deeply involved in the trafficking organization and that it's a huge international operation, not local, as she said. As far as I'm concerned, a deal is off the table. The only information we need from her is how things worked day-to-day but if she won't give it to us, I believe Servino will. I'd like to confront her with the facts."

"You're not going to show me this proof?"

"I think it's safer if you don't know right now."

Brooks' eyebrows went up. "Really? You think someone might try to kill me if I know the details?"

Corelli met her gaze. "Trust me."

Brooks looked from her to Parker and seeing an equally grim face, nodded slowly. "Let me scan it so I know what I'm talking about. It'll also help me formulate a case against Phillips and whomever else is involved."

Corelli wavered. She knew Brooks was trustworthy but she wanted to limit those who knew details.

Parker spoke up. "I think Natalie needs the gist of it so maybe you could give her an overview."

An overview would probably be safe. "Okay Natalie, but nothing in writing, not even in your notes. I'm serious. This could be deadly," Corelli said. "Let's find an empty room and I'll give you the highlights. Once we've got it under control, you'll see everything."

It only took fifteen minutes to brief Brooks but they sat and talked about it a few minutes more. "Let's go talk to Phillips and see how much she'll reveal once she knows we're onto her."

They found Warfield talking on his phone, ignoring Phillips. Corelli sensed tension in the air and presumed Warfield had tried to talk some sense into his client. Phillips eyed them warily as they settled at the table but averted her eyes at the intensity of Corelli's gaze. She jumped when Corelli's voice broke the silence.

"So let's finish this. Ms. Phillips, you've repeatedly lied to us. You named Dumayne and Blecker as the head of the trafficking operation but you failed to include your name as the third member of the Petit Triumvirate." Phillips turned ashen. "And you lied when we asked if the trafficking operation was part of a larger, national group. Actually, it's part of the Triumvirate Sexualem Parvulus, an international group." Phillips swayed and would have slipped off her chair if Warfield hadn't grabbed her.

As red faced as his client was pale, Warfield appeared ready to kill someone. "What are you talking about?"

Corelli turned to Phillips. "Perhaps Ms. Phillips wants to enlighten you because we're done. Our offer of a deal is off the table. Ernesto Servino, Ms. Phillips accomplice and boyfriend, will be able to give us all the information we need on the day-to-day operation. The proof we have on her trafficking activities will put her away for a long, long time." Corelli shuffled her papers. "And then of course, there are the possible murder charges. First of the two girls who died making a snuff film so Ms. Phillips and friends could make even more money than they did prostituting them. And, it seems to me that retaining control of two lucrative businesses like selling children for rape and selling child porn is an excellent motive for murdering your partners." Corelli took a breath and glared at Phillips. "So was Senator Stanerd collateral damage or was he part of it?"

Phillips' eyes were wild. Her breath was coming in short gasps. "I'm going to vomit."

Brooks shoved the wastebasket at her.

Warfield looked furious. "Let's take a ten-minute break to allow my client to regain control."

It pleased Corelli to see Warfield responding to Phillips the same way her team responded. Every criminal lied about what they'd done but they eventually accepted reality and cooperated with their defense attorney but Phillips had continued to stonewall him. He was too professional to just walk away but if he didn't get a grip on his rage, they'd have another murder on their hands.

Brooks glared at Corelli. "I didn't think you were going to mention the potential murder charges. Can you prove she killed those three? And the girls?"

Corelli held her hands up as if to ward off an attack. "We've been so focused on the trafficking that we haven't seriously considered her for the murders but I meant what I said. It seems like a good motive to me. What do you think, Parker?"

"We were thinking she facilitated his raping children but was on the sidelines of the business. And being in the middle of a dispute over money didn't seem like a strong enough motive. But this new information puts her in a different category. Now we know she was playing in the big leagues, running a large-scale criminal operation, and if changing the locks was part of his plan to push her out, I'd say it's a very strong motive. But I can't think of anything we've found that points to her. As for the girls, her emails implicate her."

Brooks leaned in close and spoke so only the two detectives could hear. "So are you really ready to walk away from her on the trafficking?"

"I believe we can squeeze Servino to get the details on the local organization. Unless Parker tells me I'm wrong or Phillips offers us lots more about the workings of the upper echelon of the Triumvirate, I'd say we walk. Parker?"

"I agree." Parker leaned against the wall, hands in pockets. "What's your take, Natalie?"

Brooks stared into space for a moment. "I don't have all the facts, but if she's lied so far why would we believe her now? I wouldn't offer her a deal. But if she gives you what you need, I'd offer to put in a good word with the judge, contingent on proof that she didn't lie and that it actually helped bring down this, um, triumvirate."

When they returned to the room, Brooks explained the terms. Warfield pushed for more but seeing they weren't bluffing, advised his client that she had lied so often that this was as good as it was going to get. Phillips agreed to write down the information Corelli requested and they left her with another yellow legal pad and stick pen.

When they were down the hall from the interview room, Warfield stopped them. "Sorry about wasting your time and mine. Some clients think they're smarter than everybody even though they hire the smartest and best criminal defense attorney in the state." He winked. "Maybe the country." As he walked away he whispered, "I owe you."

Parker laughed. "Wow. He owes us. A Warfield chip is like gold."

Corelli punched Parker's arm. "Yeah, that and a Metro Card will get us on the subway." She turned to Brooks. "We'll call you when we see what she comes up with."

"Do you need me with the other one, Servino?" Brooks asked.

"Nah. We have enough to encourage him to share."

Servino rolled over quickly. He'd settled for a public defender when he couldn't find anyone else, and though the young attorney tried to intervene, Servino panicked when they read him his rights and confronted him with their knowledge of the Triumvirate Sexualem Parvulus and the Petit Triumvirate. Hearing that Phillips was in custody and talking spurred him on to share. At first he painted himself as just a tiny cog in the operation, but after they let him know they were aware of where he fit, there was no stopping his verbal diarrhea. Although the attorney kept bringing up a deal and they kept saying it wasn't possible, Servino did a brain dump of everything he knew about the workings of his part of the machine and about the Phillips, Blecker, Dumayne Triumvirate.

CHAPTER THIRTY-FIVE

"Yo, Corelli, we got a hit on the camera search." Dietz handed her a couple of grainy photographs of a black car, one showed the dented rear fender and the other the license plate. "It's a Mercedes registered to the Harlem Calvary Church of Christ, and according to their records, it's assigned to Darnell Mason, one of the supervisors of the church's security guards. The second person in the car appears to be a woman. It may not be related but Detective Kim's nights watching the Dumayne house have paid off. A guy picked up Mrs. Dumayne late last night and brought her back around five this morning. She got a good look at him and ran his plate earlier. It belonged to that Mercedes. She identified Darnell Mason from his driver's license."

"Pick them up. Parker and I are going out for coffee and then we'll find a quiet place to think and read the reports you've received in the last few days. And Dietz, please get me the earring that was found in the closet with the girls."

"Sure thing. We were just getting ready to call in a coffee order so unless you're dying to go out, give me your order."

Corelli didn't hesitate. The air would feel good for five minutes and then she would be freezing. "I'll have the biggest black coffee they have and a plain donut."

Dietz made a note. "What about you, Parker?"

"I'll have a large cappuccino and a pain au chocolat."

"A pan of what?"

"It's like a croissant but with chocolate in it. You do know what a croissant is, don't you, Dietz?"

"Don't be a wiseass, Parker." Dietz added her order to his list. He handed a stack of reports to Parker. "The captain is out of the office this afternoon if you want privacy. I'll have someone bring the coffee there when it arrives."

Parker sat on the sofa in Captain Winfry's office, notebook out, yellow pad ready while Corelli paced and stretched, trying to limber up after so much sitting. "What did Jessie say about Ben Fine?"

"When I explained what we have and how we want to handle it, he reiterated that he'd trust Fine with his life, and Annie's and mine. He's absolutely sure Fine will not let politics get in the way of breaking up the trafficking ring. Jessie is going to arrange a meeting as soon as Fine's available." Parker watched Corelli bend from the waist. "Any thoughts on how to present it to Fine?"

Corelli straightened and dropped to the sofa next to Parker. "I've been thinking about that. Verbally, without giving him the books or anything in writing. Once he's on board, we go to Neil and Broderick. Hopefully, they'll rubberstamp our plan so we can turn it over to Fine and cross our fingers."

"Will Fine go for that?"

"Does he have a choice? This will be the biggest FBI takedown operation in I don't know how long, and we have what's needed for them to pull it off. I think he'll play by our rules, at least until we give him control."

Parker laughed. "You're right. I hope we get to play some role."

"We'll make that part of the deal. But for now we have three murders to solve. Ironically, I thought we'd solve the murders before we figured out the trafficking, but what do I know? Let's see if we have anything helpful." Corelli picked up a report.

The silence as they made their way through the stack of reports was only interrupted by the delivery of their coffees until Parker spoke. "This might be what we're looking for. Forlini was finally able to catch a couple of Blecker's neighbors at home." Corelli looked up. "A Mr. Savage coming home sometime after ten o'clock the night of the murder saw Phillips and Servino leaving the house. He stopped to watch because they were yelling at someone in the house but he couldn't see or hear the other person. They drove away in a car idling in front." Parker jotted a note on the yellow pad in front of her. "That seems to indicate someone in the house was alive, but of course they could've been faking it to create that impression."

"Interesting." Something niggled at Corelli. "Didn't we have something that told us they were still alive at 10:15?"

Parker thought for a minute. "You're right. T'Wayne Johnson said he got lost in Staten Island after picking up the girls and was almost an hour and a half late. Dumayne called him several times, the last a little while before he got there to find out where he was. Both phones had a record of the calls. And of course, he saw Dumayne when he dropped the girls off. Damn, I thought we had them."

CHAPTER THIRTY-SIX

Dietz came by to let them know Francine Dumayne and Darnell Mason were waiting in separate interview rooms. "How long have they been here?" Corelli wanted them to sweat a little.

Dietz glanced at the wall clock. "About ten minutes."

"Let's give them some time to worry. Unless the captain is back, Parker and I are going to continue to work here."

"It's all yours. I brought you the latest reports." He handed her the reports and showed her an envelope addressed to her. "You keep leaving this in the conference room. What should I do with it?"

She recognized Darla North's handwriting. "Give it to me." Corelli put the reports on the coffee table in front of the sofa and dumped the contents of Darla's envelope. As she looked through the relatively small pile of blurry copies of twenty-five-year-old newspaper articles, the only thing that caught her eye was a photograph of the family of Teresa Walker, an eleven-year-old girl who was allegedly raped by a church deacon named Maurice Dumayne Williams. This was the case Darla had mentioned. She studied the photo of Mr. and Mrs. Walker, the girl, and Darnell, her twin brother who looked lost. The boy's name caught her attention but Darnell wasn't that unusual a name. She put the article aside and turned to the latest reports.

Two hours later she turned to Parker. "Ready to go at our suspects? I thought we'd start with Francine Dumayne."

The bleary-eyed young woman lifted her head off the table when they opened the door to the interview room. "Why am I here? I answered all your questions."

Parker waited until she and Corelli were seated across from Dumayne. "Not all our questions, Francine. We know the mystery man you've been spending your evenings with is Darnell Mason. Would you like to talk about it?"

"I know what you're thinking but I already told you we're just friends. I recognized his accent the first time he drove me to church and it turned out he's from Atlanta and we had an acquaintance in common."

"You were out pretty late last night with your...friend."

"I needed someone to talk to and he picked me up. He took me to a bar in New Jersey and we were there until they closed. It was just conversation. I'm sure he can give you the name and they'll confirm what I said."

"Did you know Mr. Mason in Atlanta?"

"No. We traveled in different circles. He's older and works in, you know, security, and my friends are all young professionals. Believe me, I'm not about to get involved with anyone for a long while and certainly not another older man."

Corelli tossed the turquoise earring on the table. "We found your earring."

Dumayne frowned. "That's not mine." She picked it up. "It's not my style. You can check my jewelry box. I would never wear something as chea—gaudy as this."

"Do you know anyone who would wear it?"

"Mrs. Wilkerson is the only woman I've spent any time with since I came north." She giggled. "I can't quite imagine her wearing that. Can you?"

"You lied to us. You said you didn't go out the night Mr. Dumayne was murdered, yet we have a witness who saw you get in a car and we have street cameras with images of you with Mr. Mason in his black Mercedes. We believe you and Mr. Mason murdered Mr. Dumayne."

"What?" The blood drained from her face. "No. We didn't. I swear." She swiped at her tears. I did lie to you. I heard a disgusting message come in on the answering machine when I was searching for my credit cards in William's office earlier in the day. Darnell picked me up around nine thirty and we were going to drive to that bar in

New Jersey, but when I told him about the message he took me right home. I got in about ten."

Corelli and Parker perked up. "What message was that?" Parker asked.

She closed her eyes. "It was that creepy Jake Blecker instructing William to have his guy pick up three kittens—not two—because they had a guest coming. He said unless I was ready to keep them busy until they were ready to fuck them, he was to have them delivered around nine so they could take care of business first." She covered her face. "I immediately thought of those disgusting pictures. I wanted to talk to Darnell about what to do."

"And did you talk to Mr. Mason?"

"No. He remembered something he had to do. Then he pulled out an old flip phone and made a phone call. I was surprised because he has an iPhone. It was brief. 'Where are you? I'm coming. We need to talk.' Then he closed the phone and apologized for being rude."

"Did he say anything else?"

"Nothing other than goodnight. He seemed distracted."

"We're going to leave you here for a while longer. Do you need anything?"

"No, they gave me coffee and a sandwich."

Corelli retrieved the newspaper photo she'd been looking at earlier. It was worth a try. Darnell Mason was sitting up straight, hands folded on the table. He gazed at them when they walked in but didn't say anything. Parker sat but Corelli leaned against the doorjamb. His eyes flicked between them.

"So," Corelli said. "We just had an interesting chat with Mrs. Dumayne."

He shifted in his chair but didn't comment. "According to the young lady, you two were pretty chummy. Were you lovers?"

He glared at her. "We're friends, nothing more."

"Really? You mean you weren't fucking her on all those late nights out."

He roared and jumped up, hands fisted. Corelli moved toward him, Parker right beside her. The door opened and Watkins loomed in the doorway. "Everything okay?"

"Yes, everything is just peachy. Georgia peachy." Corelli had baited him to see whether she could rattle his placid demeanor. She wasn't surprised to find anger just below the surface.

"Sorry." Mason relaxed his hands and then backed into the chair. "Francine is a lovely young woman trapped by a monster. She needed someone to talk to and we have Atlanta in common. Some of those

late nights we just drove around talking, others we talked in a bar in New Jersey where it was unlikely anyone would recognize her."

The tension eased and Watkins withdrew. "Do you recognize this?" She put the earring on the table.

"Oh, Gladiola was looking for that. Did you find it in the car?"

"Gladiola?" Corelli tipped her head at the mirror signaling she wanted the woman brought in, then put the newspaper clipping in front of him. "Do you recognize these people?"

He ran his finger over the photo. "How did you find this?"

Corelli gave him a minute to remember. "Why do you go by Mason rather than Walker?"

He looked up. "My father started drinking after the rape and he eventually just disappeared. I took my mom's maiden name to punish him. It was the only weapon I had." He pushed out a harsh sound. "But he committed suicide soon after Teresa ended her life so he never knew I insulted him."

Corelli spoke softly. "So you came to New York to murder the rapist? How did you find him?"

"Purely by chance. His marriage to Francine was big news in Atlanta's Black community, and by chance, I saw clips of the wedding on TV. I recognized him immediately. But they had already left Atlanta. When a buddy of mine mentioned his uncle was an elder in Dumayne's church I got a letter of introduction and came here. I've already told you the rest of the story."

"What was your plan?"

"I didn't have one. It was so long ago and he seemed legit so I started to doubt myself. Then I heard from Mrs. Wilkerson that Dumayne was still up to no good with the children. And when Gladiola showed me the pictures she found, I knew I had to kill him."

He sounded relieved to be getting this off his chest. Corelli couldn't imagine carrying that anger and guilt around for almost twenty-five years. Her breath caught. Shit. She was carrying anger and guilt over Marnie's death. It was only two years but if she didn't do something about it soon, twenty-five years would zip by and she'd find herself an old woman whose life and her chance for happiness with Brett had slipped away. She looked up at the sound of Parker clearing her throat. *Nice Corelli. Why not analyze yourself in the middle of questioning a killer?*

"So you must have been in a rage when Francine told you about the children being delivered to the child rapists? Did you turn around, get your gun, then lay in wait with Francine until you figured they were in the middle of raping the girls?"

"Francine wasn't involved. When she told me about the phone call, I took her home. I felt bad because I could see she needed to talk."

He was being too forthcoming. What was she missing? "She said you called someone. Who?" She needed him to say it.

"Gladiola. She hates him as much as I do. She was just finishing up at the office so I picked her up there. We were on the way to Blecker's house when a guy turned too wide and hit the rear fender of my car. A cop was right there so I had to stop. I was sweating. I had a gun in the trunk and I knew I was in trouble if he searched the car." He looked Parker in the eye. "You know a Black man is never sure how these situations are going to end. It took forever to exchange insurance information and the cop took his time running both our licenses and writing up an accident report."

Damn. The lazy-ass cop probably hadn't gotten around to filing the report yet or it would have come up when they checked out Mason.

Unaware of Corelli's brief mental detour Mason continued. "And then, even though it was the other guy's fault, he lectured me about driving in the snow and ice because I'm from Atlanta. It was eleven-fifteen when we were on our way again."

He blew out a breath, then locked onto Corelli's eyes. "You probably won't believe this."

"Try us."

"While I was trying to divert my thoughts from being killed by the cop, I visualized killing Dumayne and I realized I couldn't do it. Maybe I could have done it when I was twelve or even twenty, but as an adult, I couldn't kill anyone, even him, in cold blood. I decided exposing him for what he was and sending him to jail would be a better punishment than death. I intended to confront him about raping my sister and make him fear I was going to pull the trigger. Gladiola wanted him dead so she wasn't happy with the change in plan." He stood.

Parker jumped up. He put his hands out. "Sorry, I need to walk a little." Parker leaned against the wall watching him.

He paced the small room for a minute. "We parked on Fifth Avenue and Seventy-Fourth Street and walked to the house. I was surprised to find the door open but I figured the element of surprise was good so we went in. We heard music and followed the sound up the stairs. When we reached the floor with the music, we nearly fell over each other. Three naked little girls were sprawled at the other end of the hall. They looked dead. I clamped my hand over Gladiola's mouth to muffle her scream. I didn't know what had happened but it didn't look good. I took the safety off my gun and we crept down the

hall to the room where the music seemed to be coming from." He bit his lip. "Dumayne, Blecker and a man I now know was Senator Stanerd were naked, lying in blood and shit. A fitting end, I thought. Gladiola turned and threw up in the hall. One of the girls made a sound and we both jumped. They were alive. We were going to take them with us but we couldn't figure out what to do with them. It was Gladiola's idea to leave them but hide them so if they woke up, they wouldn't see the horror."

"Where did you hide them?"

"We took them to the top floor and put them in a closet. We figured if they woke up they might stay upstairs. But then we moved a piece of furniture in front of it to be sure they didn't wander."

"What if no one had thought to look behind that chest?"

"We agreed we'd wait a day and call if the bodies weren't discovered. But after we talked to you the next day, we decided to let you know about the girls. My accent is easily recognizable so Gladiola left a message. Did you get it?"

"Did either of you go in the room with the dead men?"

"No. It was obvious they were dead so we just left them. After we hid the girls we ran out and got into the car as fast as we could."

"What about the message?"

"What?" He stared at her as if she'd spoken gibberish. "Oh. You mean the message we read about in the newspaper? We wondered about that. If it was there, neither of us noticed it."

"Did you see or hear anyone in the house other than the girls? Or on the street?"

"Not in the house. I thought I saw someone on the street when we walked back to the car but it must have been the shadows. We didn't meet anyone."

Corelli studied Mason. "Quite a story. But you thirsted twenty-five years for revenge. Why should we believe you didn't kill him?"

He shrugged. "It's the truth. I thought I could, but I couldn't. And a much sweeter revenge would have been to see him spend a long time in prison."

Gladiola Foster was jumpy as hell when they entered. Good. Maybe they'd get to the truth faster. Her story was similar to Darnell Mason's. She was freaked out by the pictures she found, disappointed that the reverend hadn't taken the porn to the police, and angry enough to want to kill the pervert. But she insisted she was behind Mason's decision not to kill him. "There was so much blood and gore. It was so horrible I turned away and threw up my dinner." She talked about being scared when she thought the girls were dead. She admitted she made the call about the girls and confirmed the location of the pay phone she'd used in Midtown. And she was happy to get her earring back. It was one of her favorites.

They left them both sitting alone in their separate interview rooms.

"Do you think we have enough to hold them, Parker?"

"They admit to being there which speaks to opportunity. As for motive, twelve-year-old Mason vowed to kill Dumayne but adult Mason said he decided jail, not death, would be the best revenge." She paged through her notes. "Kelly Dexter said she heard Mason say, 'I'm glad I decided not to,' which kind of supports his statement. The gun taken from Mason when they picked him up hasn't been fired recently but they'll test it. And they've both volunteered to give us DNA. They were in the house about twenty minutes. How much time does it take to shoot three men, carry three children up three flights of stairs, hide them, run down four flights of stairs and jog to your car? Foster confirmed she was wearing high heels. Talk about amateurs. Who wears high heels to go murder someone?"

Corelli listened to Parker, then mused out loud. "Senator Parker said he saw two people run out of the house after he discovered the bodies. And Kelly Dexter corroborated that statement. That the senator made no mention of the vomit could be attributed to his anxiety but I can't imagine not remembering the girls. Dexter saw the vomit but not the girls. That confirms Mason and Foster's account of hiding them. And calling the tip line to be sure they were discovered supports their story."

Her quick intake of breath told Corelli that Parker's thoughts hadn't taken the same path as those hovering in her mind for the last few days. "You really think he—?" Parker interrupted herself, as if she couldn't even say the words. She rubbed her temples and seemed to go inward, probably reviewing what they knew. "I'm sure that article could have driven him to murder. But did he know about it in advance? If not, why would he have brought a gun? And if he murdered the men and put the girls in the hall, wouldn't he expect Neil and Broderick to notice them? If Mason and Foster murdered them, she might have vomited so it would have been there but they could have been upstairs with the girls when the senator arrived. He did say a noise from upstairs caused him to run out of the house." She looked at Corelli. "On the other hand, as you said, the music was really loud. Could he have heard movement from two floors above? As

I recall, the chest of drawers didn't make much noise when we moved it." She shook her head. "I think we need more information."

"I agree," Corelli paused. "Will you be all right if it's him?"

"I would be sad, not because there's any love lost between us but because he spent his whole adult life striving to become the kind of man he admired and he's worked so hard to achieve what he's achieved. It makes me angry that scum like Blecker could take that away from him, or any human being, in the blink of an eye. And for what? To appoint another perverted Supreme Court justice or to satisfy some outlandish whim of a morally corrupt president?" Parker hesitated at the door of the conference room. "He's still my uncle." She said it softly but Corelli could hear her pain.

Family. Love them or hate them, blood counted for something even when you don't want it to. "We need to have another run at the senator. I'll have Dietz call his office to find out when he's expected back in the city."

Parker blew out a breath. "I can still do my job." She took out her phone and made the call. "The senate is breaking for Thanksgiving so he'll be back in the city Tuesday night. In the meantime, should we get warrants to search their apartments? Mason and Foster, I mean. Since they said they didn't go in the room, we might find shoes or clothing with blood."

"Good idea."

Parker's phone rang. "Hey, Jess." She listened a minute. "Okay." She ended the call. "Fine will meet us at Hattie's around ten this evening."

"See if you could arrange for Randall and Jessie to meet us there an hour or so earlier to talk about the senator."

They spent the next couple of hours making multiple copies of the five books plus an extra copy of the page of rapists' names that included Fine's boss at the FBI, the page with the top-level organization chart of the Triumvirate Sexualem Parvulus and the page with the high-level organization chart of the Petit Triumvirates.

Corelli felt that frisson of excitement that often came when they were close to breaking a case. She had no doubt they would launch the FBI investigation into the trafficking organization tonight. And her gut told her they were close on the murders. In her mind, the senator was looking better and better for it. But a part of her didn't want it to be Parker's uncle. She didn't give a damn about him but she knew it would hurt Parker.

CHAPTER THIRTY-SEVEN

Randall Young hesitated in the entrance to Hattie's and searched the crowd. When he spotted them he waved and made a motion asking if they needed drinks. The three of them raised their glasses indicating they were fine. Drink in hand, he touched Jessie's shoulder, greeted Corelli, and kissed Parker's cheek before sitting.

Since the DNA test had confirmed Randall's belief that he was Parker's birth father, the two had become affectionate friends. Parker loved to hear his stories about her mother but her interest didn't extend to her uncle. Now, though, the senator was looming large in their investigation and they needed to figure out if he could be pushed to murder.

Corelli enjoyed the group's easy chatter for about ten minutes before getting to the point of tonight's meeting. "So, your assignment tonight, if you choose to take it, is to help us understand Senator Aloysius T. Parker but you are not allowed to ask us questions."

Parker grinned. Corelli's play on the words of the old TV program seemed to tickle her.

She'd never thought of herself as grim but maybe she had been since Afghanistan and the undercover operation. Corelli filed that thought and focused on Randall. "Tell us what you remember about the senator before you went into the service?"

"He was five years older than Tasha and me so I really didn't know him, but all us boys wanted to be like him. Teachers held Aloysius the soft-spoken, respectful, brilliant Black kid up as an inspiration for us, but we also knew him as A.T. the guy who ran with the toughest gang, pushed drugs, carried a gun and beat up anybody dumb enough to challenge him. I learned from him that you could be smart and get good grades, yet be strong enough not to take shit from anyone. That's how you survived in those days."

"What can you tell us about his gang persona? Did he have a gun? Did he ever kill anyone?"

Randall scratched his head and stared into space. "When I was in the sixth or seventh grade the owner of a liquor store was killed during a robbery and word on the street was that A.T. did it. He would have been a senior in high school. I know for sure he almost killed a guy with his fists." His gaze rested on Parker. "And he was physically abusive to Tasha and her older sister Tiffany. It was all about his image. If they did poorly in school or hung out with guys, he beat them and the guys."

"Anything else?" Corelli asked.

Randall shook his head. "Once he went off to college, he was rarely around and I didn't give him much thought."

"What about you, Jess. Know anything?"

"He was an up and coming lawyer when I started on the beat in Harlem. I didn't know he was related to P.J. until Annie and I tried to adopt her. In my opinion, if it wasn't for his political aspirations, he wouldn't have wasted a second thought on her." He covered Parker's hand. "I heard the stories about his stealing, bullying, and threatening with his fists or a gun, and the one about him killing a liquor store owner before he left for college. I looked into the police report of the robbery and killing but it happened late at night and there were no witnesses. He and several other jocks from the neighborhood were questioned but there was no evidence to support any of them doing it."

"So he was a member of a gang, knew how to use his fists and a gun to get what he wanted, and possibly killed a man. Right?"

"Yes." Randall and Jessie spoke simultaneously.

"Thank you both. That helps us." She signaled the waitress for another round for everyone. Jessie changed the topic. "Once you two tie up this case, Annie and I would like you all, including you, Randall, with dates if you have someone you'd like to bring, to come to dinner at our house." Mention of the case led to mentioning they had a meeting in a few minutes and Randall took his leave. Parker walked him to the entrance and embraced him before turning back to the table.

The universe seemed to be doing something with fathers these days. Simone had called her last night to invite her and Brett to dinner with their mother and father. She'd questioned her sister about how and why the invitation had been extended since up until she was shot, her father, meekly followed by her mother, had disowned her for being a lesbian, or for being a detective or for being in the military. She wasn't sure but it came down to condemnation of her doing men's work and loving women. He'd cried at the hospital and visited her a couple of times at home but since she hadn't died she figured things had gone back to normal.

Parker elbowed her. "You all right?"

Parker and Jess knew about her family drama so she felt okay talking about it with them. "Just thinking. Brett and I got invited to dinner with my parents."

"Wow. Did you accept?" Parker sounded happy for her.

"I have to discuss it with Brett, of course, but I told Simone we'd talk after we close this case."

"So when do I get to spend some time with Brett?" Jessie met Corelli's eyes.

She smiled. "I'll bring her to dinner at your house."

The three of them were kicking around the murder suspects when Ben Fine strolled in wearing jeans, a lightweight blue sweater and a navy blazer rather than the FBI uniform of black suit, white shirt and tie. He didn't look like a man expecting to be handed the opportunity to take down a huge child trafficking network. Of course, he didn't know yet.

Fine didn't waste any time. "What have you got for me?" He focused on Corelli but they'd agreed earlier that Parker would be the one to put the offer on the table.

Parker clasped her hands on top of the three pages they'd prepared for him. "We've got the takedown of your life, if you agree to our terms."

He stared at her as if her words didn't make sense and he had to translate. He switched his gaze from Parker to Jessie to Corelli and back to Parker. "You have my full attention, Detective Parker."

"We have the trafficking ring in our sights. We could take down the local group, meaning the group that runs the Northeast region."

"Region?" His eyebrows shot up. "And you want my help?"

"Geez, shut up and listen, Ben," Jessie said.

"Oh. Sorry." Fine sat back. "I've been working on this forever and getting nowhere. I'll do whatever you need. Please go on."

Parker stared at him. "You may not be so anxious when you let me finish what I have to say." Fine seemed to vibrate in his chair but he didn't interrupt. Parker slid the copy of the Triumvirate Sexualem Parvulus organization chart across the table. "As you can see it's a pyramid. At the top is the Triumvirate Sexualem Parvulus led by three men who control local organizations called Petit Triumvirates all over the world. The United States is divided into six Petit Triumvirates. Our local Petit Triumvirate covers the Northeast, from Maine to Washington, DC. We're talking to you because NYPD doesn't have the resources to handle an international takedown. Any questions so far?"

"You mentioned terms. If the issue is credit or if you want in on your local group takedown, I'm sure the powers that be will agree to that."

Parker glanced at Corelli. Seeing no objection on Corelli's face, she slid the list of names across the table." Fine put on his glasses to read the small neat handwriting and using his finger to mark the rows, he read down the page. Three quarters of the way down, he stopped. His finger travelled across the entire line, job title, home address, bank information, and wife's name. He traced that line of data twice. "I'll be a motherfu...." His face was blazing, she could almost see smoke coming out of his ears. "Kevin Smythe, my boss, has insisted unless we catch people in the act, we can't get involved. Now I see why. The bastard is a customer, and a frequent one, according to the total spent in the previous six months. I understand your concern."

Parker met his gaze. "We're concerned he'll bury the investigation or just pick up a few low-level operatives. So if you're going to take it on, it means going rogue to an extent."

He blanched. He glanced at Jessie, then looked into his brandy but his glass was empty. Jessie waved to a passing waitress and pointed to Fine. She tossed a two-finger salute and a couple of minutes later slid a new drink in front of him. He took a slug. "I'm not sure how to do that with something this large. I need time."

"Corelli, why don't you outline the approach we think will work?" Parker said.

"What if we got your boss out of the way?"

Corelli willed him to focus. His commitment was critical. She was determined to take down the whole damn organization, not just the local Petit Triumvirate and only the FBI could do that. Fine's gaze settled on Corelli. "Commissioner Neil invites the Director of the FBI to NYC for a private meeting. But the Chief of Police, Chief of Detectives, and Parker and I are also there. We present the case just as Parker did for you except he may need a little more detail. Hopefully, after he sees your boss on the list of rapists, he'll understand the need to move him out of the way. We'll suggest that he creates an urgent need for Smythe in Washington and appoints you to lead the agency's takedown of the entire group internationally. We want NYPD to be a part of the takedown." She gave him a minute to consider the plan. "What do you think?"

He made no attempt to hide behind the usual bland FBI façade and his emotions—anger, fear, and excitement followed by determination were displayed for all to see. "It's worth a try. But I think we need to be sure Kevin is the only FBI biggie involved in this before inviting the Director. Since you may not recognize who's who in the FBI, I suggest we go over the whole list of names together before you issue the invitation."

Corelli and Parker had discussed this earlier so they'd brought the full list. "Okay. But it needs to be done now because we scheduled a meeting with Neil and Broderick for first thing in the morning." Parker changed seats with Jessie and placed a copy of the complete list on the table in front of her and Fine. They worked through the list silently, except for an occasional angry "fuck" as Fine recognized the name of a supposed upstanding politician or other citizen.

CHAPTER THIRTY-EIGHT

Brett was reading on the sofa when Corelli got home. Having her there made coming home feel like coming home. This is what she wanted—this love, this relationship, the comfort of coming home at the end of a shitty day to welcoming and loving arms, to a woman who helped her laugh and cry and forget the horrors she dealt with. She was ready to confront the demons she needed to confront in order to have Brett fully in her life. She poured her feelings into the welcome home kiss and hoped Brett understood the depth of the feelings.

Brett served her leftovers and a hot cup of tea. They talked about their jobs, laughing at the absurdity of people, hands touching, eyes connecting, and Corelli relaxed. After, as Brett cleaned up, Corelli's gaze went to the picture of her and Marnie in their dress uniforms on the bookcase. Even in the photograph the glow of their happiness was blinding. They'd been deeply in love. Now she was deeply in love with Brett. She repeated the pledge she and Marnie had made to each other before leaving for Afghanistan and allowed herself to feel the truth that Marnie would want her to live and be happy. She glanced at the picture again, then texted Major Magarelli to ask for the schedule of PTSD groups. That done, they went downstairs to bed. It was getting harder and harder just to cuddle but she wasn't ready yet for anything more. For the first time in ages she slept for four consecutive hours and then managed to fall back to sleep for another two hours after Brett wrapped around her.

Parker arrived at seven thirty to pick her up for the eight-a.m. meeting with Commissioner Neil and Chief Broderick. They dropped Brett at her Wall Street office then swung uptown to One Police Plaza. They'd purposely scheduled the meeting early so if Neil agreed with the plan, he could get the ball rolling with the FBI Director. Broderick was thrilled at the idea of exporting the takedown to the FBI. Neil argued that Corelli and Parker should get the credit, since they did the work. After they reassured him they were fine sharing the credit for the local takedown, he agreed to reach out to the Director of the FBI.

By the time they arrived at the station, Corelli had a text from Magarelli with the schedule of her PTSD groups and an invitation to show up at any group that fit her schedule. Parker had a text from Neil's secretary. The FBI Director was expected to arrive at Neil's office at six p.m. and they and the other guests should arrive at six-fifteen.

With the trafficking aspect of the case in motion, it was time to turn their attention to the murder. "Are we in agreement that the senator and Mason and Foster are the only suspects left standing?"

"We are," Parker said. "I'd like to reread their statements, and the forensic and autopsy reports unless you have another plan?"

They read in companionable silence for several hours before Corelli asked Parker to summarize what they knew about Mason and Foster and draw a conclusion as to their guilt. Parker reviewed their statements and tied them in with Kelly Dexter's account of seeing them and the senator's mention of them. The only new information was in the forensic reports. They confirmed the vomit contained the remains of the pizza Foster said she'd eaten while working late with Wilkerson. Strands of her long wiry blond/brown hair were found in the vomit, in the hall, on the stairs leading upstairs, on the bed in the room where they hid the girls, in the closet and on the blanket used to cover the girls, but none were found inside the room with the dead men. Her fingerprints and those of Mason were found on the doorjamb of the murder room, on the staircase bannisters, on the chest and on the closet door. None were found in the murder room. "So we can confirm Foster didn't kill them. Given the angle of the bodies and the bullet wounds, the killer would have had to be standing in the room. There's no trace of Mason in there so in my opinion he's off the hook for the murders too."

Corelli rubbed her eyes. "That leaves Senator Parker." Charging a senator was tricky at best. The newspapers and TV stations that usually published Senator Parker's lies about her were calling for her removal from the case. Was the senator getting nervous, egging on the media behind the scenes because the investigation hadn't come up with a fall guy as he'd hoped? "Forensics shows he was in the room but we knew that. His shoes had blood on them but he told us he walked in it. We need something solid to bring to the ADA. Not having other suspects is not proof."

Dietz stopped by. "Senator Parker's office called. He'll be back late tonight so I got him to agree to come down here around noon tomorrow. I hope that's good."

"Thanks, Dietz, it's fine."

"We located the case file for the Harlem liquor store owner. It was pretty thin, not much evidence. They interviewed the senator and a few other neighborhood kids but that's as far as it went. I passed the name of the gal who was the last to sign the case out to Internal Affairs."

"Thanks," Corelli said. "We're going to head out for a while. Call if you need us."

Parker picked her up at the door. "Brooklyn? You want to go to Gianna's house?"

Corelli wasn't looking forward to the conversation with Gianna. "I need to tell her what we found."

All was quiet at Gianna's house. Greene opened the door and reported that the girls were taking a nap and Gianna was reading in the living room. Gianna jumped up to greet them.

"Sorry to bother you."

"It's all right. You caught me in a quiet moment but I have to start prepping dinner in a few minutes. I'm cooking for up to eleven people these days so I like to start early. The girls love learning but they tire easily so I make them nap before helping me prep the dinner. Gabriella is in her room and Francesca and Giancarlo have after school activities. Simone and Nicky will be here later."

It was clear she was proud of the girls and the depth of her feeling for them came through. What had she done? Gianna was one of the most loving and generous people she'd ever met. She should have known it wouldn't take her long to get attached to the girls, especially since they seemed to feel the same way about her. Simone said the girls were following Gabriella's lead and had started calling Gianna mommy. "Let's sit and talk."

Gianna tensed. Her older sister knew her well and understood she wasn't bringing good news. "We found the girls' records. They're sketchy at best. Crissy was one of the many abandoned children on the streets in Argentina picked up by a recruiter for the organization. They estimated she was three years old so we have an approximate date of birth but no way to find her parents. Maria and Teresa were sold to a recruiter in Belarus, by a man who claimed to be their father. The file only contains their first names, dates of birth and his first name so there's no way to locate their parents either."

"What will happen to the girls?" Gianna didn't seem as upset as Corelli expected.

"They'll go into the system. Into foster care."

Gianna's smile was brilliant. "We want to foster them. Marco, Giancarlo, Francesca and I talked this over and we want them to stay with us. Gabriella agrees. Do you think it's possible?"

Corelli checked Parker to see if she'd had any idea this was coming but she looked dumbfounded. "There's a process but I'm sure you would qualify. Are you sure?"

Gianna clasped Corelli's hand. "I've never done anything as important or as fulfilling as helping these three beautiful girls."

Tears stung Corelli's eyes. "Wow." Her mind immediately took off trying to figure out how to make this work. "If all goes well, the threat to them will disappear in three to four weeks. In the meantime, Parker and I will talk to the powers that be to do this legally but under the radar so they and you all are protected. Do you think Dr. Court will support it?"

Gianna grinned. "She's a hundred percent behind it."

She should have known Gianna would have thought this through and made an ally of the psychiatrist. "That will be a big help. Foster care is big on separate bedrooms. Have you thought about that?"

"We've discussed it. Francesca and Giancarlo have been bugging us for months to finish the fourth floor of the house so they can have a teen den to themselves. Marco has already gotten some cost and time estimates from contractors and as soon as we decide which to use, we'll start construction. They can finish it in two to four weeks. So the teenagers will move upstairs and we'll have their bedrooms plus the guest room for the girls. Dr. Court feels it's important for Maria and Teresa to be in one room, so we're good. Of course, I have no idea when they'll feel comfortable sleeping separate from Gabby, but when they do, their rooms will be there."

Corelli pulled Gianna into a hug. "I didn't see this coming but I'm happy to acquire three nieces and I'm looking forward to getting to know them. We have to get back but I'll keep you posted."

Parker was grinning as she steered the car through the streets on the way to the highway. "I gather you were blindsided by this too?"

"Oh, you could tell?" Corelli smiled. "I shouldn't have been, knowing Gianna."

"She's the warmest, most loving and generous person I've ever met," Parker said. "She's made me feel like part of your family, not easy for me."

Gianna and Parker had become friends. So had Parker and Brett. She was the only one who was half in and half out. She was still putting up walls while Parker was slowly letting her in. Hopefully the PTSD group would help her get back to the woman she used to be, but in the meantime she had a job to do. "I'm thinking we need to put out that we found three girls alive in the house but they died from an overdose. What do you think?"

"I think it's brilliant. That will protect them from being found if any traffickers escape capture. When?"

"Let's see how things unfold."

The meeting with FBI Director Waterman was over by seven. He was skeptical but listened politely as Parker presented their case and proposed the solution. When Corelli handed him the book with the names of the men who used the services of the traffickers and pointed out Kevin Smythe and several powerful men, he paged through slowly, jaw dropping at some of the names, and acknowledged the highly sensitive nature of the operation. After Corelli reviewed the structure of the Triumvirate Sexualem Parvulus, with the names of the leaders of the various Petit Triumvirates around the world, he was totally on board. He agreed to remove Smythe to protect the investigation but only agreed to Fine heading the FBI's takedown task force after Corelli and Parker made the case. Apparently Smythe had been extremely negative about Fine.

Before he left One Police Plaza Director Waterman called Smythe and instructed him to pack for a few weeks and be in Washington tomorrow morning first thing. He also arranged to meet Agent Fine for dinner to appoint him head of the global task force and arrange to have a team ready to work with the NYPD in the morning. The NYPD brass accepted Corelli and Parker's recommendation that the Special Victims Division head up the NYPD's takedown task force.

"Wow." Parker was grinning when they walked to the car. "We did it."

"Yeah, we did. We'll still be involved but others can do the heavy lifting." Corelli felt Parker's gaze on her. Ordinarily she'd be fighting for a piece of the action but she'd concluded she really did need more healing time and visions of sailing on a blue sea danced in her head. "C'mon, I need you to drop me at my PTSD group."

"Your...PTSD group?" Parker punched her arm. "I'll be damned. You admit you have PTSD?"

Corelli loved shocking Parker. She grinned but kept walking to their car. "I'm not admitting anything. Just checking it out."

CHAPTER THIRTY-NINE

In the morning, Corelli and Parker went directly to One Police Plaza to brief the first meeting of the Joint FBI and NYPD Child Trafficking Task Force. The small auditorium was buzzing when they entered, and the buzz ratcheted up in volume when Agent Ben Fine, now Acting Assistant Director of the FBI's New York Field Office, and about twenty agents showed up in the conference room. Besides Corelli, Parker and the brass involved last night, only Fine and Chief Gina Forte, the NYPD's Task Force leader, knew why they were there in the room but the troops understood it was important.

Parker and Corelli briefed the group for an hour, presenting all they knew. Chief Forte, from the Special Victims Division, and Ben Fine gave an overview of how they planned to work together. Both walked out with copies of the books found in Blecker's house. The originals would remain locked in evidence against Marianne Phillips, Ernesto Servino and any others they arrested in the takedown. Before leaving Ben took them aside to thank them and promised to keep them in the loop about the entire worldwide effort. It was out of their hands now.

"As soon as information starts coming out about the children involved, I want to leak a couple of stories. One, that the church had pictures of Dumayne having sex with girls before he was murdered but didn't act on them. Another that when Dumayne, Blecker and Stanerd were found they were naked and had just raped three girls. And, third, that the three girls died from the drugs they were given."

"Burying the leak about the girls in the news about the child trafficking arrests is brilliant, Parker said. "I bet Darla would be happy to help."

Corelli put her head back on the car seat and closed her eyes. "I don't know where to go with the murder investigation. After we go over the senator's statement with him, we'll take a fresh look at everything we have. We must have missed something. But we need fresh eyes looking at the evidence to be sure. What do you think about pulling a team together?"

"Good idea. I'd include ADA Brooks if she can spare the time plus Ndep, Watkins, Kim and Forlini."

"That would be a good mix of perspectives. Let's stop for coffee. I need a boost before we meet with the senator." The truth was she knew it was necessary but she was feeling down about turning over the trafficking investigation to others. She wanted to personally destroy every one of the men and woman involved in hurting innocent children. Standing by and watching was never her strong suit.

Of course the senator kept them waiting an hour. When he finally showed up he was angry and arrogant. "I hope you have a good reason for forcing me to come down here, Detective Corelli."

She let him rant, then asked Watkins to escort him to the interview room. She was doing this by the book so Watkins, not Parker, would be in the interview room with her. She lingered behind a few minutes hoping to aggravate him so he would slip and give her something. He was still protesting when she entered the room. "Please sit, Senator Parker. We can get through this pretty quickly." He sat across from her, clearly not happy. "We're trying to get your view of events to help us corroborate the story of the two people you saw running out of the house."

He brightened and leaned forward. "You found them?"

"We have. So the door was open when you went in. Was it still open when you ran out?"

"It must have been. I don't remember stopping to open it."

She wanted to ease him into his story. "Can we assume you left it open?"

"Yes. I was scared."

She could see him relax. He could handle this. "Describe what you saw when you got to the floor where you found the bodies. Try to visualize the hall."

He closed his eyes. "The music was really loud. I could tell it was coming from the other end of the hall."

"Was the hall lit?"

"Yes. It was bright enough that I could see all the way to the end."

"Was there anything on the floor? Did you trip on anything?"

He frowned. "No. The floor was perfectly clear. I had no problem walking down to the room where the...you know, the bodies were."

"Was the music still on?"

"Yes. As I said it was blasting so loud I thought they were having a party."

"Was the door to that room open?"

His fingers danced on the table. "No." His fingers stopped. "Sorry, yes, it was open."

"Great, this is really helpful. Did you go in?"

His fingers started to tap dance again. His face reddened. "I've already told you in detail what I did. I was shocked and I stopped in the doorway. It took me a while to take it in. Then I went in to check the pulse of each of the men. When—"

"Which pulse points did you check? The same on all three?"

He stared down at her, taking his time to think about it. "Is this a trick question?"

"What? Why would I try to trick you, sir?"

"I checked the carotid arteries on all three and then I heard someone moving around upstairs and I ran out."

"What did you hear?"

He shrugged. "I don't know. Maybe feet shuffling, somebody walking?"

"And the movement was loud enough so you were able to hear it over the blasting music?"

Remarkable self-control. He didn't flinch. "I must have because I froze thinking the killer was there and I ran out of the house. You said you found the killers. Ask them what they were doing to make so much noise."

"You were upset but you still managed to avoid the vomit and the children in the hall?" For just a second he looked unsure but he recovered quickly.

"Are you crazy? What children?" He glared at her. "I saw no vomit. Now if you'll excuse me—"

She opened the folder she'd brought in with her and slid a copy of the blackmail article across the table. He paled. His hand shook as he picked it up. "What is this?" His gaze drifted over it. "Another article attacking me? I'm used to them."

"This one seems to be particularly damning. When I read it I thought it could destroy your career. Blecker planned to blackmail you with it. That's why you went there that night. Wasn't it?"

"I told you I don't know why I was asked to go there."

"You found them raping those little girls, asked them to put them out in the hall, and then listened to what they said. They wanted to control you and they threatened to destroy you if you didn't vote the way they wanted. You were in a rage. How dare they. You ordered the music on to cover the sound and shot them in cold blood. Didn't you?"

He remained silent, looked her in the eye but the tapping of his foot was a tell.

"I'm sure you were upset. Any normal person would be upset at murdering three people in cold blood. Yet you were cool enough to collect the copies of the article and take them with you. You didn't hear anybody in the house. You ran because you killed them." She decided to risk it. "We found the copies of the articles in the garbage can in front of the house you stopped by to catch your breath and figure out what to do." She tapped the table to get his attention. "You know, if you'd just gone home and not involved yourself or if you made an anonymous 911 call we'd probably have never found you. But you thought you were smarter than the cops. You thought you could control the investigation just like you control everything in your life."

"That's outrageous. I'm a U.S. senator. You can't treat me like this. You're nothing but a racist cop and I'll have your job for this attack." He stood and turned toward the door.

A knock and the door swung open. A grim-faced Parker glared at her uncle. "Good call, Corelli," she said handing Corelli a sheet of paper.

"Don't be rude, Penelope, you're acting like a...a common cop." His disgust and his condescension came through loud and clear.

Parker ignored him. She closed the door softly. Corelli scanned the page. Holy shit. "Sit, senator."

"I will not. You have no reason to hold me against my will."

"Read him his rights, Detective Watkins." Watkins looked as shocked as the senator but took his copy of Miranda out of his wallet and read it, asking the senator to sign that he understood each statement.

"Can you explain how it is that the gun used to murder your sister Tasha Parker almost thirty years ago was also used to murder Becker, Dumayne, and Stanerd?"

The blood drained from his face. "What has that got to do with me?" He used his most imperious voice as if that would stop her from arresting him.

"Quite a coincidence if it doesn't, don't you think?" She met his eyes. "Aloysius T. Parker, you are under arrest for the murders of Tasha Parker, Jake Blecker, William Dumayne and Harrison Stanerd."

"NO!" he commanded, as if he had a say in whether they arrested him.

She stood. "Book him." She faced the mirror. "Get someone in here to help Watkins take care of our guest."

"I want a lawyer. I'll have your badge for this."

"Let him make his call, then book him."

She went in search of Parker. Corelli strode into the conference room, not sure what to say to Parker but feeling like it was necessary to support her in some way. "Where's Parker?"

Dietz looked up from the computer. "She said we need search warrants for Senator Parker's apartment, garage, storage unit and office. I was gonna ask one of the guys to do them but she volunteered." He looked around. "She said she'd do them at her desk."

Corelli smiled. Parker knew she couldn't participate in the search but she'd figured out a way to be involved in convicting her uncle. Parker was channeling her anger. But it was the hurt Corelli was worried about.

CHAPTER FORTY

Corelli fought to calm herself as she rang the bell at Annie and Jessie's house. They'd met Brett in the hospital and Brett had been there when they'd visited her at home but coming to dinner at their house felt different, like a coming out of sorts. Annie answered the door, Jess right behind her.

"Chiara, I'm so happy you could come." Annie embraced Chiara. A hug from her always felt like coming home.

"Annie, I don't know if you remember..." She hadn't actually thought about how to introduce Brett. She pulled her close. "My girlfriend, Brett Cummings. Brett, you met Annie and Jessie Isaacs at the hospital."

Annie smiled warmly at Brett. "Of course, I remember." She opened her arms and Brett didn't hesitate to accept the invitation for a hug. "I'm so glad you found each other."

Corelli blinked back the tears that threatened. The approval of Marnie's friends meant more to her than she'd realized.

Jess stepped around Annie and hugged Brett. "I agree. You picked a winner, Brett." He squeezed Chiara's arm. "Please come in, the others are here." He led them into the living room. A solemn Parker was sitting next to Gloria Ndep, and, whoa, they were holding hands.

Corelli forced herself to not stare. Randall was on the other side of Parker with a woman Corelli didn't know.

Corelli tipped her head. "Parker." Brett embraced Parker. She looked from Parker to Corelli. "Since it's a holiday do you think you two could try and use first names?"

Everyone laughed. "In that case, I'm P.J. and this is Gloria," Parker said, and held out a hand.

Corelli took her hand. "I'm Chiara." She smiled at Ndep. "Good to see you Gloria. This is my girlfriend, Brett." She was going to have to focus to remember to use first names.

Parker introduced Chiara and Brett to Yolanda Mercato, Randall's date.

They laughed about many things and cried over a few, like Chiara's Marnie and Parker's mom. It was serendipitous timing that dinner with Annie and Jessie had morphed into Thanksgiving dinner so today Parker was surrounded by people who cared about her. Learning that her uncle had very likely murdered her mother and left her, a three-year-old, alone with the body was devastating. That he didn't even have the humanity to make an anonymous 911 call to ensure she didn't die along with his sister stunned her. She was reeling. But she was also appreciating anew the love and support and stability that Jessie and Annie had provided. And over the course of the day Annie's wonderful food and the warmth of love and friendship seemed to revive her. Chiara was happy to see the caring connection between P.J. and Gloria and happy, for some reason, to spend her first holiday with Brett in the company of Jess and Annie who had known and loved Marnie too.

As wonderful as Thanksgiving Day was, Friday was a workday for Corelli and Parker. They had lots of loose ends to tie up and evidence found during the execution of the senator's search warrants to sift through. Much to Corelli's surprise, they'd found the gun used in the four murders, Tasha Parker's wallet with her ID and a copy of Blecker's article in the senator's locker in a Harlem storage facility. If Parker hadn't known about her uncle's locker and included it in the warrants, they would never have found the final nail in the case.

Aloysius T. Parker was being held without bail, awaiting trial for the murder of his sister and another for the murder of the three men. He broke when Corelli confronted him with the gun they'd found in his storage unit. "Stanerd had insisted we meet privately that night in New York City. But it wasn't until I received a copy of the article by messenger early in the day that I knew he was going to try to blackmail me. I had no idea Dumayne and Blecker were in on it. I told my secretary I'd forgotten some papers at home and took a taxi to my storage unit to get my gun. I thought I might be able to scare him.

"I arrived earlier than they'd expected. And needless to say I was stunned to walk in and find them naked, raping little girls. The bastards weren't even embarrassed. I asked them to put the girls in the hall and get dressed so we could talk like civilized men. They laughed and made racist comments about me not being so civilized. They moved the girls but didn't dress. They sat there with their...with everything hanging out and I felt disrespected, which I'm sure they intended. I thought I could reason with them but they ridiculed my arguments.

"And Stanerd interrupted me. 'Shut up. From now on I decide how you vote and what you say. Starting immediately you will no longer speak against the package of bills I recently proposed.'

"I considered these bills radical, racist and un-American but they saw them as a means to enhance their wealth and power. Desperate, I flashed my gun and threatened them.

"'Ooh, scary.'" Blecker laughed. The others followed his lead. 'You belong to us *boy*. And unless you put down the gun, I'll release the article to the media in the morning.' They laughed again. I don't know whether it was the racial slur or the laughter or the idea of being controlled by pedophile thugs that pushed me over the edge but my finger seemed to press the trigger of its own accord. I guess I was temporarily insane. I don't know how long I stood in that room after I shot them but I eventually regained awareness and checked their carotids to make sure they were dead. Then I panicked and ran out of the house."

So he confessed to the murders, announced his temporary insanity defense and then hired Louden Warfield III to defend him. Needing to be in control as usual.

But he denied killing Tasha. According to him she called him but by the time he got around to going to her apartment she was dead. The gun was on the floor and he picked it up without thinking but then realized his prints were on it. He took the gun with him and held on to it in case he ever needed it.

He couldn't explain why he didn't report his sister's murder or why he left his three-year-old niece alone with the body of her mother and didn't do anything to ensure her safety. His claim that he ordered Dumayne to move the three girls out to the hall so they wouldn't see him kill the men, fit with the story told by Mason and Foster. Though not killing his niece and the three girls seemed to indicate some redeeming human feelings, Corelli thought something else was at play. Maybe children didn't threaten his humongous ego or maybe it was the men who put the girls in the hall to ensure they didn't witness the blackmail.

Knowing Parker felt exposed by the publicity about her uncle being charged with murdering her mother, about him leaving three-year-old her alone with the body for days, Corelli kept them out of the office as much as possible. Though colleagues like Dietz, Watkins, Forlini, Kim, and Maynard were supportive, it helped that people who loved Parker rallied around her. Not just Randall, Jessie, Annie, and Gloria, but also Gianna, Simone, Nicky and Brett. Encouraged by her PTSD group, Corelli made an effort to be there for her.

Fine asked to meet with them and Jessie at Hattie's, so Friday night after they settled in with drinks he got down to business. "Taking down this operation is a monumental project and while I have a huge team to coordinate the worldwide effort, I don't have people I can bounce things off of and trust to give me straight feedback. It's unorthodox and it would have to be just between us, but I need you three to fill that role."

"Parker and I have some slack time right now so we can do it." Perfect. An opportunity to be involved, influence the direction, yet not be bogged down with the weight of the project.

Jessie chewed his lip. "I'd have to participate as my other duties allow, if that's okay?"

Fine sat back and blew out a breath. "Two out of three isn't bad. Whatever time you have will be appreciated, Jessie."

They spent the next several weeks working with ADA Brooks to ensure the cases built against Senator Parker, Marianne Phillips and Ernesto Servino were airtight, meeting with Ben on an as-needed basis and attending Task Force planning meetings. And then the takedown happened. Corelli and Parker were in the FBI war room watching a mixture of live and video feeds of the coordinated effort to take down every Triumvirate group nationally and internationally at virtually the same time. Though some of the men and women who profited from selling human beings for sex managed to escape and some committed suicide rather than face their shame, the huge majority were arrested and their names were released to the media. Just as important, thousands of girls, boys and women were liberated. It was thrilling to know they'd made it happen. They received a standing ovation as they left the FBI office and then again at the stationhouse.

Phase Two of the takedown, a major effort to get the victims back to their homes or find homes for them, kicked off immediately. Though they knew Phase Three, the arrest of the men who paid to rape children, would be difficult, men all over the world were being picked up and charged.

One of the first things Corelli did that evening was call Darla North to give her the story about Blecker, Dumayne and Stanerd having been murdered while raping three little girls who died from the drugs they were given. She and Parker also anonymously tipped off various reporters that the church had pictures of Dumayne raping little girls before he was murdered but did not give them to the police and the celebratory funeral for Dumayne was held despite knowing he was a rapist.

And closer to home, Corelli was thrilled to bring Gianna and Marco news that their request to be foster parents for the three girls had been approved. Commissioner Neil had personally worked with the powers-that-be to fast-track the process and he had called her two days after the takedown to let her know it was done. Gianna was already investigating the process for adopting the girls.

Relaxing in Brett's arms that evening, they talked about the takedown and Brett was her usual effusive self. "I'm so proud." She touched Chiara's face. "But what's making you sad?"

Chiara leaned into Brett's strength. "The two dead girls."

Brett gently rubbed her back. "Given the circumstances a funeral and burial in a marked grave was the best you could do for them. That the Corelli clan and so many police and private citizens saw them laid to rest was all your doing. Instead of feeling guilty about them, think of all the other children you helped. And think about your three new nieces. You've done more than your share."

A couple of days after the trafficking case hit the news, Corelli's cell vibrated. It was Amari DeAndre. "Detective Corelli, I've been gobbling up the news and I'm in awe of what you and Detective Parker did for all those abused children. I've decided to contribute all of the profit from my holiday concert to charities that help them."

"That's wonderful, Ms. DeAndre—"

"Please call me Amari. I know about Simone and Nicky and Joseph." Her voice dropped. "I don't have any family so I'm always curious. Tell me about yours."

"We're pretty boring." Corelli laughed. "In addition to Simone and Nicky, I have four teenage nieces and nephews who adore your music."

"Oh, I want to hear all about them."

Corelli described the teenagers. "I also have six younger nieces and nephews." She hesitated. For some reason, she wanted to share this with Amari. And she knew in her gut Amari could be trusted. "This is not to be shared ever, Amari, but three of those six are three little girls between five and ten years old we found in Blecker's house the night of the murder. They'd been raped." Amari gasped. "My sister Gianna and her husband Marco have become their foster parents and they intend to adopt them."

"Detective Corelli, I'm honored you trust me enough to share that. Thank you. Please let me do something for your family." Corelli could hear the tears in Amari's voice.

"Call me Chiara. And contributing money to help the victims of child trafficking is more than enough."

"It's just a little thing but I'd love to invite your whole family, at least those old enough to attend, to the holiday concert between Christmas and New Year's Eve at the Barclay Center in Brooklyn as my guests."

By the time they ended the conversation, Amari had accepted the invitation for her and Kelly to spend Christmas day with the Corelli clan and Corelli had promised to call DeAndre with the total number of tickets she should reserve.

Christmas for Chiara was all about family. She didn't know whether it was her nearly dying or Brett's warm personality but her parents had welcomed Brett as her partner. For the first time in years she was looking forward to sharing both Christmas Eve and Christmas Day with her entire family. And this year the family included not just Brett, but her priest brother, Father Bart, P.J. and Gloria and Amari and Kelly. The four women arrived Christmas Day with gifts for everyone. The younger crowd was giddy to have Amari in their midst. Amari also spent time talking to Gianna and Marco and the girls who still stuck close to their mommy while the other children ran and played. From time to time Francesca, Giancarlo and Gabriella sat with the girls urging them to play a game or held their hands and walked them around.

And so several nights later, Corelli was standing huddled in her coat with the wind and rain and sleet whipping around her. The cold and the feeling of waiting brought to mind standing on the pier that freezing day seven weeks ago. Tonight was different though. This time she was dressed appropriately for the weather. And she was here for pleasure, as were the hundreds of excited people standing nearby.

Brett poked her in the side. "You just shivered. Are you sure you're all right waiting outside in the cold? Maybe I could—"

"Is the Corelli family here?" A young woman called out from the doorway. Corelli raised her hand. The woman waved the group into the Barclay Center.

The sixteen of them settled into the complimentary front row seats DeAndre had reserved for them. It was an unlikely group. Gianna and Marco with their two teenagers. Joseph and Patrizia with their two teenagers. And, Simone and Nicky, the two twenty-year-olds, with their dates, Tony and Will. Parker had brought Gloria Ndep. Corelli hadn't asked but they seemed serious. Everyone was in high spirits.

And then Amari was on stage, beautiful and vibrant. Her first song had the crowd up on its feet singing along. At the end of it, she flashed her gorgeous smile. "Hello, New York. Did you all have a Merry Christmas?" She smiled and waited for the crowd to quiet. "I'm thrilled to be here. And so happy to see all of you. We've got a great show for you tonight. But before we go on I want to take a minute to talk about something serious. Child sex trafficking. You may have seen the recent news about the arrests of hundreds of people involved with an international child trafficking ring and the recovery of several thousand children sold to predators. All the profits from tonight's show and ten percent of my profits next year will go to an organization that will support getting those children back to their families or into new families." She waited for the roar of approval to die down. "I have two very special guests in the audience tonight. Please welcome NYPD Detective Chiara Corelli and Detective P.J. Parker who are responsible for exposing the sex trafficking ring. Chiara and P.J., you are my heroes. Thank you. Also, I'm so happy to see my six super fans again, Simone, Nicky, Francesca, Giancarlo, Sal and Elena." She stared at their little group until her gaze found the two people she was seeking. "And finally, Gianna and Marco, the world needs more people with huge hearts like yours. I'm so happy to share this evening with all of you." She blew a kiss. The lights dimmed and the concert took off.

After the last encore, their escort arrived to bring them back to a combination holiday and post-concert party. The atmosphere was festive. Hors d'oeuvres and champagne were passed, the tables were loaded with real food and the bars served soda as well as hard liquor. They ate and drank, danced and socialized with Amari and her band and other singers, musicians, and notables at the party. Even Kelly Dexter was friendly as Amari kept returning to their group. It was a special night for Chiara, not just the youngsters in the family. She felt more connected to her sisters and brothers-in-law and her nieces and nephews than she had for ages. And she had Brett, who they all adored. Tonight was a sort of coming out. Other than Thanksgiving and Christmas with friends and family, their relationship had been private but tonight they were out in public as a couple being affectionate even though Amari had warned that the press would be at the party. For once, she smiled for the cameras. When Chiara's energy began to fade she begged off and watched Brett dance. Well that answered that question of whether Brett liked to dance as much as Marnie. She didn't miss anyone in their little party and even danced several times with Amari who made a point of dancing with the whole family.

Watching Brett and her family and friends enjoying themselves warmed her and she couldn't help smiling. Seeing her smile, Brett joined her. "What's so amusing?"

"Not amusing. Being here with you, with my family, makes me happy." She pulled Brett closer, enjoying the warmth and the arousal being near her always generated. A few more days and they'd fly to Tortola in the British Virgin Islands for two weeks of sailing and getting to know each other in new ways.

She'd been disappointed to find out that the catamaran Brett chartered came with a captain and a chef, a lesbian couple. She'd expected it to be just the two of them with Brett captaining the boat. But Brett explained she didn't want to worry about meals or charts or anything to do with sailing the boat. She wanted to focus totally on Chiara, on being together. She assured Chiara that even with the crew they would have total privacy, both on the boat and off in the many secluded coves where they would sail, swim, picnic—whatever.

Chiara couldn't stop thinking about the *whatever*. She couldn't wait to be alone with Brett. She couldn't stop fantasizing about making love in the hot sand, in a secluded cove surrounded by turquoise water. Then later… on the deck in the moonlight making love.

Bella Books, Inc.

Women. Books. Even Better Together.

P.O. Box 10543
Tallahassee, FL 32302

Phone: 800-729-4992
www.bellabooks.com